D0843416

DEADLY
SWEET

▲▲▲▲▲▲▲▲▲▲▲▲

Also by Sterling Watson

Blind Tongues
Weep No More My Brother
The Calling

DEADLY SWEET

▲▲▲▲▲▲▲▲▲▲▲▲▲▲▲▲

Sterling Watson

POCKET BOOKS

New York   London   Toronto   Sydney   Tokyo   Singapore

This book is a work of fiction. Names, characters, places, and incidents are either products of the author's imagination or are used fictitiously. Any resemblance to actual events or locales or persons, living or dead, is entirely coincidental.

POCKET BOOKS, a division of Simon & Schuster Inc.
1230 Avenue of the Americas, New York, NY 10020

Copyright © 1994 by Sterling Watson

Library of Congress Cataloging-in-Publication Data

Watson, Sterling.
    Deadly sweet / Sterling Watson.
        p.   cm.
    ISBN 0-671-87135-8
    I. Title.
PS3573.A858D4   1994
813'.54—dc20   94-8740
                                                               CIP

First Pocket Books hardcover printing October 1994

10 9 8 7 6 5 4 3 2 1

POCKET and colophon are registered trademarks of
Simon & Schuster Inc.

Printed in the U.S.A.

For Megan
Who knows the artist's necessity

The author wishes to thank Jamie Hastreiter for tireless and patient assistance with research for this and other books; Bill Miles, of Billy's Sliding School, for advice about politics and for allowing his good name to be abused in the cause of fiction; Ron Methot for information about flying and some terrific pegs from center field; Bob Breslin for legal and marine assistance; Dennis Lehane for his insightful and generous criticism; finally, and most especially, Judith Weber and Nat Sobel, whose understanding of fiction exceeds even their patience with erring authors.

DEADLY
SWEET

▲▲▲▲▲▲▲▲▲▲▲▲

1

Corey Darrow had a million-dollar voice.

A voice that kept Eddie Priest from hanging up. Putting his hangover back to bed.

For the second time she said, "Is this Mr. Priest? Edward Priest . . . ?" Carefully, like she was reading Eddie's name from the back of one of Raymer Harney's dog-eared business cards. The ones that came from the greasy wallet that still held one ancient, hopeful condom.

". . . this is Corey Darrow."

She was careful with the music of her voice. Eddie held the receiver three inches from an ear that felt like a wound.

"What are you," he asked, "on the radio? You do voice for a living? You sound like . . . an angel." Eddie knowing he made no sense. His brain singing the song of too much Bacardi and lime.

"That's not very original, Mr. Priest, but thank you."

"Welcome."

"No," she said, "I'm not on the radio. I work for the state. People do seem to like my voice."

That was when Eddie's stomach did the Mary Lou Retton. He had time to say, "Can you call back, say, five minutes?" Running to the bathroom to kneel and worship the American Standard toilet bowl.

He seemed to remember going back to the Hurricane Bar after Raymer Harney's departure. He seemed to remember meeting a woman there. The Hurricane served your Bacardi and lime with a paper umbrella in it. Eddie had lined up the little umbrellas on the bar during a long talk about two divorces, both of them hers.

A long walk on the beach and more talk about Men. Eddie's one or two earnest attempts to explain his species to the woman's anger. And finally Eddie's admission that he knew nothing about Men, only some things about himself and a few other isolated and probably unrepresentative tripodal life forms. And the woman, Anne by this time, pretty, smart, and damaged, standing under a streetlight by her car looking at him like she'd expected it all along. That he could not adequately account for himself.

Then back to the Hurricane where all reason and restraint had given way to more umbrellas.

When the phone rang again, Eddie was still kneeling at the shrine of indoor convenience, dry-heaving. He crawled to the tub, ran cold water across the back of his neck, drank some, and waited to see if he could hold it down.

"Five minutes by my watch," Corey Darrow said. "Look, I'm in a phone booth and there's a guy here been counting his change for ten minutes. He keeps pushing quarters around in his hand and looking at me like I might have some he could use. Quarters, I mean."

Eddie said, "Sorry, I had a bad night. It's taking me a while to get . . ."

Corey Darrow said, "If this is a bad time I can . . ."

"No, it's all right." Eddie was seeing all those miles of two-lane blacktop Raymer had driven to ask for a favor. Would Eddie talk to Corey Darrow? For old time's sake?

Eddie and Raymer had played football together at the state university. Gone to law school together. Raymer had graduated cheerfully at the bottom of their class, failed the bar examination, clerked for a while, then drifted into insurance investigation.

At the Hurricane Bar he'd reminded Eddie of football, all the guys bigger than Eddie he'd knocked down and peed on so Eddie could catch passes and get written up in the newspapers. Raymer said he'd made Eddie famous.

Now the woman had driven that same road. It would be worse than cold to send her home without at least talking to her, and hell, Eddie wanted to meet the voice. Look into those scared-of-nothing eyes he'd seen in the newspaper photo Raymer had shown him.

"Where's your phone booth?"

She said, "I'm looking around. I see a sign that says Maximo Moorings. That mean anything to you?"

Eddie said, "I've got some things to do on my boat. It's near where you are. You mind if I work a little while we talk?"

She said she didn't mind at all. Eddie gave her directions. She said, "Thanks. I mean, I appreciate this. Very much, Mr. Priest."

That's when he heard it. It was in the long sigh she gave into the phone, a shiver in the wires. She could keep it out of her eyes but not her voice. She was afraid of something.

"Call me Eddie," he said.

"I'll see you in a little while then, . . . Eddie."

Corey Darrow opened the glass door of the phone booth and pushed past the man with the coins in his hand. She took his dirty look. Gave him back her best country-girl bite-my-butt. He wasn't the one. The man who had been following her.

There were times when she thought the man was just a feeling. Just a part of this whole thing: The Bad Man. Mr. Figment. He was all the grins and ogles and sudden silences when she came around a corner into a group of men at the

3

office. A sort of collective male malevolence that had gathered into one cheap white suit, one old white convertible, a pair of mirror-lens sunshades, and a very dark tan.

But the guy was real. The car, all of it. She was certain of it now. He'd passed her twice on the long drive up. The second time, he'd stared at her, horsing the wheel with one hand, the other patting the door of the car as the wind snatched the sleeve of his greasy white suit coat. He'd looked over at her, a big grin spreading his mahogany cheeks. But no eyes. Only those mirror lenses and her seeing herself in them, small and divided in two, and then the man flooring the big Caddy and cutting in front of her in the rocking rip of wind and sound.

She had to pull over at a rest stop and get out and walk awhile to make her knees stop shaking. She held her scarf under the cool water from a stand pipe and washed her face. Opened her blouse to scrub the sudden sharp odor of fear from under her arms.

Now she was in St. Petersburg. She looked up and down the highway. Nothing but more of the butt-ugly strip she'd been driving since Sarasota. Shopping centers like the links in a chain. They'd start with a Kmart and end with an Eckerd Drug and then, a mile down the road, another Kmart and the same three or four stores in between. And all of them doing business. Enough Canadian blue heads and slack-jawed, gawking Yankees and Brits in short white socks and plastic sandals walking in with currency that beat the hell out of U.S. dollars and walking out with ice chests and nose caps and postcards with gators on them pulling the bikini pants off some drugged-out slut with an air-brushed behind.

Butt ugly, Corey Darrow thought. She'd be glad to get back to Okee County. A place good for getting through if you were a tourist on the way to Miami or Stuart or Palm Beach. Not a place to live unless you ran cattle or grew sod or sugar cane or worked for somebody who did.

Or maybe you worked for the state like Corey Darrow did, you and a few other "young professionals." The yuppies of a big, wet county, a dark green place on a green

4

map, with some four-lane cutting through it carrying people, and that one giant thing, the Big Lake, as clear from up there, the astrounauts had said, as a. . . . She couldn't remember what the astrounauts had said.

At the marina, she parked near a restaurant on pilings with windows looking out on a tidal basin full of blue canvas and gleaming white fiberglass. Hundreds of boats. The colors seemed to throb. A square half mile of expensive pleasure.

She found the dockmaster's office, a tiny cubicle in the maze of boardwalks. A rangy guy with bleached-out eyes and hands that had been cut and healed so many times they looked like cauliflower. He checked the map on his wall, took her outside, and pointed into the forest of rolling aluminum poles and stiletto outriggers. "Look for a small sailboat," the man told her. "Row 7, slip 19. It's a Ranger 23."

Priest was up on the bow when she got there, kneeling, doing something with a wrench and a can of WD-40. She stopped to watch him. Her breathing easier now, thinking, The Bad Man isn't here. Hasn't found this forest of masts and swinging, banging lines.

She liked watching the man who hadn't seen her yet, and she liked his calm, handsome face. The way he stuck his tongue in the corner of his mouth like a kid when he turned the wrench. It was cool under the big tin roof of the marina and the moving air carried the smell of salt and gasoline and mildewy canvas. She liked it.

She thought about stepping on a boat, and tossing off the mooring lines, or whatever you called them, and just sailing away. Away from her own palmetto and scrub oak country the tourists shot through with their brains on cruise control. Away from all the trouble she'd found.

Eddie was trying to loosen a stuck turnbuckle when he felt Corey Darrow's weight. He turned as the boat rocked and saw her crouching in the cockpit. She hadn't even used the spring line to pull the boat to her. It was a long jump.

She stood up now, smiling, then not just smiling. Something more there, mostly in her eyes. A sudden thing, surprising her too and making the color rise in her face. And Eddie could feel the heat in his own cheeks. His eyes sending back that same thing.

"Oh-oh," she said. "What is it you're supposed to say? Permission to come aboard, sir?"

Eddie stood and flexed his knees, sore from the hard gelcoat. "You're suppose to say it before you jump."

He told himself not to stare, but it did no good. He felt a hardening in his throat like he had to cough and couldn't. Like his heart had crawled into his throat and was climbing. He felt a little light-headed.

She let go of his eyes and looked around at the boat.

He'd bought the Ranger for nine hundred dollars from an old guy who'd sailed her all over the Caribbean. A guy who said she needed, maybe, a little renovation. Told Eddie about the four good headsails he was throwing in, the solid hull. Didn't make them like that anymore, all those layers of fiberglass. You couldn't hole this boat, no, sir, not on Florida sand bottoms. Not like you could the floating onion skins they built nowadays.

The guy hadn't mentioned the leaky through-hulls, the rotted wiring, the chain plates ripping loose from a punky bulkhead amidships. He hadn't said anything about the cracked swages and frozen turnbuckles and worn clevis pins.

They'd met in a bar, traded sailing stories. Eddie had liked the guy. Maybe felt sorry for him, the way his hands shook when he picked up his neat *anejo* rum and the way his eyes left the room when he talked about blue water sailing. Eddie wrote the guy a check right there. How could you go wrong for nine hundred bucks and a guy who takes your check in a bar?

He watched Corey Darrow complete her survey of the Ranger. She let her hands trail along the laminated mahogany tiller, looked up at the boom, the new blue sail cover. "Interesting," she said, giving him those green eyes.

Eddie nodded. "She's a lot of work."

After Eddie had actually seen the boat he'd bought for nine hundred bucks, he'd decided it was all right. She would steal a lot of free time. Time that needed stealing after Miriam had left him and the house in the suburbs to go off in search of something she called self-actualization. A thing they had in California apparently. That was two years ago. Eddie had taken his time with the boat work. It kept him from stacking too many umbrellas at the Hurricane Bar.

He'd named the Ranger for the way he'd bought her: *Sight Unseen.* Someday, he was going to paint her name on the transom.

Corey Darrow said, "You call it she?" Her voice was some

kind of music Eddie couldn't describe. She said, "You still do that? In this age of elevated consciousnesses."

"She's a she," Eddie said. "I guess I missed the elevator. Does it pass this way again?" He sat on one of the cockpit lockers, looking at the woman. Unable to stop looking. He said, "I'm a persistent guy. Maybe I'll catch it next time. Go way up there. Consciousnesswise, I mean."

She sat down, her knees almost touching his. She wore Levis, Reeboks, and a white cotton blouse, tucked in. She had a nice waist. A lot of women her age didn't have them. They'd stopped tucking in at thirty or so. Started going straight from shoulder to hip. In fact, everything he could see of her was good.

The scared-of-nothing eyes were a dark emerald. The wild, curly hair was the same color as the mahogany tiller that supported her arm now. She had long graceful fingers and good ankles. Good is what you like. Hers had a certain runner's ropy look, tapering up to a softness. Eddie wanted to see the calf, the knee.

"Well," she said, "where I come from, persistence is still a virtue." She laughed. "And most of the consciousnesses are still at sea level."

She watched him. He could see she meant it, about persistence, wasn't playing with him. And she was sizing him up, tired boat, persistence, and all. He decided not to ask any questions. Let her tell her story when she wanted to.

"Work," she said.

"I'm sorry?"

"You said you wanted to work while we talked. Go ahead and work. Don't worry about me."

Eddie removed the hatch cover and took Corey Darrow's hand and led her to it, standing with her in the escaping heat from the cabin. Old mattresses, decomposing foam rubber, things giving in to fungus and corroding salt air. "You stand down here," he said. "Careful on those steps."

She kept his hand on the way down but didn't really need it. She stood facing him, head and shoulders visible. He

8

lifted the top off the locker where she'd been sitting. "This," he said, kneeling, "is a job I've been avoiding."

"What is it?" she asked.

"Guy I bought the boat from must have had her slipped under a tree. Lot of needles and leaves and stuff washed into the scuppers. It's all clogged up in here, but that's not the worst part."

"What's the worst part?" Humor in the voice behind him. Indulging the male in his strange pursuits.

Eddie told her that the things above her head, the wooden things up there that held the two shrouds apart, were called spreaders. If she'd look at them, she'd see that they had been the roost of a large aquatic bird. She'd know this by certain signs they exhibited. He told her that the bird, probably a cormorant, had hunted from its perch and then defecated on the deck.

"That's all in here too," he said, reaching down with a pair of channel lock pliers to remove the clamp from one of the scupper hoses. Positioning a bucket under the hose.

When the rusted clamp broke loose, the ooze escaped with a gaseous thump. Eddie jumped back from the stink.

"Wow," said Corey Darrow from the cabin behind him, "that's powerful. And they say sailing is glamorous."

"We haven't got to the glamorous part yet."

"What's that?"

"Why don't we take her out to Shell Key, run some water through this scupper system. See if the kicker kicks and sails'll stand up to some wind. Maybe swim a little. If you got time, that is?"

"Time is something I've got plenty of," the voice behind him low, musical, like an instrument they hadn't invented yet. Or maybe one somebody'd played eons ago and lost. The archaeologists hadn't dug it up yet. To listen to it, Eddie thought, really listen, you'd have to lash yourself to the mast.

She said, "I didn't expect to get the special treatment."

"Here we have the good and the bad," Eddie said, lifting the reeking bucket and easing it over the side. "You're here for the bird lime. You get to stay for the fun."

"You dump that stuff over the side?" she said. Reluctance in the voice.

"Yeah," Eddie said, "there are things down there that eat it. Nature's way."

"I didn't bring a suit," she said.

"Excuse me?"

"For swimming. No suit."

"People don't use them at Shell Key. It's famous for that."

Eddie was glad he still had his back to her. He knelt for a second bucket of nausea. He wondered what her eyes were saying about swimming without a suit.

He liked it that she hadn't asked him if there was a Mrs. Priest somewhere, a first mate for the *Sight Unseen*. He thought about what he'd say if she did ask. How Miriam had gone off to California in the third or fourth wave of Seekers since the Age of Aquarius. How he'd told her that people had been going to California since some goof discovered gold at Sutter's Mill, and nobody had found El Dorado yet. They'd found some great water views, a brutal cost of living, and some wonderful ethnic restaurants, but no El Dorado. He'd said one seacoast was as good as another, and this one didn't have a bunch of lunatics on it looking for an ionic reversion. Things like that.

And Miriam correcting him: "Eddie, it was a convergence, not a reversion. And that's not what I want. I want to discover who I really am. What I should do with the time I've got left. There isn't a lot of it, you know. Time left." Beautiful Miriam, decent Miriam. Sitting across from him at breakfast, patiently explaining the end of their life together.

And Corey Darrow hadn't asked him to explain.

He said, "I always carry an extra suit for a guest." He hoped he'd gotten the right kind of regret into his tone.

It was quiet in the cabin, then Corey Darrow said, "If you have a guest, maybe she'll need it. I was here for the bird lime. I'm one of the crew."

Eddie rinsed out the bucket, turned, and looked at her. It was like rising from a deep dive and finding yourself not in air, but in those eyes.

3

▲▲▲▲▲▲▲▲▲▲▲▲▲▲▲▲▲▲

The Governor was late. And more than his usual ten minutes. Sawnie saw an aide carrying a water pitcher and a
bowl of Valencia oranges to the conference table. The
woman must have come from the second-floor cafeteria.
Sometimes the Governor stopped there for a chat with Amos
Tillman, the fry cook. Amos hailed from the Governor's
home county, and Governor Billy Miles was fond of telling
the newspapers that Amos advised him in important policy
matters. The truth was that Amos ran the capitol sports
pool. Maybe the Governor was down there making another
deposit in Amos's retirement fund.

Sawnie stopped the young woman. "You didn't see him
on your way up here, did you?"

The aide was one of a thousand pretty girls with degrees
in poly sci who schooled to Tallahassee like game fish on a
chum trail. They swam in the wake of power for a few years
then went on back to Yeehaw Junction and got married.

11

Most of them, anyway. A few, like Sawnie, stayed on and grew wise in the waters. The aide slopped ice water on Sawnie's Ann Taylor pumps and said, "Nobody down there but Amos, counting his winnings."

Sawnie watched the woman hurry to the front and start primping a stack of press releases. Pitchers of juice and bowls of oranges were spaced along the table. The Governor liked to be photographed with Florida's cash crops. Once she'd even seen him gnaw a stalk of sugar cane for the cameras. Emergency dental work after that one. And twice she'd had to prevent him from having his picture taken with a life-size Mickey Mouse.

Sawnie snuck a glance at her watch and looked at the choir of yuppies, alcoholics, and movie-stars-to-be that was known as the capitol press corps. They filled eight rows of folding chairs with about one brain for every two pairs of bright red suspenders. Talking heads wired to cameras. Out in the parking lot, the satellite trucks were lined up like pop stands. Bob Dollar, Channel 10 newshawk, unhooked himself and walked over to her.

"Hey, Sawnie," he said. "Where's old Wild Billy?" He tapped his gold Rolex with a buffed forefinger. Dollar considered himself a world-class charmer. He was legendary for the swath he had cut through the ranks of young staffers who thought that sleeping with the fourth estate could get you somewhere. He'd even hit on Sawnie a couple of times.

She leaned toward him. "This is off the record, Bob."

Dollar nodded, but she didn't begin until he had tucked his note pad and Mont Blanc pen into his jacket pocket.

"He's on the phone," she said. "The President wants another conference about those off-shore leases." She watched Dollar's soap idol face. First rule: Never say you don't know where the Governor is. Second: When you invent one, make it bigger than the one the Governor is currently missing. Bob Dollar's eyebrows arched at Sawnie's oil whopper.

"Interesting," he said. Sawnie could feel his vibrating baritone on the skin of her face. Dollar called his voice "the Instrument." He squeezed her upper arm and said, "I'd like to get together and talk about an in-depth, personal profile of you, Sawnie. You know"—he raised his soft, clean hands, framing his words for her—"the woman closest to the Governor. What *is* she really like? Hell"—he laughed, dropping his hands—"what's the Governor *really* like? Nobody knows him better than you, Sawnie." He winked at her.

She stepped back and smiled. She could hear the swell of noise in the hallway that meant Governor Wild Billy Miles had finally arrived. She said, "Thanks, Bob, but I'll stay offscreen. You start making news out of me, I won't be able to help you with the Governor." She nodded toward the doorway where the Governor's big voice boomed. Dollar hurried back to his cameraman.

Sawnie pushed her way through the gaggle of legislative staffers and reporters to the curtained alcove behind the head table. She waited by the men's room door. Through the curtains, she could see members of both houses drifting in. And she would see them on the six o'clock news tonight, saying, "I met with the Governor today, and . . ."

The Governor shook loose from the crowd, announcing loudly enough to be heard in the back that he had to go to the *necesario*. Sawnie caught him in the alcove. "Bet you got a story to tell."

"Not really." He lowered his voice. "I just stopped for a little game of eight ball." He stepped into the tiny bathroom, leaving the door open. She heard his urine begin to flow.

When he'd finished, she handed him his speech. "Pool?"

"Yeah," he said, "On the way in, I saw these Negro boys out in front of Earl's Pool Hall. You know it, down there on Decatur Avenue? I used to stop in there for a game when I was in the Senate. I told Clarence to pull over. I got out and asked who'd like to shoot some eight ball with the Governor." He winked at her. "Nobody plays eight ball like a Negro." Sawnie closed one eye. She'd told him a hundred times that Negro was out—hell, black was out now. African-American was in. His answer was that Negro had been good enough for Martin Luther King, Jr. That made it good enough for him.

13

"So," she said, "you threw the gauntlet to the studs on Decatur Avenue. What'd they say?"

"Well," he said, "one of them, the big one, said he didn't believe I was anybody's Governor, but he wouldn't mind taking some money off a cross-eyed white man."

"You been drinking?"

"No, ma'am." He opened the folder that held the speech, glancing at it. "And I'm only a little cross-eyed. At least not so you'd notice."

"So what happened?" She leaned close to smell his breath.

"He took a bunch of it," the Governor said, grinning like a Halloween pumpkin. "Money, I mean."

He walked past her and pushed through the curtains and did a little skip step to enter on the run. Let them see the energy, but never appear to be in a hurry. Three feet behind him, she stepped into the hot glare of the lights.

She had once asked the Governor how he thought it looked to have her behind him all the time, a woman like her. "It looks good," he had said. "Makes 'em think an old codger like me can still get it up." He'd winked at her, done a little shuffle step to show her he was only joking. But she knew there was something to it. And she knew he could still get it up.

She looked around the room at the other aides, most of them women, most of them more than presentable. One or two Miss Winter Garden Orange Juices or Miss Plant City Strawberries sat in the line against the wall with their knees carefully together and their faces neutrally composed.

Governor Wild Billy Miles opened the folder she'd handed him, looked into it, frowned, and set it aside. "Well," he said, "you all know why we're here. I'm not gonna give you any civics lesson. This great nation of ours took a census in 1990, and to nobody's particular surprise, the busycrats in Washington discovered that down here in the Sunshine State we are up to our ..."

Sawnie closed her eyes. Please don't, she thought.

"... *eyeballs* in pilgrims ..."

Thank you, she whispered.

"They come in the night and they come in the daytime. They come on buses and in cars, and riding the trains and on the planes that ply our beautiful blue skies. They come bringing wives and children and what the sociocrats are pleased to call the extended family and they come bringing bags and baggage, hopes and dreams, and they come needing our schools for their children, and, of course, we welcome them . . ."

She opened her eyes. Something was happening in the room now. The old thing. Somehow the stale air of business as usual had been blown away by the Governor's earnest, homely voice. Even the politicians roosting in the back were really listening. The cameras whirred and the hot lights burnt into the Governor's pale blue eyes and onto the tanned planes of his country boy face, and fifty pens scribbled. ". . . but they come needing our roads and our water and God help them, our police and our firefighters and our prisons too . . ." Sawnie thinking, This is like a day in some church way down at the end of a white sand road.

This is what he has, she realized. The thing that had made her stay with him, put up with the delays and the sophomoric shenanigans, and the times when his mouth got him in trouble she didn't need. He could make people worship with him in the church of political possibility.

People put aside their cynicism and listened to him. As corny as he was, as half-baked in some of his ideas, and as impractical as he was, they listened. His gift was the essence of politics: a person saying, Look, we can't build it perfect, but we can build it pretty damned good. What do you say?

Years ago, as a girl swimming to power, Sawnie had said yes, and she hadn't looked back.

Now the Governor lifted a hand and thoughtfully scratched the shock of fading red hair that looked like something a child had glued to the freckled forehead of an aging Howdy Doody. His voice cracked a little, slipping upward a register. "The framers of our great Constitution in their wisdom," he said, "knew that this land would grow." He stopped and grinned into the lights. "Although, Lord

15

knows, they didn't foresee it growing the way we have it down here in sunny Florida. The Constitution guarantees three rights—and you know them by heart—but every citizen believes he's really got four: life, liberty, the pursuit of happiness, and a little piece of the state of Florida where he can spend his declining years doing the pursuing."

The room erupted into applause and laughter. The Governor grinned, blinking at the camera flashes as though he had no idea what was funny. Finally, he shrugged and said, "And we welcome them ... And the way we grow in America is fair and equal because our forefathers did something right. They invited everyone to the table. After every census, members of both political parties redraw our legislative boundaries, state and federal. People of goodwill sit down together and work out a plan that balances the political interests of grower and developer, biologist and banker, native and latecomer, Republican and Democrat."

The Governor stopped and pushed his glasses down and looked out at his audience. He waited for complete quiet. When the only sounds in the room were the hum of minicam motors and the buzz of fluorescent lights, he refitted the glasses to the bridge of his nose. "Most of you know where the new districts will go; they'll ring the state. They'll embrace the water where the people go, and in some places, like down in South Florida, where the Everglades, our great River of Grass, and Miami rub elbows, they'll hold some strange bedfellows.

"I'm talking about competing interests: cane growers and environmentalists and folks that want to build houses. And I'm going to promise you something right now. Nobody's going to pollute or destroy wild habitat or bank a windfall dollar because of the way these boundaries are drawn. Not in Florida. Not anymore."

The Governor paused again, looked at the back of the room, shielding his eyes from the harsh lights. Sawnie could see him find what he wanted. The men he had appointed to the Reapportionment Committee. "Today we take the first step to ensure the fairness of this process. The first step is that first man of goodwill . . ."

The Governor named the members of the committee and they waved or smiled diffidently, or just stared their confidence into the eyes of Governor Miles. But already the excitement was waning. The excitement was the Governor, not this committee of his. Sawnie looked at her watch. She had a briefing to prepare for the Governor's paper on the repeal of the luxury tax, a tax that was killing the boating industry.

When the reporters crowded to the front, questioning the committee, Sawnie caught the Governor's forearm. "You really ought to think before you get real specific about who's screwing who down there in the cane country. You know that, don't you?" She'd never quite given up hope that the Governor would learn something about damage control.

"Oh, hell," he said, "everybody knows it already. Might as well draw some lines in the mud." He smiled at two reporters. One of them shouted a question and the Governor raised a hand to cup his ear, smiled, shook his head. He called it the deaf trick, said he'd learned it from a former president.

He turned back to her. "Tonight?" he said. "Your place? Give an old man a thrill?"

Sawnie gave back a professional smile. Nodded.

4

Eddie steered the *Sight Unseen* out through the Pass-a-Grille Channel, ran south along the outside of Shell Key, and then circled back into Bunces Pass. It was an area of varying depths, so he put Corey Darrow at the tiller and went up to the bow to read the bottom and give her hand signals. She steered to his flagging arms, through the grass beds and shallows and he felt the keel scrape only once. "Oops! Sorry!" she called.

"Gets rid of the barnacles," he shouted back.

Eddie was glad they had things to do. The wind and the effort explained the color in their cheeks, and mostly they avoided each other's eyes.

When they found the channel, a thirty-foot-wide cut that ran along the estuarine side of the key, he scuttled back and cut the Mercury outboard, brought her up into the wind, and tossed in the Danforth.

"You want to swim out?" he asked. "Make sure the anchor is set?"

She made her this-girl-wasn't-born-yesterday face, then gazed past him at Shell Key, a low, sere barrier island ringed by wide platinum beaches. Here and there a cluster of Australian pines, a lot of palmetto and cactus. And no people.

A big motor sailer made her way through the Pass-a-Grille Channel toward the Gulf. Powerboats and jet skis out on Mullet Key, looking like blue and red and white sparks skipping up the curved horizon and then sliding down again. Nothing much else on a weekday.

"I don't usually go naked with strange men," she said.

Eddie looked at the anchor line. "We may be drifting," he said, trying to look worried. "Besides, I'm not strange. I got all the usual parts." He touched himself in various places. "See. Head. Heart. Arms. Legs."

She smiled, shaking her head. Then she surprised him. The glimpse he got of those emerald eyes told him she was surprising herself too. "All right," she said, "Mr. Normal. Turn around."

Eddie edged around her toward the cabin, leaned into the hatchway, and looked up at the rusted running lights and the bent telltale at the top of the mast. He'd have to get a bosun's chair, go up there, and replace them. A lot of work, this boat.

He felt the *Sight Unseen* rock, then heard a splash. He turned and saw Corey Darrow's clothes in a small neat pile on the cockpit bench. Bra and panties folded and underneath the jeans and blouse. She was just rising now in a corona of bubbles. Tossing her head back, throwing water in a long arc that caught the sunlight.

She called, "God, it's wonderful. So cool." Her voice held delight and mischief. Whatever it was that worried her was gone from her face. She steadied herself on the anchor line and watched him. "Well, what are you waiting for. We got to check this thing, see if we're drifting."

Eddie wasn't going to ask her to turn her back. And he wasn't going to turn his either. Show her his butt while he

19

bent to pull off his socks. So he got out of his clothes while she watched, the expression on her face like she was in a supermarket, looking for the ripest tomato. This one? No. This one? No. Giving each tomato a good squeeze. When he mounted the transom and dove, the last thing he saw was that question in her eyes. Good tomato? Bad tomato?

Corey Darrow watched him surface. He grabbed the anchor line next to her, his warm flank brushing hers in the slick salt. She didn't know what to say. This was close. It stopped her voice, made her thoughts dreamy-strange. She wanted to ask him to swim around the island with her. Maybe stroke out into the Gulf a couple of miles. It was crazy, but hell, it was how she felt.

She could feel the smile on her face, and the word *delirious* came to her. She drew the word out in her mind's eye, seeing it as a motion of sinuous forms in a warm element, *dee-leer-ee-us*. After this long month of menace—her job, her friends, the whole town suddenly alien. And an hour ago the Bad Man in the white car. After all this, a cool ocean. Here in this blue suspension between land and air, in this floating no-place, she felt so far from trouble.

She wanted to tell him about watching him strip and dive but wasn't sure she could make it clear. His strong back bending in the sun, the white curve of his buttocks, and the dark, curly clump of his sex. Hell, maybe there *was* something wrong with the anchor. All she could think of to say was, "Let's check it. The anchor. Okay?"

He laughed and said, "Okay." They pulled themselves along the anchor line and he did a surface dive and she followed his tanned back and legs and hard white buttocks down through the slanting shafts of light to the sandy bottom where the anchor was buried out of sight. No, they weren't drifting. She looked at him, bubbles escaping from the corner of his mouth, saw him smiling, shrugging in the cool gloom, and then pointing up, rising and her following. He treaded water, a little out of breath. "I guess we're okay," he said. She nodded. He turned and swam back to the anchor line, and she did too, taking hold opposite him. Both of them kicking and breathing. Steady, excited. She looked into his eyes and saw what she'd seen at the marina when she'd watched him kneeling at the front of the boat. There was no hate in him, nothing to be afraid of. She felt his hand take her waist and pull her toward him.

"Wait a minute," she said. She smiled at him. It was the smile you smile in a dream. She could see it on her own face. She put her head under and kicked, surfaced on his side of the anchor line, pressing herself against the hot length of him, feeling the coarse hair of his chest in the slick salt, feeling her nipples harden, those dead giveaways. She let her hand slide down his flank, move toward the middle of him.

He circled her with his arms, holding her against the taut line and she could see his eyes asking permission. She could feel his penis pressing. She kissed him, soft at first, then with more need and more still. She could lift her knees, press them to his hips, wrapping him. She had seen him inspecting her ankles back at the marina. She could lock her ankles behind him and feel him warm and hard and sudden inside her. Inside her, moving, like the sea. And all of it comfort, comfort, comfort.

She didn't. She looked into his asking eyes and shook her head sadly and pulled away. She swam strongly toward the shore and after a few strokes looked back and saw him following her.

They swam ashore and walked halfway around the island and back again.

"You're sure this is all right?" she asked. "This Adam and Eve thing?"

He squeezed her hand. "People do it. That's all I said. I didn't say it was all right. I'm sure of very little."

She stopped, looked at him, out at the Pass-a-Grille Channel, a shrimper plowing toward the Gulf, a thirty-foot Cape Dory coming in. At Mullet Key two miles to the south the usual flotilla of pleasure craft. In the sky, an F-16 burning its way toward MacDill. She said, "I *know* it's not legal. I just want to know if it's all right."

Eddie swung around in front of her, still holding her hand. God, she was beautiful. She was turning a little pink in the sun, had fine crystals of salt on her forehead and cheeks. Her mahogany hair in a twist across her right shoulder. He leaned into the smell of Corey Darrow. No perfume, soap, nothing but what came from her pores after she had kissed him and swum in the Gulf of Mexico, an effluvium impossible to describe. And like impossibility, a drug.

"It's all right with me," he said. "Once in a while the Marine Patrol stops in here and busts a couple of bare-ass shell hunters. But they're not real persistent about it. Too busy with the cocaine trade."

She put both hands on his chest and gave him a strong, exasperated shove. "You *are* a lawyer. Everything's a little bit of this and a little of that and a lot of maybe."

He fell back into step beside her. "Corey, what is it? What did you want to see me about?"

She stopped walking, pulled him by the hand back into her face. Kissed him in a way that felt final. A way he liked and didn't like. "Not here," she said, "not like this." She meant her own nakedness. "I don't want to talk about it when I'm . . . like this."

5

▲▲▲▲▲▲▲▲▲▲▲▲▲▲▲▲▲▲

Eddie put the ice chest on the cockpit deck between them and laid out the dinner he had brought from the marina deli. Two Heinekens, a pound of smoked swordfish, some Norwegian flatbread, a bunch of flame grapes, and a wedge of Camembert. Corey Darrow touched the white crust on the cheese with her finger. "What *is* that?"

Eddie told her it was a Camembert.

She smiled. "Down in Okee City at Parson's Stop 'N Shop, they sell the old solid Velveeta and the new kind in the squeeze bottle. The locals are pretty excited about the new stuff."

He opened the two beers, handed her one.

"What did Raymer tell you about me?" Corey Darrow asked.

"Only that you wanted to talk to me." She watched him, wary. She'd said "about me" the way a country girl would. Worried about her reputation.

Eddie leaned back against the rail. "He mentioned a charge of sexual harassment. Said it was about 'that ecology stuff.' " Eddie smeared some Camembert on a piece of flatbread, stuck a grape in the middle, and popped it into his mouth. He washed it down with the yeasty Heineken, remembering his meeting with Raymer in the Hurricane Bar.

Raymer and Eddie had talked small for a while, quietly remembering old football games. When they'd finished a couple of good seasons and some alcohol, Eddie had said, "Raymer, what's this about?"

Raymer scratched his fifty-inch chest, looked lost for a moment, and said, "You ask me, they invented feminism so ugly girls would have something to do."

Raymer was like that. The graceful transition wasn't in him.

A whippet-faced brunette lifted her chin sharply when Raymer said the F word. Or maybe it was the U word. Or maybe there was another word in there that was bothering them this year. She looked at Raymer like she might have to speak to the management.

Raymer said, "But this one ain't ugly. Come to think of it"—Raymer knocked back his whiskey, ice clattering against his yellow buck teeth—"she ain't a feminist either." He turned to Eddie. "Just a good old girl in trouble. For some reason, she's calling it sexual harassment. I told her you'd talk to her."

Eddie said, "What do you mean, she's calling it sexual harassment? Don't they have rules, guidelines down in Okee County?"

Raymer turned his third bourbon slowly on the bar. The half-moons of cleat scars studded Raymer's huge hands. "Most of that county, all they got is cowboys, cattle, and cane fields. Migrant labor. They got Indians too, Miccosuki mostly. And rattlesnakes. Big around as your thigh, the snakes down there. Will you talk to her?" Raymer looked at him, asking for a favor Eddie didn't owe.

Eddie looked at the glittering bottles across the bar. For

24

a couple of months now, maybe three evenings a week, he'd found himself standing at this polished zinc bar drinking something with a paper umbrella in it and watching the sun set. Happy to think of himself as dormant. Waiting to see what the next phase would be.

He said, "I still don't see what the problem is. She's got a complaint, she takes it to the authorities. She goes through channels."

Raymer sighed, sipped his whiskey, and pulled a newspaper clipping from his pocket. When Raymer put it face down on the bar, saving it, Eddie knew the woman in the photo was no snake.

"The key question here, Raymer, is why me? We keep doing the lambada around it."

"This is right up your alley. You'll see when you talk to her."

"What's my alley, Raymer?"

Raymer sounded embarrassed now. "You know, that ecology stuff. Save the Florida panther. Hell, save the panther's urine. Analyze it for Epstein-Barr syndrome. Extract chromosomes from it and clone panthers for the twenty-first century. I don't know. It's her wants to talk to you, not me." He looked at Eddie over the rim of his glass. "I'm supposed to set up a meeting. Remind you I used to protect you from deranged pituitary cases that wanted to knock your dick off."

Eddie said, "You don't know what *exactly* this has to do with 'that ecology stuff'?"

"She didn't seem to want to tell me, so I didn't seem to want to know. If she says there's a connection between harassment and panther piss, I believe her."

Eddie tasted the Bacardi again, with its background of Persian lime. It was the taste of his dormancy. "I don't practice law anymore, Raymer. I sell boats. I like it. You meet a better class of people when you take out a forty-three-foot Hunter for a little sunset check ride. The people you meet are *not guilty* as a rule. That's about as close as I get to ecology anymore."

Raymer turned the newspaper clipping over, slid it across the bar. Trump card. He said, "Her name's Corey Darrow." The headline read: Water Management Official Accused of Improprieties. The woman's large dark eyes looked straight back at the camera, scared of nothing. Big hair, dark, wild, and curly. She was no snake.

Raymer had measured Eddie's reaction to the picture. "I told you she wasn't ugly."

Corey Darrow watched Eddie swallow the Heineken, then she looked back over her shoulder at Shell Key and the Gulf. Way out, a phosphate carrier was plowing toward the Tampa roadstead. Eddie could see the yellow and black pilot boat leave the dock at Egmont Key, making for its rendezvous with the ship. The sea breeze was beginning to blow, stirring Corey's hair. Tapping the points of her white shirt collar against the tanned skin of her throat.

"I only said that about sexual harassment because they wouldn't leave me alone. All of a sudden I was the punch line of all the jokes. It had to stop. I went to my boss, Clinton Reynolds. Clinton's the division head. The next thing I know, he's got me talking to the district ombudsman about making a formal complaint. The district ombudsman is six feet tall, weighs two hundred and thirty pounds, and has a mustache. Her name is Francine Borden. Wears NOW buttons on both lapels.

"They all thought it was funny, the men I mean. Francine Borden starts talking about class action suits and getting the ACLU involved and wants me to talk to my co-workers about joining me in the fight and pretty soon I'm the laughing stock of the county. I mean I'm competing with Francine for that position.

"I talk to Clinton again, and he says, 'That's what she's there for, little lady. To help you out. That's why the state pays her that big salary.' He's talking real solemnlike, but he's delighted I'm associated with Francine. He knows how that makes me look."

Eddie said, "Wait a minute. You lost me back where they

wouldn't leave you alone. What happened to make them start doing these things?"

"I found something in the computer. I guess I should say I *didn't* find it. Somebody deleted one of my files. It was a form 16 stroke 10. It's a form we have to fill out when somebody comes into the office and asks for information. We're a government agency and a lot of what we know is open to the public. Information gathering and dissemination is one of the services we provide. The 16 stroke 10 is just routine.

"When I saw this one was missing, I got the log-in rosters and looked at the user codes. Our files are input by Marcy Ransom. She's just a . . . well, she's a drone. She can sit at the green screen all day typing and listening to the local country station and humming 'Honky-Tonk Angel' or something and not go crazy. I figured maybe Marcy'd dumped the file. But it wasn't her code. It was Clinton Reynolds's.

"I went back to him. Said, 'Look, Clinton, somebody goofed. Maybe Marcy's finally gone around the bend. She dumped one of my visitor's reports.' I knew Marcy didn't do it. Like I said, her user code wasn't on it.

"Clinton says, 'So? What's the problem?' I had to laugh, thinking about Clinton stretching himself to the limits of his computer skills. Sitting there with an open software manual and typing with his lips moving. Finally, I said, 'Clinton, you dumped the file. This is your code, not Marcy's. What's going on here?'

"Clinton goes all red in his already hypertensive face and tells me, 'Forget it, missy. If you know what's good for you.'

"Well, I did. Forget it, I mean. For about three days. Then I saw the article in the newspaper. How they found the bicycle, all smashed to hell out on one of the service roads in the east county. How they didn't find *him*. No trace. How they figure it was a hit and run, maybe a rock truck running overloaded, avoiding the weigh station on U.S. 41. How they think he must of been lying out there a week before a gator crawled out of the canal and drug him in. I didn't *like* it."

Corey's outrage was loud, echoing off the shoreline, the

low wall of Australian pines a hundred yards west. Eddie watched her, the set jaw, the compressed lips, the fury that made her green eyes small and dark. He'd seen it before. Had sat behind a lawyer's desk and seen it a lot of times. The ordinary man or woman suddenly fed up, the red-lined anger, burnt to the top of what ordinary could take. Pissed off, fuming, ready to do something. Usually, the wrong thing.

Quieter now, she said, "I decided to ask around. I talked to a few people in the agency, down at the courthouse. Nobody knows anything. Nobody wants to talk about it. Everybody says, 'Don't mess with it, girl. It's way over your head.'

"Then I start getting the dirty notes on my desk and the guys tell me they're reading about me on the men's room wall. I get phone calls from a couple of bozos that say they heard I was a good-time girl. All of a sudden I'm hearing from every asshole with a dick and an ax to grind."

She watched Eddie. Her anger had stopped the Heineken halfway to his mouth.

"Sorry," she said. "I guess that's pretty hard talk for a girl that went to vacation Bible school every summer till she was in tenth grade."

Eddie shrugged. Finished his beer. Picked hers up, handed it to her. "Drink up," he said. "This stuff's too good to waste."

She accepted the beer, took a long pull. She looked at him. "We got this all assbackwards, didn't we?"

Eddie knew what she meant. Didn't want to say so. Didn't even nod.

She kept talking, her anger rising. "I come to you on a professional basis, referred by a colleague, and we end up skinny-dipping and doing the desert island number. I guess you think I'm a real country bimbo."

6

▲▲▲▲▲▲▲▲▲▲▲▲▲▲▲▲▲▲

Eddie said, "I was thinking about getting a new set of Michelins."

"Tires?" she said. Anger streaming at him from those emerald eyes. "You were thinking about *tires?*"

"Yes," he said quietly. "I was thinking about driving all those miles down to Okee City. Hell, maybe relocating. Maybe halfway. Naples. I've heard Naples is good. I get a little place on the beach. We meet on weekends. We eat grilled swordfish in a restaurant on the water, maybe take the *Sight Unseen* out for an evening cruise. Then we come home to the wind blowing through the jalousies. Or the miniblinds. What the hell. Those are just the details. The point is, I was thinking about changing my life."

When he finished, he realized that he'd meant what he said. That it came from the way her eyes had worked on him since the moment she'd jumped aboard the *Sight Unseen*. From her voice. And from a deep part of him, a place

29

he had thought he'd lost after Miriam had stroked off looking for the El Dorado of human potential.

Corey Darrow's angry eyes cooled. She lifted her beer and sipped. Then the little smile came on. "Whoa, now, buster. Let's not take out any licenses or get any blood tests."

Eddie put some Camembert on flatbread, crowned it with a red flame grape, and handed it to her. "All right," he said. "We won't do that yet. Tell me the rest of this thing with your boss and the guy who visited. It's the same guy the gator dragged into the canal, right?"

She looked at him for a long time, then looked around at the sky and water, shaking her head slowly at the place where she found herself. "Did Raymer show you the clipping?"

Eddie nodded.

"I wake up one morning, and I'm in the paper. A bunch of vague stuff about improprieties, all from unnamed sources, and I'm the one accused of altering state records. I call the paper, nobody'll talk to me. They're all taking cover back there behind the First Amendment. All high-minded and scared shitless. And they're sure not scared of me.

"Goddamn it!" She flung her empty bottle over the side, skipping it on the crest of a swell.

Eddie watched the bottle fill with water, waiting for her.

She looked at the hand that had thrown the bottle, covered it with the other one, wrung them. Then she made two hard little fists. "He was a little guy, dressed like some kind of movie extra from *Out of Africa* or something. He actually had a pith helmet. Khaki shirt and shorts, canvas puttees, jungle boots, the whole bit. And he wore those round wire-rimmed, milk bottle glasses that went out with John Lennon. Kept taking them off, breathing on them, and wiping them on his shirt. He wipes, they come up dirtier than before. He didn't smell all that good either."

"What did he want?" Eddie picturing this beautiful woman in a government office with a strange little man who was going to die under the wheels of a rock truck.

"Like I said, it was a routine request. He wanted information about local soil chemistry. I pulled up some stuff on the computer, printed it out for him. He got real excited."

"He got excited? About soil chemistry?"

"That's what I said. His eyes got real big behind those magnifying lenses and his face—he had a terrible sunburn—it got even redder. He started breathing hard, biting his fingernails. I'm waiting to see if he wants anything else, and he looks at me and, I swear, I get the impression he doesn't want me to see he's excited."

Eddie thinking, maybe it was you. Maybe you excited him, Corey Darrow. Eddie knew how that could happen. He said, "Who was he? You get visitors like that all the time?"

"That's the thing. He didn't say. Not exactly. I could tell by the way he talked—he asked me specifically about pH levels in the sand substratum—he wasn't just John Q. Citizen. The guy had some expertise."

Eddie looked at her, the gemstone eyes, the wild dark hair and the black Irish complexion. She was back there, reliving the moment, the mystery. He said, "Then somebody deletes the file. They find the guy's bike, but they don't find him. You ask about it and you get the treatment? Is that it?"

"Almost," she said quietly.

"Who else have you talked to about this? Besides your boss and Raymer Harney."

"Nobody much. I mentioned it a time or two here and there. Real casual. All of a sudden I'm Gloria Steinem in a shit storm."

"You said almost?"

"Yeah," she said. "What I mean is, I saw the guy *again*. I saw him *after* he asked about the pH in our lovely local sand substratum. And it was *after* something else too. It was after they said he was hit by the truck. He came in late in the afternoon on a Friday. Most of the division is already out starting another lost weekend. I'm signing some payroll vouchers for our consultants. I look up and there's the guy walking past my doorway. I stick my head out in the hall. He's going into Clinton's office. I go down there. What the hell, I'm taking vouchers to the cashier's office. I pass the door, I hear Clinton raise his voice."

"Words?" Eddie asked. "You get any words?"

She shook her head. "Just noises. Two guys who aren't happy with each other."

"Did you see the guy leave? The little guy?"

"Yes," she said, her voice low and sorry. Like she wished she hadn't seen him leave. Or wished she'd followed him.

Eddie finished his Heineken, feeling sleek, skin-taut under the last of the sun, satisfied. The feeling that never lasted but always promised to. He said, "Why did Raymer think we ought to get together?"

The question surprised her, and not happily. She watched him a while before answering.

"He told me about you and that stand of red mangroves in Calabria County. How you got the state in on it and stopped them from building." She looked at him deep now, hard. "Raymer said you couldn't be bought."

Eddie nodded, thanking Raymer, remembering.

Eddie had been the legal representative of a grass-roots nature advocacy group called Florida Green. A bunch of old sixties lefties, kids who'd heard John Denver sing "Rocky Mountain High" too many times and an assortment of dropouts from the Sierra Club and the Audubon Society who believed that stronger measures were needed to stop environmental rape. Eddie had been hired to do the legal work. He had turned over some rocks in the streambeds of corporate America to see what would crawl out from underneath. What crawled wasn't pretty.

The opposition had accused him of industrial espionage. But Eddie hadn't taped any locks or planted any bugs. His secret was Martha Weinstein.

He had gone to law school with Martha. Martha had gone into corporate law. Somewhere along a very steep earning curve, she'd developed a conscience. She'd started leaking documents to Eddie Priest, the attorney for Florida Green. And things had gotten ugly.

The Calabria County episode had earned Eddie a certain

kind of notoriety. Along with the newspaper stories and one
or two spots on the local news, he'd had his share of anonymous letters. Letters that asked him why he wanted to inter-
fere with honest commerce. Letters that purported to be
from "decent working people." Letters that speculated about
the bones that might be rattling in Eddie's closet. Phone
calls at midnight from men who talked matter-of-factly
about dismemberment, about troublemakers who ended up
as frozen hunks of chum in the bait shops of Marathon and
Islamorada. And he'd heard from one particular guy, a guy
named Ernesto.

Eddie sold boats for a living now.

Corey Darrow said, "Raymer bragged he knew you, big
football star and all. The guy that caught the One-Second
Pass. So I asked him to set this up. I told him I needed
a lawyer."

Eddie said, "My law practice is permanently temporarily closed."

"Permanently temporarily?"

"It means I pay my corporate fees every year and keep
up my membership in the bar association. I'm still an attorney in good standing, and I sell boats for a living."

"Why?" she asked. "Why is that?" Eddie watched her
eyes. Wasn't sure what was in them. She wasn't exactly
disappointed. He thought maybe more interested than disappointed. Here was a man who had changed his life.
Wanted to change it more, with her. He considered telling
her about Ernesto Plar. Martha Weinstein. What had
happened.

"I like boats," he said. "A lifetime love affair. You sell
sailboats, you spend a lot of time on the water. Out of sight
of land. You meet some very nice people. Sailors are gener-
ally a pretty good bunch." He smiled. A little self-
advertisement.

"And anyway," he said, "you don't need a lawyer. You
haven't been fired. They fire you, *then* you sue them."

He watched her face, not sure how she was handling this.
She was waiting, careful, taking it all in.

"But," he said, "I pack a hell of a lunch. What do you say we make this a regular thing: the ride, the swim, the walk, the smoked swordfish?"

Corey Darrow's eyes crashed. She left him and went inside, rethinking some things. It scared him. He'd blown it. When she lifted her eyes out of that inward sight, they were different, dull. Hell, they were scared.

She said, "There's one thing I didn't say. There's a guy following me. At least I think he is. He passed me twice on the way up here. Weird-looking guy. Big shock of black hair, big white grin. And real dark. A sun god type in a Don Johnson suit and silk T-shirt. Drives a big white convertible."

"Maybe," Eddie said, "the guy just likes to pass beautiful women on secondary roads. Something to do on a long drive."

"No," Corey Darrow said. "I got this feeling about him. It's not a good feeling. Francine Borden would tell me to get more rational, get out of this woman's intuition thing. But there it is. I got a feeling the guy wants to hurt me." She watched the last of the light. Waiting. Eddie didn't know what to say. He got up, stowed the fragments of lunch, and started the Mercury outboard. It would be tricky getting out on a falling tide through those grass flats and sandbars.

Eddie kept busy, steering by his memories of how they had got here. He doubted that anybody was following Corey Darrow. She was a government girl who'd asked some awkward questions about her boss. She was marching to a different drummer. Using some crude methods, the bubbas were calling her back to the ranks. Come back to the parade, Corey Darrow. That was all it was. And that would make anyone a little paranoid.

And the weird guy with the dark tan and the white car?

Eddie had spent hours listening to people hype their troubles, thinking they were elevating their compensation too. Maybe she'd invented the weird guy as a last shot at getting Eddie interested. Clients had done stranger things.

No, he decided, not this one. This one was no hype artist. This one believed it about the tanned guy. Believed he was after her. Eddie didn't.

She sat against the rail, the wind tossing her curls. Content apparently with his silence. When Corey Darrow leaned back and closed her eyes, Eddie thought about intuition.

The week before she disappeared, Martha Weinstein had called him, said she'd had a dream. Something bad had happened to her in the dream.

What? Eddie had asked. Picturing Martha standing in the phone booth she always used. Pretty, small, scholarly Martha in a phone booth two blocks from her office.

"Meet me, the usual place," Martha had said. She hung up.

In the little Greek restaurant where they always met, the corner booth, she settled her Coach briefcase beside her, opened it, handed him the last set of photocopies. They were aerial photos of a remote mangrove coastline. It could have been anywhere, but it wasn't. At the upper left margin of one of the shots, you could just make out the Mule Island ferry slip. The photos were taken from a chase plane, flying above a second aircraft. The one spraying the herbicide.

The photos had been taken two years before the planned starting date of the construction project. Six months before the passage of the Wetlands Protection Act.

Eddie put his hand on the documents. Martha put her hand on his, the first time she'd ever touched him. The last. She said, "I know you want to sleep with me. I want you to know I want the same thing. I think it's important not to bullshit about a thing like that."

Eddie nodded.

Martha smiled. "But we can't. Not while we're doing this. You understand?

Sure, Eddie had said. Of course, she was right. His eyes said she was right about the other thing, too.

Over coffee and baklava, he asked her again about the dream.

"I don't know," she said. "It wasn't that specific. They never are." Her voice diving, going deep. Her large dark eyes getting tight and frightened. She was lying to him.

Finally, she said, "But something's going to happen."

Eddie'd asked her if this had happened before. The dream thing. The thing that wasn't specific.

She'd said she had to go, had to get back to work. Good-bye, she'd said. And meant it.

Eddie believed in intuition. And feared it. It was a thing to avoid if you could.

In the rising dark, Eddie steered for the bright lights atop the Hurricane Bar. He planned to put the boat up for the night Bristol fashion and say good-bye to Corey Darrow on the dock. Tell her he'd had a beautiful day and he hoped she'd had one too. That he wanted more like it. Hoped she did. Mention the Michelins again, the drive down to see her.

Corey opened her eyes. "Feels good," she said, "the wind. The way she moves over the waves." She laughed. "You got me doing it, now. Calling a boat she." She reached out her warm bare foot and rested it on the top of his. Where it fit. He remembered her ankles kicking ahead of him in the swells as she swam for land. She said, "Francine Borden'd have a vapor if she could see me now."

"Nobody here but us swimmers," Eddie said.

Eddie strung out a hundred yards of silver wake behind them before he said, "A guy came to ask you about soil chemistry. Later, he disappeared. The cops found his bicycle, they think he got hit by a rock truck. They've got an estimated time of death and you saw the guy *after* that time. You heard him yelling in your boss's office and then your boss deleted the file that proved the guy was there. Is that about right?"

Across from him in the half dark, she nodded.

"And you know there are a hundred ways this could all be completely innocent, right?"

"Sure," she said. "That's why they want me to shut up.

36

Because it's all completely innocent." It was Eddie's turn to nod.

"So," she said, "you think I should just forget about this. It's nothing, right?"

Eddie switched hands on the tiller. He didn't think there was enough light for her to see his face. "That's what I think," he said.

7

▲▲▲▲▲▲▲▲▲▲▲▲▲▲▲▲▲▲

Harry W. Feather stood in the phone booth, watching the woman say good-bye to the guy with the sailboat. Like a couple of high school kids on their first date. No, wait a minute here! The guy was kissing her. Giving her a good, solid kissing. Going steady these two. No first-date jitters here. Heavy petting, steamy backseat stuff.

Funny thing was, they didn't say much. Must have taken care of business out on the boat. Nothing left to say on good old terra firma.

Harry W. Feather dialed the number and waited. They'd planned the phone call, but Harry knew the man would make him wait. Put him in his place. The man answered on the ninth ring, "Coltis here." Always answered that way.

Harry thinking, I'm supposed to be happy I don't get some secretary, some flunky out there at the agribusiness empire of Lofton Coltis.

Harry couldn't keep the sarcasm out of his voice. "Yeah,

well, it's Harry W. Feather at this end. The Cowgirl met some guy at a marina. They went out on his boat. Four hours I'm cooling my heels in a restaurant bar trying not to puke from all the fish nets and little dockside villages made of balsa wood. Some bimbo coming up to me every ten minutes, asking me if my party's arrived yet. Do I want an appetizer? I'm telling her I bought the bar stool with the whiskey I'm drinking. Can't she leave me the fuck alone?"

Coltis blew a big, tired sigh. Big agribusiness guy, Napoleon of Commerce. No time for Harry Feather's problems. Coltis said, "I'm buying your time at a pretty handsome rate, Feather. Be polite to the ladies in the restaurant. Use those manners your momma taught you. Do whatever it takes."

Tone of authority. Used to being obeyed. No questions. Complain and you're out. Some Juan or Etienne, no green card, takes your place cutting the cane.

Harry W. Feather said, "Whatever it takes, Lofton." Using the first name, knowing Coltis would hate it. "I gotta go now. The bitch is getting in her car."

Harry W. Feather watched the woman walk right past his big white Caddy, not recognizing it. Still drunk on her sea captain. His intoxicating presence. He said to Coltis, "Call you when I get back."

"Don't bother," Coltis said, tired. Long day in the cane fields, watching over the stoop labor. Counting trips to the water bucket, making sure nobody took too long in the port-o-potty. Big management decisions.

Good old Coltis, University of Florida and Harvard Business School. Coltis's old daddy sends him to Harvard to take a little country out of the boy. Put him on the Charles River, get the smell of pig shit out of his nose. Let him smell the Yankee shit floating in that icy water. Make him long for his old Okee City home. All those acres nobody could shit on but a Coltis.

Harry W. Feather didn't say anything. He'd been told not to bother. "And, Feather," Coltis said, "you're not poaching gators here. You're not dynamiting shad. This is serious.

You graduate with this one. Don't hurt the woman, but scare her very well. Scare her so she knows it's deliberate. So she makes the connection we want her to make. Then she'll do the right thing. You do it right, Harry, and we move you up." Coltis cradled the phone so gently Harry didn't even hear a click.

Hoboy! Harry W. Feather thought. Moving up. He wondered what Coltis had in mind for him. Wondered if the guy knew his real worth. Harry W. Feather had read all the books from that Harvard MBA. In fact, had read the very books Coltis had held in his own hands. Harry's mother, Amelia W. Feather, had smuggled them out of Coltis's study, swiping them one at a time when she cleaned up.

Maybe Harry had only seen pictures of Cambridge, the icy Charles, but he'd read the books, crunched the numbers. He knew up from down, in from out, in the world of finance. So what did old Coltis mean when he said, You move up? It was something he'd have to think about. Ponder.

Coltis was dangerous. The more you knew about him, the more dangerous he was. Not like a gator or a moccasin. With them, knowledge gave you an edge. With Coltis, you had to be careful what you discovered. Sometimes you had to play dumb, be invisible. Harry W. Feather was good at that. He'd watched the old men, learned it from them. They could disappear right in front of your face.

One minute you look, there's an old guy drinking from a paper bag, leaning up against the front of a minute market on U.S. 41. Middle of the Glades. Noon. Nobody else around. No car to drive. You look away and back again, the guy's gone. Blank wall. The older they were, the more they remembered about the old days, the better they did the disappearing act.

Harry walked to the Caddy. He was getting in when the boat guy walked by. And, hoboy! Harry recognized the guy! Eddie Priest, big-time ex-football player. Carrying a canvas bag from the boat. Serious sailor's look on his face. Or maybe it was a serious pussy look. Cowgirl pussy. The guy walked with a limp, khaki shorts, two big scars on the left knee. Frankenstein scars, zippers. Guy used to catch passes, score touchdowns. Harry remembered the games on TV when he was a teenager. Remembered the guy's name, what he looked like in a football uniform.

Guy still had some gristle on him, maybe a little belly, but plenty of meat stacked in the right places. Handsome football star face. Tanned, the guy, but white underneath, white as the belly of a bottom feeder. White to the core of his bushwah soul.

Harry W. Feather slid down in his seat as the guy passed. Invisible. Wouldn't do to be seen here. What he really wanted to do was talk to the guy. Get in his face, make him see Harry W. Feather. Hey, man. You have good sailing out there today? Nice, what you call it, breezes and things? Good zephyrs? See the guy's goofy smile get brittle.

Harry W. Feather liked to puzzle them. Good policy. The guy saying, Pretty good breezes. Nice day. How 'bout you? You a sailor?

Harry W. Feather smiling, laughing. Jerking his thumb at the Caddy. Me, I sail in the land yacht there. She can still sail. I'm out there on the old blue highways doing ninety. Got the wind in my face. I'm yelling, "Abaft, you swabbies. Man the pork rinds, and bring her about in the boom." Nautical stuff like that. It's fun. Passes the time on the long drive.

Yeah, well . . . , the guy says, shifting his weight in that phony-confident jock way. Smile rotting off his face. Not knowing what to make of old Harry. Well, that was the point. They had to guess and Harry didn't.

The Former Football Great was unlocking his car now. Some Japanese hunk of grunt. Nagasaki Nut Bucket.

When the Former Great was gone, Harry W. Feather backed the Caddy out. Leaving the parking lot, Harry got a little rubber, essence of Goodyear, perfume of burning brake bands, eau de Citgo. He liked to horse the big Caddy around.

The sunset was a gorgeous blood orange when Harry took the approach to the Sunshine Skyway Bridge, big ugly hump of a thing out there in the dusk, lights shining up its big spider legs. Pretty spectacular, the tourists said. Go to St. Pete, see the bridge. Drive over the bridge and stop at the top. Let the wind blow your blue hair straight out behind you. Cause a ten-car pileup. What the hell, it's what you came for. You gotta look.

He caught the Cowgirl at the top of the southbound span. The sun setting over the Gulf, a pale moon rising over Tampa Bay. Couple of phosphate ships anchored in the roads off Egmont Key, lit up like Christmas, waiting to take the channel in the morning when the pilots shook off their union restrictions. Harry W. Feather knew all about the commerce of the Tampa Bay area. Hell, he'd read it all, studied it. All part of his preparation for a better life.

He fell in behind the Cowgirl's blue Ford Explorer. Keeping his distance. Lot of vehicle for a Cowgirl. And brand new. He hated the thought of it getting scratched. Good solid American rolling stock. If it got scratched, the Cowgirl would get the blues.

8

Lofton Coltis watched Clinton Reynolds park his Mercedes under the long windbreak of Australian pines. The pines sheltered the western approach to Coltis's house from winds that swept unimpeded three hundred miles across south central Florida from the Gulf of Mexico. They blew a full ten miles on Coltis land before reaching this house. Reynolds got out of the Benz and stood watching the house where Coltis waited.

Coltis could see Clinton's gold Rolex flash in the setting sun; the car, the watch, the Armani suit, all of them to mask the essential fact of Clinton Reynolds. That he was a jumped-up grit in a patronage job he didn't understand, a tall and angular body that housed a mental homunculus whose only ambition was to suck the tit of bureaucracy until senility forced him to retire. And this nonentity had decided to do Lofton Coltis a favor.

Coltis did not want Reynolds in the house. Did not want

that ambling, perfumed pretension inside the simple country
house his grandfather had built from Georgia heartpine,
lumber shipped to him eighty years ago on steel rails Henry
Flagler had laid across the virgin pine barrens. Coltis
stepped outside, stood waiting in simple contrast to Clinton
Reynolds. Coltis a tall, lean, white-haired man in tan whipcord trousers, a white cotton shirt, and old work boots.

Clinton Reynolds stopped a few feet from Lofton Coltis
and shaded his eyes from the sun.

Finally, Reynolds said, "How are you, Mr. Coltis? It's
been a while since I seen you."

Since you *have* seen me, Clinton. Coltis thinking, Didn't
they teach you anything in that school my daddy's taxes
bought?

"Walk with me, Clinton," Coltis said. Starting across the
yard toward a row of sheds and outbuildings. Clinton fell
into step beside him. "Sure, Mr. Coltis, only"—looking at
the Rolex—"I don't have a lot of time. I got to . . ."

"You've got time for a little walk, Clinton. A little talk
about the favor you did for me."

"Aw, Mr. Coltis, that was just something I . . ." Clinton's
voice different now, rising. His pigeon chest not feeding the
voice enough air. Rising and getting smaller.

"Just something, Clinton? I'll say it was just something."

They had reached the edge of the sodded yard. Out here,
things got a little marshy this time of year. Coltis enjoyed
the soft feel of the earth under his boots, the sinking in. He
liked seeing Clinton mired to his socks in the black muck
that paid the bills. Clinton's glove-thin Italian tassel loafers
disappearing. Liked hearing Clinton's breathing drop down
from his porcine nostrils to his open mouth.

"Mr. Coltis, I didn't . . ."

Coltis raised a hand. "Just a minute, Clinton. Let's just
step along here in silence a moment. We don't have far to
go. Just out to the shed there. I've got something to do, a
chore, and we can talk while I do it. That all right with
you, Clinton?"

Coltis walked into a shed that housed on an old tractor-

drawn sprayer tank. He walked past the rusted sides of the
five-hundred-gallon tank, past its long-flattened tires to a
scarred and wealed bench that stood under the shed's single
window. Through the window Coltis could see the asphalt
airstrip where the two Agwagon crop dusters were tethered.
He stood at the bench, staring at the two airplanes.

"When I was kid, Clinton, I used to drive the sprayer
behind you. In the summertime, I'd go out barebacked like
the buck I was and do a ten-hour shift pulling that sprayer
with somebody named Juan or José walking behind me at
the end of the hose, spraying the crop. You picture that,
Clinton?"

"Sure can, Mr. Coltis." The voice up in choirboy range
now.

Coltis didn't look at Clinton. He was looking into the past.

"We'd turn at the ends of the rows, Clinton, sometimes
I'd get sprayed. Or I'd drive through a cloud of the stuff, a
mist on the wind, something like that. You picture it?"

Clinton said he did, he pictured it right good or something
like that. Coltis wasn't listening to him. He knelt and lifted
an old grapefruit crate from under the bench and removed
a five-gallon can from it and a pair of heavy black rubber
gloves. "This is what we sprayed, Clinton." He put on the
gloves and used one thick rubber finger to wipe dust from
the label on the can. "You see that, Clinton?"

Clinton leaned close. "Parathion," he said. "It says parathion, don't it?"

Coltis turned away from the window. The two airplanes
tied down to steel spikes driven into the asphalt had long
ago replaced the tractor-drawn sprayer. "It does indeed,"
he said, "and Clinton, the government says I can't use this
anymore. Hell, it kills army worms and locusts and the
medfly. It kills just about everything that crawls and flies
and eats a man's crops, but the government says I can't use
it. I used to pull that sprayer and get wet with the stuff and
breathe it in and that was thirty years ago and it hasn't hurt
me, and you know what, Clinton . . . ?"

Clinton said he'd sure like to know what. He sure would.

Coltis said, "The government won't even let me get rid of that sprayer because of the residue she holds. They'd come out here and wrap the whole damn thing in space-age plastic and bury it in a salt mine in Utah and send me the bill if they knew about it. And, Clinton, God only knows what they'd do with this." Indicating the gallon of poison.

Clinton said he didn't have any idea about any of this. Not one.

"This, Clinton, is what an honest farmer is up against these days." Coltis pried the lid off the old gallon can of parathion. The lovely smell he remembered bloomed into the hot airless shed. You wanted to know why kids sniffed glue, abused household substances, all you had to do was sniff this stuff. It was powerful. He turned to face Clinton. The heat had made Clinton's armpits meet in the middle of his Armani suit. His tassel loafers had thick rinds of mud around them. His eyes were smaller than usual and full of the question he had lived with since birth. What have I done to deserve this?

Coltis said, "Clinton, you decided to do me a favor. You wanted me to think well of you. Hell, you probably think of yourself as a man with a future in this county. A man like you always thinks he's got a future. He thinks about patronage, influence. Nothing straight, direct. His mind moves like a snake. So you decided to do me a favor. You didn't think to ask me if I wanted the favor. You didn't think to ask me what effect the favor might have on *my* future. You didn't think because that's the way you are, Clinton. A snake can't see what's flying way up there, coming from way, way off. A snake has what I would call a vision of the immediate."

Clinton had found something in his rolling thoughts. "I fixed it, Mr. Coltis. I did. That girl is completely . . . discredited." Clinton struggling with a polysyllable. "You saw what I told the paper about her."

"No, Clinton. *You* saw what *I* told the paper."

Coltis himself had written the news about the girl. But it had been sheer luck that he'd heard about her in time to

46

phone the newspaper. Explain the situation to some friends of his. How the girl had taken it upon herself to alter state records. What she hoped to gain, Coltis certainly couldn't say. How she was blaming it on her boss, Clinton Reynolds. But it was only a temporary solution. He'd had to craft a more permanent one.

Coltis reached into the old gallon can and gouged out a handful of parathion. It was blue-black, the consistency of axle grease, and it had that pretty smell. A high, heady odor that hinted of the fantastic scenes they said people sometimes witnessed at the moment of death. He held the cold, blue-black gelatin in his hand. "Like I told you, Clinton, I used to get this stuff all over me, back when a boy did a man's work. It never hurt me." He held out his hand to Clinton Reynolds. "Shake," he said. Saying it like you would to a very tall dog.

Clinton stood there trembling, a good head taller than Coltis, those pig-dark eyes dilated, the sallow, fish-belly complexion reddening, a hank of greased hair fallen across a low forehead. Trembling, wondering if there was any way out of this. And the capacity for wonder failing him utterly.

Coltis said, "I want to make a bargain with you, Clinton, and I want to shake on it." Holding out his gloved hand.

Coltis had made a bet with himself that Clinton would shake hands. That he was so conditioned to servitude that he would reach out and take the black glove. But Clinton's hand only hovered in the air between them, unable to cross the last inches. No matter, Coltis thought. The thing that kept Clinton from obeying him was the same thing that had made Clinton destroy the computer file. It was the thing that had to be punished.

Coltis struck quickly. Like the mouth of a snake, the heavy glove seized Clinton's hand. A good firm grip. "I'm glad we had this talk, Clinton." Lofton Coltis held the hand hard, the way his grandfather had taught him to do when he was just a shirttail boy shaking hands with grown men. Getting to know the world. As Clinton started to buck and jump, Coltis could feel the black gelatin oozing between his fingers. Enough parathion in their two hands, if Coltis remembered the measure correctly, to charge the sprayer tank three times, three thousand gallons. "And, Clinton, don't do me any more favors. That's our bargain. Not unless I ask you to, that is."

He let Clinton's hand go and tossed the heavy glove onto the bench. He was halfway back to the house when he heard Clinton's running feet behind him, then heard Clinton stop to vomit, screaming the name of his Jesus into the country silence. Then he heard the Benz start and Clinton tore away.

9

▲▲▲▲▲▲▲▲▲▲▲▲▲▲▲▲▲▲

The headlights had been behind her for an hour now. She'd first noticed them at the cutoff to Zolfo Springs. She couldn't make out the car behind the glow, but she knew it was the same one that had followed her for an hour. What the hell, she'd told herself. This old two-lane at night. Not so many opportunities to pass. But she'd been passed twice. She'd seen them both coming, gaining on her. But this third car, the one behind her now, kept exactly the same distance from her whether she speeded up or slowed down.

The first car that passed her was a big black Oldsmobile. Two women in it, talking a mile a minute in the glimpse Corey got. One holding a lit cigarette, gesturing with it. The two of them blasting past on their way home from a weekend in Naples. Heading back to the farm for another week of cooking collards and washing Delbert's socks, picking the cockleburs out of them before tossing them into the Kenmore.

Next, a pickup full of sleepy migrants. She'd slowed down to forty-five, forced the truck to pass her. An old GMC that probably wouldn't do more than fifty. But the driver had tripped his brights at her and powered on around. Mexicans, the parents and their oldest son in the cab and a bunch of stair-step kids in the truck bed, the youngest curled up on big sister's lap. All their eyes glowing in her headlights, watching her with that sullen passivity as the truck pulled away.

And the car behind her slowed, kept its distance. That was when Corey Darrow got scared.

Harry W. Feather had it planned. He'd watched the road carefully on the way north, not sure what he was looking for at first, then the thing coming together in his mind, exactly how to do it. The elevated roadbed, almost a dike, the hard rain he'd driven through wetting the soft, narrow shoulders. The sharp slope to the ditch and then the ditch itself. A canal really. He'd liked it on the way down, guessed it'd go at least five, six feet deep. You wanted to scare somebody, that was the place.

After he'd seen the canal, he decided to pass the Cowgirl, play with her a little. Let her see his face. He'd put on the big wraparound aviators with the mirror lenses, pulled out to pass, looked over at her. The last human face. The face of Harry W. Feather. Flying that big Cadillac and smiling at her. Giving her the celebrity grins.

That was the trip north.

Now Harry W. Feather saw the old, dead Esso station coming out of the dark. Rusted red gas pumps with their white glass globes. They were his landmark. Time to do it, Harry. Time to get righteous. He pulled out and stood on the firewall, blowing a cloud of unburnt gas and black smoke out of the Caddy's pipes. He loved that. Wretched excess. He was almost alongside the blue Explorer when the bitch caught on and hit the gas. That Ford could go. Maybe not like the Caddy, but she was going to make a race of it. Good. Fine. Mr. Coltis had said he wanted the woman to

50

be afraid. At speeds above seventy, water was as hard as concrete. Harry knew the physics of fear.

When Corey Darrow saw the lights move at her, she was almost relieved. She punched the Ford up to seventy and reached over, popped the glove box. Driving with one hand, groping for the heavy revolver Raymer Harney had given her. A loaner, he'd called it. Whatever.

She remembered meeting him at the Cane Cutter Bar and asking, "Did you bring it," and his face going all B-movie serious and him saying, "Follow me out back in about three minutes." Then he got up to leave.

Out back, a couple of cane cutters were drinking shine from a quart jar and some cowboy had his girlfriend or somebody's girlfriend up against the wall, running his hand up the slit in her skirt. And Corey saying, "Raymer, what are we doing out here?"

And Raymer handing her the stainless-steel Smith & Wesson .357 Magnum. Warm from inside his polyester pocket. "Here it is," he said. And then, "I still don't get it, Corey. Why you think you need a handgun."

After she felt how heavy it was, that serious weight, she hoped even harder that she didn't need it.

"Put it in your bag, Corey," Raymer had said. "Don't wave it around out here, for God sakes. And one more thing. It's clean."

"Clean? Clean, Raymer?"

"It's not registered. Serial numbers ground off. As far as the authorities know, it doesn't exist."

"Is that good?"

"Good and bad. A person uses it, dumps it, nobody traces it back to that person. That person gets caught with it. Deep dirt."

"So, if I use it . . . ?" Corey searched for Raymer's eyes in the dark.

"You get rid of it quick."

She found the gun now in there among the dusty maps and old Kleenex dispensers. She put the gun between her

51

legs and pushed the Explorer up to eighty. Hell, as scared as she was, maybe she could outrun those lights.

The Caddy backfired and Harry W. Feather promised himself he would have a serious talk with Boner Harkness at Fender Mender Auto Body and Repair. Boner had tuned her up especially for this trip. Boner had promised she'd go like there was no tomorrow, like she was burning rocket fuel, like Fireball Roberts was driving her. Well, Harry W. Feather was having a hard time catching a Cowgirl in a new Ford Explorer. Harry kicked the accelerator a couple of times, trying to get the last few R fucking P fucking M's out of the old girl. He needed them. It was only two more miles to the place. The spot he'd chosen, where the dike was highest and the dark, sulfurous ditch was deepest. Then he saw the Explorer skid.

Maybe the Cowgirl had hit a patch of oil, a place where some dusty butt Mexican had blown the engine of his crapmobile. Happened all the time. Or maybe the Cowgirl just couldn't take the heat.

Watching the Explorer fishtail across the northbound lane and then back south, its brake lights coming on, Harry pictured her in there clinging to the wheel until her store-bought fingernails popped off. Ping! Ping! Those nails hitting the dash like little bullets. Scared to death.

But she got the thing right, flying straight and level, and Harry knew he had to get up there and do it now, before she got another couple of hundred RPMs out of that Ford mill. He kicked the Caddy again, made her belch, moan, resist, then give in, giving him another hundred, then another two and he was alongside the Cowgirl. Looking over, smiling, edging over toward her, crossing the center line. *Seeing it.* Holy shit! Look out, Harry! Watch it, boy!

Corey Darrow lifted the .357 Smith and showed it to him, held it against the window. Trying to keep her hand from shaking. Fighting to hold the Explorer on the road with her right hand. She could only take her eyes from the road for an instant, but she saw the surprise in his face. Maybe fear there too. Good. Good for you, Corey. Scared the fucker. Kicked him right in his psychic testicles. Girls with guns. Why not?

She was still shaking from the skid. A rabbit. Goddammit, a rabbit. Right across in front of her and her risking twenty thousand dollars worth of a brand-new Ford and her own priceless life to avoid killing a damned rabbit. Corey, what is wrong with you? What is wrong with you?

Instinct. Instinct is wrong. Mine is for life, not death. Mine is to be careful. Too many years of learning to care. The eye sees the bunny, the hand jerks the wheel. God, she'd almost hit the ditch for a bunny. But she hadn't. She'd gotten it straight again. Gotten it back on the road and now she was showing the guy the stainless .357. Giving him something to think about. The two of them shooting down that lonely, narrow highway at ninety in the middle of the night.

Did she dare look over again? Had to. The guy was waving at her, driving with one hand, leaning toward his open window. Those mirror eyes. In the backlash of their combined headlights she could see how dark he was. That tan. Sun Worshiper. The Bad Man. The man who had been following her.

She lowered the pistol, holding the Ford tight, and with the pistol butt touched the button that opened the window. It hummed down and the nightswamp rushed in, warm and rotting and somehow sexy. Yes, sexy. Making her nipples hard. Corey rested the pistol barrel on the windowsill and asked herself if she had what it took to pull the trigger. Send something across the three feet that separated them, something to let the guy know how serious she was about staying in her lane. Then she saw the rabbit. Not another one. The same one. The one she had swerved to miss. She pulled the gun in and closed the window.

Harry couldn't believe his luck. The Cowgirl, surprisingly resourceful, had just pulled that heavy hitter back into the car. He wished he could have seen the look in her eyes.

That animal terror. Harry daring her to shoot and then that giving in, giving up. God, that was sexy. It was what a man wanted from a woman. Finally, that was it. He inched the Caddy over toward her. The thing was to do it without touching. In essence, make her do herself. Just keep taking up the space, strangling her, eating up the good road, until her right front tire skipped the asphalt, hit the sickening, sucking mud, and the top-heavy Ford went in.

He took road, but she held her own. Not looking at him. Harry leaning toward the window, whacking his hand on the steering wheel. Whacking and shouting, "Move over! Give me some room here! Don't hog the road!" The place he'd planned for her was less than a quarter mile ahead. A few seconds at this speed. Harry, if you can't do it pretty, do it ugly. He edged the Caddy and felt the shiver of metal as his right front bumper kissed her left wheel well. And then?

She was gone. Disappeared.

He let the Caddy wind down. Good old girl. Done him proud after all. Maybe he wouldn't have to have that talk with Boner Harkness about the quality of American workmanship. He didn't touch the brakes until he'd coasted a mile. In his rearview, he could still see the column of steam hissing up from the ditch. All that hot metal in all that cool water. Even at this distance, it was pretty spectacular. Harry stopped, executed the difficult maneuver of U-turning the Caddy on the narrow road, and started back to have a look. What hath Harry wrought?

Corey Darrow couldn't move her legs. And after the bite of the seat belt, she was hurt above her waist. She couldn't tell. A collarbone? Maybe the left shoulder dislocated? First, there had been an enormous pressure and noise, an impact distributed through her entire body. Later, after a few moments passed, she began to separate the areas of pain. The left leg below the knee, the right at midthigh. The left arm. She wanted to see her legs but couldn't. The car was filling with water. She had one good hand left.

She didn't know what to do. The water was in her lap, the car lying on the driver's side, tilting at an angle of maybe thirty degrees. She'd heard you were supposed to turn off the ignition, but if she did that, she wouldn't be able to get the window open, crawl out. She had one good hand and she used it, reaching across her torso, broken edges grinding in her shoulder, and pushed the power window button. The window hummed down and the water poured in. Oh, shit, Corey. Oh, shit.

She tried to rise in the seat, tried to lift herself. Couldn't. No energy now. Too much pain. Paralysis rising from her lower back, cold into her chest. The water filling the car. She could see outside, across the windowsill. See the level of the ditch. Maybe, just maybe. She waited as the water touched her breasts, her neck, her chin. She arched her back, lifted her chin. She could do it. Thank God. Keep her mouth and nose, her eyes, out of the water. She could wait this way. As long as she could stay awake, she could wait this way. Wait for somebody to come.

She had a dream. There were rabbits. Hundreds of them. Rabbits everywhere. Big ones and little ones. They crowded around her, rubbed against her legs like cats and she knelt to pet them. Pet store rabbits, impossibly plump and clean. One of them spoke to her. "In the animal kingdom," the rabbit said, an old male with a stubble under his chin like a man's gray beard, "there are two kinds. Those who pursue and those who are pursued. Nature gives each its skill. Things are not as dangerous as they might seem. Remember that."

She woke up knowing that someone was coming. Thank God, she thought. Thank God and so soon. I didn't have to wait here so long. I had only one dream. I am still breathing. But her neck, her back, were howling already from holding up her head. She was starting to tremble.

Then she saw the mirror lenses, the man standing on the road above her. And she understood something. The man was an Indian. What did they call them nowadays, out there in the world where minorities changed their names every ten years? They called them Native Americans. This man was not some sun-addicted beach god, he was a Seminole Indian. Or a Miccosuki. She remembered it as a kid, passing the signs on old 41: Airboat Rides. Alligator Wrestling.

Going in there with her parents and watching the Indians, eyes sullen, sitting under lean-tos of thatched palmetto fronds, weaving cloth to sell or carving curios and her waiting with her parents in the heat and dust, drinking a Coke from a tall red machine that sat alone in a clearing, its back to a single power pole. Her eyes following the wires until they were out of sight along the road that connected this place to the highway. Finally, her mother whispering to her father that she wanted to leave. *"Now,* please." And her father saying, too loud, "Wait a minute, Harriet. I come all the way out here, I'm gone see a man wrestle a gator like the sign said." Her father standing there with his wallet in his hand.

Finally, at some unseen signal, an old man had climbed into the muddy pen. The gator so sleepy from sun or drugs that all he'd do was roll over and slowly lash his tail. Still it had scared her. Not the fact of animal and man meeting like that, belly to belly. Not the obvious lethality of both nor the likeness of their slow, serious movements. She had seen herself in the eyes of the old man as he had walked to the pen. A little white girl drinking a Coke in the hot sun. A little white girl who had somehow crawled out of the wallet in the hands of the white man with the nervous grin on his face.

She came back now from that sun-hammered, hopeless place to see the Indian walking into the ditch. Getting his shoes, his pants wet. He was waist deep in it, coming toward her in an aura of moonlight. Maybe it would be all right now. Maybe. Corey Darrow let herself hope it that way. He smiled as he came, perfect white teeth in a face almost black in the moonlight. When he got to the car window, his body pushed water over the sill and into her mouth. That was all the margin she had. An inch for her eyes and mouth. She coughed, spit. Tasted the swampsex.

She heard him say, "There now, Cowgirl. Take it easy now. Let's see what we can do for you."

She closed her eyes and took a deep breath of the spicy nightswamp air and saw herself making love with Eddie Priest in the Gulf of Mexico. Then she remembered the kingdom of rabbits.

Harry W. Feather reached down and gently tangled his fingers in the Cowgirl's hair. It was muddy and wet, but it was good hair. Not too coarse and still smelling of whatever she washed it with. Something perfumey he liked. She was classy for a country girl. He'd seen her around town. Harry W. Feather leaning invisible against the front of the Citizens and Southern Bank, watching her pass. She had some class. She didn't wear stockings as thick as sausage casings or jewelry that made her look like a walking chandelier from a Holiday Inn or shoes you could kick field goals in.

She was a cut above the other Cowgirls, this one. He rested his hand on the hot, hard globe of her skull and thought about it for a minute. Maybe even regretted it a little. Thought about what they might have done, him and this one. Saw himself forcing her over to the side of the road, pulling her out of the Explorer into the Caddy. Talking to her, real sweet, voguing with the Harry W. Feather charm school attitude. The whole ball of wax. Telling her, maybe, what the W stood for. Harry White Feather. That he was a prince of the Creek Nation, that he had ancestors going back to before the migration of the Creek from the Piedmont region. That his grandfathers had shed the blood of white men in General Gaines's army. Charm her right out of those tasteful, county bureaucrat clothes she was wearing and get her on his side. Make a friend. An ally. Things like that happened all the time. People having changes of heart.

But it was just a dream. Harry W. Feather stopped having it now. It wouldn't work. Too late. Harry was thinking of Lofton Coltis. Mr. Coltis wouldn't care for this much. Harry had done a lot more than scare the woman. Maybe if she hadn't shown him the gun, threatened him. Maybe if she

57

hadn't done that, Harry would have let her go with a good scaring. And maybe not.

Harry W. Feather held the Cowgirl's head, listened to her breathing, felt her tremble under his hand, fighting for every breath now. Gutsy. Tough. A lot to be admired here.

He held her head under until the trembling stopped.

10

▲▲▲▲▲▲▲▲▲▲▲▲▲▲▲▲▲▲▲

At first, they'd met in the Governor's mansion. It was safe. She had every official reason to be with him there, day or night. But the Governor had decided he wanted a little risk with his tryst. So, risk it was. Sawnie owned a cabin near Kulawaaka Spring about forty miles out of town. An old hunting camp. After the Governor's successful run for a second term, she'd used her bonus money as a down payment on the shack and its five acres. The place reminded her of her father. Come to think of it, the Governor did too, but she didn't want to think about that any too carefully. Not tonight, anyway.

She walked around the place, getting it ready. Kicking on the old air conditioner, cracking some ice into a bowl, setting out the whiskey. When she saw the headlights of the Governor's Jeep Wagoneer sweep across the windows, she poured their ritual bourbons. Sipping hers, she stood at the window and watched him get out of the Jeep under the damp swags of Spanish moss that hung from a hundred-year-old live oak. He stretched and looked back up the sand track that snaked through the oaks and cypresses. Then he leaned back into the Jeep, took something from the seat, and stuck it under his coat. He looked at her window, waved.

When they'd planned this the first time, she'd told him she didn't think he could get out of town without some reporter following him. "I can see it now," she'd said, " 'Governor Caught with Senior Aide in Love Cabin. Issues Usual Denials.' " He'd said he could do it and he had every time so far.

She'd finally got him to tell her how he did it.

He kept the Jeep in a long-term parking garage not far from the capitol. It was registered under the name of Mr. Effingdam Wright, one of the Governor's little jokes. Mr. Wright was a tall, bald-headed man with a big globe of forehead, a very dramatic handle-bar mustache, and an unenviable complexion. Mr. Wright had had some sort of accident and walked with a cane. Sawnie had asked the Governor what he thought the people of the state of Florida would say about it if he ever got caught wearing his Effingdam Wright disguise.

"Well," he'd said, "I should say they'd admire my persistence in the pursuit of love, if not my originality in the matter of protective coloration."

When she heard his boots scuffing on the front porch, she picked up his bourbon and walked over to let him in. The first thing through the door was his Effingdam Wright face, a not very artful rubber mask, complete with Groucho glasses and the drooping bandito mustache. The genius of it was that the parking garage attendant, a man selected for his position by Amos Tillman, the Governor's bookie, was legally blind. The Governor snuck out through the kitchen and rode to the underground garage lying on the backseat of Amos Tillman's ancient Buick.

The blind attendant always showed Mr. Wright a great deal of courtesy. The two of them being persons of infirmity.

She took Mr. Wright's face from the Governor's hand and gave him a glass of bourbon.

"What's that you're hiding under your coat, Governor?" She hung Mr. Wright on the hat rack by the door.

He sipped the bourbon and turned his back to her. "Never you mind about that. All in good time." He took off his jacket, leaving the surprise, whatever it was, wrapped up. Just like him. Always full of surprises. Surprises that cost her weeks of damage control.

He came to her now, smiling, stopped a few feet away, tossed back the rest of the bourbon and opened his arms. She stepped into them. Feeling him rest his chin on the top of her head and begin to sing to her, some lullaby he had invented, some nonsense thing from the powerful source of language that was his political fuel. She closed her eyes, her face pressed to his neck, listening through her skin.

The voice was the thing that had captured her early, made her believe in him. Had kept her with him all these years. And it was hearing him singing a strange, sad melody from his hospital bed when he had awakened from the surgery after the plane crash; it was that melody that had seduced her. Long before he was physically able to become her lover, all through his long convalescence, she had known they would make love. It was there in the song he sang.

Now their lovemaking was slow and sweet. She lay holding his moving body, her eyes closed, feeling his rhythm in her, matching it, the two of them one creature on its long swim. They slept together.

When she surfaced, he was sitting at the table by the window, nude, looking out at the dripping trees. A ground fog had come in and now the big oaks that shaded the tin roof formed drops the size of robin's eggs and shed them. The drops fell and broke and it was to this percussion that Sawnie awoke. It was coffee-dark at night out here under these oaks; not even the light of a full moon could filter through. From down by the spring, she heard a whippoorwill cry. It didn't say "Whippoorwill." It spoke a legal phrase to Sawnie's ear, something like "To whit, to where?" ending as a question. She thought of it as the lawyer bird, part of the music of this illegal love.

She turned her head a little and watched him, not wanting to break his reverie. He had the bourbon bottle on the table and he'd made a considerable dent in it. He reached for it now to pour again, and she watched his long, white frame stretch and relax.

She knew what he was thinking.

The Governor's wife, India Lindfors Miles, had been killed in the plane crash. She and the Governor and their pilot had been en route to a field trail for quail dogs in southern Georgia when their twin-engine Cessna 310 had gone down in a storm. The pilot had died instantly, but the Governor and his wife had been able to crawl from the wreckage and fashion a shelter from clothing and parts of the aircraft. When they had been found the second day after the crash, the Governor was in a coma and India was lying dead with her head in the crook of his arm.

After his long recovery, after they had become lovers, he had told Sawnie the last thing his wife had said to him. Lying there in pain, then in the rising numbness, she had said, "I'm going now, Billy, but I want you to know it's been a good ride. A very damned good ride." The Governor had whispered as best he could: "Don't be silly. You're not going anywhere." But she was, and he had known she was. And he had lain there feeling her go, then feeling her gone, cold and gone, and then he had gone himself, into a coma, wishing for death.

Now Sawnie watched him sit naked, drinking, lean and bleached as an ancient white heron, and looking out the window into the night. And she knew he was thinking about India. He had told her that being with her brought it all back. "Well, then," she had said, "maybe you shouldn't be with me. Maybe you shouldn't bring it back." And he had looked at her hard, angry: "No," shaking her by her shoulders like she was a little girl, "no, don't ever say that. It *should* be like death. A little like death. Every time it should be that way, just a little."

Maybe she had understood, maybe not. She knew she had something that was important to him. As important as anything. Anything but politics.

"What you doing?" he said, his words a little bourbon loose.

She stretched in the warm bed. "How'd you know I was awake?"

He laughed, but with an edge. "Man don't know when his woman's awake, he's in trouble."

She laughed too, softly and without any edge. His calling her his woman, his knowledge of her. These were things of his vanity and she let him have them. Wouldn't have tolerated them for a minute in a man her own age. But you didn't change the course of an old river. This man thing of his was bred in the bone and he would live and die with it.

"You want to talk about it?" She meant India, the crash, his wounds, the long scars on his chest and legs, and the ones inside too, the real disfigurements that no one but she had seen. The things he sang about when he made sad love to her.

He waved the hand that held the bourbon, slopping some of it on the floor. "No," he said. "Ain't you wondering what's in my coat?"

"I'll start wondering at Christmastime. For now you can pour me a drink."

He walked over to the bottle of Heaven Hill and poured, tall and white-naked and moving with a stiffness that was half age and injury and half natural dignity. He came back with her drink and his coat. She took the drink and watched him open the coat and take out a folder. In spite of herself she was disappointed. No diamond necklace, no emerald brooch to match her eyes. No, and there never would be. He thought such things were sentimental slop. He'd told her that he'd never bought his wife jewelry. After he'd given India his mother's Purdey shotgun, anything else would have been anticlimactic. She could buy her own trinkets. India had been a wing shot of legendary deadliness.

Sawnie had told him that she'd rather shoot lobbyists than little birds and she liked men who remembered her birthday. He'd said, "Girl, I'll give you myself when we've got time and a lot of interesting work to do with the rest of your life and if that isn't enough, well, you can keep the job and find someone else to tickle your fancy."

"Open it," he said. She looked into his eyes, thinking, Not here, not now, not work.

It was a government form, the one you filled out if you planned to run for public office in the state of Florida.

"What's this? You planning to run for a third term? There's just the little matter of a constitutional prohibition against it."

"Read it," he said, almost angry.

She picked it up, lay back on the pillow, and looked it over. On the second page, at the bottom, someone had typed in her name. She looked at him. "What the . . ."

"That's right, Sawnie. You. You're going to be what the good Lord made you to be. Not some glorified gopher for a fossil like me, but the natural born Solon you are. And you're going to do it with my support. All of it."

"I can't . . ."

"Of course you can, and you will."

He smiled now, watching her. Some test she had to pass. She looked into his eyes until she was certain he was serious. Then she let herself smile too, let herself think about it, imagine it a little. Hell, why not. Who knew the government, the lobbies, business and industry, the press, even the people, better than she did? The answer was, nobody. Not even the man who had misspelled her name "Sarnie" at the bottom of this form. That man was the Governor and it was the first typing he'd done in a very long time. Her smile got a little wider.

She said, "What are you thinking about? That state house seat from Calabria County? The one old Milford Samuelson's retiring from? That could be an interesting race."

He frowned. Shook his head. She had disappointed him. He picked up the bourbon bottle and slopped some in both of their glasses, spilling a little on the sheets of the bed she thought of as theirs.

"No, hell, Sawnie." He reached out and touched her head. "Think about it."

She tried to think about it. Not much happened. And a sip of the good hot bourbon didn't help. Finally she shook her head.

He frowned harder, drank his whiskey in an angry way. This thing had him all stirred up. And there was more going on than his giving her a gift, his support, his acknowledgment of her buried ambition. She wasn't sure about the rest of it, but she knew she had to handle him easy. She waited, her eyes open to his.

"You kept your residency down there in that godforsaken east Jesus county of yours, didn't you? Isn't that what you told me?"

She nodded. It was true. She had kept her residency in Okee County for tax reasons and partly because she could never believe this Tallahassee thing was real. Nobody really lived in the state capitol. People flew in to do the business of government and flew out to some real life somewhere else.

"And you don't know what I'm talking about here, girl?"

"If I do, I'm keeping it well concealed." She tried to get him to smile at her puzzlement.

"I'm not talking about some piddling seat in the house. I'm talking about the United States Congress, girl. There's gonna be a new congressional district down your way when this reapportionment thing gets done and you're gonna file for it. And win it. I'm going to be all over this state supporting you."

He got up from the bed and walked to the chair where he had left his clothes. Left her paralyzed in the hot grip of surprise. Damn! The U.S. Congress. Damn, but she wanted it. She could feel it now in every limb, a pleasant, growing vibration, urgent and long overdue.

He was dressing quietly, his back to her. When he turned

around, stumbling a little from the bourbon, his face was grim. "Thing is, and you know it as well as I do, you got to have clean skirts. Not a speck of mud on them, girl."

She pulled the sheets up around her neck. Maybe that was a cold night wind from the open window where the Governor had sat looking out at his thoughts. "Well," she said, "there's a sort of an irony here, isn't there? About the size of a grizzly bear, I'd say."

He stood over her, dressed now, the empty bourbon glass in one hand, and the ridiculous rubber face of Mr. Wright hanging from the other. "You could call it that," he said. "I guess you could call *me* the mud on your skirts. But you got too big a future for *this* now." He swept his hand at the little cabin: "You can do too much good now. It might sound corny as hell to someone your age, but the truth is, I've got to give you up for the good of your career and for the good of this state. End of goddamn speech."

She loved him, and how much? So much that she'd kept it from herself. When people said a woman could have it all, she always thought, You can have only what you can do well. A career or a marriage, not both. This little shack in the woods had owned a marriage and now, losing it, she knew it for the first time.

She turned away. She didn't want him to see that her eyes were wet. She whispered, "You had to get drunk to tell me, didn't you?" She didn't know why she said it or what else to say, except thank you. Thank you for the good news and the bad news. Thank you for the knife that cuts my bonds and cuts my flesh too. She wiped her eyes on the sheet and turned back, managing a smile as he stood over her.

To the rubber face of Mr. Effingdam Wright, she said, "You better get on out of here before I make an ass of myself more than I already have. It's late."

He leaned down and kissed her. She said, "And don't get caught swerving all over the road. Some state trooper'll have a heart attack when he sees your driver's license."

"Straight as an arrow," he said, his voice no longer slurred. The thing he'd needed the bourbon for was finished now. At the door, he stopped. "The deadline's in two weeks. There's a nine-thousand-dollar filing fee. I'll float you a loan if you need it."

When his engine sounds had died away in the dripping trees, Sawnie lay thinking about the future. What it might hold. And the past too. The Governor's voice when he'd appointed the reapportionment committee, that old rambunctious prayer of politics. That song he could get the people to share with him. He'd been singing to her in that room in the capitol, telling her that the hymn and the prayer were hers now.

11

▲▲▲▲▲▲▲▲▲▲▲▲▲▲▲▲▲▲▲

Thunder woke Eddie Priest at midnight. The Gulf of Mexico was throwing horizontal rain. He went out to the old sleeping porch and stood in a pool of rainwater, cranking the jalousies down. A laughing couple came running from Pass-a-Grille Beach into the corona of a streetlight. Two senior citizens, they held hands, the woman's silver hair lank and streaming. Some second childhood tryst rained out.

Eddie watched the two get into a BMW and drive away. He went to the tiny bathroom at the end of the sleeping porch for a towel to wipe up the gray-painted oak floor. Why did people paint good oak floors? This beach bungalow, whose second floor he rented, had owned a hundred treasures. A succession of sojourners had painted them or modernized them or removed them to antique sellers. He stood pushing the towel around with his bare foot, shivering in the storm wind from ten thousand feet up. He was thinking about the dream.

The dream had begun with Corey Darrow's dive. The bubbles streaming around her, her long hair throwing an arc of water into the setting sun. Then her legs a hot ring around him. The two of them at home in each other, the same sleek, mad water animal. Doing, in the dream, what they hadn't done in reality. Then the woman had broken from him. Some signal of his flesh causing her to separate. Eddie not knowing what it was. The words "What have I done?" forming in his mind as the water grew colder and then suddenly deadly cold and Eddie swimming for the transom of the *Sight Unseen* and heaving himself over, collapsing, shivering on the deck, then rising to look out and Corey Darrow gone.

And then waking to thunder and wind and this wet towel under his foot.

It took only a minute for the sleepy long-distance operator to get the number for him. Charming, he thought. Down in Okee Country they had real people drawling phone numbers. They hadn't yet hired the electronic voice that pumped out numbers with eerie plosions of robot breath.

He dialed Corey Darrow and felt a certain joy when he heard her say hello and was about to answer when he realized she was a recorded message. When the message ended with a cheery "Wait for the beep," he said, "Corey? It's Eddie. If you're there, please pick up. I know it's late, but I ..."

He was about to say, "I had to call," but it didn't sound right. And he wasn't going to mention the dream. The dream didn't amount to anything but some partly digested Camembert and his feeling a little bad about the way it had ended out on the boat. His not wanting her trouble, not really believing it *was* trouble, and her seeing this and going silent and then later kissing him good-bye with a surprising warmth and saying, "Get those tires. Those Michelins. You hear?"

And him saying, "Damn right I will. Next weekend. Another island. Same activity?"

And the shyness in her eyes while they both remembered

kissing in the water. Nothing shy about the kissing. The beep caught him debating what to say. "I had to call"? It was the truth.

He dialed the number again, heard the message. That voice. She could make a million dollars with it. He said, "I had to call. I'm sorry it's so late. You must still be asleep. Or maybe you stopped at a motel. Anyway, I just wanted to say I . . . meant it about next weekend. And listen . . ." BEEEEEP.

He dialed again. "Listen," he said, "let's talk again about that problem you mentioned . . . I mean I didn't feel right about leaving it where it is. Maybe there is something I can do about . . ." BEEEEP.

Eddie imagined her standing there angry in the dark. Hearing his messages but not wanting to pick up. Maybe not so much angry as proud. Still feeling the bruise of his rebuff. Or maybe it was the country girl standing there, rethinking her reputation and the too hasty embrace she had given a man who owned a leaky boat. Who had taken her out to a deserted island and talked her out of her panties.

Or maybe she wasn't there. He put the phone down. Maybe she hadn't made it home. Fatigue had overtaken her on that lonely road and she'd stopped for the night. That had to be it. She wouldn't stand there and listen to him fumble. Not the woman with that voice.

Or maybe she was out somewhere, helling around, trying to forget about Eddie Priest and his boat and an island where the sun went down memorably and a country girl shouldn't have.

The rain was pounding hard on the jalousies. The wind keening like the demented backup singers of the band in Bedlam. The cold wind felt good on the sunburn Eddie had acquired with Corey Darrow. He'd call again in the morning. He finished drying the floor with his foot and went back to bed.

Harry W. Feather stood in the dark listening to the Cowgirl's answering machine, waiting to see if the Former Football Great was going to call again, keep on swelling the cash flow of AT&T. When nothing happened, he replayed the messages. And kept replaying them, standing there alone in the darkness of his very first home invasion. He loved the way the Former Great sounded. The guy whimpering, "I *had* to call."

Harry had been five miles from the scene of the crime when he'd felt it, that lingering sense of the thing done quickly and not well. Oh shit, Harry, *the gun!* The stainless-steel piece the woman had waved at him. He had to admit there was a moment when he thought she might just reach out and touch someone, smoke some ordnance old Harry's way. But no, by golly, she hadn't. Made him lose all respect for her, at least until she made a brave show of it at the end. Holding her head up like that, spitting and sputtering. So fierce to keep the air coming.

So Harry had thrown the Caddy into a smoking half-circle and headed back hard. Thinking of the Ford Explorer coming out of the ditch at the end of a wrecker's cable, all weedy and still hot and steaming and the water pouring out of the cab and Sheriff Bryce Nailor standing there with his thumbs in his belt and his gut spilling over so he couldn't see his Redwing boots, and there it is, lying on the floorboard. That pretty stainless piece. So Harry was heading back to the muck and mire. He was going fishing for that pistol. Make things look righteous.

He was half a mile away when headlights rounded the curve and he decided hauling ass was the better part of valor. Another smoking U-turn. It would just have to *seem* curious, a dead bureaucrat with a gun in her car. And, hey, maybe it wouldn't be all that damaging. Harry started playing with it. Building the scenario. Doing it the Hollywood way. What is this pretty girl doing with a gun that causes her to leave the asphalt at ninety? He could see it on "A Current Affair." Bizarre Sex Leads to Highway Tragedy. Gun sales going over the top.

But he couldn't make himself happy with storytelling for long, because Lofton Coltis wasn't going to like it. Not this story. Coltis would call it the metaphorical equivalent of dynamiting catfish. Something very, very smartass like that. Something to remind Harry W. Feather that in Coltis's eyes he was only a couple of notches up the food chain from a bottom feeder. So, Harry W. Feather pulled the Caddy over beside the sign that welcomed visitors to Okee City and thought things over.

It was a little after midnight and the flat landscape lay in almost total darkness. The farmers and shopkeepers of Okee City were long since dreaming the dreams of stupidity and a general failure of the imagination. Bryce Nailor, the sheriff, would be out on the southern approach to town where he could tune in a Miami country station. He'd be half asleep in the music or looking at crotch shots in *Club Magazine*. When somebody finally did stop and find the Cowgirl and get to a phone, the call would go to the sheriff's dispatcher. She'd call the town's single EMR unit at the county clinic and then get ahold of Bryce. Bryce would put down his magazine and quiet the swelling in his pants and then Harry W. Feather would hear the sirens loop-looping across the silent, swampy fields of Okee City. That's how it would go. The night was quiet. Harry W. Feather figured he had time to go to the Cowgirl's house.

It wasn't at all what it was cracked up to be, home invasion. In the perfect home invasion, there would be people *in* the house. There'd be a prom queen who'd walk in on Harry W. Feather rubbing the sleep from her eyes. Maybe wearing a filmy nightie. Or some broncing buck would come home from a long night of titty-hawking and catch Harry W. Feather with the prom queen's panties under his nose. This was far from the perfect first time. Harry reminded himself that he wasn't here for the thrill. He was here because he had fucked up.

Harry had on his AIDS fighter's rubber gloves. The Cowgirl had left a back window unlocked. People were like that out in the country. What the hoo-hah, maybe he'd find some hard copy. Coltis believed the woman might have printed out the file. Harry didn't know what was in the file. Just that it had made Coltis so pissed off at Clinton Reynolds that he'd threatened to castrate him with a machete. Harry's mother, Amelia W. Feather, had heard them on the phone. She'd thought it was funny, said she'd nearbout had to stuff her dust rag in her mouth to keep from laughing out loud at what the refined Mr. Coltis had said to Clinton Reynolds.

So, maybe Harry W. Feather would find something here. Something to sweeten the pot a little, take the edge off old Coltis's pique when he read in the county fishwrapper that Clinton's assistant, Corey Darrow, had been dredged out of a canal with a .357 Magnum in her car.

Harry found some matches in the kitchen and walked through the house, striking them. The Cowgirl had taste, all right. A little too severe for Harry, a little too modern, but good all the same. In the bedroom, the usual collection of pictures. Mom and Dad, a couple of used-up farmers, mealy looking white people. And wait, here's the Cowgirl. Several shots of her. One picture, she's in her band uniform carrying a saxophone. Another, she's a cheerleader. That letter sweater and short skirt, those cute little saddle shoes and the, what did they call them? Pom-poms? She's laughing in both shots. Harry didn't see how a girl could toot in the band and do the Block That Kick shit too. You sure had to be versatile at Okee City High. And the Cowgirl was a looker, even in high school.

The family history, yes, but no documents.

So Harry played the messages again, listening to that moony, scared thing in the big jock's voice. "I *had* to call," the Former Great said. Half a day out on a boat and the guy was absolutely P-whipped. Had the scared thing already. Scared he'd lost his girl. God but love *did* make fools of people.

12

▲▲▲▲▲▲▲▲▲▲▲▲▲▲▲▲▲▲▲▲

Boner Harkness pulled the tow cable down to the ditch and waded into the cool water. He didn't like this one damn bit. The steel cable was heavy and burred. In the rush, he'd left his gloves back at the shop and now the little steel prickles were cutting into his hands and Bryce Nailor was just standing up there on the shoulder watching with his big arms folded across his silver sheriff's star.

The paramedics had come and gone. One of them, a short, wiry guy with that dead gleam in his eyes that you got from too many stiffs and too much blood, had told Sheriff Nailor that she'd been dead for half an hour, maybe forty-five minutes. Talking quietly, ignoring Boner. Nothing they could do, the guy said. He'd reached in, unfastened the seat belts, but there wasn't room down there to open the door. It made no sense to drag a corpse out through the window. The paramedic's blue jumpsuit wet to the waist, the guy picking ditch muck from his pant leg, still had his rubber glove on. Tells Bryce Nailor to call Blessings Funeral Home. Bryce, Mr. Forensic Genius, says he already did. Says he called the minute he saw her.

Boner had to put his head under water to attach the big hook. It took two tries. After the first, he leaned against the still-hot grill of the big blue Ford and let himself look into the cab for the first time. He could see the top of the woman's head, swaying with the movement of the water. Her hair floating out around her, some of it out the window now, shining in Bryce Nailor's headlights.

"Whyn't you come on down here and help me," he called to Bryce. "Can't you see I can't get this hook set right?"

Bryce Nailor just recrossed his arms and looked down at his boots, kicked a piece of roadside junk off into the dark.

"Hurry up, Boner. You got to have her up here when the meat wagon comes. Old Draper ain't gone get his only suit wet messing with a stiff that's up to her eyes in ditchwater."

Bryce Nailor looked off at the horizon. As if he could see anything that way. As if it wasn't the middle of the goddamn night.

Boner got her hooked on the second try. Came up spitting that stinking piss water and wishing he didn't have to drive this tow truck, didn't have to live in this middle-of-nowhere town, didn't have to handle this cable without his gloves.

He climbed out of the muck and jumped himself up and down to sling off as much water as he could and then drove the truck another twenty yards down the shoulder to let out more cable. It was going to be a tricky pull. She'd have to come up parallel to the road, slow and steady, or, full of water, she'd turn over. Maybe go bottom up.

Boner seeing the woman's hair now in his mind's eye, dragging along the bottom of the ditch because he pulled her all wrong.

But Boner pulled her right and when the Blessings Funeral Home hearse arrived, he was standing by the winch watching the water slowly leak out of the Explorer. Bryce Nailor had gone over to look inside, but Boner stayed by the truck. He knew he didn't want to see the woman's face.

Old Draper got out of the big Lincoln hearse. Lifting a knee up with both hands and dropping one foot on the ground, then the other. Bryce Nailor, at the Explorer's window, whispered, "Holy shit! Mr. Draper. Come 'ere an' look at this."

Old man Draper, who had seen everything, who would probably live long enough to see Boner and Bryce Nailor naked on the marble slab in his basement, dipped his head a couple of times and spit snuff and shuffled slowly over to the Explorer. He was too short to look in without climbing up on the running board. What he saw didn't shake him much. Maybe his throat, which always seemed to make swallowing motions, gobbled a couple of times extra. That was enough for Boner.

Something had reached out to him, something that wanted him to join the two men at the door of the Ford. Wanted him to see the woman.

When Bryce Nailor opened the door, the rest of the water splashed out. Bryce Nailor jumped back and Boner, standing beside him now, had to reach out and stop the woman from tumbling out. Her shoulder was cold in his hand and his stomach contracted at the touch of her. But it would be worse, much worse, to let go and see her lying at his feet, water seeping from her hair onto the road. So he pushed against her cold weight and felt her left arm slowly fall from her lap and saw it. A stainless-steel pistol in her left hand. Close enough for him to read: Smith & Wesson. Her white fingers frozen around it. Trigger finger in the killing place. And the thing cocked.

Boner standing there with his left hand on the door and his right on the woman's shoulder and the shiny pistol barrel pointed at his big toe. "Holy shit," he whispered, "Bryce, Mr. Draper, help me."

"No, hell," said Bryce Nailor, "you got her, Boner. Just ease her on out of there."

Boner feeling the little wounds from the steel cable, watching the blood from his cut hands leaching into the white fabric of the woman's shirt. "I can't," he said.

76

Because of her face. Because of her eyes. Open. The look in them.

"I got to let her go now."

Already loosening his grip on the woman's shoulder. Their two fleshes repelling each other in a way that made the remains of Boner's supper drill at the back of his throat.

When he'd said, "let her go," he had heard, somewhere behind him, a long way off it seemed, both of them start running. Mr. Draper scraping his palsied old feet on the asphalt, and Bryce Nailor's big legs stretching out, his boots scuffing hard down the road.

Goddamn them, Boner thought. Letting go. Letting her go because he had to, because of the rising nausea and seeing, as he turned, tried to run, out of the corner of his eye, her arm leading her down as she fell limp and loose, the silver barrel headed for the asphalt. Boner only half turned, not even properly running yet when the shock and the flash and the outrageous noise lifted him into the night.

13

▲▲▲▲▲▲▲▲▲▲▲▲▲▲▲▲▲

The cocktail waitress said, "Again?"

Eddie Priest had had enough of a lot of things, but he nodded, said, "Again."

The waitress said, "That's a Turkey up, ice water back." She looked at Raymer Harney. "How 'bout you, Raymer?" Her name tag, said, "Your Server Is Glyneice." She had on a fringed denim skirt and green suede cowboy boots, a black Death From Above T-shirt. There was a conspicuous absence of underwear. And there were six fresh stitches over her right eye.

Raymer looked at Eddie. "Sure. Why not."

Glyneice said, "That's a Maker and branch." She walked to the bar, an artwork constructed of dried sugar cane stalks and palm fronds stapled to a two-by-four frame. The motif of the Cane Cutter Bar was, in Raymer's words, "sort of a Tiki kind of thing, you know?"

Eddie knew. He looked around at the crossed machetes

on the walls, the two stuffed rattlesnakes over the bar—one of them with red nail polish on its fangs to simulate blood—and the collection of Haitian and Mexican laborers, local studs, and dating couples from the Okee City gentry. The jukebox was playing "Cowboy Logic." Eddie and Raymer had come here straight from Corey Darrow's funeral.

"How'd she get them?" Eddie asked. "Glyneice, I mean."

"Get what?" Raymer closed one eye, tilted his head in the old way of an inebriate who wonders if his companion is drunk.

"The stitches, Raymer."

"Oh! All's I heard was that she 'had to show that bitch.' I don't know what bitch. I don't know what was demonstrated. I only heard that she had to . . ."

Glyneice arrived with the next round. Eddie put his numb hands flat on the table, looked at them, then up at Raymer. Christ, he thought, did I really ask how Glyneice got her stitches?

They had quit talking about Corey's funeral long ago.

When Raymer Harney had showed up that morning, Eddie had just sold a forty-foot Cape Dory to a farmer named Arn Engstrom.

Raymer had stepped out of his car onto the dock looking way too serious for the kind of day Eddie was having. Some kind of apology in Raymer's eyes. Eddie had given Corey Darrow some advice: Had Raymer come back to ask him to change his mind?

Eddie had given the Engstroms the traditional stocking-feet tour of the Cape Dory and Mr. Engstrom had written the check. Now that tall, hawk-faced farmer and his wife were climbing back aboard the Cape Dory with their shoes on. What the hell. You own it, you wear what you want. Wear nothing if you want. Eddie smiled, picturing them, the farmer and the farmer's wife, sailing off into the tropical sunset, naked as God made them. Burning those white Wisconsin winters from their skins.

Raymer said, "How are you, buddy?"

"Raymer," Eddie said, his eyes still holding those happy scenes of the Engstroms, his right hand holding the check. He wanted to relish the moment. "What the hell are you doing here?"

It was eleven o'clock in the morning and Raymer looked like he'd slept in his suit. Eddie put the check in his pocket. The Cape Dory rocked gently under the weight of her new owners. He said, "Let's go to my office."

Eddie sat behind his desk, propped up his feet. Raymer took one of the mate's chairs by the big floor-to-ceiling window. All the bright blues and yellows and greens of the marina pouring in behind him. Raymer's eyes wouldn't meet Eddie's. "What can I do for you, Raymer?" Eddie wanting his moment with the check, the exhilaration, not to mention three months' rent and all the Mount Gay he could drink. With or without the paper umbrellas. Those new Michelins. And Corey Darrow.

"She's dead, Eddie. They pulled her out of a canal last night."

"Who's dead?"

But he knew or was beginning to feel the knowledge, cold and hard and stuck in his throat like a bone. "Pulled who out of a canal?"

"Corey Darrow." Raymer waited, watching him with those eyes full of apology. Eddie had to stand up. But standing, he found that his legs had gone watery. All he could think to do was take the check out of his pocket, drop it in the desk drawer. Then thinking, I don't want this with Raymer Harney. I want to be alone with this.

He was about to excuse himself when he saw that Raymer had been crying. The red, swollen eyes, the raw nostrils. Raymer pulled out a wadded hanky, stared into it, trying to control himself. Raymer had been more to Corey Darrow than a contact, someone who had arranged a meeting with Eddie Priest.

"You mean she never made it home?" Dumb, Eddie thought. A stupid question. Noises to buy time, time to think. Bury the bone somehow.

"She went off the road," Raymer said. " 'Bout five miles from town." Raymer thrust his long legs out into the room, his heels skidding on the Persian rug. "They said she went in a little before midnight. That's when her watch stopped."

Eddie's head swarming with questions. His voice loud, angry now. "Damnit, *who said?* What else did *they* tell you?"

Raymer pulled his legs in, hunching over them with both hands on his tree-trunk thighs. "I talked to Boner Harkness, drives the tow truck. He pulled her out. Him and Bryce Nailor. He's the sheriff."

"Raymer, I don't give a fuck about two grits named Boner and Nailor. I want you to tell me what happened to the woman." Call her the woman. Push her away a little.

"All's we know now is that she went in. The shoulder was soft. It rained last night. There's a canal by the road right along there. Water runs twelve feet deep in some spots. Hell, some folks fish in there. I went out this morning and looked at the tracks. She must of just lost control, hooked her right front off the asphalt, hit mud, and slipped into the ditch."

"What about . . . Corey? How did they find her? How did she . . . ?"

Raymer hurried now, hunched over, staring at the whorls in the rug. The words spilling out. "Still in her belts." Raymer's voice thinned to a squeak. "She must of been hurt too bad to get herself unbuckled. Bryce said it looked like she had broken bones and some internal injuries."

"It *looked* like?"

"He said she was pretty bad, Eddie. The county M.E. ain't looked at her yet. That's tomorrow."

"Autopsy?"

"Standard."

"You said you went out there, right?"

"I went out there this morning. Before I left to come down here. She was a friend of mine." In Eddie's mind's eye, Raymer stood on the asphalt of a country road. He'd risen before light and stood there in the dark, looking at the place where Corey Darrow had gone in. Mourning a friend.

81

"What else did you see? Did you see anything unusual?"

"No, not really."

"Not *really*, Raymer. Not really?"

"Well, like I said. I looked at the tracks. Walked them back up the road—it's a straight stretch there. There was some, not exactly skidmarks, just fresh rubber running straight about a hundred yards to the place where she hooked her right front off the hard road. I don't know how to account for that. If she'd skidded, they would have been fishtails, but the marks go straight. You'd think she fell asleep and drove off the road. But that wouldn't leave rubber. It's almost like she accelerated straight at the ditch."

"Would she fall asleep?" Eddie was seeing Corey now, disoriented, waking up too late with a foot pressed hard to the accelerator pedal. The black water coming at her.

"You tell me. You were the last one with her." Raymer dug his fingers into his thighs and lifted his eyes from the rug. The investigator in him rising out of mourning. Aiming his country smarts at Eddie. "How much did she drink, Eddie? What kind of . . . condition was she in when she left here?"

"She was fine, Raymer. She'd had one beer. One with me anyway. She was tired, we both were, but she wasn't exhausted."

"Well," Raymer said, heaving a sigh, "that ain't all. When they pulled her out, her left arm was broken but she had a gun in her left hand. A .357 Magnum. A Smith."

Something wrong now, something barbed in Raymer's eyes, cutting deep. Something Raymer didn't want to say.

"In her hand? Not in the car, not under the seat. In her hand?"

"It was in her hand, Eddie. And it went off. Boner Harkness, the tow truck driver, got about half the slug in the back of his leg after it deflected up off the road. Lucky he's not dead, you ask me. The morgue attendant had to pry the pistol loose from her fingers when they got her back to the county clinic. Her finger was frozen on the trigger."

Eddie looked out the window at the rainbow of colors—

blinding white boats with their bootstriping and bottom
paint, blue and maroon and yellow canvas, club pennants
from all over the world. Blue sky and blue water. All of it
going gray now. Gray like the view in the eye of a storm.

The Engstroms were climbing down the ladder. Eddie
could see the shy smile on the woman's face. A bit of a
dance in the way the long farmer walked beside his wife.
They were starting a new life.

Raymer said, "Eddie, there's something you ain't telling
me. She was something to you, Corey. Something happened.
She wasn't just somebody you met because I asked you to."

Eddie looked at Raymer, hating him for a second, then
forgetting it. Raymer was just the messenger. Raymer was
his friend. And Corey's.

"She was somebody, Raymer. Somebody I wanted to get
to know better."

Eddie and Raymer had driven back to Okee City, caravan
style. Eddie in his Celica, staring at the smoking rear end
of Raymer's old Buick, trying to think about nothing as the
cattle country gave way to an ocean of green sugar cane.
He'd listened to a lot of sad songs on the country stations
and thought about Corey, what it might have been like with
her, and thought, This is the least I can do. Be counted
among the mourners, if anybody's counting.

He'd imagined a little country church service, a congrega-
tion of maybe two hundred, the cortege to the graveyard a
long, traffic-stopping line of pickup trucks and Chevys full
of old ladies in organdy dresses. Lace-bordered hankies
pressed to their eyes.

He wasn't ready for it to be just he and Raymer. The two
of them and the old guy who ran the town's funeral parlor.
A guy named Draper with a face like a wrinkled paper bag
and the suspicion of a limp. Walking with a wince in his
face as though years of handing out cheap sympathy had
made him want some himself. And the two kids who handled the shovels.

Eddie and Raymer looking at each other across Corey's

box. Carrying her with the two kids across the flat, marshy ground to the muddy hole. Nothing pretty about it.

Eddie muttering, "Didn't she have any friends?" Raymer looking across at him, sweating from the effort. His words coming out in wheezy puffs. "She had them. They just didn't come. Word got around it wasn't the thing to do."

Eddie asking, "What about that boss of hers? What's his name?"

"Clinton Reynolds." Raymer wheezing. "I don't see a weasel anywhere, do you?"

And then the old guy, Draper, hauling out the Bible and doing his bit as the representative of heaven. Solemnly explaining to them that he *was* ordained. Then reading the stuff about how the grass grew up green and got cut down. Eddie could never remember where those lines came from, but they always shot him right through the heart. Both barrels, one for the green grass and one for the scythe.

Eddie poured the shot of Wild Turkey into his throat and felt it scald down, giving his heart a little arrhythmic tickle, a scary hint of stoppage. Then he sipped the stinking sulfurous fluid they called water in Okee City. Raymer was staring into his whiskey. There was not a damned thing left to say.

Glyneice seemed to rock to a stop at their tableside, her stitches blurred. "Whatta you say, boys? Another time for old Glyneice?"

Eddie was about to say, "For you, anything," when he realized that Raymer was asking to be excused, looking with urgency at the men's room door and mumbling something about what a man's gotta do. Eddie didn't want to think about what was on the other side of the men's room door. A slit trench?

Glyneice stepped out of Raymer's way. She reached up and touched her stitches, smiling.

Eddie said, "I guess not. That last one topped the tanks." He reached into his wallet and took out a fifty that had

84

recently belonged to a farmer named Engstrom. A guy whose life had changed. Glyneice took it, examined it.

"That ought to do it," Eddie said.

She smiled. "It ought to."

The front door of the Cane Cutter Bar opened and Corey Darrow walked in.

14

▲▲▲▲▲▲▲▲▲▲▲▲▲▲▲▲▲▲

Eddie looked at the empty shot glass on the table. Closed his eyes. Counted. Opened them. Looked at the woman again. At the glass. Something that came from the distillery? Something you couldn't taste or smell, a chemical mistake that made you see things. Made you believe a dead woman walked. Walked into the Cane Cutter Bar in a charcoal Ellen Tracy suit and a string of pearls. He was about to get up, go to Corey. But she stopped just inside the door and her green eyes passed across his face like he was furniture.

Eddie pushed himself up and followed her to the bar. He took a stool a few yards from where she stood waiting, tapping a quarter on the bar. The bartender was drawing beers, lining them up on Glyneice's tray for a table of Haitians. Eddie waited. He had to hear the voice.

When the bartender finished, she said, "Excuse me. Do you have a phone I can use?" She lifted the quarter, showing him she wasn't asking for anything free. And it *was* the voice, that million-dollar music he'd last heard when he'd said good-bye to her at the marina. Telling her not to worry. That things weren't as bad as she thought they were.

The bartender pointed to the hallway that led to the back door and Corey followed his directions. Eddie pushed off from the stool, checked the men's room door for Raymer, and followed her to the phone.

She fed the machine and dialed and he stood a few feet away, watching. She had to have seen him by now. What the hell was going on? She stood facing the wall, listening. Nobody answering. Her face full of concentration. When she hung up, opened her purse, and dropped the quarter into it, Eddie stepped into her path.

"What are you doing?" he said. "You *saw* me. I *know* you saw me."

She looked up at him, snapped the purse shut. The surprise in her eyes changing to hard resolve. Then the voice. "Look, I don't know what you think . . ."

"Corey," he said, "it's me, Eddie. For Christ's sake, what are you doing?"

She looked at him for a long time. Finally, she said, "I'm not Corey. Corey's dead." She looked over his shoulder at the hallway, the bar. "You must not be from around here. If you were, you'd know that."

Now he could see it. Could start to see it. Even hear it a little. The difference. The eyes maybe a little wider apart and not so extreme in their emerald color. The lips thinner, slightly more severe. The hair a shade lighter, but the same wild Irish curls. The voice a little deeper, a more serious music. He said, "I thought . . ."

"I know what you thought. A lot of people used to think it. I'm Corey's sister. My name's Sawnie."

She held out her hand and he took it, already trying to convince himself she was not his second chance.

Sawnie Darrow had missed her sister's funeral and she hated it. Hated the time they'd sat on the runway in Tallahassee, listening to the announcements from the cockpit, the pilot's voice getting more and more testy as he told them about problems with the aircraft's communications equipment. "Folks, it's better to fix it on the ground than in the air." So she got out of Tally an hour late and landed in Sarasota and called the man, Draper, at the funeral home, told him she was chartering an airplane. That he could go ahead with the plans. She'd make it on time.

Then the flash squall from the Gulf, socking in the charter air terminal in Sarasota and Sawnie trying to talk the charter pilot into flying anyway, the two of them standing in the hangar beside the Beach Seneca, costing Sawnie God knew how much, and the guy looking at his watch, stepping out into the rain to look up, then telling her about FAA regulations and how he couldn't fly even if he wanted to and he certainly didn't, not with the possibility of windshear you got near these summer storms.

And finally getting into the air at four o'clock with forty minutes to make it and Sawnie's last phone call to the strange old man, Draper, in Okee City. Telling him to go ahead, she'd be there. She'd make it somehow. When the second storm hit them, sweat sprang from the pilot's hairline and dripped into his shirt collar. She knew she shouldn't talk to him, so she held her wild thoughts in while he horsed the Seneca away from the white-water clouds. Finally, the feeling of grace when the wheels hit, skidding, and she could see the rain slicing across the little runway in a sudden flash of lightning. They had diverted to a country field near Zolfo Springs.

In the little terminal, the pilot stared at her with grim resentment. "Lady, we came in on nonusable fuel. You know that?"

Sawnie had no idea what he meant. His hand shaking, slopping his coffee onto his big aviator's watch, and him telling her they'd used so much gas flying around these clouds, avoiding those windshear conditions, he'd had to go into his reserve fuel. That left him three gallons to find the airport, the runway, and get down. "Lady," he said, "I was running out of fuel, altitude, and ideas. That's the worst rain I ever flew in. Nobody should fly in rain like that."

Sawnie thinking, They are burying my sister, and I'm not going to make it. Not going to be there to see my dear sister go into that earth as black as Cuban coffee and just as fragrant, earth that seeped up between our bare toes in the summertime when we ran to meet Daddy coming home from work at the end of the long road where the mailbox said Darrow in red paint that dripped from the letters. She felt a deep, breaking sadness. It pulled her toward the country night, toward her sister, even though it was too late to do the last decent thing, the only thing left for Corey.

She looked at the pilot and smiled and put her hand on the rim of his shaking coffee cup to still it and said, "What the hell. You gotta die sometime."

She walked off then to get into the rental car they had found for her, but only after she'd mentioned the Governor's name three times (as she had promised herself she would never do in personal emergencies), hearing the pilot behind her muttering, "Another lunatic."

Now she was sitting in a bar in Okee City taking what comfort she could from the story two strangers could tell her about how they had put her beloved baby sister, Corey, into the black earth. And the comfort, it turned out, was not much.

"You mean *nobody* came?" she asked for the second time.

The big one with the basset hound eyes shook his head and looked at the door of the bar in a way that told her he'd rather not sit through any more of her questioning.

The other one, smaller, better looking, had something in him. More than the whiskey he had drunk, more than the anger he obviously felt at Corey's lonely funeral: something in him that kept his eyes from meeting hers. So she kept looking at him, sipping her vodka and tonic, kept asking *him* the questions.

"Tell me again how you knew my sister." She leaned forward, picking his locks with her eyes.

*   *   *

89

Eddie looked at Raymer, back at the woman who was not Corey, but looked almost exactly like her. Who was a twin, but not identical, but almost, or something like that. Or so she had told them. He wondered why she hadn't cried yet. Why Corey hadn't mentioned a sister. Wondered why Raymer hadn't told him there was one. And most of all, wondered how much he should say about why he was here.

He turned his shot glass on the table and said, "She came to see me in St. Pete. We met there, got to know each other a little. When I heard she was dead"—indicating Raymer with a sway of his head—"I drove down for the funeral. I figured it was the least I could do."

That last, the least part, had not sounded right. Had been somehow callous, though Eddie had not intended it to be. He'd tried for the last half hour to be careful, because he'd had too much to drink and because careful was right with a bereaved sister, but this woman didn't play the part of the bereaved. She acted more like a prosecuting attorney. And Eddie didn't like where that put him and Raymer.

She looked at Raymer now, but she spoke to Eddie. "You heard from Raymer she was dead? He called you?"

Her eyes let go of Raymer, picked up Eddie's again. That strong green beam. "Look," he said, "I don't know . . . What I mean is, there's something we haven't told you."

Raymer chimed in. "Right. That's right." Leaning forward now, serious. Very serious about letting Eddie carry the ball here.

Eddie going ahead. "Your sister was in some kind of trouble. That's what she came to see me about."

There was nothing left to do but tell it, Corey's trip to St. Pete, the afternoon on the boat, and Corey's confused story about a deleted computer file and a strange little man who went missing. When he finished, Corey's sister looked at him for a long time. Taking a couple of slow sips of her drink and watching him.

Finally, she said, "That's it? That's everything?"

Eddie had no idea how it was going to feel until he said

90

it. The thing he hadn't even told Raymer. "She said she thought someone was following her." It felt rotten.

He remembered Corey saying the man had been tanned. A Don Johnson imitation, she'd called him.

"A guy with a dark tan, driving an old car. A big one." He tried to keep his voice level, scrubbed of any judgment about Corey's fear. Tried to meet the woman's gaze.

Corey's sister looked down at her drink. Eddie was glad to have the green eyes let go. The eyes so much like Corey's. Looking into her vodka and tonic, she said, "Why you, Mr. Priest? Why did my sister tell you all this?"

Eddie gave Raymer a look that woke up the remnant of coherence Raymer had left. Raymer told the woman how he had made the introduction. That Corey had wanted to talk to Eddie. Raymer mentioned "that ecology stuff" again. Eddie watched the woman take this in. Raymer's version of Eddie's credentials. She didn't take it well.

Eddie said, "Look, I'm retired from the law. I sell boats for a living." Eddie thinking, Martha Weinstein would have liked this woman. Martha'd had the same seriousness, the same . . . something.

He remembered Ernesto's first phone call. Ernesto suggesting that Eddie ought to keep his nose where it belonged. Unless he wanted somebody to stick a 14 ought hook through it and go trolling for sharks in the Gulf Stream.

Eddie said, "I told Corey I didn't know anything about what's going on down here. She said that was all right and she left."

He tried to keep his voice down where things were just sad and weary, but he was getting angry now because of Martha. The way history repeated itself.

"Then Raymer told me about the accident."

Again the woman watched him for a long time. He could see in her eyes the years of weighing people and their trouble. She had the scales in there. *Fair Weight. No Springs.* He could see himself in there, registering very light. Very light indeed. She shook her head, knocked back the dregs of her vodka and tonic, and shucked a ten-dollar bill out of her

Coach bag. She crossed her arms across her chest. A chest that reminded him of Corey's. "You rotten rat bastard," she whispered. Acid and ice, that whisper.

Eddie glanced at Raymer, but she wasn't including Raymer. This was rat bastard singular.

"My sister told you she was in trouble and you didn't do a goddamned thing about it."

She kept breathing it at him, the soft, mean whisper. "And now she's dead."

She got up and walked out into the night.

Eddie looked at Raymer, who wouldn't meet his eyes. He looked around the bar, his head ballooning with a fierce and sudden ache. Warning him about the hangover they would share tomorrow. The Haitians and Mexicans had long since gone. The jukebox was silent. The girls who got prettier at closing time had all gone off with the studs they'd been sharing for years. Glyneice of the fresh red stitches was leaning against the bar, counting her tips.

For maybe the hundredth time since yesterday, Eddie thought about the things he could have done differently. Things that might have kept Sawnie Darrow from calling him a fatherless rodent. He saw himself following Corey Darrow home, getting out of the car in front of some country house she lived in and telling her, See, no one is following you. Nothing to worry about. And maybe that would have saved her. And maybe it would only have postponed what happened. He saw himself telling her he'd make some calls, look into this thing, get back to her. Saying, I'll take your case. And saw his phone calls yielding nothing, or worse, stirring up more trouble.

Now there could be no worse trouble for Corey Darrow. Now there was Sawnie Darrow and the trouble in Eddie's own head.

"Goddamn it," Raymer muttered. There were tears on Raymer's cheeks. "That pistol, Eddie. I gave it to her. I didn't tell you. She asked me for it and I gave it to her. They pull her out of a canal and she's holding it in her hand."

Eddie knew the tears weren't there just because Raymer

had given a dead woman a handgun. "What else, Raymer? Tell me."

Raymer rubbed the back of his neck, shook his head until his cheeks rolled. "Damn it!" he said. "It's an illegal weapon. A piece I took off an arson suspect. The guy had ground the numbers off it."

Eddie watched Raymer rub his eyes now. Rub those bad memories in there. "Eddie, she said she needed protection but I didn't want it traced back to me. How's it gonna be for me I give her a piece and she caps some guy that calls her a feminazi?"

Eddie rubbed his own eyes. It was late. His head banging hard, Eddie thought, At least we didn't tell the sister about the pistol. Plenty of time for that tomorrow.

15

▲▲▲▲▲▲▲▲▲▲▲▲▲▲▲▲▲

Harry W. Feather was thinking about love. How it made fools of people. He didn't want that to happen to him. Not again. And he'd heard that Moira B. Breath had come home. He wanted to see her. She was one of his biggest moments, was Moira. She'd been his first woman, in the cool shadows of a cane brake beside a canal. The first of many and in many ways the best.

He was fourteen. Moira had said she was thirteen and ready for him, but he'd later heard from friends that she was twelve. He'd made the beast with a little girl who had bucked and wiggled under him like a snake in boiling water, making noises in his ears that he heard for days afterward. Never had forgotten. Not words, unless they were words she made up. Unless she spoke a language he knew nothing about. He'd been a fool for Moira, all right.

He drove out toward the Miccosuki reservation land. If Moira B. Breath was back, she'd be out there somewhere,

94

down one of those swamp-mucky back trails with a double-wide trailer at the dead end of it. A trailer perching on cinder blocks with a gasoline generator chugging away and a pickup truck sitting out front. Moira's father, Donny L. Shanks, had gone into the trailer rental business, and Harry knew where most of Donny's properties were.

He found Moira on the third try in the maze of roads he knew as well as anybody. He'd only had to turn the Caddy around twice and get out once to bleed some air from a rear tire stuck in sucking mud. The mosquitoes a sudden, singing smoke around his head, a hundred torments, half of them finding their way back into the car with him. He parked beside Moira's Nissan pickup, knowing it by the Barnard College sticker on the rear window. He'd heard about that, her going off to college. There'd even been a piece about her in the *Miami Herald*. Miccosuki Girl Wins Barnard Scholarship.

Harry sat in the dark of the Caddy. He lit a cigarette for the mosquitoes and thought about this. It didn't look right. The yard was neatly raked and sprinkled with a bed of Australian pine needles. To his right, he could see a half-acre vegetable garden, collard leaves, lemon grass, and banana plants gleaming emerald in the moonlight. No junk, no clutter. No gasoline generator. The wick of a hurricane lantern flickered in one of the trailer windows.

When the light went out, Harry was out of the Caddy and crouched, cupping his cigarette in a curved palm. He watched the trailer, the windows, the front door. Nothing. More of the same. He was about to rise when something slid past the side of the trailer, low to the ground, coming. At least he thought so. With the speed of fear, he got back in the Caddy, locked the doors, and pulled his piece, a Llama nine-millimeter, from under the seat.

Holy shit! A face at the window. But not a face. A dog. A big one. Slapping its big feet at his window. Wanting in. A curiously silent dog. Harry W. Feather worked the slide on the Llama and pointed it straight at the big face. Someone knocked.

On the other window. He turned, lowering the pistol. "Harry W. Feather," she called. Her face close, hot breath on the glass. Twirling a finger to signal that he should lower the window. It was Moira. In the moonlight, she was still twelve years old, still a bucking, wiggling, yipping feral thing. He reached over and unlocked the door, sticking the piece back under the floor mat. "Get in," he whispered.

She shook her head, kept twirling the finger. He hit the button and the Caddy's window hummed down. She stuck her head in, and there it was, powerful, awful, a stink Harry had not known in years, not since his grandfather, Tom W. Feather, had died. It was some concoction of decaying hyacinth blossoms and raccoon musk the old men had used to keep the mosquitoes off. And it worked. Kept everybody else off too. Way off. He was glad Moira wasn't getting into the car. He looked to his right. The dog was gone now.

"I can't get in," Moira said, "Footnote wouldn't like it. He hates cars."

"Footnote?" Harry stared at her. She was different. He could see that now. He just couldn't see how.

"Footnote," she said, reaching down, pulling the animal up, its front paws on the window. Harry's hackles buzzed the full twelve volts. His batteries bubbled until sweat broke in his palms. It was no dog. It was a goddamned panther. A Florida panther. Maybe the last goddamn Florida panther, for all Harry knew. He looked at Moira with a new respect. She probably knew.

"He got hit by a car. Some two-wrist. Heading for Miami to see dolphins jump through hoops. Some shit like that. Probably didn't even see old Footnote crossing the road. Signs all over down there."

She pointed toward U.S. 41, the stink from her wafting into the car, mixed now with the mysterious hot odor of the big beast that stared at him. Eyes a lot like Moira's, come to think of it. "I'm taking care of him till he's ready to hunt again," Moira said.

Harry thinking, He looks ready to me. All he could say was, "I've seen the signs, Moira."

Moira looked at the interior of the big Caddy. "You drive that stretch of 41, Harry, you take it slow, okay?"

Jesus. He hadn't seen her in five, no, seven years, and all she had to say was, "Take it slow, Harry. Drive carefully." He nodded. He couldn't get used to the panther, on its hind legs, staring at him, a gossamer string of spit dripping from its jaws onto the Caddy's windowsill.

Harry said, "Hey, Moira. What do you say you put old Footnote . . . Footnote, is it?"

She nodded, solemn.

"Put old Footnote away, wherever it is you put him for the night. You and me catch up on what's been happening since the last time we seen, I mean *saw*, each other."

Harry figured he could put up with the smell. Or maybe get her to wash it off. Hell, they could take a shower together and *he'd* wash it off. Why not. A public service.

She watched him. Eyes that had more than a passing kinship with that cat's eyes. Finally, she nodded. "But you'll have to let Footnote get to know you. If he thinks you're all right, you can come in." She watched him. He nodded, already resenting it. What a man had to do for a little human warmth.

"And Harry W. Feather," she said, "I don't put Footnote away. Footnote stays with me. He's always with me. Until I send him back to hunt. Okay?" Her eyes were earnest, feral. The same eyes that had looked up at him from a bed of Australian pine needles in the brake beside the canal, enjoying him, communicating a need.

Inside the trailer, it was like a library. The walls were lined with books, magazines, maps, computer printouts, and official-looking reports with government seals on them. Harry considered himself an educated man. Self-taught. *Autodidact and Proud of It*—that would be his bumper sticker. But he felt the first constrictions of claustrophobia at his throat when he looked at Moira's walls of paper.

She had a desk set up off the tiny kitchen, a computer on it. She'd told him she had to drive down to the gas station a couple of times a day and pay five bucks to plug in her battery pack, recharge it.

"No shit," Harry said, "what are you, writing a book or something?"

"Something like that," she said, going all quiet and mysterious.

He looked down at his hand, still slippery and reeking of panther saliva. He hadn't liked it one bit, the way Moira had decided the big cat would get to know Harry. "Go ahead," she'd told him, the two of them standing by Harry's car. "Kneel down and let him take it in his mouth. Taste it. He isn't going to hurt you. Not unless he thinks you're a threat to me."

And Harry kneeling, holding out his hand. The beast sniffing it, taking it in his big hot mouth, just holding it there, one second from amputation and those eyes looking into Harry's, speculating. Harry thinking, Holy shit, how I'd like to be a threat. Be your worst nightmare, you mangy, testosterone-bloated meow-meow. Stick that Llama in your ear and give you the cosmic Q-Tip. The big brain reamer.

The cat's tongue was like shark's skin. No, more like a wood rasp. The big fangs rested heavily on the veins on the back of Harry's hand. Tomorrow, he'd have bruises. Like some poor puke who did needle drugs. The beast's breath smelled like rotting meat. This, Harry realized, when the cat finally spit him out, was a rival. A rival. Oh, yes, indeed.

Now the cat was lying over by the door, blocking the only exit, and Moira was in the kitchen pouring Harry a drink. Harry watched her moving around. She looked good, even in that silly dress. Some sort of back-to-your-roots Miccosuki rag. What did they teach them up there at Barnard? Wasn't there a course in Basic Bloomingdale's, Intermediate I. Magnin? Was it all burning the midnight books up there at old Barnard? No social life? No doing the wild thing with freshmen from Columbia?

She looked like something out of a picture some two-wrist had taken fifty years ago. A Miccosuki woman standing in front of a palmetto-thatched chickee. Her dead eyes offering hand-beaded belts. Only Moira was thin, her body as lithe and sweet-moving as it had been when she was twelve, and her eyes weren't dead. They sparked.

She was Moira B. Breath, the B. for Big. The old women told the story of Moira's mother giving birth. About how Moira hadn't needed the traditional slap on her pretty little butt. No, sir. Little Moira had taken a huge breath, inflated those fine little lungs, and let out a scream you could hear all the way to Tampa. Moira Big Breath was her name. She'd been screaming ever since.

Harry said, "Moira, you gonna have a drink with me, right? You not gonna make me drink alone?"

Moira looked him in the eye and said, "Harry W. Feather, you aren't going to get me drunk and fuck me." She glanced at the doorway where the big cat lay with its ugly face on its crossed paws. Staring at Harry. She said, "Footnote wouldn't like it."

"Wouldn't like what?" Harry knowing what she meant but asking anyway.

"You fucking me. The getting me drunk part wouldn't bother him one way or the other, but Footnote has a real proprietary thing for me. I think it's even a little bit sexual. After all, I saved his life."

"Tell me about that," Harry said. "How you did that?" He sipped his bourbon, tried to look interested.

Moira started telling about how she was on her way to plug in her computer at the gas station on 41 and she'd seen something moving in the weeds at the side of the road. And there's this giant cat, this panther with a broken right foreleg. And this cat is not about to let Moira get near it. She's got it backed up against a ditch bank and she's scared to death and the cat's scared to death and dehydrated and smells like it's pissed all over itself and maybe it's gonna die any minute or attack her or drown itself in the ditch and all she can think is she's got to help. Got to get the thing back home.

"I stayed there squatting in the sun for four hours," Moira said.

"So how'd you do it finally?" Harry asked, sipping, trying to get the Barnard girl to cut to the chase.

Moira B. Breath looked at him for a long time. Calm. What the New Age bozos called "centered." Coming straight at him out of her own specific gravity. Finally, she smiled and said, "We established a common language."

Harry didn't laugh. He was proud of himself for that. Didn't spit the bourbon in a fine mist in her face from laughing. He was a Miccosuki warrior and he had self-control. Self-control was part of the whole schtick. He said, "Tell me about it, this language." Very calm. Sipping his sour mash. Convinced now that Moira B. Breath was at least two cans shy a six-pack.

"I can't." Moira shrugged. "I'm writing a book about it."

Hoboy, thought Harry. The Jane Goodall of Everglades National Park. Miccosuki Witch Doctress, Moira B. Breath.

"I can tell you this," Moira said. "After I learned to talk to him, Footnote got up and walked to my car. Dragged himself there on three legs, got in the front seat, and rode home with me. That's when I went to the library in Everglades City and got the book on first aid. Learned how to set bones. That boy over there . . ." She pointed to Footnote. The big ugly cat lay staring at Harry like he wanted to get up, walk over, and say, "You and me, bud, outside. Right now. Best man takes the keys to the trailer."

". . . that boy over there," Moira said, "he's brave. He let me set that foreleg without anesthetic." Moira looked pointedly at the glass of whiskey in Harry's hand. The anesthetic Harry needed.

Moira said, "I told him it would hurt. I'd do the best I could. I'd be gentle, but it would hurt. He took it. Didn't move. Didn't make a sound. That's bravery," Moira B. Breath said. "The world needs a whole lot more of that." Moira's eyes with their roots in that still center of hers.

Harry didn't believe it. The part about the bone. Oh, there was no denying she was living with a panther. Hell, maybe the last Florida panther. Not even the Fish and Game Commission biologists could say how many were left. Couldn't be more than a handful. Mangy, inbred, bearing the diseases of a gene pool turned in on itself.

Harry pictured the big cat wandering the glades looking for companionship, seeking the love that made fools, and one night seeing two lights coming fast and God knows what the big cat thinks as it steps out on U.S. 41 in front of a rocketing Pontiac from Thief River Falls, Minnesota. The sickening thump. Old Sven and Huldah in there yelling, "Holy shit! What was that?"

Well, she had one, a panther, old Moira did. Maybe the last one. But Harry didn't believe the part about the bone. She was lying about that. She'd taken the animal to a vet somewhere, convinced the guy to set the bone. If there ever had been a broken leg. Hell, maybe she'd bought the animal from somebody. Out West they called them mountain lions. They had a lot of them out there.

Harry W. Feather, self-taught man, autodidact and proud of it, said, "Is that what they taught you up there at Barnard College? What you did with that scholarship? Establish a common language with the Florida panther? How to set panther bones? Stuff like that?"

Moira stood up and the cat was instantly on its feet. It was like her shadow. Harry wasn't too drunk to know that he had to stop this "it" thing. The cat was not an "it." It was a *he*. Some very substantial proof of that fact was swinging under the beast's tail.

Moira said, "It's time for you to leave, Harry. It's late and you're tired. I don't know if it was good to see you. I'll have to think about that. And Harry?"

Harry was standing at the door, looking down at the panther. The panther was making up his mind whether or not to get out of Harry's way.

"Harry," she said, "that's what they taught me at Barnard. To *think* about things. Once you start thinking, it's hard to stop."

"So, what do you think about, Moira Big Breath? Other than it might not be good to see me?" Harry knowing the question was stupid but unable to keep himself from asking.

101

Sterling Watson

Moira let her hand rest on the big animal's head. Fingers sinuously stroking. She said, "I think I hate that fucking highway out there, Harry. I'm as far away from it here as I can get and be on Indian land and I can still hear it at night. Those fucking cars going to Miami. I think I'm going to take it." She waved her free hand, the one that wasn't communicating with the panther, waved it at the books and papers and maps that lined the walls. At the computer. "That's what this is about, Harry. An Indian girl goes to Barnard College, she doesn't come back home and drink Mad Dog and swap food stamps for lottery tickets. She learns the panther's language and she takes back the road that tried to kill him."

Sitting in the Caddy, firing it up, the mosquitoes in there with him, singing their bloodsucking song, Harry shook his head and wondered if he'd heard her right. Moira B. Breath was going to take back the highway? The highway that tried to kill the panther?

102

16

▲▲▲▲▲▲▲▲▲▲▲▲▲▲▲▲▲

In the morning half-light, with his hangover rising like a grizzly out of hibernation, nothing to eat but his brains, Eddie started ringing the changes on his guilty bells.

Ernesto's voice was a deep resonant baritone, a voice that had made Eddie conjure a face. The face was Mayan, inscrutable. It belonged to a tall, bronzed man whose large brown eyes would say the last thing Eddie would know in this world.

Then Ernesto showed up in the office one day. Noon, Eddie's secretary was out to lunch. Eddie looked up and double-took this dapper Latino man who looked like a bank teller or maybe a slightly overweight dance instructor at Arthur Murray. The guy was about five seven in his conservative cordovan shoes and he was carrying a white cardboard box tied with a burgundy ribbon. The kind of box a dozen roses came in. He introduced himself as Ernesto Plar.

"I'm the guy," he said, "been calling you on the phone."

And Eddie thought, Jesus, this is what I was afraid of? This is the voice that threatens to cut off my hands? My worst nightmare come to life at noon on a Friday? A little fat guy holding a flower box?

Eddie's anger bloomed, but the impulse to bury a fist in the man's face gave way to curiosity.

"Mind if I smoke?" the guy asked. Taking out a pack of Merits.

"I'd rather you didn't," Eddie said.

Ernesto nodded politely, put the cigarettes away.

"So?" Eddie said, stepping from behind the desk. Eddie, six feet and change, looking down at this little Latino man, thinking how the phone had magnified this guy, made a monster of him in Eddie's imagination. Developing a theory about the size of fear, how it shrinks when you seek its source.

Ernesto handed him the box. "Open it, Mr. Priest." Ernesto looked very grave.

Inside the box, a clot of wilted branches. Eddie couldn't tell what the hell they were. Not flowers. That was certain. Some kind of joke. Some symbolism. Not a very good smell.

"Don't you recognize it?"

"No," Eddie said.

"Your red mangroves, Mr. Priest. Your precious red mangroves. Funny you don't even know what they look like. Seems like you would, you don't want nobody to even touch one. Cut one down. Make room for a nice house for somebody to live in. Somebody with a wife and kids and a job, all that."

"Yeah, well," Eddie said. The smell rising out of the box. Eddie about to say something about the principle of the thing. How you don't have to recognize a wilted red mangrove branch on sight to know it's important. To know why the state of Florida needs them.

"I think you better dig down in there, man," Ernesto said. He meant the box, the bouquet of dead mangroves. "You not finished yet," Ernesto said. "You need to keep looking what I brought you. You need to think about it."

Eddie took the mangroves out, lifting the dead stalks one by one. And Ernesto slipped out of the room.

Later that day the news that Martha Weinstein had disappeared. On her way to work. Her car found in a supermarket parking lot. No sign of a struggle.

Lying in the half-dark on Raymer Harney's couch, Eddie remembered the way Sawnie Darrow had looked at him in the bar. Questioning him like a tough prosecutor. Sometimes asking Raymer the questions but looking at Eddie all the time.

He realized that he had wanted to tell Sawnie Darrow about Ernesto. Not mention Martha, just tell her about the Latino guy who had called to ask if he'd like to go fishing. As the bait.

In the two years since he'd left lawyering, he'd told the story a few times in bars or to clients at the marina. He'd thought maybe telling the story would be therapy. So he told it funny. How the guy, Ernesto, had taken his time, explaining exactly how he would put Eddie's head on a 14 ought hook. "I think I go in one eye with that hook, Mr. Priest, out the other. Right to left. Work it in easy, work it through. That way, you keep that goofy look on your face. That look I see in the newspapers. What you think about my, what you call it, technique?" Eddie working on the accent, the deep, grave baritone. Doing a little Marlon Brando. Some of that "I coulda been a cadenza" gravel in his throat.

In bars, when he'd had his third Bacardi and lime, the story was useful. It was the easy shorthand of a sea change. It was how you climb down the social ladder and up the income scale. How you go from environmental crusader to purveyor of wind-powered boats to people who bring their garbage home with them. If they don't get drunk and throw it over the side.

Finally, he'd stopped telling it. It hadn't felt good, leaving out the Martha part. It wasn't the therapy he needed. He knew he should have put his fist through Ernesto's face. Therapy in retrospect.

One of his guilty bells, a new one, bright and shiny and loud, rang a question: Where had the woman spent the night?

Raymer had mentioned the De Soto Hotel, said it was the only place in town. She must have gone there. She must have had one hell of a time. Sleeping alone in this little town with her sister stiffening into the ground not far away. And thinking that she hadn't even been there to drop the traditional rose on the coffin lid. Eddie rolled out in the dark, waiting on unsteady legs to see if his stomach would ride level. When it did, he took a quick shower and pulled on some clothes.

The desk clerk told him that Sawnie Darrow hadn't registered at the De Soto Hotel. Eddie asked for a phone book. When he'd found Corey's address, he asked for directions. The sleepy clerk drew him a map. "It's out in the country, but I think you can find it all right."

Eddie wondered what *wouldn't* be out in the country around here.

Corey's house was about three miles out of town at the end of a winding sand track on a little bluff overlooking some pasture land. It was light enough when Eddie got there to see a salt lick off in the ground fog and some rotting sheds and outbuildings. An old farm. Apparently, Corey had renovated the pine and tin-roofed farmhouse. Sawnie Darrow's rented Corsica stood in the dooryard. Eddie parked behind it and walked toward the front door.

It was years since he'd hunted, but you didn't forget the sound of someone working the slide on a pump shotgun. He stopped, one foot ahead of the other, scared and wondering whether to raise his hands. After some shallow breathing and an examination of options, he said, "Don't shoot and I'll give you a discount on a good used boat."

He looked to his right as the woman stepped out from under a dripping oak. She was wearing knee-length rubber Wellington boots and a fawn hunting jacket with a quilted shoulder pad. The Remington pumper was aimed at his face.

"Look," Eddie said, "this isn't doing anything good for my hangover."

She thought about it for a moment, then lowered the gun. Eddie was gratified to hear the little click when she put the safety back on. His stomach was riding a heavy swell, a confused sea. He excused himself and stepped into a bank of ground fog and vomited. The woman waited quietly behind him. When he was finished, he said, "You got anything inside that changes the taste in a man's mouth? You know how it is in the morning."

"I know some of it," she said and walked past him, carrying the shotgun in a practiced way. He followed her into the house.

She gave him coffee in Corey's kitchen.

Sipping the good bean and watching her over the steaming cup, he asked, "You been out hunting?"

"I went for a walk. I couldn't sleep."

"You always carry heavy ordnance when you walk?"

She looked at him with those prosecutorial eyes. Why did he say these things? Or, better, why did he say them exactly as he did? "Look," he said, "I came over to apologize for last night. It wasn't very . . . sensitive of me to . . ."

"Fuck your sensitivity," she said. "I went out with the shotgun because I think someone's been in the house. I was looking for footprints, tire tracks, something." She sipped her coffee, watching him over the cup's rim. "I caught you and your sensitivity on my sister's property. You've said you're sorry and I agree. You can go now."

Eddie said, "Did you find anything . . . disturbed?" He was about to say "missing," but, hell, how would this woman know what was missing here?

"No. There are tire tracks out there and footprints, but I don't know what they mean." She looked off into the dark house. "It's just a feeling I have." She stood up. "You ready?"

She was a woman practiced in getting rid of what she didn't want. Eddie could see that. And he could guess that somehow the two sisters had gotten rid of each other, or maybe just one of them had. He looked down at his unfinished coffee. "You haven't seen your sister in a while, have you?"

She looked at him, at her coffee, sat back down. Her eyes were hard to read now. She wasn't the prosecutor anymore. The question had hurt and she was protecting the place where it had gone in.

She said, "What did you do with my sister that day? When she came to see you?"

"My question first."

She pushed herself away from the table, took her empty cup to the old porcelain percolator on the propane stove, and filled it. Then she picked up the shotgun from the countertop and looked at Eddie like he was vermin getting a reprieve. She worked the slide three times, expertly shucking three bright red shells onto the countertop. She collected them, put them in her jacket pocket, and then stowed the gun in a cabinet by the kitchen door. She put her cup on the table and sat down again.

"Look," she said, "I don't like you. From all appearances you're some kind of sleazy opportunist who got involved with my sister the day she died. You couldn't have known her, not much anyway. Why don't you have the decency to leave this thing alone."

Eddie thought about it. Maybe he *was* an opportunist. Taking the opportunity to work out his guilty feelings about Corey, a woman he had known very briefly and, he believed, very well.

"Tough," he said. "You're very tough. You put the gun away, then you give it to me with both barrels. Okay, the sleazy opportunist is dead. Now, whose question gets answered first?"

"Mine," she said. "And I am tough. I eat assholes like you for breakfast. Don't forget it."

"Jesus," he said, "assholes for breakfast. And I'm the one who puked."

She didn't laugh, but he thought she smiled. Maybe just in her eyes. He said, "It's exactly what I told you last night.

Raymer sent her. She asked if I knew anything about a guy who disappeared down here in sugargator county. She thought I was in the loop. I told her I just sold boats."

"Did you sleep with my sister?"

Gone the smile. The eyes, two mean green gemstones.

Eddie didn't answer.

Sawnie Darrow shook her head in what looked exactly like disgust. When she was finished, he said, "What about my question?"

"All right," she said, "I hadn't seen my sister in a long time." She wasn't going to give any more.

"Why not?"

"That's not your business."

"Is it yours who your sister ... ?"

"My sister didn't *love* you!"

"Maybe not." Eddie stood. "Look, I wanted to do the right thing. I think I've done it. I'll be out of your life by this afternoon."

Eddie walked to the door. Sawnie Darrow stayed at the kitchen table, her back to him. The phone rang. She rose and answered it.

"It's for you." She handed him the phone like it was something he'd dropped on his way in.

Raymer said, "Eddie, buddy, you gave me a scare leaving like that."

"Didn't take you long to find me." Eddie looked at Sawnie. She was frankly listening. He was afraid she was as beautiful as Corey. He was afraid of it.

Raymer said, "Well, finding people's what I do. Look, I called the sheriff's office. They said I could have a look at the Ford. You want to go?"

"The Ford?" Eddie was watching Sawnie watch him.

"Eddie, I'm talking about the Ford that went in the canal. Corey's Ford!"

"Yeah, I want to go with you." He watched Sawnie. "To see the Ford. And I got someone here who wants to make it a threesome."

When he hung up, Sawnie Darrow bit her lower lip and

shook her head. Then she said, "Give me a minute to get out of these boots."

When she returned from the bedroom, ready to go with him, she stopped him in the doorway. Leveled those prosecutorial eyes at him.

"Why did you quit the law?"

She wanted an answer right then. Like the answer would be her ticket to get in the car with him. Go see her sister's Ford. If he didn't talk, she wouldn't go. She was a lot like Martha, all right.

Eddie walked past her out to the car. After a while she followed him.

17

▲▲▲▲▲▲▲▲▲▲▲▲▲▲▲▲▲

I bet that hurts."

Harry W. Feather stood in the shade of the tin awning of Boner Harkness's Fender Mender Auto Body and Repair. He was watching Boner move around in that very painful way.

"You goddamn right it hurts," Boner said. Boner stopped to pluck at the elastic bandage that covered his right leg from ankle to knee. The bandage and the swelling underneath it made the leg twice as thick as his left. Harry could see the blue streaks of infection spreading across the top of Boner's right foot. Boner was wearing one steel-toed black work boot and an unlaced tennis shoe. He had even cut off the leg of his khaki pants because he couldn't stand anything touching him.

"Tell me again," Harry said, "about the emergency room."

Boner was standing by Harry's big Caddy convertible. Out there in the morning sun, sweating. Calculating the estimate Harry had requested. "Ain't much to tell," Boner said. "What I already told you. That nigger welfare doctor at the county clinic is digging around in my leg for lead. About three hours he's in there and he keeps telling me it's gone hurt. 'I am afraid these weel hurt you now, a leetle, Meester Harkness.' And I'm lying there with my goddamn fingers digging about six inches into that steel table and I'm telling myself, Boner, don't scream. You can't scream in front of no nigger with a French accent."

Harry watched Boner carefully circle the Caddy, scribbling figures on a clipboard. Harry didn't like it when Boner stopped and let his fingers slip across the streak of blue paint on the right front wheel well. That night it hadn't felt like much, the little kiss his Caddy had given the Cowgirl's blue Ford to send it onto the soft shoulder, but out here in the light of day, that kiss was real visible.

Boner wrote some more, leaned his swollen butt against Harry's car and said, "I can paint her for three hundred dollars even. That's if you go white over white."

"Sure," said Harry. "Whatever's right."

Boner looked up at him, surprised that he wasn't going to haggle about the money. What Coltis was paying him, Harry could buy a new Cadillac. Hell, two of them. Three. But he liked the old one. It was a thing of, well, sentiment.

Boner said, "How'd you get her dinged like this anyway?"

Oh, shit, Boner, Harry thought, bad question. He said, "Boner, you know how people behave in parking lots these days. They aren't careful. They don't look out where they're going."

Boner said, "That don't look like . . ." then noticed Harry, really noticed what was in his eyes. What Harry wanted Boner to see there. Harry said, "I guess you seen just about every kind of ding on a car, haven't you, Boner."

Boner nodding, his throat pumping on nothing, lifting his greasy chin. He took a step away from Harry's car.

Harry said, "And you can tell from just looking it's one of those parking lot encounters. Some housewife throws open her door and it skims right along old Harry's right front there and she don't leave a note on his windshield. She don't wait for him to come out of the store where he's shopping. She just takes off like the irresponsible citizen she is. That the way you see it, Boner?"

Harry watching with the thing in his eyes. The thing for Boner to see.

"It looks like that to me, Harry." Boner took another step away from the car, looking at the clipboard, down at his swollen leg. "What about two-fifty for that job, Harry? You think three hundred's too high?"

"No, Boner. Fair's fair and three hundred is fair for the job."

Old Boner breathing normally again. Beginning to anyway.

Harry watched the leg. Always had been fascinated by the details of illnesses, photos of gunshot wounds, lesions, sores, and the chancres of tropical diseases. Things that swelled and smelled, things that oozed.

Harry had his own library of illustrated medical books, case studies. Hell, there were some pretty radical things right there in good old *National Geographic*. Harry's favorite of all was a small fish that thrived in South American rivers. This fish had gills that opened like an umbrella. This fish was attracted to human urine. It loved human urine and whenever a human being urinated in the South American river where this fish lived, the little fish swam up that stream of urine, entered the human being's body, yes, sir, by you-know-what doorway. And it opened those umbrella gills with their little needle points. And this fish had found a home. No way to evict, short of surgery. Death by uremic poisoning in a matter of hours.

Harry loved the strangeness of the little fish. What in God's name was evolution thinking about when it invented a fish that killed by swimming up the human urinary tract? What kind of weird genetic guarantee was buried in that fish's brain?

Harry looked at Boner's leg, the blue streaks creeping

across the foot, and there, above the bandage, moving up the thigh.

"Did they get it all out?" he asked. Composing his face in sympathy.

"You mean the lead?"

Harry nodded. Serious. Concerned.

"Well, yeah. I mean, I think so. Most of it anyway. Maybe they was some little ..."

"Because, Boner, you got to get all that lead out of there when there's a gunshot wound, because, you see, a person can get lead poisoning. And lead poisoning is not something to be fucked with. Not by a long way."

"You think I ought to go back to Dr. Merseault and ask him about it, Harry?" Boner looking worried. Boner's hand touching the bandaged leg, not really touching it though, just hovering over it here and there.

Harry said, "Sure, Boner, if you trust him. I mean he's a Haitian and all. Persons of color is what they call us now. Indians and Haitians. Hell, they got good medical schools in Haiti. What I heard anyway. Very fine educational setup, they got. Go on back and ask him about those blue streaks there, the ones on the top of your foot. Ask him if those are normal. But don't go today, Boner."

Harry gave Boner the keys to the Caddy. "You paint her this morning, Boner. Okay?" The thing in eyes. The thing that Boner understood. Understood now, because Boner had opened the door of the Cowgirl's Ford and seen her eyes. Had told Harry all about it.

"Sure, Harry." Boner's voice was very small. Hardly a thing to be heard. "I can't finish her this morning, but I can get her done by tomorrow, late."

Harry pointed to the dinged fender. "You sand her good, Boner. Take her right down to the primer. And you start this morning. You understand me?"

"Sure, Harry."

Harry had thought about taking the car out of town, maybe down to Miami to get the work done. But he'd decided on Boner. In Miami, he'd have to wait in line. Down there, he didn't own anybody like Boner. The job could take a week. And hell, down there it might look funny, a Micco-suki with a vintage Caddy, some blue paint on the front. Somebody might remember, might snap a Polaroid or two of the car. Classic Cadillac. Harry could own somebody down there, sure, but it took time to establish the kind of relationship he had with Boner Harkness.

When that crazy fucking Miccosuki, Harry W. Feather, was gone, Boner Harnkess sank against the scraped fender of the old Caddy and regretted his entire life. It was bad enough he had to go around carrying the name Boner, and all because of that yearbook picture. Bad enough he had to spend his life fixing the old junkers brought in by Mexican and Haitian migrants who couldn't afford to do anything but keep fixing what couldn't be fixed. Bad enough that he had to paint cars, coating his lungs with solvents and primer dust all the damned day long. But now, he had lead frag-ments in his leg from ankle to knee and this crazy Indian wanted him to paint the Caddy he'd painted not even a year ago. And all because of one little scratch on the fender.

Boner eased himself into the Caddy and drove it into the paint bay and sat there in the cool shade. He leaned back on the leather seats and thought about the woman, those dead eyes he'd been seeing every time he closed his own. The question in those eyes.

And that damned Bryce Nailor leaving him there with her staring at him. And that pistol hitting the asphalt and the rush of noise and light and then the pain, numb at first and then sharp, and him having to convince Bryce Nailor to call the rescue truck again. And Bryce: "They ain't gone come back here twice in one night, Boner. Just get in that truck and drive yourself to the clinic. You ain't hurt bad."

And Boner pointing at his shoe, the pool of dark, hot blood he was standing in. A little steam rising down there and him saying, "Look. Look." All he could think of to say. And old man Draper finally scraping back from where he was hiding behind Boner's truck. "Why, Boner, I believe she got you in the tibial artery." The old man's eyes measuring him for that slab in the basement of the funeral home.

Then Bryce pulling off Boner's own belt and wrapping it around his leg in that annoyed way Bryce had and saying, "Damn it, if you bleed all over my cruiser, you the one gone clean it up."

In the shade of the paint bay, Boner let his hand rest on the top of his thigh. His leg felt like it was made of boiling metal. The skin wanted to split from the swelling. Boner couldn't help it. He started to cry.

He saw himself for the ten thousandth time at the senior prom, dancing with Melissa Belanger, slow dancing, close in the dark. And the thing. The thing happening and then the guy with the camera taking pictures for the yearbook. The guy says, "Hey, Bill? Bill Harkness? Give us a smile!" And Boner turns and smiles and the camera flashes and then it's May and there it is for the whole town to see and laugh at for the rest of Boner's natural life.

There it is crawling down his trouser leg, bulging like it wants light and air, wants Melissa as bad as an eighteen-year-old woody can want, and it's a week before graduation and people are coming up to him asking him to sign the picture. *No, Boner, lower. Sign it right down there, right next to . . . it.*

And all of a sudden the girls won't talk to him. They walk right by him on the sidewalk, give him that sour, PM-essy look. Half of them been putting their toes in their ears in the back seat of somebody's Chevy since they were soph-omores and they won't talk to Bill Harkness anymore be-cause some guy took a picture of him in a state of nature.

And Melissa Belanger. Oh, God, if Boner felt sorry for anyone more than himself, it was Melissa. She'd left town before the end of June. She'd left at night. Hadn't even called Bill Harkness to say good-bye. But Melissa had done all right. Eventually. Last he'd heard, she was selling real estate in Naples. Doing very well for herself. Boner would bet she didn't wake up nights standing in a pool of light at the prom holding hands with the guy that grew the beast.

Standing with Bill Harkness whose name would be forever afterward . . . Boner.

Boner wiped his eyes and pushed himself carefully out of the Caddy's front seat. He'd been crying a lot lately, just suddenly starting it, and telling himself it was the pain, but he knew it wasn't the pain. It was the dead woman's eyes. And it was everything.

In the little storeroom off the paint bay, he was looking for the half can of Oyster Shell White he had used on the Caddy a year ago, when he saw it. Staring at the shelves of cans, a little bit of color daubed on each label so he could find one at a glance. There it was, the blue color he had just seen on Harry W. Feather's fender. It was a Ford blue. It was the same blue he had pulled out of that canal. It was the brand-new blue of Corey Darrow's Explorer.

Boner lost his balance. He slid down the wall in the dusty, cramped storeroom, spread-eagled, his leg screaming. The tears starting again. Oh, Boner, what have you got yourself into now? If it wasn't the woman looking at him, those pale green eyes asking him that necessary question he couldn't answer, it was Harry W. Feather, removing those mirror shades.

Harry stopping the conversation and just staring until Boner saw what was there to see in those damned dirt-black Indian eyes. What was there to see? Nothing.

Exactly that, nothing. An emptiness so far and deep that it scared you the way you were scared out in the Gulf, out of sight of land, with hundreds, maybe thousands of feet of water under you and an empty sky over your head. It was an emptiness that anything could fill, absolutely anything. And that, Boner decided, hearing himself whimper now and unable to stop it, that was what was so bad about it. Any whim Harry W. Feather had, any little thing that occurred to him, that thing could happen to you. It could happen to you if it filled that empty place in Harry W. Feather for just long enough.

18

▲▲▲▲▲▲▲▲▲▲▲▲▲▲▲▲

Walking behind the rat-faced sheriff's deputy, Sawnie saw the blue Ford Explorer standing in the hot morning sun at the back of the lot where they kept abandoned vehicles. She hurried ahead, leaving the three men behind. Walking fast as though she could open the door and find Corey inside and ... *do* something about this.

All night long and all morning, her inborn need to act had raged without an object. She was the woman who managed things for the most powerful man in the state and all she had done for thirty-six hours, the most important day and a half of her life, was miss connections and chew her knuckles and, yes, goddamn it, weep like a soap opera boob.

She heard the deputy behind her, talking to the big fat man, Rayford, Raymer somebody? Saying, "Here she is. Right where they unhooked her. It's a shame, a brand-new vehicle like that."

She spun and gave the deputy her hottest stare. He nod-

ded to her and excused himself to his fat friend, Rayburn.
The two men watched the deputy go, then the lawyer, if
that's what he really was, started walking a circle around
the Ford. He trailed his hand along its gleaming sides and
she hated it. Like he was touching Corey.

She looked up at the empty blue heavens, already brutally
hot at nine o'clock, and said to herself, "Take it easy, Sawnie. Get your wits about you."

The lawyer was about to open the passenger door. She
stepped forward, wanted to be there for it. As though what
would escape was the last of her sister's presence on this
earth. But in the burst of hot, already fetid air, there was
nothing of Corey. Only mud and the quick beginnings of
the rot that this climate gave every wet thing left to stand
in the sun. Hell, this whole county was wet and standing
in the sun and its people and its crops and its politics all
had a sweet-rotten softness.

Some of the contents of Corey's purse lay on the seat—
sodden Kleenexes, a check-cashing card, a tube of lipstick.
A tampon that had bloomed open and released its string
tail. Three inches of water stood on the floorboards and the
windows inside were smeared a pale green.

The water had been high enough to cover Corey's head.
She closed her eyes and listened to the lawyer breathing
next to her. In the dark, she tried to call back that northern
person, the capable Sawnie Darrow of the Governor's office.
She opened her eyes and turned to him, and in that other
woman's hard, official voice, she said, "Tell me what you
see."

Eddie knew he had to be careful. It was hot and his bour-
bon-scorched stomach was none too easy in the ditch stink
from the Ford. And the woman was challenging him again,
her eyes demanding something that he no longer owned.
Something he had sold with his first big boat. A thing he
hadn't missed much until this moment.

"Raymer," he called, "tell us what the deputy said."

Eddie kept his eyes on the woman's face. Neither of them

looked at Raymer. He heard Raymer step close. Clear his throat.

"They found her still in her seat belts. The county M.E. said she had a badly broken left arm and a dislocated left shoulder. Possibly broken ribs and a back injury. Some internal injuries from being thrown against the belts."

"What killed her, Raymer?" Eddie conscious now that his own voice came from the courtrooms of long ago.

Raymer stopped. Eddie's eyes had not left the woman's face. Raymer watched the two of them. Finally, he said, "She drowned."

Eddie thought about it. Corey going in, the impact, the spray of water up the windshield, the brutal stop, then the water rushing in and Corey taking stock of her injuries, of what she had left. The damage was to Corey's left side, the arm she'd have to use to heave open the door. That or reach across with the right, which could be just as hard. Maybe she'd just decided to sit there, wait, hope someone came along. Maybe she'd thought the water wasn't too high, she could make it; then she'd lost consciousness. Maybe she'd been unconscious all along.

And in her left hand, Eddie thought, there's a .357 Magnum. Cocked. She doesn't let go of it going in. Can't have picked it up after the crash. She's driving with it in her hand, and after the impact, she can't lift it, can't fire out the window to signal someone. But she doesn't let it go. Not even to struggle with the belts. What does that say? What does it say? It says she needs the gun. Even after the crash, she needs it.

And what could Eddie say right now? He looked at the woman but spoke to Raymer. "How could she drown? She was hurt but she'd have adrenaline going for her. The truck came to rest upright. After it filled with water, why couldn't she unhook the belts, crawl through the window?" Eddie watched the sister's eyes, seeing the pain in them, and something else now, the thing he hoped to see. As bad as this was, he could see her intelligence rising.

Raymer sighed. "I don't know, Eddie. The doc said shock

probably. The impact stunned her, and she drowned. It happens."

"And you went out to the scene, is that right?"

Raymer said, yes, he'd gone out the morning it happened, stood there in the dark with a flashlight looking at the burnt rubber tracks heading straight off the road like she'd accelerated into the canal.

The woman finally broke from Eddie's eyes. She turned to Raymer, including him for the first time. "Will they check the truck, see if there was anything wrong with it? See if it malfunctioned?"

Raymer said, "They wouldn't normally. Not unless there was some problem involving the insurance. We can have it done if you want."

The woman nodded. "I want."

Raymer said, "There's a Ford dealership over in Crescent City."

Eddie thought she was ready now and so he took her arm and she fell into step with him. On the driver's side, he said, "Look at this."

He showed her the streak of white paint on the left front wheel weel. She reached out and touched it, picked at its crusty edge with a fingernail. She looked up at him. "What is it?"

On the other side of Eddie, Raymer whistled low and slow. "Lord, Lord!" he said.

Eddie said, "I don't know. Maybe she ran into somebody on her way down to see me. Maybe she stopped somewhere for a cup of coffee and somebody scraped her in a parking lot. It couldn't have been much of an impact."

Sawnie Darrow's eyes, softer now, less angry but just as scary, looked their question at him. "But you don't think it happened in any parking lot, do you?"

Eddie looked at Raymer until Raymer nodded. Eddie told Sawnie Darrow about the Smith & Wesson .357 Magnum they'd found in Corey's hand. Cocked. She listened, then nodded, then nodded again, harder. Then she said, "Good,

good." Eddie wasn't sure, but he thought she meant it was good that her sister had died with a weapon in her hand.

He said, "I don't think it was any parking lot. I think there's a guy somewhere with a very dark tan who drives a big white car. I think he ran your sister off the road." Eddie was sure of it now. Knew it. A tanned guy with a flashy smile had followed Corey Darrow in a big white car like she'd said he would, followed her south, looking for the right time and the right place.

He said, "I think this explains those tire marks Raymer saw. Two cars going fast. One leaning on the other. Corey steering left against a car pushing her right. She's not swerving, but her tires are slipping sideways, burning as she goes off the pavement."

Eddie closed his eyes in the heat and saw it. The two speeding machines kissing, the one shouldering the other, Corey's tires smoking. All the ugly physics of murder. He opened his eyes.

He didn't know what to expect from the woman. Tears maybe. Maybe she'd faint. It was hot enough and the stink from the Ford was as close as he wanted to get on a hungover morning to the smell of death. All she did was look at him in that careful, evaluating way. Her eyes asking if he was right for some job she was imagining, some subcontract from the strange connection these sisters must have had. Then she looked at Raymer, asking the same question. When Raymer looked back at her for a while with that steady Deputy Dawg squint, she said to both of them, "What do we do now?"

Eddie said, "Raymer?"

Raymer shrugged. "We start looking for a tanned guy who drives a big white car . . . with a streak of Ford blue on it."

19

▲▲▲▲▲▲▲▲▲▲▲▲▲▲▲▲

Harry W. Feather stepped behind the palmetto clump and put the Zeiss field glasses back into their leather case. Damn, but the woman looked like a certain person, a person he had reason to believe was dead. It had given him quite a start at first. Then he'd remembered the photographs in the little family shrine in the Cowgirl's house. Of course! The two lookers, a saxophonist and a cheerleader. You *couldn't* do both: march in the band and sis-boom-bah on the side-lines. They were twins, not identical, but sororal. Harry W. Feather, graduate of the University of Life, believed that was the word for the two girls. Sororal twins.

Harry got back into his rented Eldorado and waited until the woman and the two men drove away. He knew the men, Raymer Harney, brainless investigator, and the Former Football Great. Guy who'd got lucky out on a boat. Two boy scouts doing the right thing. It was touching. Harry was touched. Somewhere in there, way down, he could feel what

123

it would be like to do somebody a favor. Free, no strings. Strange was how it would feel. Take a woman whose sister was recently deceased out to inspect the death vehicle? Strange.

Harry W. Feather thought about driving back to Boner's body shop. Take a look at that fender. Make sure old Boner started right there. That big electric sander biting her all the way down to the sheet metal. But that would be stupid. He had to stay away from Boner and the Caddy for a while because the Former Great might have seen him in it at the marina that day. Harry didn't think so. They guy was too hot for the Cowgirl to notice anything but the swelling in his Levis.

Boner would work fast if Boner knew what was good for him. If Boner wanted to keep on sanding and painting and driving that tow truck. Harry was going to visit Mr. Lofton Coltis.

Lofton Coltis watched the yellow school buses draw up along the black mud road. The doors swung open and the dark faces poured out, talking in that excited, musical way. All these years, and Coltis still couldn't understand them half the time. Jamaicans, Haitians, Mexicans. The Tower of Babel toppled into his cane field.

His hands, three hundred of them stood, by the buses looking at the field of cane that stretched on, unfenced, for a mile. Coltis liked the metallic sound these men made when they moved. Like a medieval army on the march. Each man wore steel foot and shin guards and a steel cuff on the hand that grasped the cane. A thick, leather glove for the machete hand.

The men spread out along the road, facing the cane, shaking themselves, massaging their muscles like runners at the starting line. Going quiet now. Taking a somber look at the day's work.

The cane looked green from the air, a fresh spring green. The color of oak leaves in April. But straight on, the stalks were gray, and up close, they were damp and tangled with weeds and smelled of the decay of the centuries that had made the deep, black loam. The cane sucked its sweetness from that mud.

Coltis gave the signal and the men surged forward, clanking like knights unhorsed in the lists, going into battle against the unending rows. Each man would confront his rows, hacking and gathering and piling up the cane behind him. Each man was expected to lay down a ton an hour or go home and tell his Maria, his Yolanda, his belle Genevieve that he couldn't cut it in the American fields. Couldn't cut and gather and lift with the men who came for the hard currency that would make them princes in their own lands.

When Coltis heard the first clatter of machetes, he turned to watch the smoking stacks of the sugar processing plant on the horizon. Black smoke rolled skyward, drifted south toward Miami on a steady breeze, thinning and going gray, then white as it climbed. He owned the controlling interest in the plant. His land stretched on behind its high, smoking stacks some twenty miles, almost to the outskirts of Dade County. In his rolling thoughts, what lay to the south was Sodom, the obscene Berlin of 1930, Caligula's Rome of bread and circuses. On clear nights, he fancied that he could see the lights of Miami flickering on the horizon. And many nights he had stood in his fields imagining he saw the fires of the final destruction of that urban cancer, Dade County.

In more controlled reflections, Coltis saw two possible fates for Miami. The first was to explode in a holocaust of color war. In this first scenario, the last act was an alliance of whites and Cubans, a marriage of convenience to defeat the more dangerous, darker people. But it was a marriage that would end in divorce. The white–Cuban coalition would kill off the more vicious but endemically disorganized blacks and then fall out.

Although Coltis had little sympathy for the canal-dwelling, barbecuing, mall-wandering white population of Dade County, it saddened him to imagine what would happen to them at the hands of the better-organized, better-financed, and fundamentally more intelligent Cubans.

A second possibility, and one that Coltis hated even more than the first, was the declaration of a state of emergency. A kind of revived New Deal in which the ills of Miami would be temporarily salved by an enormous, slovenly welfare behemoth. Armies of functionaries frantically trying to keep the colored factions from each other's throats with barricades of tax money. A bureaucracy that would continue to pay until Dade County became a collection of Balkan states, Cuban, black, white, Jewish, Haitian, Colombian, gay, and lesbian. All of them squatting on what they saw as their rights and all exacting county, state, and federal tribute.

Coltis stood at the center of an enormous agribusiness empire whose southern border was a banana republic. Its instability threatened him and his neighbors, the state he loved and the country whose decline and fall he saw nightly in his dreams.

And that behemoth bureaucracy with its regulations and its mountains of paperwork was already reaching toward him from Miami and from Tallahassee, telling him what he could and could not do on his own land.

Harry W. Feather said, "Excuse me, Mr. Coltis."

Coltis lowered his eyes from the horizon where the smoke of boiling sugar drifted toward Miami and looked at the Indian in his ridiculous getup. White linen sport coat, a light blue silk shirt with no collar, and some blousey green silk trousers. And those glove leather shoes. Coltis was pleased to see them sinking under the Indian's weight into the sweet black muck. "What is it, Feather?"

"There's been an accident. I'm afraid the girl's dead, and . . ."

Coltis's eyes stopped Feather's foolish voice. He knew that Corey Darrow was dead. Precious little happened in Okee County that he didn't know about. "She wasn't supposed to die. I told you to send her a message. Only a message."

Feather looked at him. Sullen, unable or unwilling to explain what had happened. The other thing that Coltis already knew: It was clean, the girl's death. Whether by luck

126

or Feather's design, it was clean. Sheriff Nailor was calling it an accident.

Feather said, "I was about to say, Mr. Coltis, before I was interrupted, that she got a sister."

Coltis hearing that little edge in the Indian's voice. That insolent edge.

"Looks just like her. I saw her this morning at the sheriff's impound lot, looking at the Ford Explorer. She was with Raymer Harney and a guy from St. Petersburg. Name of Eddie Priest. Used to play football with Raymer at the university. Maybe you remember him."

Sometimes Coltis thought he liked the Indian. Because Feather stood up to him. *Before I was interrupted.* Coltis liked that. It took some testicularity to talk to Lofton Coltis that way. Coltis had acquired Feather through Feather's mother, a good, reliable woman, his housekeeper. She was tickled pink, or whatever color she turned when she was tickled, that her son was working for Coltis. She saw it as the first step up for her handsome, gifted boy. Well, it was a step somewhere, and the boy *was* good-looking in a smarmy way. Gifted? Coltis doubted that his mother understood exactly where her boy's talents lay.

Coltis let the Indian stand there, sinking, watching Coltis's eyes. Finally, he said, "I'll call Raymer's supervisor at Dixie Fidelity and see what he's up to."

The Indian nodded, waited.

Coltis said, "I guess old Billy Darrow did have two daughters. I'll check into that too." Coltis wasn't much of a football fan. He wasn't going to worry about a guy who used to run up and down a field carrying an inflated pig's bladder.

Coltis watched the Indian closely. Waiting to see if Feather thought there was more to worry about. If there was, then the Indian had kept something from him. Not much went on in the Indian's eyes. You might call them empty. Maybe something a little deranged way down in there. Something very useful. The Indian said, "All right, Mr. Coltis. I thought it was best to tell you what I saw. You want me to just sit tight for now?"

"That's right, Feather. Sit tight. Sit any way you like. Just don't do anything freelance, like Clinton did. By the way, have you seen Clinton lately?"

Coltis smiled while Feather looked at him for a moment, trying to pick his locks. Feather said, "I saw him. He's wearing a glove. It's hot as hell and Mr. Clinton Reynolds, Water Management Director, is wearing a white cotton glove on his right hand. What you call it, a gardening glove. He didn't look too good either. Pale. Sweaty."

Coltis wanted the details, exactly how Clinton Reynolds looked, but he decided against the questions. "That is strange," he said, "wearing one glove on a hot morning in June."

Coltis watched the Indian stand in front of him now, the black muck almost to his shoe tops. Feather had not looked down. Coltis liked that. Feather was proud. And hell, with what Coltis was paying him, he could afford to buy a whole carload of those silly Italian slippers in every sickening color he wanted. Most people would have looked down.

Coltis said, "Yes, you just sit tight. I'll find out about the sister and then we'll talk. I appreciated what you did for me and I've shown my appreciation. But Feather . . .?"

"Yes, Mr. Coltis?"

"I don't want to see you out here again. I don't want to have another meeting like this. Do you understand?" The Indian's eyes going sullen now.

"I spoke to your secretary," Feather said. "She told me where to find you. I just assumed . . ."

"Assumptions, Feather. I am awash in a sea of other people's assumptions and it is getting harder and harder for me to swim. Look, Feather, I like you. You know that. I don't want to be hard here. I don't want to patronize. I understand your position and I think you understand mine. That's one of the reasons I like you. I would have thought you'd realize that we can't be seen together."

Coltis watched the rows of clattering, hacking men. The

best cutters had already slashed fifty yards into the cane, their neat, herring-boned stacks behind them. Occasionally, one of them would stop chopping, straighten his back, stretch, and look at Coltis. He knew that the Haitians called him *faucon*, Hawk, for his piercing eyes. They feared him. Coltis let his eyes fall to Feather. "Not even out here . . . with these people. All right?"

Coltis liked the way the Indian set his jaw and nodded. No arguments. No pissing and mewling. What he didn't like was Feather's not telling him about the gun they'd found in the dead girl's hand. Maybe it was just bad luck, something Feather couldn't have prevented. However it had happened, it was the first unclean thing. Coltis hoped it would be the last. He turned away to watch the cutters. But he listened as Feather pulled his shoes out of the mud with two good sucking noises and walked off to his car.

Marked with Coltis's urine, Harry W. Feather sat in the rented Eldorado, watching the cutters slash and stack the cane. Thinking about the way Coltis had insulted him.

"All right?" Coltis asking him. Sure it was all right. He'd wanted to tell Coltis about how it had happened, his and Cowgirl's rocketing steel, that brief kiss of metal, and then the Cowgirl suddenly gone. A column of steam behind him in the ditch. How it was an accident. How he regretted it, felt bad, all that. See what Coltis would say about things getting out of hand like that. You could learn a lot about a man from the way he acted when things got out of hand. But Coltis wasn't having any of it.

And Harry had planned to tell Coltis about the pistol. About going back to look for the computer file and not finding it. Had planned to, but it was the wrong time and the wrong place. Some etiquette they didn't teach in the University of Life. Harry W. Feather guilty of a social infraction. He had presented himself in the man's field, soiling the man's presence with his own red Indian self. Didn't he *know* they couldn't be seen together?

Now he did.

20

▲▲▲▲▲▲▲▲▲▲▲▲▲▲▲▲

Sawnie wandered her sister's house, opening drawers, searching closets, examining documents. She told herself it was a search for clues (even the word sounded futile and melodramatic), but it was really her punishment for the time and distance she had put between herself and a beloved sister.

She stood now at Corey's bedroom closet and fingered the lapel of the fawn hunting coat she had worn the morning the lawyer, Priest, had come. She remembered the shiver that had seized her when she had put it on, wrapping herself in the still-fresh odors of her sister's body. The perfume was White Linen. The underscent was the sweat of a working farm woman, a hunter. It had made her dizzy, standing there in the foggy dawn with the shotgun in her hand.

She riffled the sleeves of Corey's blouses and blazers. Grays and blues, all dour and official. The labels from malls

130

and boutiques in Miami. No place to buy decent clothes in Okee City. She closed the closet door, wondering: Who was this estranged sister of mine? It was only a three-hour drive to meet for lunch, a night of catching up in some highway motel. We didn't do it. Why?

Sawnie lay down on her sister's bed and remembered the thing she had in common with the Governor: sudden violent death. The thing that had driven her out of this county and made her hate the thought of coming back to it.

Her parents had been killed in a midnight collision at a lonely crossroads when she and Corey were twenty. A drunken cane cutter's pickup had crossed to their side. Sawnie was a senior at Florida State, Corey was already clerking at the Water Management Agency. Corey had spent two years at Miami Dade Junior College, but she'd missed the country. Sawnie was different. From the windows of the FSU Political Science classroom building, she could watch the construction of the new state capitol building, a concrete and steel colossus rising skyward. She dreamt of taking her diploma there.

After the phone call that had brought Sawnie home for a double funeral and a division of property, the two sisters learned that their father's estate was in trouble. They found liens and mortgages in drawers and markers for personal loans scrawled on scraps of paper with their father's notations of partial payments and renegotiated terms. The names on the scraps became faces at the door, men who waited a day or two and then came by, saying they were sorry, but . . .

After a long night of talk and, finally, of heated argument, Corey had decided to marry herself to the long work of saving the family house and land. A work that would commit her to the county indefinitely. She had asked Sawnie to join her.

Now, lying on Corey's bed, a bed inherited from their parents, a bed where Corey must have lain planning her endless financial rear guard action, Sawnie remembered telling Corey that she saw herself doing something else.

Something big. A thing that couldn't be done in this cane and sod and cattle county. There was only one place for Sawnie Darrow in this long, strange circus of a state. Tallahassee.

Sawnie still ached recalling Corey's eyes, the recognition in them that Sawnie had harbored this thing, the difference between them, for years, saving it for this moment.

The sisters had called and written for a while after that, shared holidays together in the family house, Corey digging out the bank statements and the markers and recounting her heroic engagements with creditors and the infinite stretching of her clerk's pay.

The sisters rising, earning more, collecting more responsibilities into their hands. And calling, visiting less often. And finally, not at all.

One thing Sawnie's search of this house had told her. Corey had killed them all—the debts, the liens, the mortgages. Every scrap of paper stamped "PAID" was neatly filed away.

She cried when she found Corey's will. The house Corey had saved now belonged to a defector named Sawnie Darrow.

Lying on Corey's bed, staring at the bars of light printed on the wall by a falling red sun, Sawnie knew she should call the Governor. He'd be anxious, worried. After he'd heard the news of Corey's death, he'd said, "My heart is with you. Take all the time you need to clear it up."

Yes, his heart was with her, and it was a big and a good heart, but he had said, "Clear it up." The meaning was plain. A sister's death should not involve anything unseemly, anything complicated in the wrong way.

What stopped her hand from reaching for the phone by Corey's bed, dialing the Governor's private number, was another of the Governor's colorful turns of phrase. He had said, "No mud on your skirts."

When the phone rang, Sawnie was burrowed deep in Corey's bed. She counted the rings, promising herself she would answer the next and then the next. Finally, she threw off the comforter and as much of the past as she could ever lose. She picked up the phone.

"Well, hello there!" the Governor said. "Finally tracked you down."

Sawnie needing a little time. "How did you find me?" Speaking in the old office voice.

"Well, let's see. They got one hotel in that little town and you're not in it. They also got directory assistance with one Darrow. It was a masterly piece of detective work." Did she hear impatience in the executive tone? Sawnie's anger rising now.

"I was going to call you," she said, cold.

"So," the Governor said, "what's going on? Has it been . . . rough?"

Sawnie remembered him lying in the hospital bed after the plane crash. Telling her about India's death, her last words. He prided himself on the way he had gotten over it, gotten on with it. For him, grief had its season. You harvested and stored away the sheaves. Then you planted a new crop.

She had to tell him she was staying here awhile. He'd know soon enough. "Well," she said, "it looks like there are some irregularities down here."

"Tell all. Your Governor is all ears."

Thinking of the Governor's preposterous cartoon ears, she laughed and it felt good.

She told him about meeting the two men in the bar, keeping her descriptions of Eddie Priest and Raymer Harney neutral. She told about going to see Corey's Ford Explorer, about the streak of white paint. What the lawyer, Priest, had said about Corey's being afraid of a man with a dark tan, a man who drove a big white car.

She told him about talking to the local sheriff, a bloated, fatuous time-server named Bryce Nailor who had found Corey in the canal. Asking the sheriff if he had any theories about what had happened. Getting nothing but a sly shake of the head, some mumbled, stale condolences.

She told the Governor about going to the county medical

examiner's office and reading the autopsy report. Finding nothing there but Corey's sad injuries and the fact that she had drowned. She told him about them offering her the photographs of Corey and her own cowardice, or fear, whatever it was that made her refuse to look at them. And telling the other two, Harney and Priest, that they'd better not look either. No one was going to look at Corey, not that way.

She told him about the gun they had found in Corey's hand. How it had gone off and shot some holes in a tow truck driver. She told him it was the gun that kept her here. She had to know why her sister had driven off the hard road into a canal with one hand on the steering wheel and the other holding a cocked .357 Magnum handgun.

"Constable Nailor has a theory about the gun," Sawnie said. "He thinks my sister was doing something weird with it. He's leaving it up to me to figure out what that is."

"He said that?" the Governor asked. "He said, 'something weird'?"

"He did," Sawnie said.

"Damn him," the Governor said, his voice low and threatening.

"Right," Corey said. "Listen, can you do something for me?"

"Just name it."

"Give me some of Lucy Watkins's time. There's something going on down here at Water Management. I want her to check it for me."

"You got her. As long as you want. I get short-staffed, I'll get some folks from the temporary pool. She's probably still in her office right now."

She thanked him. Listened to his breathing for a space.

Finally, he said it: "You know I can't get along without you too long, Sawnie."

"I thought you didn't want any mud on my skirts."

He laughed. "I'm not talking about *that*. I'm talking about the efficient running of an office the taxpayers are paying for."

"Let's see," she said. "The taxpayers. Seems like those are the folks you like to call 'a great unbrained gaggle of gator puppies.'"

"Did I say that?"

"You did."

"Spinbabe, did you give any more thought to that document I typed your name on? You know the deadline is coming up."

He meant the new seat in the U.S. House. His plan for her future. Sawnie saw her name at the bottom of that page he'd brought to the cabin in the woods, misspelled in the Governor's lousy typing. Saw herself again speaking to the sun-lit, uplifted faces of her fellow Floridians, telling them her vision of the future. And then she saw herself explaining to the press the time she'd spent in her old hometown throwing hers and the Governor's weight around, sticking her nose into the strange circumstances of a sister's death. A sister who'd died with a gun in her hand.

She said, "Yeah, I thought about it. I have to stay here awhile longer and take care of my baby sister."

The Governor waited a space, then he said, "Sure. I understand. When you get it all taken care of, you come on home. We got work to do together."

Lucy Watkins was in her office. Sawnie asked her to find out what she could about the computers at Water Management in Okee County. Use her superhacker skills to access the database.

"What are we looking for, Sawnie?"

Lucy's voice was full of sympathy and the perpetual anxiety of the dedicated technocrat. Sawnie said, "A file that's been dumped. Didn't you tell me once you could retrieve most deleted files?"

Lucy said, "Most people don't know deleted files aren't really gone. They're still out there in electronic limbo, sort of lost in ionic space. I can use my famous utilities program to look for the file you want."

"Good," Sawnie said. "I knew I could count on you, Lucy."

"*Any* deleted file, Sawnie. That covers a lot of territory."

"Not just any file. You're looking for a file my sister entered and somebody else deleted. My sister's name was Corey Darrow."

21

▲▲▲▲▲▲▲▲▲▲▲▲▲▲▲▲▲▲

Eddie stretched and yawned on the front seat of Raymer's old Buick and watched the unending sea of cane. He and Raymer had been at it for two hours now, driving and looking for . . . God knew what.

Making good on their promise to Sawnie Darrow, they'd gone down everything that could, by any abuse of language, be called a road. They'd stared at shotgun cracker shacks, people living in old cars, and migrants camped out with canvas stretched across the beds of pickup trucks. They'd done a sociological survey of Okee City and environs and the results weren't pretty. It seemed like the only thing they hadn't seen was a house or a trailer or a store or a bar with a big white car parked in front of it. A car with a little streak of blue on the right front.

Raymer was talking about his work.

". . . so there's this labor contractor, well-known guy around here. Supplies cutters to the cane growers. He puts in a claim on a Key Man insurance policy. It doesn't smell right, so I start asking some questions. It turns out to be a beauty, a real beauty. This contractor, he picks up five or six hitchhikers and derelicts. He gives them liquor and offers them jobs. The pissbums, they don't know what's going on. They think they're signing employment contracts. But what they signed, they signed . . ."

"Policies," Eddie said.

Raymer: "What?"

"Policies. I said, they signed policies."

"Who's robbing this train?"

"Sorry. You are."

The cane, the junk cars, the rust and the rot rolling by.

"So, they sign policies as Key Men in this contractor's organization. Men he can't afford to lose without major damage to his cash flow.

"The first Key Man falls out the back of a speeding pickup. Two other Key Men in the same truck can't explain exactly how it happened. The second guy gets bitten by a coral snake way out in the boonies. The snake bites him three times, both feet and one hand. You know the odds of that happening?"

"The odds are long, Raymer."

"So this labor contractor, big-time criminal brain, he's asking fifty thou a pop for his derelicts."

Eddie watched the cane, the trailers, the cars, looking for white car, big white car, thinking about the phone call he'd made to the marina before going on this mission with Raymer.

When Hanson's secretary answered, Eddie'd asked to speak to her boss.

"I think he's out showing that Beneteau, Mr. Priest. To one of your clients, I think. You want me to go get him?"

"No," Eddie said. "Just tell him I won't be back for a couple more days."

George Hanson was the marina sales manager. Hanson's secretary was a pretty black woman named Sophie. Eddie liked her. Watching her get picked up after work by a succession of well-heeled, massive gentlemen he later learned were the defensive backfield of the Tampa Bay Buccaneers. Sophie said, "He's not going to like it. You're his top guy this month in commissions."

Yeah, Eddie thought. Key Man. He said, "Tell him I'm enjoying the commission on that Cape Dory. Tell him there was a lot of stress associated with that sale and I need a few days to relax."

"Yeah," Sophie said. "That stress'll kill ya. What's her name, that stress?"

Eddie thought about it. "Her name is Sawnie Darrow."

Sophie laughed. "I'll tell him."

Eddie remembered the morning with Sawnie Darrow. Raymer had been there too, but Eddie hadn't noticed him much. Raymer had been washed out of the picture by whatever it was that came from the woman. Eddie couldn't keep his eyes off her. And when those green eyes looked at him, he couldn't meet them. It was like being a schoolboy again. Words like *smitten* kept occurring to him.

Even in the medical examiner's office when they passed around the brown envelope with the horror show pictures of Corey. Sawnie grabbing them from his hand, telling him he wasn't going to look. Nobody was. Eddie thinking, I'm looking at you. So beautiful! And later, walking out of the place thinking, What kind of man am I to sit there with pictures of dead Corey in my hand and this goofy lump in my throat for her beautiful, angry sister?

"What's got into you?" Raymer said.

Eddie stretched again on the car seat. Raymer's sofa had written its name on Eddie's lumbar region. Its name was Torquemada.

"Nothing," Eddie said. "Keep talking. I'm listening."

"Like hell you are."

"No, really, I am."

"I know what you got on your mind, buddy."

"There!" Eddie said, turning to look back. The place

they'd just passed. The hand-painted sign hanging from a punk tree limb.

"What?" Raymer slowed.

"What do you do if you got a blue streak on your big white car? What do you do, Raymer?"

Raymer the storyteller looked annoyed, confused. "I don't know. What do I do?"

Eddie turned, pointed at the sign: Harkness Fender Mender Auto Body and Repair.

"Shit," whispered Raymer, pulling a U-turn. "Why didn't I think of that?"

Raymer drove into the yard and there it was, sitting in one of the paint bays. A big white Cadillac convertible. No sign of life at the auto body shop. It was after five. Eddie figured the owner had probably beat foot for the day.

Raymer said, "I make it early seventies. A real land yacht."

"You know who it belongs to?"

"Everybody does. Guy named Harry Feather. Indian guy. A Miccosuki."

Zingo! Corey had said a guy with a very dark tan. Don Johnson type. Hell, Johnson could play an Indian. Eddie said, "Let's go see the guy. This Harry Feather. What you say?"

Eddie and Raymer got out, walked over to the paint bay to get a closer look. Raymer didn't go inside the bay, didn't touch the car, so Eddie didn't either. Eddie could see that the gleaming white paint wasn't dry yet.

Raymer looked down, picked up one foot, then the other. Black mud already oozing up the sides of his cheap wingtips. Sweat through his suit. Grime on his hound-dog face. "I'm beat, Eddie. What you say to some dinner, a couple bumps of old Uncle Jack Daniel's? We go see the guy in the morning."

"The car's already painted?"

"It looks that way."

"You know what that means?"

Raymer looked at Eddie like he'd just been asked how

many fingers Eddie was holding up. "I know what it *might* mean, Eddie. Let's not jump to any conclusions."

"What we do," Eddie said, "is start with the guy that painted the car. Ask him if he saw a little streak of blue on the left front."

Raymer sighed and lifted his feet again. "So," he said, "you starting a new career. Gonna show old Raymer how to investigate a suspicious circumstance? You noticed I'm not calling it a crime?"

Eddie just looked at him. "First I'm gonna teach old Raymer how to make coffee. Then maybe some things about what the human body can reasonably be expected to take from a sofa. Then maybe we'll move to the crime thing."

Raymer sighed, lifted one foot, then the other. "My old dogs are tired, but they can smell the hunt." Raymer started toward the Buick. "You want to call the woman? Get her in on this?"

"Naw," Eddie said. "I say *we* talk to Mr. Harkness, just the two of us."

Eddie thinking he needed a break from those green eyes. The way they made him feel. What they made him want to do.

22

▲▲▲▲▲▲▲▲▲▲▲▲▲▲▲▲▲▲▲

Boner Harkness's leg was burning. The skin above and below the bandage was stretched as tight as a sausage casing. It was a deep blue at the edges of the bandage and angry red where the tendrils of his pain reached upward. The tendrils were into his groin now, and they held his toes in a hot hard grasp. And God almighty, the pain!

Boner had used up all the Darvon the Haitian doctor had given him. He'd started on the Valium his mother had left in the medicine chest before she'd gone off to live with her sister in Valdosta. With the last of the Valium he'd had no recourse but to go to whiskey, and whiskey did very little good. The pain sang in his ears and thumped in his chest and invaded everything he thought. It was becoming a voice and it wanted to talk to him. He couldn't make it out yet, but the message was clarifying as the pitch climbed higher, higher like an approaching siren, like a mosquito in his ear.

Boner saw the headlights wash across the front of his

trailer and then heard the engine quit. He heard two doors open and close. If it was two, at least it wasn't that crazy goddamn Harry Feather. The thing about Feather, you never saw him with another person.

Boner raised the bottle of Heaven Hill and took a long drink, then went to the window and lifted the shade. He recognized Raymer Harney. The town was talking about Raymer and some friend of his from out of town. Saying they were snooping around, asking questions, bothering people. Well, good luck to them. Anybody talked to them about Okee City business would end up cooking in a ten-thousand-gallon vat of sugar cane. A little hide and tallow to give your Dixie Crystals extra flavor.

Boner knew they were here to talk to him about Feather's car. But old Boner was in the clear. He had finished the job in record time. He'd ground the blue scrape on the right front wheel well right down to the shiny metal. They'd have to find that blue in the powder on the floor of the paint bay. They had forensic science nowdays, the cops did. Boner had seen it on TV. But he doubted like hell they could find that blue in all those layers of dust.

Even so, when the doorbell rang, Boner Harkness jumped. And jumping aroused the voice in his flaming leg. When he walked to the door, he was wiping tears from his eyes.

Eddie stood back and let Raymer hit the doorbell another good squawk. They had seen Mr. Harkness lift the shade and look out at them. Mr. Harkness, locally known as Boner for some comical reasons Raymer had explained to Eddie in the car. Eddie figured he'd let Raymer lead the way here. Raymer being acquainted with local customs. Eddie wasn't ready for what he saw when Harkness opened the door.

"Hey there, Boner," Raymer said. "Can we come in? Talk to you a little bit?"

"I ain't got no Key Man insurance, Raymer." The voice angry and strange too, a little unhooked back in the throat. "We ain't got nare thing to talk about."

Standing behind Raymer, Eddie got a whiff of something

seriously unpleasant. Then Harkness opened the door a little more and Eddie saw the leg, the swelling, the discoloration. A fifth of bourbon hung by its neck from Harkness's right hand.

Eddie stepped out from behind Raymer. "What you say to parting with a little of that whiskey, Mr. Harkness?"

Where Eddie came from, no swain could refuse a call to hospitality involving his bourbon and another man's thirst. It would be a declaration of outright dislike.

Harkness looked at Eddie, then at Raymer, then shifted his weight, wincing, on the injured leg. Then he turned, leaving them at the door. Eddie nudged Raymer from behind.

Inside, the stink was overpowering. And it was coming from underneath those yellowing bandages. Eddie had to suppress the urge to lift his coat lapel and apply it to his nose.

The walls were lined with unpainted pine shelves full of greasy car repair manuals, and the floor was covered with AstroTurf. There was a big-screen TV and a stack of girlie magazines. It was all there, work and play. Harkness was in the little kitchen searching for two clean glasses. Eddie hoped the search was not futile.

When Harkness poured the bourbon, Eddie and Raymer settled on the orange Naugahyde sofa, Harkness standing over them.

"Sit down, Boner," Raymer said. "Join us."

"Can't," Harkness said. "She won't bend." Indicating the leg. Poking it, in fact, with an index finger that was curiously indifferent. Treating the leg like a thing already separate from the self of Harkness.

Eddie said, "Mr. Harkness, I don't know much about medical things, but that leg looks bad to me. Have you been back to see the doctor since the night the gun went off?"

What happened in Harkness's eyes was large and mysterious and frightening. It wasn't Eddie's mentioning the doctor that caused a recognition in those washed-out blue disks. It was "the night the gun went off." Harkness blinked, drank from the bottle, and snapped his head back as if to throw off the memory. The night he pulled Corey out of the canal and she got her strange revenge.

"Can't," Harkness said. "I went to that damned Haitian doctor *one time* and look at me." Poking the leg again as though it belonged to someone else.

Raymer said, "Boner, I was driving by your shop and I saw Harry Feather's car. Looked like you painted his car. Is that right?"

"I painted it. Anything wrong with that?"

"No, hell," Raymer said, looking into his glass. Taking some of the bourbon in a gingerly way. "A man's got to make a living. Only thing is, it's got to be a legal living. A man can't conceal evidence of a crime."

"What crime?" Harkness's voice was too loud. He wasn't looking at Raymer. He was watching the leg as though it had asked a question.

"I think you know what I mean, Boner." Raymer sipped. Eddie couldn't bring himself to touch his lips to his glass. It was good enough just to hold it under his nose.

"You two get on out of here. I ain't telling you anything about Harry Feather's car. I painted it and the last time I looked there wasn't nothing illegal about painting a car."

Raymer smiling now, looking at Eddie over his glass. And Harkness poking the leg with his finger, an angry look on his face as though the leg had just made a damaging admission about Feather's car.

Raymer pushed himself up. "All right, Boner. We'll go."

Eddie rose, followed Raymer to the door. Looking at the place where the fresh air started. Raymer stopped, turned back.

"Boner, I was you, I wouldn't tell Feather we were here."

Harkness nodded, but not at Raymer. At the leg.

Raymer said, "And I wouldn't tell him we asked about that blue streak on the front of the Caddy."

It brought Boner around or back. It woke him up. His face drained a little. His voice went tight in his throat. "You didn't. You didn't ask about it."

"Didn't I?" Raymer said. "Sorry. It gets confusing."

"It?" Boner asked, his eyes narrowing.

"*It*, Boner," Raymer said. "*It.*"

"You mean that blue streak?"

"Right. That's what I mean."

"Told you I didn't see no blue streak."

"Sorry," Raymer said. "It got confusing again."

Boner smiled. He understood confusion.

Raymer said, "I'm with Eddie here, Boner. I think you ought to take that leg back to Doc Merseault. It looks bad to me. And Boner?"

"Yeah?" Harkness watching the leg again, waiting for it to speak.

"That leg smells worse than a hog pen at farrowing time."

Harkness not listening to Raymer, bent at the waist, inclining his ear to the leg.

Outside, Raymer said, "How'd I do?"

"All right by my lights," Eddie said. "He's obviously scared peeless of this guy Feather. He gets scareder, maybe he'll let a grand jury overhear him and his leg talking about it."

They got into Raymer's black Buick. Raymer said, "Feather's a scary guy. He doesn't have all the things people usually get with their human card. He's shy two or three essential components. One of them is giving a shit whether you live or die."

Raymer cranked the Buick. "And we're a long way from a grand jury, my friend."

Raymer guided the Buick down the winding mud track through the cane fields. "What you say we go to the Cane Cutter? End the day with a drink of *clean* whiskey?"

Eddie nodded. "My dance card is empty."

Out on the hard road, Eddie asked, "What you think about the blue?"

"Oh, yeah," Raymer said, horsing the Buick in a tight side step around a dead possum. "Boner saw the blue, all right."

23

▲▲▲▲▲▲▲▲▲▲▲▲▲▲▲▲▲▲▲

Harry W. Feather was on pus patrol. He had ransacked his
entire collection of medical literature, all his old copies of *Geographic* and the *National Enquirer*. It was absorbing and infor-
mative reading, but he hadn't come up with anything useful.

Now, in *The Lancet*, he'd found an article about an African
wasp that laid her eggs in the tissue on the crown of the
human head. She was a deft and delicate little bird and you
didn't have to be bald to become her children's nursery.
When the larvae hatched, they feasted under the scalp, making first an itch, then a quite considerable headache, and,
finally, a brain fever that sent you raving into the jungle,
where you became paralyzed. The perfect host.

It was all very damned interesting, but it wasn't what
Harry W. Feather needed. His library had failed him. He
poured himself a glass of Rebel Yell and walked out to the
little cypress deck he'd built to overlook the canal. He stood
at the rail watching the night.

This was about as good as it got out here on Indian land. The canal was flowing fast a few yards below him, its surface broken by bait fish. The sky was a fine blue-black and starry. The breeze was fresh enough to keep the mosquitoes off and the humidity was bearable. Like they used to say in that missionary church his mother took him to before she gave him up for raising by her television and his reading habits, "This is a night the Lord has made."

No, sir, no, ma'am, it didn't get better than this on Indian land, because Indian land was mostly water.

Along the far bank of the canal, a fish hawk skimmed the surface, dipped her talons, and raked a hand-sized bream out of the tannic water. And Harry saw the flash and roil of something big snapping in the bird's wake. Something by God going for that bird and not missing her by much. He switched on the powerful deck lights and the big gator's red eyes came on like the hellfire beacons they were. And Harry had his inspiration. Suddenly, he knew exactly what he needed.

He'd been baiting the gator for weeks now. The first time, he'd run over a possum not thirty yards from his front door. Didn't want rotting meat in his dooryard, so he'd thrown it in the canal. He was turning away when he'd heard the quiet, efficient sluicing of the gator's big jaws.

Harry had seen gators feed plenty of times, liked the way they approached from the side, opened their jaws and used the suction of inrushing water to stall the struggling prey. Then the powerful swivel of neck and the crashing jaws. That lightening clamp. And this gator was big. Harry guessed him at twenty feet, at least two thousand pounds. In mating season, he'd heard the gator roar. Roaring and throwing his weight around out there to get on the good side of some mother gator.

The gator and the dead possum and the fish hawk and all that rot and seething out there in the night had given Harry W. Feather his idea. He walked back inside and grabbed the keys to the big old Caddy. Lord, he had missed that car. Even if it was just for one day.

* * *

148

Harry parked a few blocks from the country clinic and walked to the alley behind the building. He stopped in the shadow of the Dumpsters and put on his AIDS fighter's rubber gloves. On the loading dock, the back door was open, but Harry couldn't see anyone inside. He waited awhile and was about to climb into the first Dumpster when a man came out dragging two heavy black plastic garbage bags. Harry stepped back into the moon shadow while the man swung the two big bags up into the Dumpster. The guy was some kind of orderly in green hospital scrubs. When he was gone, Harry climbed up into the Dumpster.

It was full of the bags, all of them tied with heavy wire strips and tagged with white paper flags. Harry lit his Bic and read one of the flags: "Danger! Hazardous Medical Waste! To Be Incinerated. Do Not Open This Container." One of those grinning death's heads that told you: POISON.

Harry recalled reading the article in the local paper. How the clinic wasn't meeting federal standards. How they had to hire a waste management firm from Miami to come up, haul the stuff away, and burn it in some high-tech inferno so it wouldn't go into the local landfill, infect the water, whatever.

Seeing that fish hawk snatch her bream out of the canal had put Harry in mind of the food chain, of the worms out there in the landfill chewing away at the town's garbage, of the water leaching out of the garbage all its special juices, and those juices going where the water went. And the water went everywhere. Nature's way.

Harry opened his Buck knife and slit the first bag. His nose told him he had hit pay dirt. With the tip of the blade, he picked his way through some pretty nasty stuff—old dressings, some suspicious plastic bags, a whole raft of syringes with their darling little needles glinting in the moonlight. But nothing to make Harry's pulse rate climb, until . . . Hoo-hah, there it was wrapped in a some gauze, the gauze stuck inside a used plasma bag. Carefully, Harry slit the bag and then the gauze, revealing his happy little find. Oh, archaeology of dung heaps! Oh, happy pus patrol!

It was a severed human finger. It was hard to tell by the light of Harry's Bic if it had belonged to a Latino person or had its deep brown color because it was so far gone in its natural processes. It stank like nothing else in the bag. Harry lifted it carefully and dropped it into the mayonnaise bottle he had brought.

By the look of things, Boner was asleep on the sofa. The leg, a pretty sight even through the window of the trailer, was propped up on some pillows. The empty bourbon bottle on the floor by Boner's right hand told the story of how Boner had managed to get some rest. To Harry W. Feather's delight, Boner had even left the front door unlocked. So far out in the country like this, so few visitors. Hell, it could be six, ten days between visitors for a guy like Boner.

Harry stood over Boner for a while, trying to get used to the smell from the bandage. Waiting to see if Boner would wake up. Finally, Harry gave him a nudge, another. Nothing. Boner was good and gone. Harry unfastened the bandage at Boner's thigh, unwrapped a few feet of it. Holy noses! Even Harry, who enjoyed nature's fundamental processes, had to go to Boner's little bathroom, find a bottle of cheap cologne, sprinkle some on a washcloth.

Holding the cologne to his nostrils, Harry kept unwrapping the bandage. The leg was a sight. Harry wished he had a camera. Some of his favorite magazines published amateur photos of women posing nude. Just your housewife down the street setting up the camera. Whacking the delayed shutter and then sprinting all ajiggle into position for the flash. Working girls whose boyfriends and husbands had snapped them looking back between their legs and smiling. Why wasn't there a section in *The Lancet* or the *New England Journal of Medicine* for photos of the kind that Harry could have taken right now?

The leg was black behind the knee and blue at the upper and lower extremes. The cracked and peeling skin looked like gator hide. The wounds had swollen and burst their sutures. They released a suppurating ooze that was a truly remarkable emerald color. And all this because Boner couldn't repose the proper faith in Dr. Merseault. Couldn't because the good doctor was a person of color.

From his pocket, Harry removed the bottle that held the decomposing finger. He had stopped on his way at a spot near the landfill, a place where even a good stiff breeze couldn't wash from the night air the heavy presence of what was underground. He had filled the bottle with ditch water. Now he took one of the syringes from the Dumpster and drew into it a solution from the bottle. He knelt beside Boner's leg and selected a site.

The largest wound was about an inch across, its jagged mouth pouted open. It would do very well. Remembering the wasp who laid her eggs in the human scalp, Harry inserted his needle. The last half inch of the needle's travel made Boner stir. But only a little, only a twitch and a groan from Boner.

Harry pushed the plunger, watching the gray-green fluid disappear from the plastic cylinder. He didn't know what the needle itself might carry, but he had read up on infections, especially hybrid infections, how difficult they were to cure. How they could sometimes defeat the finest of antibiotics. Harry W. Feather drew the needle out, picked up the finger bottle, and stood, watching Boner sleep. Boner seemed to be dreaming a long talk with someone. His lips and eyelids moving. A lot of REMs going on there.

Harry wondered if he, Harry W. Feather, was in Boner's dream. He turned off the air conditioner. The heat would help things grow. He whispered good-bye to Boner and left.

Down the road, he stopped and tossed the finger and the syringe into a canal. Stood for a moment in the moonlight, watching the bait fish stir the surface where the finger had gone in.

In Boner's dream, the band was playing "Unchained Melody." It was the last dance of the senior prom. Bill Harkness was dancing with Melissa Belanger. Dancing slow and close. Already thinking about what might happen after the music stopped and the couples drifted from the floor. Thinking about Bill Harkness getting lucky with Melissa Belanger in the back seat of a brand-new, midnight blue Chevrolet Impala. How sweet that would be.

The song was ending. Melissa swung away from him, their arms linked. His limbs held the warm memory of Melissa's long length. He closed his eyes for a moment as the last chords echoed through the open doors of the high school gym into the warm night. Then came the flash.

24

That's him. That's Feather," Raymer said, poking Eddie's forearm with a cleat-scarred finger.

Eddie and Raymer were on their second Maker's Mark. Glyneice was delivering with a reassuring regularity. The Cane Cutter was doing a brisk business with the blue-collar drinker who had not made it home for supper. Too early yet for the dating couples and the sharking singles.

Eddie looked at the door when Raymer's finger dented him. Yes, the guy could be an Indian, but not pure blood. Had to be some bleachy genes in there somewhere. The guy looked a little like Paul Newman playing Hombre. Eddie watched Feather walk to the men's room.

It bothered him that the guy had probably been there the day he'd met Corey. It felt dirty that Feather might have seen him still in Corey's spell. And then followed her.

Feather came cruising out of the men's room still zipping

his fly. His eyes lit up, his lips moving with some song to himself. The guy on some kind of high, wired. Drunk maybe, Eddie thought. Or coked? High on life? People all over the Cane Cutter coming up from their drinks, looking at Feather, then burrowing down lower than before. The crowd reaction: This guy is dangerous.

Eddie wondered why Feather had run Corey off the road. What could Feather have to do with a computer file and some guy who'd come to town asking about pH levels in the local sand substratum?

Watching Feather walk to the bar, Eddie felt something starting in his own limbic system. Feather knew he was here. The strut, the stud strut from the men's room. Feather hadn't gone in that way, and it wasn't the relief of a good strong piss that had brought him back out on a macho buzz. It was Eddie here. Feather had come out saying, Hey, bud. You're sitting in my booth.

A little sweat broke on Eddie's forehead. You didn't meet guys like Feather selling forty-two footers out of Hanson's Marina.

Raymer stood up. In a reflex Eddie did too.

Sawnie Darrow came walking across the Cane Cutter toward them. All eyes turning to watch her now. Eddie catching Feather in the corner of his eye. Feather was the only one in the bar *not* looking at Sawnie. The only one not stunned at the likeness: Damn she looks like Corey!

That did it. Feather was convicted. He had killed Corey. Eddie knew it and knew he'd have to do something about it. And he knew Raymer was right. They were a long way from a grand jury. And even if Boner Harkness was willing to say that he'd seen blue paint on Feather's Cadillac, what did they have?

There was some confusion about where Sawnie would sit. Eddie thought she wanted to sit beside him. And didn't want to. And didn't want to hurt Raymer's feelings. Fuck Raymer. Eddie moved over. Smelling the woman's perfume. Something subtle and expensive. Something that married her natural scent.

She sat down, not looking at Eddie, her hands folded on the table. Finally, she said, "What the hell. I couldn't stay out there moping around Corey's place all night. What is there to *do* in this goddamn town?"

Eddie and Raymer looked at their drinks.

Sawnie didn't look at the lawyer, Priest. She watched Raymer's face, feeling her own strained smile, waiting for someone to say something that would ease them into an evening of drink and conversation. She was tired of being alone in Corey's house with the memories, the sadness. And feeling the Governor, far off, calling her back to a job, a future he wanted to shape for her. Now she wanted to pour some bourbon on those hot circuits. She wanted a blank two or three hours.

And maybe she was ready to admit to herself that she wanted the company of Eddie Priest. That she'd liked the way he'd handled himself today at the sheriff's office and with the medical examiner. Quiet, competent, not pushing, not oversolicitous of her. Asking her what she wanted to do next. Acknowledging her ownership of grief, but not concealing his own. Sawnie had begun to believe his own might be real.

Priest signaled the waitress. The woman, a real Okee City homegirl, sidled over and said, "Do it again? The usual?"

Priest nodded, looked at Sawnie. "And for the lady?"

All right, Sawnie thought. I'll be your lady tonight. In this place, ladies don't have to think. She smiled big and bright. "Bring me what the gents are drinking. And, Glyneice, I'm behind. Make it a double."

Harry W. Feather didn't like the way the Former Great had looked at him. He didn't like that goddamned confidence. Where did you get that? Out on the gridiron? Out there, you get hit and you eat some grass, maybe, and some fatass in a striped shirt blows a whistle and they bring out the golf cart. Truck you off for some X-rays. Then you're back for the second half. I mean, *shit,* that ain't real. That's Nintendo life.

Harry just flat didn't like the guy. One dog in another dog's face. Meat breath to meat breath. He knocked back his peppermint schnapps, feeling the sweet sting go warm into the middle of him. He pushed away from the bar.

Sawnie was saying, ". . . so I do whatever the Governor needs. I guess you could call me a political generalist. That's what I like about the job. The variety."

Eddie watching Feather walk across the room. Thinking, oh boy, the variety.

Feather stopped at their table, stood there grinning, those weird eyes stuck on bright, drumming his fingers on his thighs, the guy all energy. He said, "Hey, ain't . . . I mean aren't you Eddie Priest? The guy that caught the One-Second Pass. What did it feel like, catching that pass?"

Raymer slowly shook his head, looking down into his drink. Sawnie Darrow watched Feather. Baffled. Not sure what to do.

Eddie looked at Feather, trying to hold the smile on his face. The guy, Feather, standing there with his finger on one of Eddie's buttons.

Eddie had relived the One-Second Pass too many times. It was the shorthand of all his casual encounters. When someone asked him, Hey, was he the guy who caught the One-Second Pass? he gave The Answer.

The Answer was memorized and The Answer had long since dimmed any real recollection. The Answer ran like a grainy game film across his mind's eye, always the same. Eddie couldn't even remember when he'd decided it was easier to replay The Answer than to go back there and search for something authentic. The Answer had sold a lot of boats.

It was raining. They had the ball on the Mizoo forty-five yard line with one second on the clock. Time for one snap of the ball. Eddie ran the down, out and down. Solly Bid-

dlemyer rolled out and did some fancy footwork at the side-
line avoiding the defensive end and then put up one of his
cannon shots. Eddie came down dragging his feet on the
end line, chalk in his shoelaces, three Tigers on his back,
and a wet pigskin teed up on his fingertips. Sixty thousand
eyes watched the ball: Would it stay on the tee? The referee
stood over him with his hands up like a tree. And pandemo-
nium, as they say.

Eddie had dislocated a finger earlier in the game, and
there was only one authentic answer to the question: What
did it feel like? It hurt.

Eddie looked down at the finger now. It was hyperex-
tended thirty degrees, a real novelty shop number. He
wanted to stick it in Feather's eye. Instead, he gave The
Answer: "It was a great moment. It felt great. Just like you'd
imagine it would."

"You were a great one," Feather said, shifting his weight.
Eddie guessed him at about one hundred eighty, all of it
pretty hard. Some gator wrestling, Cadillac horsing gristle
in there.

Feather showing no signs of leaving. Standing there in
an orange silk T-shirt and a white linen sport coat, the
coat collar grimy from rubbing his bare neck. Wearing
floppy pleated chinos. Some kind of rubber-soled lobster
pink espadrilles. Looked like he'd fallen off Carmen Mi-
randa's head.

Feather looking at Sawnie now. "I bet the lady is thrilled
to be sitting here with the guy that caught the One-Second
Pass? Am I right? Thrilled?" Boring in at Sawnie with those
switched-on eyes, all that hyped-up energy. Sawnie looking
away now.

Eddie pushed back in his seat, working the bent finger,
then drawing it into a fist. "Look," he said, "we're having
a little drink here. And . . ."

Feather raising a hand. Traffic cop, social director. Doing
the right thing. "Hey," he said, the voice high, pinched in
his throat, his face getting a little pale, "I know what you

157

mean, man. I do. A couple gents like you don't get ahold of class pussy like this every day so I'll just . . ."

Eddie was out of the booth, somehow going over Sawnie without touching her, coming straight from the lizard that squatted at the top of his spinal column. The reptile that lived to serve the god Adrenaline. He had a handful of Feather's orange silk shirt, had it wadded under Feather's chin, Feather's feet leaving the floor. Out there in the realms of Ordinary Happy Hour, a place Eddie had definitively departed, the bar was going crazy. People running for the door, women screaming, Glyneice sliding to a stop with a tray of beers. The beers doing what Isaac Newton had said they would do when the tray stopped moving.

Eddie had Feather's back to the bar, had his chin back. Liking it. Words coming to him now. Something about inviting Feather back to the booth, suggesting he apologize to the lady. Then the lizard unfurled its tail, flicking it up into Eddie's cortex. The lizard's question: Where are this guy's hands?

Eddie let go, shoved himself backward into a bow just as the bright arc of the Buck knife swept from right to left. He looked down at the floor where, but for two inches of his own good sense, his intestines would be steaming among the peanut shells. He looked at Feather.

Feather was smiling, already closing the knife. Eddie backed off another step and the world around him took on shape and sound. He could hear Raymer, somewhere behind him. "Look out. He's got a knife!"

It was fun, Harry W. Feather thought. A good test. Now he knew what the guy had. What the guy had was pretty good. No match for Harry W. Feather of course, but pretty good. And the guy had done some serious damage to his silk shirt. This wouldn't do. There would be recompense. You didn't handle a person like this in front of other people. It was embarrassing.

Harry W. Feather put the knife back in his pocket. He

pointed a finger at the Former Great's face. Like aiming a deer rifle. He stared down the length of his arm into the Former Great's eyes until he was sure the Former Great understood him. Knew it all, down to the very last little detail.

No exit. No end. No running. No rules.

When Harry could see the sad acknowledgment in the guy's eyes, he dropped his arm and made a slow circle toward the woman. The big stupid jock turned with him, the two of them swinging on the radius of the circle Harry was drawing. The jock kept his eyes on Harry's smile.

When Harry got to the booth, he turned. Just gave the Former Great his back. Fuck the guy. Let him bring what he had. He looked at the woman. Put his hands on the table and leaned down to her. "Ma'am, I'm sorry. What I said was an ... unfortunate remark. It was a violation, and I offer you my apology. You *are* a very attractive woman, but what I said was crude. What you got to understand, though, is this is a crude place. You live here, after a while, you don't know how to talk to nice people anymore. But hey, you know that. You grew up around here."

Harry pushed up, stood looking down at the woman and the shit-scared Raymer Harney. "And one other thing. I want to tell you I'm sorry about what happened to your sister. She was a very nice person."

Harry watched the woman to see what she'd do with this. She surprised him. Not like the Former Great. Everything the Former Great did was right from The Plan. All dumb jocks were born to The Plan. They had to live it. No choice. You do this and I gotta do that. That's why Harry had almost spilled the Former Great's sweetmeats with his Buck knife. It wasn't part of the plan for your opponent to pull steel when you grab his shirt, shove him back against the bar.

This woman was a little different. For one thing, she wasn't scared. For another, she recognized him.

Not him. Not Harry W. Feather as such. But she knew

the idea, the *ideal* of a Harry W. Feather. She'd met Harry
W. Feather before somewhere. Harry was certain of that. He
didn't know if it gave her anything to bring. Maybe it did.
He said, "Hey, I'm sorry. What can I tell you?"

Harry W. Feather left the bar without looking back at the
Former Great. He didn't have to look. He could imagine
everything the guy would ever do.

25

▲▲▲▲▲▲▲▲▲▲▲▲▲▲▲▲

Sawnie said, "Would you like to come in for a nightcap?"
"Of course."

Eddie hadn't followed her to Corey's house just to do the right thing. He *needed* a drink. She put the key in the lock, turned. "I own this house now. Did you know that?" Her voice was sad.

She left him at the door and went around the house checking the locks. Eddie walked to the kitchen and waited.

After Harry Feather had cock-strutted out of the Cane Cutter, every eye in the place had examined Eddie and Sawnie and Raymer for a count of, maybe, fifty. Then the talking started, loud, agitated. You could hear men all over the room telling their favorite bar fight stories in English, Spanish, and Creole.

Only it hadn't been a fight. Not really. Eddie had been in a few, and he knew it. What it had been was a warning. Not a warning about what might happen, but about what

161

was inevitable. That is, unless Eddie could find a way to get back to before. Before he'd agreed to spend a day with Corey on the *Sight Unseen*.

Sawnie came into the kitchen and started searching the cabinets. "I offered you a drink," she muttered. "I guess I better produce."

Eddie said, "Maybe she didn't keep booze in the house." He liked the way Sawnie moved, the efficiency, the grace. She found the Early Times in a pantry cabinet. "Here it is," she said, "right next to the cider vinegar."

Eddie thinking how strange it was that he wanted to take her in his arms only minutes after almost having his guts aired by a Miccosuki with a Buck knife and an attitude. Strange because now it was like a first date. They were doing small talk. Eddie's hands shaking a little. Sawnie had her back to him, cracking the ice trays, pouring the whiskey.

When she turned, Eddie couldn't meet those gemstone eyes. She slid the whiskey in front of him and he pretended to find something floating in it. Dipped his little finger in, pretended to lift something out. He was holding the nonexistent thing up to the light, examining it, when she said, "Look, we have to talk."

Eddie licked his finger and looked at her. Not sure why this took more courage than it had taken to grab Feather by his lounge lizard shirt. He said, "You're right about that."

Now that his eyes were in hers, he was falling hard. He was dizzy with her. She was too much of all the good things that were so bad. The good things that promised to last and never did.

He wondered what she was getting from his own washed-out, pale blue eyes. He got up and offered her his hand. She looked at it, took it, and he drew her into his arms. Holding her close, he moved her across the living room. It was like they were dancing, and when they got to the bedroom doorway, both of them saw Corey in it. The music stopped.

She leaned against him for a long time, breathing hard. He couldn't see her eyes but knew they were closed tight like his own. And behind them were her imaginings of what it would be like with him in that room and how she'd feel afterward. After she'd been his second Darrow sister.

She drew her fingers slowly across the back of his neck and pulled away from him. She went back to the table and sat down.

Nothing coy about her hand on his neck, everything exploratory about it. Her way of saying, Maybe we'll touch again.

Eddie opened his eyes, dizzy. Got his balance and sat down across from her.

"Look," she said, "I appreciated what you did back there in the bar. But you shouldn't have done it."

Eddie knew she was right. And he knew several more reasons than she did why she was right, but he asked it anyway. "Why not?"

"Because you could have been hurt. Badly hurt over a word. A word that didn't bother me at . . ."

"It wasn't just a word." Eddie didn't like interrupting her, but he had to. "It was the first word. There's gonna be a lot more. I was telling him I know that."

She went into his eyes again. For a long time, staring. Deciding. She backed out saying, "I like you. I didn't at first, and I hope you'll forgive that. But now I do. You're a good man. An ethical man."

Eddie winced. "I don't know," he said. "I just sell boats and try not to do the wrong thing. Sometimes that's right."

She liked it, what he'd said. She knocked back her bourbon and dropped them both another portion. She nodded. "It's as good a creed as most I've heard. How come you quit practicing law."

"Because of a guy named Ernesto."

She watched him, waiting for the story. Only now he couldn't tell it. Realized he'd told it for the last time. And realized something else: Feather was Ernesto. The big reaction back at the Cane Cutter, grabbing Feather by the silk shirt; it was about Ernesto. About that thing out there, the nameless dread. The guy who could get your number from

163

directory assistance. Cold call you up. Stir up your imagination enough to change your life.

Yes, Feather was Ernesto with breath that smelled like peppermint schnapps and it had felt good, so very damned good to get a big knuckle-popping handful of Ernesto and shove his ass back up against the bar. And it had felt good to have enough of the good lizard left, crouching there above your hypothalamus to jump back just in time to avoid the bright sweep of the Buck knife.

It was a kind of ethics.

"So who's Ernesto?" Sawnie sipped her bourbon. Her eyes like that hand across his neck, exploring him.

"Just a guy," Eddie said. "A guy who offered me a job selling boats."

She looked at him again for a long time. Going way in. In so far it hurt. Then she said, "I know that guy. Feather." Taking a big drink, a slug that stopped her voice, made her eyes water. Made her lift a pretty, knotted fist to her mouth and cough.

"I don't mean him, personally. Just guys like him. You get them in politics. They've got a lot more polish, but they're the same thing under the clothes. You know?" Her eyes were guarded now. A little scared.

Eddie nodded. Not really knowing, not liking it that she'd said "under the clothes." Not wanting to imagine her knowing what was under Feather's ridiculous tropical costume.

"So," he said, "where does that leave us?"

She smiled at him. A sad smile. "I was about to say, 'in a world of shit?' "

Eddie laughed. "Maybe not."

Eddie told her about his and Raymer's visit to Boner Harkness's trailer. About finding the big white Caddy, freshly painted. About his thinking maybe they could work Boner off against Feather. Work on Boner's fear a little. Rock and a hard place. Get him to tell about the blue streak on the white car.

She looked a little sick, taking it in. A little bit worse for the information. "Jesus Christ," she whispered. "I think you're saying Feather killed Corey."

"We don't know that yet."

Sawnie took the bottle and slopped some bourbon into her glass. It seemed to Eddie that she drank through gritted teeth. "We know it," she said. "Oh, yes, we do."

Eddie reached out and stopped the glass on its way to her mouth. Feeling the resistance in her hand, seeing it in her eyes. Finally she gave in and let him settle the glass on the table.

He said, "I like you too. I liked you way back when you called me a rat bastard."

She drew a big breath and sighed it out. She looked tired and sad. The man who had killed her sister had called her class pussy in a migrant bar in Okee City. She said, "Would you stay here tonight? Please?"

Eddie saw her look over at the sofa. He'd noticed it on the way in. It was a hell of a lot better than Raymer's torture rack.

She said, "I don't mean you and me." Explaining it carefully. "I don't mean *do* anything. I just mean stay here so I'll sleep safe. Would you do that?" Eddie saw her sneak a look at the windows, at what might be out there on a night like this. On any night. It was a new world out there.

"Sure," he said, "so you'll sleep safe."

But not sure. Not sure how safe she would be with him here. How safe either of them would ever be with Harry W. Feather out there.

She got up, moving differently now. Not so efficient, not so definite, now that she knew the face, the eyes that had watched Corey's Ford go into a canal.

She put the bourbon away, and Eddie followed her to a linen closet. Watched her get out some sheets and a blanket. She was on her way to make up his sofa when he took the stuff from her. "I can do it," he said. "You go on to bed."

But she didn't. She stood watching him botch the job of making a bed. When he was finished, he sat down, testing the lumps. "Not bad," he said.

She sat in Corey's matching love seat.

Eddie thinking, What the hell. Deciding to ask her. "Look," he said, "you're the Governor's right-hand woman. Why don't you just call up the FDLE, get them to take some names down at the sheriff's office? Find a creative reason to haul Feather in. Put him in the puke tank with some big cutter named Julio that drinks mescal and shaves with his machete. Let him think about his life a little. See what shakes down after a month or two. In there with Julio. Maybe he's not so tough after all."

The way she looked at him, Eddie couldn't tell if she was tired or disappointed. Guessing disappointed. She knew Feather was tough. She could see Feather handling Julio without much trouble.

Then Eddie saw something else, something way down in. Something she didn't want him to see. Maybe it was the Governor in there. She didn't like his mentioning her Tallahassee connections.

"No," she said. "I don't think so." She got up and started toward the bedroom. "I think we have to do this without any help from the Governor."

When she was gone, her door closed, the house quiet, Eddie walked around, checking locks again, thinking, We do this? Do what exactly? He went to the kitchen and found the shotgun in the broom closet where Sawnie had stored it the first morning he'd visited her. One lump he wouldn't mind sleeping with.

In Corey's dark, quiet bedroom, with the good man, Priest, sleeping outside her door, Sawnie called Lucy Watkins in Tallahassee.

"I hope I didn't wake you, Lucy?"

A sigh. "God knows I've got no social life, Sawnie, but I don't go to bed *this* early."

Sawnie looked at Corey's bedside clock. It was ten o'clock and felt like three A.M. Now she remembered that it always seemed later in the country. A lot of things were different here. And enough had happened today to fill a week. "You

get anything?" she asked. Sawnie could hear one of Lucy's
Siamese cats yowling in the background.

"Yes and no." Lucy's voice taking on the concentrated
excitement you heard when Lucy's computer attacked a
problem. "I accessed the database down there in Okee
County. It was a piece of cake. Modemed right in there. A
junior high school hacker could crack their records. They
ought to hire a consultant, get some security. Hell, they
could get me cheap. The Governor sure does."

"That's great, Lucy." Sawnie knowing you couldn't rush
Lucy.

"I had to access the organizational charts to find who
worked with your sister. Then I went to the user codes.
Then I went for all the deletes, starting with the recent ones
and going backward. There's no file like the one you want.
Nothing your sister entered was deleted. Not by her or anybody else." Lucy's voice changing a little. One of the cats
whining at her ankles.

"Yes, Lucy?"

"Sawnie, there's a problem. I found an internal security
file that shows somebody was under investigation for improprieties. Improper use of a county vehicle, purloining
postage stamps, misusing a cellular phone. A lot of chicken
shit stuff. The kind of stuff everybody does. Innocent
enough until you make an enemy. Somebody wants to make
you look like you been feeding at the public trough."

Sawnie said, "Who is it? Who's under investigation?"

Lucy crooned to the cat, "There, there, precious. Mommy
feed in a minute."

To Sawnie: "Corey Darrow."

Well, Sawnie thought, they can't hurt Corey now. Not
anymore they can't.

Lucy's voice smaller now and filling up with that perpetual anxiety. "Listen, Sawnie, I want to make sure you understand this. I'm not telling you there never was a file. Only
that I couldn't find it."

She said, "Lucy, I'm confused. I thought you could retrieve a deleted file. I thought that was pretty simple for you."

"I can in most cases. Anybody dumb enough to set up a system like the one they got down there probably wouldn't know how to really deep-six a file. All I can tell you is either the file never existed or somebody got very smart very fast."

"Thanks, Lucy. I owe you."

"All right, precious, Mommy feed now," Lucy sang. "It's nothing, Sawnie. Take me out to lunch when you get back. When *do* you get back?"

"I don't know, Lucy. Let's hope soon."

26

▲▲▲▲▲▲▲▲▲▲▲▲▲▲▲▲▲▲▲

Harry W. Feather watched the Cowgirl's sister though the bedroom window. Enough space between the blinds to see a slice of her pretty face, her pretty mouth moving. She looked disappointed. You had to figure that was good. Or did you? Harry was confused about it. He wondered who she was calling. Wondered if Coltis Almighty would decide to share the information with him. Whatever it was he had learned about this class lady from out of town. Lady wearing some cane cutter's yearly wage in clothes and jewelry.

She had to be somebody important. Maybe she was married to some rich guy. That was usually how the ladies got the fancy clothes and the big baubles. She was driving a shitty rented Corsica, nothing to learn from there. Just one of Detroit's mistakes.

And she had the Former Great in there with her. But not *in* there. The Former Great was staying in some other part of the house. Harry W. Feather imagined the touching scene.

169

"Not tonight, sweetie, I'm too tired. Encountering that rude man, that dislikable person of color, has given me the vapors. I just don't think that I will invite you into my boudoir tonight. I hope that is congenial with you, my dear?"

Something like that. Then the Cowgirl's sister who is, for Harry W. Feather's money, even more beautiful than the Cowgirl herself, goes off to her bedroom trailing a long silk scarf after her. Her wrist pressed to her forehead. Leaving the Former Great to take his hank on the couch.

Harry backed away from the window and walked the hundred yards out to where he'd parked the Caddy. He stood with the Caddy's door open, smoking a Dunhill and thinking. He remembered Coltis telling him how they couldn't meet where people could see them. Insulting him that way. He decided to drive out and see Coltis. Ask the big guy about the woman. Hell, they were associates now, and Harry had a right to know things. He couldn't be left in the dark like this, outside the window looking in.

Harry W. Feather parked beside his mother's battered Ford Ranger pickup under the Australian pines at the back of one of Coltis's outbuildings. The house was lit up like a Christmas tree. Coltis's dooryard had been turned into a parking lot that sported some pretty serious rolling stock. Harry counted three Benzes, the big ones, four Cadillacs, a vintage Lincoln Continental, the Kennedy model, same car they shot the president in, and at least six of the bigger Buicks and Oldsmobiles. One guy was driving a Rolls-Royce Silver Arrow. Coltis was having one hell of a party.

Harry took the long way around to the kitchen door, letting his fingers trail across the shiny hoods of the expensive automobiles. Music and laughter came from the house. It wasn't his kind of music. It was that Frank Sinatra, Wayne Newton, summer wind comes blowin' in ooby-dooby shit. It probably wasn't Harry's kind of laughter either.

Amelia W. Feather jumped when Harry came in the back door very quiet like he was learning to do. Amelia W. Feather turned back to the stove. "You scared me, Harry.

You shouldn't sneak up like that. I'm an old woman." She was stirring something that smelled pretty good. The kitchen counters were covered with all the stuff she'd fixed for the party and here she was, still humping a hot stove.

Old whore, Harry thought. "Sorry, Mom," he said. "Just habit. Moving slow and quiet. Just the old Miccosuki habit. Old habits die hard."

He was sure he heard it, his mother sniffing her contempt at him. Thinking what she thought about him. That she'd had to work for white men to keep him in dirty magazines and quarters for video games. That he was raised by a convenience store on highway 41, not by his good old Indian momma.

"Momma," he said, "how come I got such angular features? How come I'm not as dark as you are? As Daddy was? How come people ask me if I'm Italian or Cuban? You got any idea about that?"

It was a conversation they'd had a hundred times. Harry always asking the same questions. Amelia W. Feather always answering the same.

"Harry," she said, "how come you talk that trash to your momma? You think that's right? You think it's nice?" Her back to him, stirring the pot.

Harry's father had run away before he was born. Had been killed by a big rig loaded with steel reinforcing rods on the way to Miami to build some condo high-rise. Stumbled drunk out in front of a truck. Harry had seen the pictures of his father. Benjamin W. Feather had been a very Indian-looking guy. No forehead, flat-nosed, almond-eyed, and dark as a coffee bean. Either Harry W. Feather had caught some serious phantom genes from way back in the Pleistocene or his momma had caught some white guy, maybe a truck driver. Some guy stopping off at one of the motels where she'd been a maid before she'd gone to work for Coltis.

"What's in the pot?" Harry asked.

"Ham gravy," Amelia W. Feather said. "For Mr. C's

breakfast. I always make it up the night before. That way I don't have to rush so much in the morning."

It made sense, Harry W. Feather thought. It made sense because his mother was getting old. Something he had noticed lately. Old enough that she had to take it easy with the dust rag and the carpet sweeper. Had to watch out when she crossed highway 41. Look both ways for the big trucks when she went to buy her Beech-Nut chewing tobacco and the latest *People* magazine.

The party people were talking, laughing on the other side of the wall. Harry couldn't make out the words. He asked Amelia W. Feather, "What's going on? How come all these people here tonight?"

"Just a party," she said, stirring. "You stay in here with me, Harry."

Just like that, Harry. Stay, Harry. Where you belong, Harry.

Harry walked over to the pass-through and lifted the sliding panel. Little hole his momma pushed the food through. Harry rested his chin on the counter and looked. It hurt his neck.

Hoboy, they were having fun. He recognized most of them, the local growers and their slack, fat wives. He'd seen them around town. He'd driven through their fields, fields that went fifty miles in every direction, watching them stand by their pickups shading their eyes in the sun while the Haitians and the Jamaicans cut the cane. Harry was looking for Coltis. It wasn't easy. He didn't want to be seen. He ground his chin into the Formica and twisted his head one way and then the other. Then he heard the voice: Coltis talking to somebody. Talking in a real soothing way Harry had never heard before. Hell, it was almost like purring. Coltis just out of Harry's sightline, talking to somebody about, what was it? Local color? No, local culture. Harry wished they'd move a little closer so he could see them. He wanted to know who Coltis talked to that way.

Amelia W. Feather put her hand on his shoulder and it made him jump. He didn't like jumping in front of her. He pulled back from the pass-through. "Get away from there, Harry," his old mother said. "I told you about that before, watching like that. Spying. You gonna get me in trouble you do that."

Harry turned and took her wrist in his right hand. He gave it enough pressure to let her know something. Something she had guessed a long time ago. He squeezed until her eyes narrowed, and she looked down at the floor. "All right, now" he said, "you go back to the goddamn ham gravy." Turning back to the little window, wanting to know who it was Coltis talked to like that.

Harry heard the soothing voice again, closer. Coltis saying, "Why don't we talk about it right now. Let's go into my study. I'm beginning to see some intriguing possibilities in what you're saying."

And then a woman said, very polished, very, what you call it, socially adroit, "Mr. Coltis, you don't want to abandon your guests."

The two of them were moving toward the study. Harry had already recognized the woman's voice.

Coltis and Moira Big Breath walked into Harry's vision.

Moira dressed in her traditional red, blue, and black Miccosuki blouse and skirt. All colorful and tricked out ethnic, Moira. Moira, the toast of the party, Harry figured. Putting that Barnard College smooth together with that tough Indian rough: Getting just the right combination to wow the big cane men. Hoboy, old Moira, rising in the world.

It put the big burn in Harry's chest. The big mean burn.

Moira Breath stood at the window looking at the night while Coltis closed the door, shutting out the party noise. Jesus, she thought, he was a smooth operator. Inviting her here like this to show all these snuff-dipping, crotch-hustling gumps and their wives that he had . . . what? The sophistication, the courage to break the old prohibition. Moira had finally decided it was just another way to show them he owned them all. Coltis throws a party, invites a squaw, and makes them come and treat her like folks. Jesus, but he was smooth.

Moira closed the curtain, turned to face him. Coltis standing over by the door, his hands on his hips, his legs spread, smiling, his eyebrows raised. Looking like he'd just trapped something and was considering what to do with it. Who he could show it to. She smiled at him big and cool. Gave him the cocktail and culture chat smile she'd learned from the philanthropy mavens on the Upper East Side and in the Village coffeehouses and in the Broadway theater bars before the shows started. At the benefits and the sensitivity seminars, all the places where they needed one, a genuine Native American.

Hell, in a way, she liked the guy. The way she liked anything that was pure, like her own Miccosuki blood. This Coltis guy was straight, two-hundred-octane white supremacy, neocolonialism, nostalgia for the empire. He was a dead white man who just didn't know he was dead. And that was his charm, the not knowing. That and his sexy, ramrod self-assurance. She thought he looked like an aging Harrison Ford. Real Hollywood material. Something out of a John Ford western, the guy who circles his arm in the air, leans forward in the saddle, and hollers, "Wagons ho!" A six-and-a-half-foot phallus from Central Casting.

It made her think of Harry Feather, the contrast. The girls at Barnard, the ones from Larchmont and Grosse Pointe, would have called Harry "attractive in a Guido kind of way." But to Moira that wasn't it. Harry wasn't just hard and lean and vital. He was something elemental, like the trees, the water. That made him dangerous. A man like that wanted to turn a woman into something elemental, a baby maker. This Coltis would probably hire someone else to make his babies for him, just like they cut his cane, made his money. He was a watcher, this Coltis. And he liked the long view. Well, Moira thought, that's what they teach at Barnard, the long view.

"So," Moira said, "you've got me all by myself, Mr. Coltis. What is it you want to talk about?"

"Oh," he said, walking over to the cordovan leather sofa, easing down in that stiff, sexy way. "I think you know what it is." He patted the sofa beside him showing her where to sit. Not too close. Just schmoozing distance. Close enough for politics.

All right, she'd play his game. She lifted her fringed squaw skirt and curtsied to him, winked. She sat down next to him and crossed her legs nice. "Is it about what I've been saying, Mr. Coltis? Some of it getting back to you? Me talking about asserting Native American rights around here. Stirring things up a little. Getting some ethnic awareness going in this county. That kind of thing?"

Moira didn't know what Coltis was on about, but she had a guess. He was afraid she'd start talking to the Haitians, the Mexicans, the Jamaicans, about conditions in those cane fields.

He smiled, looked into her eyes. And she looked into his. His were a cool, pale blue. That dangerous American blue. It wasn't the dark blue of the flag, not the blue of the arterial blood American boys had spilled all around the globe in wars with the dark likes of Moira. No, his was the paler, subtler blue of the ink that was used on financial instruments and deeds and wills. It was the blue of a certain kind of wealth. Not the crude green wealth that was wadded in somebody's sweaty pocket. This was the blue riches that reposed in banks and brokerage houses, sleeping until the economy shrugged in its favor. Yes, Moira decided, Coltis's eyes were the color of very old money. She liked the color. And maybe she could take some of it from him.

"Sure," Lofton Coltis said, keeping his voice low, his tone moderate. "I've heard some of what you've been saying. Not a lot goes on in this county I don't hear about." He gestured at the dark windows, the vast night beyond, the land he owned. He hoped his eyes, his manner, showed the woman the responsibility, the heavy weight that came with owning.

"What did you think about them, my guests?" he asked

her. He leaned toward her a little, showing her that he cared what she thought of his friends.

She gave him that smile again, Little Miss Mischief.

"Why, I think they're all very nice. They've certainly been gracious to me ... tonight."

Coltis knew she was playing a scene with him: New York snot comes home. This was guerrilla theater to her. She was going to give him enough rope to hang himself. Let him make an ass of himself and laugh behind those dark, backlit eyes. So be it. It didn't matter where they started. Outcomes, Coltis had learned, were what mattered.

Coltis smiled. "The men here tonight represent one hundred thousand acres roughly, a fifty-mile-wide strip of land that stretches unbroken from the Gulf of Mexico to the Atlantic Ocean." But no, he thought, that was an exaggeration. There were two sandy beaches, east and west, and on them an infestation of fools in obscene bathing suits stewing themselves in tropical oils and desiccating their kidneys with candy drinks made of rum and tequila. This band of fools girdled the state. They broke what would have been a mighty symmetry of farmland stretching from salt to salt.

But he continued, "They're important men, powerful men, and they came here to meet you. To show you their goodwill, and, of course, they hope you won't do anything that damages their interests. It really is as simple as that."

"So that's it?" The beautiful woman with the ocher skin and the pretty ankles uncrossed and recrossed her legs. She said, "They came to see who's not going to damage their interests?" She smiled again, but Coltis thought he saw something come loose at the edges of her smile. The certainty unraveling a little. She laughed. "What are they going to do if I have the wrong plans? Am I going to have an accident? Is that it? This county has a history of accidents happening. Labor organizers have accidents, social workers in the migrant camps. People disappear around here, Mr. Coltis. Something gonna happen to old Moira?" She laughed, and to Coltis it sounded a little like the dry rustle of the cane leaves when they caught fire.

Coltis leaned forward again and looked at her very seriously. "Of course not. I think they'd just like to know that you can be reasonable. That we can talk about some things. Get on common ground."

"You're right about that, Mr. Coltis. It's about ground. It's about ground you got and we don't. Ground you took away from us. Ground we want back. What you think about that?"

"I think we can come to some kind of an agreement about ... public works. Projects that benefit everybody around here. I'm hoping we can get together on this without a lot of noise in the press. Why make a bunch of lawyers and journalists happy? You see what I mean?"

She watched him, smiling. And maybe it was a smile he could work with. A smile of accommodation, compromise. Maybe. It was certainly not the New York snot smile. She'd put that one back in her bag of tricks. Coltis said, "We've lived in harmony with the Miccosuki for a long time. I see no reason for that to change."

Moira saw what he meant. Common ground. Harmony. He was offering a deal, he and his friends. And they had the power to make things happen. Big things. They were the guys with the Tallahassee phone numbers in their heads. Moira thought about telling him what she had in mind— the concessions, the highway tolls, the reversions of ownership of lands to the tribe. Moira going around to trailers and shacks on Indian land collecting the faded deeds and papers from the old men, collecting the rights that had been slicked and lawyered and taxed and cheated away from them. Maybe they could work together, maybe he meant what he said. She'd learned up there in cold New York that it was bad manners to talk business at a party.

"All right," Moira said, "let's start small."

"Small is good," Coltis said. "A lot of big things start that way."

"I'll bet you don't even know you've got a mound on your land. Not a mile from here. Measures at least an acre in circumference. It showed up on some aerial photographs. They put it on the State Survey of Native American Archaeological Sites."

"You'd lose the bet," Coltis said.

"I'd . . .?"

"I know about it. My family has known about it since we came to this land in the mid-1800s. What about it?"

"We want it back. It belongs to the Indian people."

"I can't imagine why you want it. It's in the middle of one of my cane fields. And besides, it can't amount to much in an archaeological way. It's exactly like hundreds of other mounds around here. It's nothing but what your ancestors threw out the back door after they finished eating. A bunch of conch shells, clam shells, turtle shells, and a few pot shards. There's nothing to it."

"I think it's a burial site," Moira said. "I think it holds the spirits of my people."

Coltis said, "I've never seen any evidence that anything but the fragments of a very meager diet are buried there. And that land is producing cane. Why don't we talk about something else. Why not a park or some other recreational facility for the tribe. I'm sure that some of us who own land around here could get together and talk about letting go of a tract for some good civic purpose. Hell, Miss Breath, I'll bet *you* something. You ask the people out there on Indian land, most of them will tell you they'd damn sure rather have a boat landing than bragging rights to a hill of broken conch shells and pot fragments."

Moira said, "I didn't think you'd see it my way, Mr. Coltis."

"At least we're talking. It's a start, isn't it?"

"It's a start," Moira said. "A small one."

"Like we said, big things start small."

We didn't say it, Moira thought. You did. Moira was thinking that big things started big.

It wasn't manners that kept her from telling him what she was thinking. She wasn't sure what stopped her. She considered it while Coltis smiled at her, while his eyes

slipped from her face to her legs and back up again. Maybe
it was what had happened in his eyes when she'd said that
thing about people disappearing in the county. Something
hard and cold in there. Whatever that thing was, it had
frozen solid when she mentioned the mound. It was only
there a second or two, and it had changed everything. And
it had scared her.

Now he reached out and took her hand, lifted it, held
it. It wasn't a handshake. Certainly not the handshake of
agreement. It was a cold caress. She didn't take her hand
away from him. She waited for him to let go, but he didn't.
Not exactly. He put her hand back in her lap, composed it
there for her. Patted it once. And she shivered, because it
was as though he had taken and given back some thing, a
little thing that belonged to him.

Harry had left the kitchen when he'd heard the study
door close. Outside in the cool darkness, he'd stood at the
study window and tried to see, to hear. It had been a night
of peeking and sneaking, a bad night, and it made his face
burn in the cool wind outside Coltis's window. He'd had to
step aside quickly when Moira had come to the window.
He'd watched her pull the curtains back, then let them drop.
All he'd seen after that were shadows gesturing inside.
He couldn't hear anything but the wind behind him in the
Australian pines. God but this brought the burn. Pulled the
burn down from his flaming face into his belly where it lay
banked and consuming. God but this standing outside was
hurting him. Making him cranky, giving him doubts,
thoughts he didn't want.

He'd stood there watching the shadows inside, thinking.
The big thing coming back to him. The big thing he loved
to think about and hated. The big thing was this: Sometimes
he let himself believe that Coltis was his real father. That
Coltis and his mother, a long time ago, before she got fat
and started pushing a dust rag around this house, no more
to Coltis than the furniture she dusted; that they'd had it
hot and hard and long and Harry was the result. Coltis his

179

father. Not some truck-driving road trash his momma had got down with some drunk afternoon in a highway 41 motel. And Harry with these hard-to-explain angular features, this movie boy face. And there was the promise he'd made to himself: to go in the front door someday and ask Coltis about it, ask him straight up, direct. Not put up with any sidestepping or doodah. Pull the Buck knife and tell Coltis: Look, let's give blood, you and me. They got ways now to test blood. The genetic thing, like that.

The party was breaking up now. Harry had to get his Caddy out of the yard before anyone saw it. He walked back to the kitchen door, opened it. "Don't worry, Momma. I'm leaving. I ain't going to get you in any trouble. Not tonight anyway."

Outside in the night with the burn in him, he drove the Caddy a half mile down to a side road. It was a good place to wait. On her way home, Moira had to pass this way.

27

▲▲▲▲▲▲▲▲▲▲▲▲▲▲▲▲▲▲

So," Harry W. Feather said, sitting in Moira Big Breath's little kitchenette, drinking bourbon. "How's himself there, the panther? He making a swift recovery? Getting over his difficulties? The psychic wound, all that?"

What Harry really wanted to do was confront Moira about what she'd said to Coltis in that study. But he had to be careful. If she and Coltis were two shadows a foot apart on the couch in that study and Harry was outside the window, well then, Harry had to be careful, that was all. He decided to concentrate on the panther. He didn't think he had to be careful about the panther.

He'd thought about it a lot, her and the panther, and he honestly believed that something unnatural was going on. He wanted to be direct. Ask her what it was about panther dick. Was it the bristly little point on that sheath of hairy skin that covered the panther's thing. Did she like it, the way that thing tickled. How come an Indian man, a Micco-

suki warrior prince, wasn't good enough for Moira. She had
to do animals, Moira? But you had to start somewhere, so
Harry was asking about the panther's mental health.

"Yes," Moira said, "he's made some progress. And I've
made some, too. You want to hear about it? You want to
listen seriously? Not make a lot of inane comments, not
interrupt me all the time." Moira's right hand trailing down
from where she sat at the little computer table, stroking the
panther's head. The goddamn panther loving it, too.

Harry looked at his own hand, lifting the bourbon glass
to his lips. Tooth marks on the back of it, gonna be bruises
soon, and smelling like whatever panthers have for breakfast. Roadkill probably.

Harry had followed Moira home from Coltis's party. He'd
knocked on her door, and she'd made him go through the
same damned humiliating thing again. Harry saying he
wouldn't do it. Not twice. Moira telling him, you want in,
you put your hand in the panther's mouth. It's your passport. Harry kneeling again, going through it again. And the
worst thing was the panther was no more interested in
doing it than Harry was. Half-hearted sandpaper tongue
lapping him. The animal looking at Harry, then up at Moira.
Both of them pussy-whipped.

"Yeah," Harry said, "I want to hear it. No interruptions.
I'll be good." Thinking maybe he could get enough bourbon
inside him to listen to this straight, no jokes. No fucking
around with Moira Goodall, the Miccosuki witch doctress.

So Moira started pulling books and articles and Xeroxes
and government pamphlets off the shelves. Stacking them
in front of Harry. Some of them were tribal documents. Indians from other states. Hell, she had Alaska in there, South
Carolina. Moira's mouth going like it was made by Black
and Decker.

"The road, I'm talking about Highway 41, Harry, the road
belongs to Indians. It's on land we own, or did until they
cheated us out of it. I'm going to do what the Indians are
doing up north. They're taking back the roads and streams
and lakes and rivers. They're taking back the fishing and

mineral rights. They're charging tolls and fees to the white man if he wants to swim or fish or camp or even drive on these lands. They thought they bought us with bingo games and concessions like untaxed cigarettes and food stamps. Wait till they start paying us a toll for every fourteen-wheeler that carries a load of toilet paper to Dade County.

"You see, it's like we're a foreign country. They signed treaties with us. Legally, we have the right to deal with them the way we would if we were a government, a sovereign state with national borders. That means road tolls, stickers to get in and out, tariffs for goods that come in, the whole thing. It's the way Indians are doing it now—the Delaware, Iroquois, Ponca, Sauk, the Fox—it's all here in these documents. The Miccosuki are living in the nineteenth century, Harry. We have to wake up. We've sold Manhattan Island for a bunch of Mardi Gras trinkets, a bunch of Walt Disney illusions. We have to get back what's ours."

She looked at him very carefully now. "Harry, they're growing sugar cane on the old burial mounds in this county. The places where our people's spirits rest. Or they dig them up, take the bones to museums. It's just one more thing that's got to stop. I'm going down to the tribal gathering in Hollywood, start talking to people down there. Important people in the tribes."

Harry wasn't sure when the smile got ahold of his face. Probably about halfway through, when he thought about Mr. Lofton Coltis and his friends, what they would do if a bunch of Miccosukis decided that their land didn't belong to them anymore. Didn't because of some old treaties signed back when Polk was in the White House and Indians were still wiping their butts with Spanish moss.

And the mounds? Everybody knew about them, at least everybody Indian did. Most people he knew had long ago decided that the archaeologists had more claim to the bones than the Miccosuki did. Hell, they were the bones of a people who had died out in the sixteenth century when the Spanish had come with guns and smallpox and measles.

The whole thing was centuries late and a ton too stupid. Harry couldn't stop his lip from curling.

"So," Moira said, "you think it's funny?" Her hand stroking the panther hard now, fast. Moira not aware that she was giving the animal a very good scrubbing. The panther looking up at her. Hey, lighten up. "I was gonna ask you to come in with me, help me on this, Harry, but it looks like you think it's a joke or something."

"Not so much funny, Moira, as impossible. You know who owns that land? Both sides of the highway, north and south, east and west? You know who had the state dig those underpasses just so his cattle and his farm equipment could pass under without having to wait for traffic? You know who that is?"

Moira's chin rising, her skin a little less red than usual. Going a little pale up there in the rarefied intellectual air. Stroking the panther hard. "I know," she said. "Lofton Coltis and that bunch of fat white men who call themselves his friends."

She shoved the stack of papers on the table, some of them falling into Harry's lap. "I've done my homework. I know who the putative owners are. I've also read the documents, the treaties, seen what the other tribes are doing. We are the *real* owners. You and me, Harry. And I want you to help me."

Moira looked into his eyes. A challenge. Do the right thing, Harry. Harry W. Feather thinking, Right, Moira. Me and you and the panther. He thought it was interesting that she hadn't mentioned going to Coltis's party. She'd sure left that out. He wondered if all this, this stack of papers in front of him, was what she and Coltis had talked about in the study. He didn't think so. He didn't think Moira was that stupid. He decided to change the subject.

"Look," he said, "I was out here the other day. Came out to see you. All dressed up in my best. Kind of a surprise for you. I knocked and all. You weren't in the trailer."

Moira's eyes going from disgust, disgust at the politically uncommitted Harry, the Indian who was white under his paint, to suspicion. The suspicious Moira was something to see. The suspicious Moira stopped petting the panther. Pulled her panther hand into her lap.

Moira said, "So what did you do then? You knocked and I wasn't around."

"There's a path. Goes back in the woods. I saw you go back there. You and him. The animal, the panther. You and him, you speak this common language. Hoboy, you go out in the woods together and you a speak that language, right, Moira?"

"Get out of here, Harry. I don't want to see you again. You're the same trash you were when you took advantage of me in the bushes by that canal. The same trash. I don't want to see you again. Ever."

The hand going down to the panther's head again. The beast waking up now, alert to what was going on. Something tense between Harry and Moira. The panther looking at Harry now like it was Harry's time to leave. Harry had seen that look in the eyes of pimps and bouncers.

Harry stood and finished his bourbon, dropped the empty glass on the pile of documents. "Something I want you to know, Moira. Something my momma told me. Imagine me growing up and never knowing it. My spirit brother is the panther."

He'd told his mother about Moira, seeing her, the panther, all that. And his mother, Amelia W. Feather, had told him, "Harry, your totem is the panther, you know that?"

It was a painful memory. His mother giving him this revelation, something he should have known long ago. It had left Harry feeling stupid.

And his mother going back to her dusting, shaking her head. "You ain't no Indian, Harry. You was raised by a convenience store and a television set and a bunch of dirty magazines. You what they call assimilated. You know that? And it's my fault. I shoulda remarried. Got you a real Miccosuki daddy." Shaking her head, dusting.

And Harry thinking, You goddamn right it's your fault. And saying, "Hey, Mom, don't worry about it. I grew up okay. I made it, you know. And I can find out all I need to know about the Indians from Moira. Hell, she's got all the books. And you know how I like to read."

She stopped shoving the rag. Sprayed it with Lemon Pledge. Looked at him, sad. "Yeah," she says, "I know how you like to read."

Referring, of course, to Harry's collection of medical literature. His little library of sores, boils, chancres, poisons, suppurations, wounds, burns, and the strange creatures that inflicted nature's punishments. "Reading's reading," he said. Tired of her now. "All of it improves the mind."

Now Moira was shaking her head just like his mother did. And she was petting the panther again.

Harry extended his arm, pointed his index finger straight at the panther, down there at Moira's feet. The panther let out something like a growl. Quiet, but definitely hostile. Harry closed one eye and brought his thumb slowly down on the top of his index finger. He smiled.

"Get out, Harry," Moira said. "You're trash. You're a product of white culture. You belong out there on 41 with the rest of the trash they haul to Miami. I don't want to see you again."

Harry wondered who she did want to see, other than the panther. He remembered those shadows in the study. Maybe Coltis was making Moira happy now.

28

▲▲▲▲▲▲▲▲▲▲▲▲▲▲▲▲▲

Eddie woke up on Sawnie's couch when he heard the newspaper hit the front door. He stumbled to the door and opened it to a wave of humid air. The sun was just cresting the horizon and it was already so hot that his chest burnt when he took a breath. On his way to the kitchen for coffee, he stopped and listened at Sawnie's closed door. All quiet inside.

The front page of the *Okee County Ledger* was devoted to an article about Mr. William Harkness, proprietor of the Fender Mender Auto Body and Repair Shop. Mr. Harkness had been discovered dead in his trailer by a pamphleteering Jehovah's Witness. A spokesman for the county clinic said that he had died suddenly of massive toxic shock resulting from an accidental gunshot wound.

Page two featured Water Management boss Clinton Reynolds. Mr. Reynolds was a very sick man. Mysteriously sick.

Eddie remembered that Mr. Reynolds had figured promi-

187

nently in the tale Corey had told. She believed that he had deleted one of her files.

Eddie noticed that his hands were shaking. He dropped the paper on the coffee table and looked at them.

The night before: The bar and Harry Feather came back to him.

He could feel the aftershock of Feather's weight in his stiff forearms and back. Had he really had Feather's feet off the floor? Maybe a hundred and eighty pounds airborne on the fuel of Eddie's adrenaline.

He was lucky he'd gotten out of that bar before the law arrived. Hell, maybe nobody had called the law. Come to think of it, maybe that was worse.

After half a cup of coffee, he decided to make the call himself. See what Sheriff Bryce Nailor had to say about Harry Feather. That Indian with a Buck knife and an attitude.

Okee City was a railroad town. It straddled the old Seaboard Coastline route. The steel rails were gone now, but you could still see the railroad right-of-way, a hump running through backyards and parks and playgrounds.

The town sported some fine old cracker houses with gingerbread and dog runs and wide verandahs and porch swings. In some of these, the old folks still sat in the evenings fanning themselves with the face of Jesus.

The town's commercial district was on its third or fourth face-lift since the stores and offices had been built out of Georgia red brick a century ago. Its flagship was the De Soto Hotel, named for a rapacious Spaniard who had marched through looking for gold, unaware that the mucky earth that mired his wagons was the real gold.

In the hotel restaurant, Eddie stopped to admire the embossed tin ceiling panels, the brass paddle fans and pecky cypress wainscoting. The air conditioner was roaring and it felt good. Eddie plucked his wet shirt away from his chest. Sheriff Bryce Nailor watched him from a booth in the back.

Eddie stepped up and started with his best: "Hot enough for you?"

"You're late." Nailor hit the crystal of his watch with a sausage forefinger. He closed one eye and regarded Eddie. Eddie knew the type and knew the regard. He imagined Nailor nestling his cheek against the walnut stock of a shotgun and closing that one eye as the quail exploded from the broom sage.

The De Soto's clientele—a table of deputies, some farmers having breakfast in town, a guy in a suit who might be the local dentist—all of them watched Eddie sit down across from the sheriff.

"You recommend the sushi, Sheriff Nailor?"

Nailor said, "You wouldn't be one of those smart-ass *Miami* lawyers, would you?"

It was peckerwood cop code for: Am I about to break bread with a person of the Judaic persuasion? Eddie said, "Naw, I'm from up in the north part of the state. Isle Hammock. You know it?"

Nailor didn't look convinced. But he smiled, a small, stingy hole in the middle of his suet cheeks. Eddie smiled back. Nailor ordered fried mullet, scrambled eggs, and grits. Eddie asked for toast, juice, and coffee.

When the food came, Eddie took the newspaper out of his pocket and unfolded it on the table. "Sheriff Nailor, don't you think it's a little strange? Your Water Management director raving out of his head in the hospital with some kind of poison in him and this auto body guy, Harkness. He's dead the same day?"

Nailor lifted a piece of mullet to his mouth and the yellow grease dripped from his knuckles. His eyes clouded with confusion or malice. He shook his head slowly.

"No, I don't think it's strange. I talked to Doc Merseault and he don't think it's strange either. You want to tell me why *you* think it's strange?"

"How's the mullet?" Eddie asked him. "When you dip it in the egg yolk?"

Nailor looked at it speculatively, sucking his teeth. "Not

189

as good as last week." Then he laughed and looked around the restaurant. "This fish *was* here last week." The table of deputies laughed the necessary laugh of the pecking order.

Eddie said, "What's strange is that Corey Darrow died under suspicious circumstances and both of these men had contact with her."

He could see that Nailor wanted to laugh again. He almost did. In fact, raised his hand to his mouth with a wiping motion that removed the mirth. "Look, Eddie, all due respect and everything. Clinton Reynolds and Miss Darrow had a problem at work. Something about a computer file, a guy who came by the Water Management office and then disappeared. We find his bicycle on a secondary road twenty miles out in the boonies. I don't know what it was about. Clinton said he didn't either. Water Management is state business. I don't mess in it. I don't think Corey had anything to do with Clinton getting poisoned. Clinton was just standing in the wrong place when one of those Agwagon crop dusters missed the cane field. It happens once in a while. Doc Merseault says Clinton's symptoms are about right for that."

Nailor ate another mullet finger and washed his mouth with coffee. He lifted his fork, picked at his cuticle with it, put it back down.

"And Boner?" Nailor said. The mirth playing again at the corners of his mouth. "All Boner did was his job. Pulled Corey out of a ditch. You might say she killed him, but the law don't allow me to charge a dead woman with shooting a man."

Eddie said, "What about this Harry Feather, getting his car painted by Harkness? There's white paint on Corey's Ford."

Now that Eddie had seen the Indian, his eyes, what was in them and what wasn't, he knew Feather had killed Corey. And Feather had a reason to want Harkness dead.

Nailor shoved himself forward, resting both hands on the table. "I sent a man out to talk to Feather. He wants to know what's wrong with having his car painted. I can't for the life of me figure out what to tell him. And between you and me, I wish more of them Indians would take pride in their possessions the way Feather does."

Eddie took a bite of toast, cold and dry as Nailor's cooperation. "And this Harkness died of some kind of weird superinfection? You buy that, sheriff?"

Nailor shrugged. "Doc Merseault said he told Boner to come back for more shots. If he had any swelling, to get in right away. Feather saw the leg when he picked up his car. Said it was real swollen. Said he told Boner he shouldn't be working on a leg like that." Nailor shook his head. "Boner wouldn't listen, would he?"

Eddie reached up and touched his nose. Bruised against the stone wall of Nailor's redneck logic. Cop's logic. He thought about the power Sawnie could summon with a phone call to Tallahassee. Oh, the fire she could light under the fat ass that supported the slow mind of Sheriff Nailor. But she'd said she wouldn't do it.

"So, tell me . . ."—Eddie struggled for sweet reason—". . . about Feather. Who *is* he anyway?"

Nailor frowned and drummed his fingers on the table. "Feather's never been in any trouble. Maybe a scrape or two down in Miami. Country boys always go down there and get themselves in Dutch. But nothing around here. Leastways nothing we could pin on his red Indian ass."

Eddie said, "What would these nothings be, the ones you can't pin on him?"

Nailor said that maybe, just maybe, Harry and a couple other gentlemen of the red persuasion had done some marijuana smuggling. Maybe they had a crop or two of their own out there in the hammock land, and maybe there had been some scamming with untaxed cigarettes and some poaching. Your out-of-season doe, your illegal gator.

But nobody'd ever been caught, and nobody out there on Indian land wanted the sheriff's office to mess in their affairs. The Miccosuki kept to themselves mostly. They didn't bother the local folks. Folks whose protection was Sheriff Nailor's sworn and sacred trust. And his paycheck.

Eddie said, "You don't call pulling a knife on somebody in a bar getting into trouble? That's not trouble in this town?"

The good sheriff looked at Eddie out of one eye again. Again it was like aiming something lethal.

"What I heard, you started the physical stuff. All Feather did was defend himself. That's what people told me."

Eddie was glad he'd left Sawnie sleeping. She'd be sitting here thinking how he'd overreacted with Feather in the bar. And Eddie was glad he'd flushed the knife out of Feather's pocket. At least that much about Feather was clear. The guy would cut before he'd talk.

Nailor opened the second eye. "I'd have to say no to your question. That's not trouble, not in the Cane Cutter. I've seen people dead on the floor in that place. But it could *lead* to trouble and I'd hate to see *you* in trouble around here, Eddie. There ain't that many folks around here that care about football."

Eddie shook his head slowly. Persistence was a virtue in football and in this game too. Eddie asked, "What does this Feather do to support himself? I mean what does he do that he can talk about? Write on a tax form?"

"I don't know, to be honest with you." Nailor pushed himself away from the table, slapped both hands on his knees, and stood, indicating that he had given a nervous city man about as much time as the local taxpayers could afford.

Eddie stood too. "You can't tell me anything he does to put a bean in the pot. Anything legal?" Eddie dropped a ten-dollar bill on the table.

Nailor grinned, picked up the ten, handed it back to Eddie. Dropped his own money in its place. "Seems like I heard he does odd jobs for Mr. Coltis. Lofton Coltis. Big agribusiness man. Sugar cane, you know what I mean?"

Eddie knew. The gray-green sea of cane that enclosed the town, flowing unbroken except by canals and peat-black roads for miles in all directions.

Nailor said, "Feather's mother keeps house for Mr. Coltis." Nailor put on his Stetson hat. "Anyway, that's what I heard."

And that was when Eddie's bells started ringing. It wasn't Ed McMahon at the door telling him he'd won the Publishers Clearing House Sweepstakes, but it was something. Nailor had just connected the guy Corey had said was following her to a man who might have something to gain from her silence. A man named Lofton Coltis.

Eddie and Nailor stepped out into the heat. The sidewalks were empty. All the street life had gone looking for shade. Nailor looked up at the pale, empty heavens and picked his front teeth with a fingernail. "By the way, the Ford agency in Crescent City called. Said there was nothing wrong with the Explorer. In their opinion, the young lady fell asleep at the wheel."

Eddie decided that Sheriff Nailor was smarter than he looked. He had managed to implicate Corey in a shooting and a poisoning. She'd accomplished both after falling asleep at the wheel and killing herself.

Eddie said, "Fell asleep with a cocked pistol in her hand?"

"It happens. And stranger things too, believe me."

"So who was this guy?" Eddie asked. "This guy that visited Water Management? The guy they found his bicycle in the boonies?"

Nailor looked at him for a long time, smiling, shaking his head at Eddie's tenacity. Nailor's red face said it was too hot for this.

"Nobody knows who he was. We think a rock truck hit him. We didn't find a body. Maybe a gator got him. There's a big canal right by the road. He left a few things in his hotel room, but nothing that got us anywhere. His prints weren't on file. We wrote him up in the newspaper, tried to get the word out on him so somebody'd call, let us know who he was, but we didn't get anything back."

"What'd you find in his room?"

Nailor wiped sweat from his face. His impatience was large and hot now. "The usual things. Clothes, a few personal items. A letter to some woman. He'd just started writing it, no address, no way to find her."

"What'd it say?"

"It said he thought he'd found something."

"What *exactly* did it say. Do you remember?"

Nailor looked up at the hot morning sun, remembering. "It said, 'Adele,' ... the woman's name was Adele ... 'Adele, I believe this time I have found it.' "

Nailor looked past Eddie at the town's one traffic light. Eddie looked back there, saw it change from red to green. When he turned back, Nailor had stepped close. Quietly, without his hearing movement, Nailor was in his face.

"I'm gone tell you something about that pistol, Eddie. Something just between you and me and the lamppost over there. That was an illegal weapon. Somebody ground the serial numbers off that pistol. Now, what in hail do you think a nice young lady like Corey Darrow is doing with a nasty little item like that?"

Eddie stood there in Nailor's mullet breath. The sun seemed to have stopped everything except Nailor's slow, gamy respiration. Eddie had no answer he could use. For his own reasons, Raymer had given Corey an untraceable weapon.

Nailor waited in Eddie's silence. Finally, he backed off a step and hooked his thumbs into his waistband. "What I think you ought to do now, Mr. Priest, is get on out of here before you cause any more trouble. You and the lady."

A car pulled up. Eddie turned. It was Sawnie in the rented Chevy. She got out looking cranky, half asleep. Eddie turned back to Nailor to say, "Here's the lady now," but Nailor was halfway across the street. Fast and silent for a big man.

Sawnie stood in front of him on the hot sidewalk, frowning. "Well? What did law enforcement have to say? You gonna tell me?"

Eddie took her arm and moved her toward the cool hotel. She pulled away. "I'm not a goddamn car, stop steering me!"

Eddie didn't let it bother him. He knew why she was

angry. She'd gone to sleep scared and woke up in an empty house. Eddie's note on the coffee table.

"Sorry," he said, "it's just a habit. My mother taught me to step to the curbside of the lady and take her arm. She's very much in my thoughts. Is old Mom."

Sawnie looked up at him, squinting in the sun. Probably thinking about his mom's bankrupt values and Eddie being some kind of troglodyte who grabbed women and shoved them around. Then softening. Softening. A boy whose mother was always in his head was, well, a good boy. She said, "I'm sorry, it's just . . ."

Across the street, Bryce Nailor opened the smoked glass door of the storefront sheriff's office, walked inside.

"You want some breakfast," Eddie said, "a cup of coffee?"

Sawnie ordered iced tea. It came in a big sweating glass clouded with sugar.

Eddie said, "You know you're off the tourist trail when they don't even ask if you want sugar in your tea."

Sawnie laughed. "It was a big deal, coming here when I was a kid. They had a candy counter by the door. I'd buy Milk Duds and Jujubes. Watch the traveling salesmen eat lunch. Once in a while, my daddy'd bring the whole family here for the Sunday after-church ham and yams special. A buck fifty a plate, all you could eat."

"You eat a lot?"

"We all did."

Eddie told her what Nailor had said about Feather working for Lofton Coltis, Mr. Big Sugar. "Remember what Corey told me? The file that disappeared. The guy asking about soil quality. I'm thinking maybe we can find that file. Maybe somebody saved a copy. Maybe this Coltis guy is in it somewhere. You see the connection I'm working on here. Feather and Coltis?"

Sawnie lifted her tea, sipped. "I see it," she said. Eddie wondering why she wasn't excited. He didn't have to wonder long.

"There's no file. I've been all over Corey's house. She

didn't save any hard copy. I had a friend of mine, does computers in Tallahassee, access the local database. She didn't find it, and if she didn't, nobody can." She looked at him. "Why would a big-time grower get involved with a sleaze like Feather? Why would they kill my sister over a computer file."

Eddie said, "Hey, I'm trying to push your suspicious buttons. I say we assume this Coltis gets something from Corey's death. Corey told me the local newspaper had her written up as the guilty party. Vague allegations about improprieties. You know who controls the newspaper in a town like this. I think we ought to look into this guy."

Sawnie stuck her finger into her iced tea, stirred, pulled it out, and sucked it. Unaware of herself, like a kid intrigued with the trick she was doing. Eddie watched the finger go back into the tea. He said, "You got any more friends in Tallahassee? Somebody who can look into a big cane grower? Guy who employs half the people in town, probably, one way or another."

"The sheriff?" Sawnie asked. "You think he employs the sheriff?"

"Like I said, one way or another."

"Maybe I got friends," she said, not the kid anymore. Serious, looking at her tea-wet finger, burying her hand now in her napkin. "We'll see if I do." She looked around the dining room, lowered her voice. "Look, Eddie. I'm from around here. It's been years, but you don't forget the name Coltis." She glanced at the windows. "Hell, it's written on half the buildings and street signs in town. When I was growing up, we called it Coltisville. You know what I mean?"

"You mean we don't mess with this guy unless we've got a good reason?"

She shook her head. "I mean we don't mess with him at all."

"So," Eddie said, "I think I'll call him. Let the big dog know the little dog's gonna piss on his perimeter."

Eddie looked at her, not wanting to make that mistake

again. Grab her elbow and steer. "Or maybe you'd like to call him."

Sawnie pushed away from the table, got her purse from the floor beside her chair. "I'll call him. I'm a dog, too. And she was my sister."

She nodded toward the pay phone, an old black model bolted to the wall by the front door. A corona of phone numbers penciled on the wall around it. "Last time I put a quarter in that phone, I was seventeen years old. I was calling Humphrey Lambert to see if he'd go to the Sadie Hawkins dance with me."

"It wasn't a quarter, it was a dime," Eddie said.

Watching her walk off to the phone. Thinking, God what legs and what a stupendous ass. Wishing she'd call Eddie Priest, invite him to the dance of life.

29

▲▲▲▲▲▲▲▲▲▲▲▲▲▲▲▲▲▲▲

Harry W. Feather wanted to go to the clinic and see Clinton Reynolds up close and personal. He wanted to buy a big spray of cut flowers, gladiolas and mums, maybe some baby's breath, a basket of fruit. Do the good-friend-in-the-sickroom thing. Get a good close look.

But he couldn't. Not with the Former Great and Raymer Harney asking questions about him. Not with Bryce Nailor sending that rat-faced deputy out to ask about the Caddy. Was there any blue paint on the right front?

Harry'd had to settle for a long talk in the Cane Cutter with a guy he knew that worked in the county clinic. Orderly or something. This guy had no medical knowledge. Practically an illiterate. Hell, Harry knew twice as much about infections and poisons from his reading as this guy did from ten years of bedpans and hauling out those big plastic garbage bags. The ones with the scary tags that said

Danger—Medical Waste. But the guy had told Harry a pretty good story. The story of Clinton Reynolds.

Harry W. Feather had bought the guy a few beers and listened carefully because Mr. Coltis was asking about Clinton.

Harry W. Feather called Lofton Coltis.

"So this guy in the bar tells me Clinton's got one hell of a set of symptoms. Some real medical journal stuff. You want to hear about it?"

Coltis's voice cool, remote as usual. "I suppose so. Yes, why not. I'm concerned about Clinton. The whole town is concerned."

"I sure hope they don't blame the growers, Mr. Coltis. You know, the pesticide thing. Duster pilot dumps his load shy of the field. Seems like they always go after the big guy. Deep pockets, all that?"

"Tell me about Clinton, Feather. I want to hear about Clinton." Something new in Coltis's voice. Something Harry liked. Call it concern. Not respect, not yet. But maybe the distance between concern and respect could be crossed. If Harry played his cards right.

"Well, Mr. Coltis, apparently we're talking about a whopping big neural deficit. This pesticide, how it kills your creepy crawlers, your bugs, it goes for the nervous system. What I heard, when it gets on people, it attacks the brain. Same family of agents they use in chemical warfare. We're talking nerve gas here."

Harry trying to keep the excitement out of his voice. Unseemly. Give the man a factual report. Do it like you'd read it in the *New England Journal of Medicine*.

Harry said, "They got an antidote. Atropine. But Clinton messed around wearing that stupid glove, didn't get in to the doc soon enough. This guy I talked to, guy works at the clinic, told me Clinton was supposed to shower three times right after it happened, put his clothes and shoes in a plastic bag. Burn them. We're talking a dangerous substance here.

199

I guess Clinton thought he was gonna be all right. I sure hope it didn't happen in one of your fields, Mr. Coltis."

"What else, Feather?" Coltis's voice no longer cool. Cold. Frozen. So remote now he wasn't even in the same county. Hard to tell now about concern and respect. "Is there more about Clinton? Is he *saying* anything?"

Harry said,"Well, this guy says sometimes Clinton's catatonic, just lies in bed stiff as a stick, then other times he raves and says he wants to die. Wants to kill himself. Like that. They got him tied down. Restrained, they call it. But I tell you, Mr. Coltis, the weird thing"—Harry thinking, the truly wonderful thing, the thing that interested Harry W. Feather—"is this thing about his brain. The doc is saying the brain sends out these confused signals, hormones, to the intestines and the liver and kidneys and they start eating themselves. They just start wasting away. It's kind of like internal starvation. Something like that."

Hoboy, Harry thought, Auschwitz on your insides. Belsen in your belly.

"Spare me the theories, Feather. It sounds like Clinton is in very serious trouble. And you say he's raving, not making any sense?"

"What I heard, Mr. Coltis."

"It's too bad. I'll have to visit him. He has no family, I'm afraid."

Harry thinking, No one to sue. Nobody to get pissed off about gross incompetence in the handling of a deadly chemical agent. No sister or aunt or little boy to go looking for some smart lawyer with a nose for the green. Looking for you, Mr. Coltis. You and your crop duster on a human bombing run.

Harry W. Feather said, "Yeah, it's too bad. I thought you'd want to know. I remembered you asking me about Clinton the other day. The day we talked in the cane field."

"Thank you, Feather. Thank you for calling. I appreciate the information. And Feather, let's have a talk soon. About your future."

"Mr. Coltis, I can come out there right now. You want

me to. I'm completely at your disposal." And thinking, Disposing, that's my line. Coltis proposes, Feather disposes. A partnership.

"Not today, Feather. But soon."

Lofton Coltis walked outside and stood in the sun waiting. He had decided to take them to the Coltis family cemetery. It was on some high ground not far away in one of his cane fields.

The woman, Corey Darrow's sister, had called, asking for a meeting. Her voice all Tallahassee official. Coltis had made a few phone calls, knew how the country girl had risen in the world. Exactly how. The Governor's special assistant, she was, and didn't know that Coltis knew it.

When they drove up, the Tallahassee woman at the wheel of a rented car, Coltis got into his old Ford pickup. In his rearview mirror, he saw them get out, awkward, looking toward the house, then at him, sitting in the truck, waiting. He could see Eddie Priest's lips move, the woman speak in response. She led the way toward his truck.

When the woman put her hand on the door, Coltis leaned over and said, "I've got to go look at one of my fields. You two might as well ride along with me."

The woman, beautiful by any standard, but a little hard for Coltis's taste, looked in at him, then back at the ex-football star. "All right, Mr. Coltis," she said. "We'd like to see one of your fields."

She slid next to him, pressing warm and sudden against his shoulder. Priest getting in on the other side and pushing the woman even closer to him. Close, that's how it was in the truck. And that's the way Coltis wanted it. It was how two men rode with a woman in a truck, putting her in the middle.

He was taking them to the place where circumstances had forced him to learn something important about himself. He called it his Mount Horeb. According to the Bible story, on Mount Horeb Moses had heard the voice from the burning bush. Coltis had a title for his own story: "The Tale of the Gypsy Botanist."

He pulled out onto an asphalt secondary road, taking his time, liking the wind in his face from the open window with its sweet burden, the odor of decaying vegetation and the coffee-rich aroma of his dark soil. "So," he said, "what did you want to talk about? Miss Darrow, is it?"

"Yes," the woman said, "it is. I'm Corey Darrow's sister. Did you know Corey?"

"Only in passing." True enough. Her passing.

Coltis turned down a muddy tractor path between gray walls of cane stalks, water-filled ditches on both sides. He drove only a hundred yards before stopping. "Let's not beat around the bush," he said pleasantly. "You're here to talk to me about your sister's death."

The woman hesitated. Then she said, Yes, yes, they were here to talk about that. Did Mr. Coltis mind?

But Coltis was already out of the cab and walking. Leaving them to catch up if they liked. He walked fifty yards down the road and stood looking out into the field. This was high ground, maybe ten feet above the average local elevation, and it was a place where the soil had always been weak. Weak in a way that no one had ever understood. It had never produced good cane.

The man had simply shown up one day at Coltis's back door, dressed in the genteel rags of a nineteenth-century African explorer—hiking boots, puttees, canvas shirt and shorts, a pith helmet, and thick milk-bottle spectacles. He'd asked for a glass of water.

Coltis had stood watching the tired and dehydrated stranger drink glass after glass of cold water, a little man about his own age with sandy hair, a brush mustache, and a hard, tensile body. Listened to him talk about his work, his passion, his quest—botany. The man was searching for a rare subtropical plant, an herb called pittisspasium.

Immediately, Coltis had liked the man. His monkish dedication, the way his strange eyes fired when he talked about

obscure plants and herbs. Even the fact that he trespassed on
Coltis land as though science conferred a right of passage, a
right that canceled laws of ownership and simple danger in
this rural country where people still shot intruders. Yes, Coltis had even liked the man's trespass.

Coltis invited him to dinner, a night of conversation between two educated men, a night of talk about books and
ideas. Invited him to spend the night. Coltis himself had
prepared dinner and, in the morning, breakfast, because
Amelia W. Feather was gone for the week, visiting an ailing
sister. It was over coffee and eggs and ham gravy that Coltis
had asked, "What is this pittisspasium? What's it look like?
Did you find any around here?"

The man's eyes going small and secret. Full of a dark
gleam that Coltis liked because he recognized it. The man
sitting there wearing the same salt-stiffened, reeking outfit
he'd taken off the night before, the rucksack on the floor
beside his chair. The man weighing Coltis's question, trying
to decide how to answer it.

Coltis smiled into the face of the Gypsy Botanist's indeci-
sion until the little man said, "Oh yes. Oh yes, Mr. Coltis. I
found it. I found a very nice carpet of it less than a mile
from where we sit right now."

"That would be on my land," Coltis said. "A mile from
here in any direction would have to be."

Coltis's guest only nodded.

Coltis was not sure why he said, "Well, finish your coffee.
Let's go see this famous, rare plant. Show me what you're
so excited about, my friend."

In the Ford truck, Coltis drove the little man to this spot,
the high, dry place he now called Mount Horeb. The place
of self-knowledge. They'd stood where Coltis was standing
right now and looked out into the cane, and the tough little
man with the sandy hair and the brush mustache had
pointed at the roots of the cane and said, "There it is, all
over the place. That little green vine. The leaves look a bit
like watercress. See it?" The Gypsy Botanist's voice quaver-
ing now with scientific excitement.

Coltis said, "Yes, I see it." Watching the strange excitement in the little man's eyes. Trying to keep from laughing aloud at his own disappointment. All this passion over a weed. A meaningless plant Coltis had ignored all his life. Something that apparently had a Latin name.

"What are you going to do with it?" Coltis asked. Something had occurred to him. Hell, maybe this little fellow would write the plant up for some botanical journal, publish an article. Maybe they'd have to name the thing *Pittisspasium Coltisiensis* because it had been found on Coltis land. But Coltis thought, No, no, they name the discovery after the discoverer. They'd name this rare little plant after the Gypsy Botanist who stood beside Coltis staring into the cane. Wiping his dirty hands nervously on his canvas shorts.

The little man said, "It's going to be remarkable. Amazing."

Coltis still smiling. Liking the man. Deciding that all passion, no matter what for, impressed him in a world full of mall-crawling drones, petty thieves, and vidiots who stared at glittering screens until their eyeballs fried. "What's going to be remarkable?" he asked.

"The company I used to work for, pharmaceuticals. They fired me a year ago because I said I believed I could find it here. In the continental United States. Because I wouldn't stop looking for it. The only place it's ever been found is along the Amazon, Orinoco country. Huge fields of it there destroyed every day. You know the rain forest? The slash-and-burn thing. You must have read about it."

Yes, Coltis had read about it. Said so. "But what's the significance of the thing? Of finding it in the U.S.?" Coltis still thinking about that little bit of fame, that small piece of scientific history.

The Gypsy Botanist's voice was barely audible. A passionate whisper, something that should have gone into a lover's ear. "Ovarian cancer," the Gypsy Botanist said.

"Ovarian cancer?" Coltis asked. Had he heard it right?

"A specific against ovarian cancer in the advanced stages. The best thing we've ever found. At least I think so. My whole research program was based on that belief. Early tests were very promising. Tumors shrinking, disappearing. I had my own lab and sixteen assistants working on it before the company got cold feet, decided it would never be commercially feasible because the goddamned Brazilians would never get their shit together. The company didn't believe it'd grow this far north. What we have here"—the little man waving his hand at the field in a way that bothered Coltis, like his saying "we" and his almost proprietary tone of voice—"what we have here, I'd say, is proof I was right. Of course, it's a slightly different strain. A heartier strain, I'd say."

The first warning bells ringing in Coltis's brain now, the sweat on his forehead, the hair rising on the back of his neck. Trying to keep the changes out of his voice. Asking, "So what will you do now? What's your next step?"

"I'll get my job back, that's what." The little man's voice hardening. Not looking up at Coltis, not taking his eyes from the carpet of green herb there under the gray cane. "I've been riding a bicycle for two weeks, did I tell you that? I don't even have a car. My goddamned car was repossessed. Did I tell you that?"

"Your job?"

"Sure. I go back, tell them it's here. Convince them to go into this thing in a big way commercially. Maybe they'll have the good sense to listen to me this time."

"And if they don't?"

"Then there's plan B. The Environmental Protection Agency. They find out this is here, they'll slap a protected flora order on it quicker than you can say Charlie Darwin."

"And what will that mean, for me, I mean? This is my land."

The little man looking up at Coltis now for the first time. Their eyes meeting now in a way far different from the way they had met last night over brandy and talk about the state of the world.

"Well," the Gypsy Botanist said, caution coming to him seconds late. "What they usually do, they ask you to wait till the thing is decided. You know, they ask you not to disturb the plant in any way until they figure out what to do about it."

"What to do about it?" Coltis thinking, They don't *ask*. Not this government we have now. And thinking about harvest time, a hundred Jamaicans and Haitians and Mexicans wading into this stand of cane in steel shin guards.

"I mean whether it can be grown elsewhere. Grown in controlled circumstances. That sometimes happens."

"But more often . . .?"

"More often . . ." The voice very small now. The eyes veiled, the little man taking a square stance, planting his scuffed boots in front of Coltis.

"More often," the Gypsy Botanist said, "they just declare the site a protected habitat. In effect, it belongs to the government after that. Oh, they'll pay you a condemnation fee. For this, it'll be a quite generous one, I'm sure."

In the last minute, Coltis had taken stock of the man again. After the idea had come firmly into his consciousness that there were acres and acres of this ugly weed spread across his vast holdings, he had looked at the sun-burned angular planes of the man's face, the hard, ropy forearms, the big, calloused hands, and the strong, thin legs. He had taken stock of the man and of himself and had known himself for the first time.

At the last, Coltis had watched carefully. Before he had taken the little gypsy into his hands, the man had looked down the road. Then up the other way, past the truck into the empty distance. Had seen that they were alone inside the gray walls of cane. And in the little gypsy's eyes, Coltis could see this. Could see his own and every man's separation, every man's aloneness under the sun.

It had been as hard to strangle the Gypsy Botanist as Coltis had thought it would be. Five minutes of the most terrible and exhilarating work Coltis had ever done.

"Mr. Coltis?" the woman called from some twenty feet away. Maybe it was too wet for her shoes where Coltis was standing. Maybe she and the ex-football player had sensed that he was not really here. That he had gone somewhere. They couldn't know he was in the past. How hard it was to break from that past now and confront their stupid questions. He raised his hand, a gesture he knew would seem strange to his two living visitors, and saluted the ghost in the cane.

Perhaps it was a salute to passion. To this place where two passions had met and one lay buried under a bright green carpet of pittisspasium. In the Coltis family plot, in a hole Coltis himself had dug and dug deep.

"Mr. Coltis!" the woman called again. She would be beside him soon, she and the ex-football player. Coltis turned to face the woman from Tallahassee.

"Look," he said. "See those stones." He meant the marble gravestones, some of them with the names lost to rain and the abrasion of grasses stirred by the wind.

The woman nodded.

"This is where my family is buried. We've had to fight to bury here. After towns get started and governments come and people start thinking about being sanitary, you have to fight all kinds of regulations to bury your dead on your own land. Did you know that?"

The woman looked at him. Her companion, the football player, looked down at his sinking feet, embarrassed or confused.

"I suppose so," the woman said. "I suppose I did know that."

Coltis remembered the last of his relatives to be buried here. His great-aunt Delia, an eccentric woman who had kept on wearing her old whale-bone corsets until they had literally come apart and hung around her in chalky, flaking fragments. Coltis, aged nine or ten, had stood here with his own father watching the laborers dig, and watching them, late in the afternoon, at the bottom of Delia's new grave, find something. And lift this thing carefully out and lay it on the fresh black earth from Delia's hole. The sweating dark-faced men looking up from the hole, watching his father for a decision.

They had found a human skull, ancient, small, and black. To his breathless boy's question, Coltis's father had said, "Oh, yes. Oh, yes, they are buried here too. The Indians used this place long before we came. And this is not the first person we have found here from the old days. The Indians made the high ground here. This whole acre is an ancient mound."

His father had smiled, his eyes clear and confident. He had pushed the skull aside with the toe of his boot. "But we are here now. It is our day, and you and I are glad for that, aren't we, son?"

Looking into the black holes that had been ancient eyes, the young Coltis had said his own quiet yes.

And after the ceremonies that had snugged Delia safely away in the earth that made the family living, the boy had come back and found the old skull where his father had tossed it, some twenty feet off into the cane. With a large stone he had brought, the boy had smashed the skull into tiny fragments. And he had thrown them to the four winds, his face burning with shame. Young as he was and stupid as he was, he had believed that all history had begun with a Coltis on this land. His hands trembled with the knowledge that time was layered and the bottom was always farther down.

"Well," Coltis said, "it doesn't matter. You aren't here to look at my dead. You're worried about your own."

The woman nodded again, emphatic. Her friend, Priest, looked frankly baffled. Coltis hoped he would stay that way. He was not sure he understood all of this himself. Things had gone far and fast, and he had not been able to control them.

It had been luck that Amelia W. Feather was gone. It had been a small matter to take the bicycle out to a lonely road at night and leave it there mangled. A small matter to instruct Clinton Reynolds to shut the woman up when she asked about the file and the disappearance of the Gypsy

Botanist. And later, a somewhat larger matter when the woman would not shut up and when Clinton had bungled the business of deleting the file, using his own rather than the woman's user code. The file, of course, was everything. Not because it proved the man had come to Water Management, but because it recorded the little man's question: about soil, a certain kind of soil whose pH level could only be found on Coltis land. And finally, it, everything, had become matters for Harry Feather. And Feather, in his way, had handled them.

It did no good now to regret what had gone wrong. Now, the only thing to do was go ahead. See the thing through to its outcome and make sure that outcome was the right one.

30

▲▲▲▲▲▲▲▲▲▲▲▲▲▲▲▲▲▲

Eddie said, "Mr. Coltis, are you all right?"

This wasn't going like he'd thought it would. He'd figured
Coltis for a country smoothy or a stonewaller. Either the
guy would serve them candied bullshit or the minimum
ration of don't-know's and sorry-can't-help-you's. But
this? The guy standing at attention, staring into the cane
for a full five minutes. Staring at the family graveyard.
Tall and thin and Gary Cooper tough-looking. Impressive
for a guy his age. Eddie guessed about fifty-five. It felt
strange to be out here alone with the guy. Surrounded by
all this green.

Eddie looked at Sawnie. She shrugged, looked around at
the fields of sugar. Her eyes asking how to get back to the
home planet. What galaxy was this anyway? About a half
mile away, a red crop duster made a pass over the cane, its
white cloud spewing, thinning, drifting down.

Coltis turned and abruptly strode past them, grinning like

he was hosting a Rotary Club dinner. He waved his arms at the gray walls of cane. "What do you think? Will she make a profit? This field?"

Following, Eddie said, "I don't know much about balance sheets for a sugar cane field, Mr. Coltis, but I heard a story about a computer file down at Water Management. Corey Darrow told me about it the day she died. She said it had something to do with you."

Coltis looked at Eddie carefully. Then at Sawnie. His Rotary smile cooling fast. "My name's on a lot of state and county documents, Mr. Priest. You'll find it on schools and libraries and scholarships, too, and in the earliest history of this state. If you look. If your *investigation* takes you farther than a story cooked up by a young woman who was, forgive me, Miss Darrow, very confused. If you want to look at the records down at Water Management, I'm sure they'll let you do it. Most of it's open to the public."

Sawnie stepped up next to Eddie now, looked down at her city shoes sinking in the mud. "I know I won't find anything *now*, Mr. Coltis. My sister's records were destroyed. I know it because she said so and my sister doesn't . . . didn't lie."

"That's right," Coltis said. "You do have the power to look into things, don't you, Miss Darrow? You have friends in high places. I bet you know everything there is in a computer about the life of this humble farmer." Coltis did a little bow, his hands in the pockets of his tan whipcord trousers. All deference, all politeness, Eddie thought, all sweet bullshit.

The red crop duster was getting closer, looking bigger, its white cloud blanketing maybe a hundred at a pass. Eddie could see the pilot look back as he banked at the end of his run, looking to see if he'd cut his spray at the right moment. Jaunty, the guy, in his leather helmet and goggles. White scarf like the Red Baron.

"I did a little checking," Sawnie said.

Coltis said, "And you're suggesting that I had something to do with the destruction of this mystery file, is that right?"

"It wasn't just a file," Sawnie said. "It was about somebody. A man who visited the Water Management office and then disappeared. You must have read about him in the paper."

"You're implying that the file was destroyed because it proved the man had been to Water Management? Why should I care about that?"

Sawnie didn't say anything, except with her high chin, the balled fists at her sides. Eddie could almost hear the tumblers in her brain rolling.

Coltis said, "And Mr. Priest. Eddie Priest of football fame. The man who caught the One-Second Pass. Beat Missouri in the Sugar Bowl. A genuine Florida celebrity. What's your interest here, Eddie?" Coltis looked straight at Sawnie when he said "interest here."

Eddie thought about calling Coltis Lofton. Getting real familiar with the guy right here. Maybe slap him on the back a good hard shot, show him what it took to beat Missouri in the Sugar Bowl.

Eddie said, "Corey Darrow was a friend. She told me about what happened to her down here. She asked me for advice."

"And what did you tell her to do?"

Eddie looked at Coltis's salt-of-the-earth face. The angular Gary Cooper good looks. Unwavering eyes. The hard, disciplined body. He decided not to lie to a liar. "I told her to forget about it."

Sensing Sawnie's reaction. Her pulling back from him miles and miles. Disappearing from that table in Corey's kitchen where they had sat drinking bourbon after almost dancing into the bedroom.

Eddie said, "I told her it was probably nothing. I told her to go home, get on with her life. The thing is, I regret that now." Eddie hoped Coltis could read his eyes. Understood the dangers of regret.

Sawnie said, "My sister was harassed." Her voice was hot and high, the voice of an angry woman, not a Tallahassee deal maker. "She was threatened. There had to be a reason for that."

"Maybe somebody down at Water Management over-reacted." Coltis's voice was soft, as close to kindness as Eddie guessed it could get. The red Agwagon's engine pop-popped off in the distance as it made its turn, preparing to come back and bomb another hundred rows, another eighty yards closer to them.

"Let's say it happened," Coltis said, "and it's regrettable. But what did I have to do with it? I'm a farmer, Miss Dar-row. I don't get into town that often. I run a business. A very big business."

Might as well do it, Eddie thought, shoot the whole wad.

"Mr. Coltis, there's a guy named Harry Feather who drives a white Cadillac. He just had the car painted. There's a streak of white paint on the left front fender of Corey Darrow's Ford Explorer. We think Corey was run off the road, pushed into that canal by somebody in a white car. She told me she believed she was being followed by a man who fits Feather's description. And we know this Feather works for you."

"Let's see," Coltis said. Not so kind now. The voice, the manner cooling again. "You've got some paint on a dead girl's car. A girl who probably fell asleep at the wheel and drove into the canal."

"People don't fall asleep in cars with guns in their hands, Mr. Coltis."

"Oh, yes," Coltis said thoughtfully, "I heard about that. A lot of people are talking about it. Lots of theories, some of them not very pretty. My own is that she took the gun from the glove box *after* she crashed. She tried to fire a signal shot but couldn't."

"And *closed* the glove box, Mr. Coltis? Seriously injured, with the water pouring in, she took the time to close that box?"

"People do strange things under stress, Eddie. I think you and the lady are behaving pretty strangely right now. You don't know how the paint got on the girl's car. You can't

prove it's from Feather's car. A girl told you she was being
followed by a man who looked like Feather, but neither of
you actually *saw* the man following her. And you believe
Feather works for me. And on the strength of this, you slan-
der my good name. A name that's been prominent in this
county since the second Seminole War."

Eddie said, "Nobody's slandering anyone, Mr. Coltis. We
came out to talk to you because Corey Darrow's reputation
has been damaged."

"Let me tell you something. Harry Feather doesn't work
for me. His mother's my housekeeper. Has been since Harry
was a shirttail boy. Harry visits his mother at my house.
Runs some errands for her but does not, in any way, work
for me."

Coltis looked up as the crop duster cut off another hundred rows, another eighty yards closer. Maybe a hundred
yards from them now. Its engine thundering suddenly on a
gust of wind. Eddie wondered if Coltis could calculate the
time they had left here. Before the white cloud included
them.

Coltis said, "I'll give you this for nothing. A man would
be a fool to have Harry Feather as his paid assassin. Feather's unstable. You never know what he'll do next. Many's
the time I've heard his poor mother complain about the boy.
Trying to get him established in some kind of career. She
hasn't had an easy time with him."

"Are you saying Feather's a criminal?" Sawnie again.
Back from her anger. But somehow alone, not here with
Eddie at all.

Coltis smiled, allowed himself an abstemious laugh. "Of
course not, Miss Darrow. Only that he's got no direction in
his life." Coltis started walking toward the truck. Eddie
looked at Sawnie. Got nothing back. Slipping on the muddy
road, he followed Coltis.

The red Agwagon roared overhead, circling for its next
pass. Eddie saw the pilot look down, clearly surprised to
see them. The plane's wings rocking a little as it powered

off. He wondered if the pilot knew he was looking down at the man who paid the bills.

On the ride back to the farmhouse, Coltis said, "Let's do a cost-benefit analysis on this thing, shall we, Miss Darrow? My risks and gains from killing your sister. Would a good businessman do it?"

Staring ahead at the road, Sawnie said, "He would if there's a benefit we haven't talked about here. Something he wanted or something he feared. Something Corey knew about . . ."

Coltis said, "And apparently didn't mention."

Sawnie turned and looked at Coltis. Still acting like Eddie wasn't here. "Who knows, Mr. Coltis? Who knows what she mentioned?"

Coltis smiled. "You know, I ought to resent this. Your coming out here asking these questions without any basis in fact. But I don't. I know you had to do it. I respect this, people doing what they have to do. I respect passion in all its forms. There've been times in my life I've had to go out on a limb. Act without time to think, reconsider. Do things I didn't know I was capable of until I did them. Sometimes with good results, sometimes not so good. I think I've been fair and generous with you."

Coltis stopped the truck in his dooryard, turned off the ignition. He sat staring at the sober old farmhouse. "I'll ask you now to take some time, reconsider what you're doing. And I'll tell you this: We won't have another one of these talks."

Sawnie pushed off from Eddie's shoulder. She was out of the truck, leaning against the window and looking back in.

"We don't need to reconsider, Mr. Coltis. We just need more facts. You were right about that at least. Thank you for showing us your field."

She was off walking toward the rental car.

Coltis put his hand on Eddie's shoulder. A curiously light touch for a man his size. "Women are like that, aren't they,

Eddie? Excitable. Prone to jump to conclusions. That's why we like them so much, isn't it?''

Eddie slid over. He was thinking Sawnie might just be excitable enough to crank up the Chevy. Let him walk home. He said, "We do like them, that's a fact.''

Coltis smiled. "What was it like, Eddie? Catching that pass with one second on the clock? All those people cheering for you?''

Eddie looked off at the field where the duster spewed its white cloud, dropping poison now where the three of them had stood a few minutes ago.

"You know what they're saying in town, Mr. Coltis?''

"No, Eddie, I don't. You going to tell me?'' Coltis smiled, shook his head. "I'd rather hear about that Missouri game.''

"They're saying the poison that got Clinton Reynolds couldn't have come from a crop duster. It's a real old variety. Something they banned years ago.''

Eddie let go of Coltis's eyes now. He did a slow, careful sweep of the farm, taking in the old house, beautiful in its simplicity, the business offices, the sheds and outbuildings. All of it neat and clean and secret. Until somebody got a search warrant.

He looked back in at Coltis, at a man with a sudden sweat on his forehead, a man not so interested now in old football games.

Coltis said, "Eddie, you know how it used to be. People weren't so careful with poisons once upon a time. Bad things are buried and dumped all over this county. Who knows what Clinton got into . . . or how?'' Coltis smiled, touched his temple. "Clinton wasn't what you'd call a mental heavyweight.''

"Thing is,'' Eddie said, "there's a guy in town says he remembers you buying a lot of this stuff. I think it's called parathion? Says you were the last of the big growers to use it.''

"Who is this guy, Eddie? What's his name?''

Eddie got out of the truck and walked, taking the lie with

him, the man he had invented who knew Coltis's poison. It
had been a risk and it had paid. The payoff was the look
in Coltis's eyes.

Eddie walked fast to catch his ride, tell Sawnie what
she'd missed.

She had no eyes for Eddie. "Jesus Christ!" she said. "He
ate our lunch." Her voice was a low, cold whisper. "The
guy tore us to pieces." Eddie would have preferred her
screaming at him. At least *looking* at him.

"Wait a minute," he said, "let me . . ."

"And you," she muttered, "you with your telling Corey
to go home. 'Forget about it. It's probably nothing.' You
never told me that one. You sure left that one out, didn't
you, you prick."

She started the car and swung it into a curve too fast,
fishtailing in the mud. She righted it just before burying her
left front wheel in a ditchbank.

"What else did you leave out?"

Eddie watched the oncoming ribbon of wet mud, balanc-
ing himself on the seat with both hands. "Nothing. That's
the whole story."

"You wait to tell me about the gun, you and Raymer.
Waiting for the right time. It's not until the second day I
hear about the paint on the car. What else are you withholding, Mr. Legal Mind? Mr. Cross-examination. Hoboy, you
really put some questions to Coltis!"

Eddie reached over and took the wheel with his left hand,
turned off the ignition with his right. The Chevy's steering
wheel locked, and he waited while Sawnie struggled with
it, waited for her to realize she'd have to stop them before
they ploughed into the cane. He was bracing himself for the
impact when she hit the brakes. "Not so hard," he whispered. "You'll skid."

They came to rest with the front bumper against the first
row of stalks. Both of them rigid on the seat. Finally, she
whispered, "Mr. Driving Instructor. Mr. Don't Stop Too
Fast."

Eddie let go of the wheel, pocketed the key, and took a deep breath. "I can't do anything right today. I ought to go back, get in bed, start the day over again."

"I'd go back further than that. I was you, I'd talk to my parents about another night under the sheets, another Eddie altogether. One with some brains and some . . ."

"Some what? What is it you're on about here? I told Corey it was probably nothing. Think about it. What did she have? She's gonna trash her whole career over some guy who gets run over by a truck, a gator drags him into a canal. I gave Corey some bad advice? Is that right?"

"*First* you fucked her. *Then* you gave her the bad advice."

"Fuck you," Eddie said. He tossed the key in Sawnie's lap and got out of the car. Stood with the door open.

He said, "I should have believed her about the guy following her. We know that now, don't we? I've got to live with it. I'm here because being here is gonna change the way I live with it. And yes, I was looking forward to seeing her again. I believe she wanted to see me, too. She told me she did anyway. She said what a woman says to a man she wants. I don't see anything wrong with it."

Eddie slammed the door, started walking. Twenty yards down, he heard the car start, the rear wheels slipping, then catching. Sawnie easing back from the cane, shifting, rolling forward.

She pulled up beside him. "I'm sorry," she said. "Get in." Looking straight ahead, her hands white on the wheel.

Eddie got in. She eased the Chevy up to speed.

"I'm sorry, too," he said. "And I don't think he tore us to pieces. Today was for the record. It's what he does next that matters."

He told her about the guy in town he'd invented. The guy who was supposed to know that Coltis had purchased parathion. Had been the last grower to use it.

Sawnie didn't like it as much as he did.

"In his eyes?" she said. "You're saying you saw it in his eyes? He killed this Clinton character?"

"That's what I'm saying." They rode in silence for a while.

"How'd you know about the poison?"

"I called the doctor."

Finally, she said, "What do we do next?"

Eddie thinking, You and me. I wish I knew. Looking over at the face that was even prettier than Corey's. Thinking that old unforgivable and unreconstructed thing: that she was beautiful when she was angry.

"We talk to Feather," he said. "Give *him* a chance to step on his dick."

31

▲▲▲▲▲▲▲▲▲▲▲▲▲▲▲▲▲▲

They drove back to Okee City without talking, Sawnie's hands clenched on the steering wheel. The road going from wet black mud to county asphalt. With Okee City's red brick facades rising out of the green horizon, coming closer, Eddie knew the thing they had to do was coming at them. A collision, sweet, he hoped, always dangerous.

At the city limits sign, she said, "You want to come to my house? Some dinner maybe?" Her voice barely a whisper, and still she didn't look at him.

Eddie said, "Sure." Not sure. Sure only of that.

When they hit the main drag, passed the sheriff's office and the De Soto Hotel, several stores, and offices with Coltis Enterprises painted on them, she said, "Where does Raymer live?"

She slowed the Chevy, pulled over. "You drive, take us there. I don't want to go back to Corey's." She held up her hands in front of her eyes. They were shaking. "Everything I look at there . . . hell, you know what I mean."

Eddie knew. She meant photo albums, crocheted doilies Aunt Martha had sent for Christmas, a footstool some boyfriend had made in industrial arts class.

When Eddie's father had died, he'd kept everything—the hunting trophies from the father-and-son field trials, the pictures of his dad coaching Pop Warner football on a north Florida cow pasture, Eddie's buckteeth sticking out the front of his helmet, his bony shins already covered with cleat scars. He'd even kept his dad's clothes.

When his mom had followed his dad five years later, the things were too many, suddenly too much. He'd called a sister in Miami and a younger brother in Alabama, read them the inventory, asked what they wanted shipped to them. He'd sent their requests air freight, rented a storage locker for a few of his football memories, some photos and trophies, one or two old jerseys, and his father's shotguns. The rest went to Goodwill Industries.

Then Miriam left and things got simpler. Eddie moved to the beach apartment. Nothing there but a table setting for two, sheets, towels, and his boat-selling clothes. He wanted to go without a history for a while, see what it felt like to invent himself every day.

Eddie drove to Raymer's and followed Sawnie up the stairs behind the garage. Inside, she said, "Not bad. Nice view of the back of the feed store."

"Raymer, you here?" Eddie called. Raymer's car was gone, but Eddie had to do this anyway. "Hey, Raymer?" he called.

He turned to Sawnie, who stood at the window looking out. "Yeah," he said, "too bad you can't see any sugar cane. With a cane view this thing would rent for a lot more."

She turned from the window, wiping the dust from Raymer's sill onto her black linen skirt. "You're right," she said. "A cane view and it'd be primo real estate."

"Raymer's out," Eddie said. "I guess I'm your host. What can I fix you for dinner?" He walked to the refrigerator. Opened it, his mind as empty as Raymer's old Frigidaire.

When he turned from the refrigerator, her back was to

him. He crossed, took her arm and turned her, held her. She let him, her arms hanging at her sides. He lifted her chin. Her eyes were closed, red. She'd cry soon.

"I always know," he said, "from the kiss. If the kiss is right, then . . .? You know what I mean?"

"I know," she said. "I'm like that too. A lot of people must be. They just don't say so."

Eddie kissed her. Just a brush, a light press. Something she could reject if she wanted to. Something she could turn away from, neither of them the worse for it. She tasted good. Her breath on his face sweet, smelling of mint and human mystery. She still hadn't opened her eyes.

He kissed her again, firm. She lifted her arms, took his shoulders, easy at first, then digging, her nails probing. She turned her head a degree, adjusting their noses, and kissed him, opening her mouth, letting him taste her deeper.

Eddie pulled her to him, pressed his right hand to her lower back, bringing her thighs to his, her breasts to his chest. Wanting every part of him to touch her, from his knees to the place where their nipples met.

"Who am I?" she whispered.

He knew what she wanted. It was the wrong thing and somehow the only thing. He loosened, let her go a little, his mind rolling. Images forming and disintegrating. A face coming into focus. A composite of Corey and Sawnie. Sawnie and Corey.

"Sawnie Darrow," he said, uncertain, his loins speaking. He pulled her back in. Kissed her hard. Her arms holding him hard, her mouth pressing.

"That's right," she whispered. "I need you."

She broke from him, took his hand, and moved toward Raymer's bedroom door. Eddie followed her down the corridor of his tunnel vision, a roaring in his temples, tumescent. He knew what she meant. She had thanked him for his farewell to Corey. She needed help making her own.

They stopped at Raymer's door, both of them surprised by the plainness. It looked like a hospital room, spare, clean, basic. A twin bed, a dresser, an armoire, a small bookcase full of paperback crime thrillers, and a TV on a small table. A blue chenille cover on the bed.

"You think he'll mind?" she said. She was squeezing his hand so hard it hurt.

"Don't care," he said.

"You think he'll come home?"

"Don't care," he said.

"You know," she said, her voice dreamy. "I had a man." She touched herself between the breasts, pressing two fingers hard there. "He's still in my heart." Eddie could see immediately, as much as he could see anything but her body, that she was not embarrassed to tell him this.

"Not anymore," Eddie said. "Not anymore he isn't."

He moved her into the room, found the key on Raymer's dresser. He locked the door.

When he turned, she was already out of her blouse. She stood bare-breasted, beautiful. Her breasts full and high, a faint blue tracery of capillaries webbing out from their dark centers. She was shivering.

He walked to her, warmed her.

After, they slept for a while. When she woke up in the cleft of his arm, moved her head, Eddie said, "What?"

"Nothing." She yawned.

"There's something," Eddie said. Coming out of his easy sleep. "I can tell. Something you want."

"Tell me why you left the law." Her voice was quiet, careful. She was looking for that ticket again. Her pass to whatever future they were going to have together. She wanted Eddie's secret.

"Not now. Not like this." He curled his arm, touched her forehead.

"Okay," she said, rolling away. "Sorry."

"Sawnie?"

"I said it's okay."

She turned back, propped herself up on one elbow, and looked down at him.

Staring at the ceiling of Raymer's room, he told her about

the development site, the litigation, the pristine coastline he'd tried to save. About Ernesto Plar and Martha Weinstein.

"That's all?" she said. "Just a bunch of dead mangroves in a box meant for flowers?"

"No," Eddie said, "that's not all. He left, Ernesto. He walked out and I'm lifting those dead mangroves out of the box one at a time. Doing what he told me. Down on my knees on the office floor doing what this little guy told me to do and in the middle of the box, on a bed of mangroves, there's a nose. I think it was a woman's nose."

"Jesus," Sawnie whispered.

"It had a hook through it," Eddie said. "A big fishing hook."

"And they never found her, Martha?"

"They never found her."

Eddie wondered if the bed felt dirty to her now. If the room seemed cheap. If she thought she might be with the wrong man.

She didn't say anything. Eddie didn't know how much time passed. When she leaned over him, her hair fanned across his face and chest. She pressed her lips to his, kissed him hard. She said, "I want you again. Can we?"

She was really Sawnie now. Corey was gone now and Martha was moving away. Going back into the cave of memory, deep under the bell tower where she'd wait for some guilty hungover dawn to ring the bells again.

Sitting in the Caddy, Harry W. Feather waited for Moira to leave for the tribal gathering in Hollywood. Going down there to sell her idea about toll booths and tariffs and Indians acting like a sovereign nation. Breathe some political fire into those Indians. Get them to stop dancing around in circles and making handy-crafts and start calling themselves Native Americans. Politicize them, that was what Moira was going to do. And maybe she had a point. Maybe Harry himself should put a little more Native in his American.

Take the thing seriously, his having a spirit brother, the panther.

It was dusk when Harry saw Moira's truck pull out onto the road she hated, the road that had hurt the panther, the road she was taking back from the state and from Mr. Lofton Coltis. Moira sitting up straight in the truck, all business. Hell, she probably had the portable computer on the seat beside her. One hand on the wheel, the other tickling away at those keys. Writing up a legal brief for the Miccosuki cause.

When Moira's truck was just a dot in the distance, Harry pulled the Caddy out from under a stand of punk trees behind the convenience store and drove to Moira's trailer.

Harry jimmied the front door, damning himself for forgetting to bring a flashlight. It was dark inside and he couldn't just reach in and turn on a light. Not in Moira's trailer. Moira was all-natural with those hurricane lanterns. Before he edged the door open, Harry pulled the Llama nine-millimeter from his waistband and worked the slide, jacking a round into the chamber. He had personally drilled the center of the lead bullet, making himself a sweet little hollow point. A dum-dum. On impact, when the flesh rushed into the hole he'd drilled, the bullet would fragment like a tiny grenade.

With the door open now, Harry worked his Bic out of his pocket. He wondered who'd have the advantage if he lit it, him or the panther. He slipped inside, his back to the wall, and waited, calming himself. Going way down into his Indian self, his ancestry, back there with those warrior princes of the Creek Nation, dark men who had spilled the blood of white men in General Gaines's army. Back there, way back, was the vision he needed to find a panther in the dark.

Harry believed the panther was here. Believed she'd left the cat behind for the weekend. Left her big boy with some roadkill to eat and firm instructions to piss in the shower stall. He stood in the dark against the wall, thinking, Maybe not, maybe she took him with her, maybe that hand that wasn't on the wheel was on the panther's head. Or maybe she had him somewhere else. Boarding with someone, some other Native American activist who wanted to build some toll booths. Get a dollar a pop from the two-wrists on their way to Miami to see dolphins jump through hoops and Cubans dance the *méringue*. One thing was sure, the place smelled like panther. Fresh panther.

Harry sniffed, hoping his nose would tell him where the animal was, but all his nose knew was twenty years of Marlboros and cheap drugs. Then Harry heard something, a slow, heavy scraping. Claws. Had to be. Off to his right, he thought, the trailer vibrating a little under the cat's movement. Harry feeling his palms get wet, his breathing go shallow, thumbing the Llama's safety again, tenth time at least. It wouldn't do to make a mistake now, not now. Harry whispered, "Here kitty, kitty, kitty."

He pushed away from the wall and stood in the middle of the narrow room, facing west, toward Moira's bedroom. That sense, way down, way back there, telling him the cat was west. He raised the Bic to strike its flint. Harry thinking, Kitty, I'm gonna put this Llama in your mouth. Make you taste it, see if it's okay, me being here like this. A passport to panther heaven.

The panther was already in the air when Harry's lighter flared. Big face, red eyes, open mouth in the muzzle, flash and shock of the Llama. The panther's weight on Harry's chest, like someone handed him an outboard motor. Said, "Here, catch!" Throwing him back, the two of them embracing, falling onto Moira's little kitchen table. Harry and the panther going down in an avalanche of books and papers. Harry lying there for a space, smiling in the dark. The panther's dead weight on his chest.

For an instant, he had felt the panther's claws bite; then they trembled, retracted.

It was a heart shot. A lucky shot, sure, but a man took his luck, good and bad. The big ugly kitty had hit him without enough juice left to sink a fang into Harry's face, give him the good raking he deserved. Give him an honorable wound he could take down to the tribal gathering. Show them around the campfire. Get down buck naked and say, "Hey, man, look at what I got the last time I met the Florida panther, man. Mean dude, the Florida panther. But not as mean as old Harry W. Feather."

Harry pushed himself up in the dark, feeling his chest hot and wet with the panther's blood. The Llama was firm in his right hand, but he'd lost the Bic. He groped for it, no rush, savoring this moment. When he found it, he lit one of Moira's hurricane lamps.

Oh, those hollow points! Those dum-dum bullets! No wonder the Geneva Convention had outlawed them. Most of the panther's chest had gone through the fist-sized hole in its back. Pieces of it, red and bone white, dripped from Moira's bedroom door. A drape of spongy red lung, oozing frothy blood, hung down the panther's belly.

Harry found some garbage bags in the kitchen, a good waterproof trench coat in the closet, and wrapped the animal, dragged him out the front door. He heaved the panther into the Caddy's trunk. He thought about going back in to blow out the hurricane lamp, decided against it. Leave a light on for Moira. She'd think her kitty did it for her. Sort of a welcome home. What the hoo-hah, they spoke the same language.

Harry lit the Bic, looked down at himself. His belly and loins covered in warm red blood. Good, good.

32

▲▲▲▲▲▲▲▲▲▲▲▲▲▲▲▲▲▲▲

Eddie followed Sawnie in his Celica. It was early dark when they got to Corey's, the last of the sun's fire fading from the cane fields. Eddie parked and walked to Sawnie's car, looked in at the woman who had just changed his life. He wasn't seeing double anymore; she was just one face. The face that had lain beneath his for three hours in Raymer's room. He leaned into her window, the smell of Raymer's bed faint on her.

"Invite me in for a drink?"

She smiled.

Inside, she picked up Corey's mail. A few bills, some junk, and a letter. From the sudden slump of her shoulders, he knew the letter was trouble. Not just a sad reminder, mail for Corey that kept coming like the fingernails of a corpse keep growing. The letter was addressed to Sawnie Darrow.

He watched her open it. Glimpsed a brief typed note. No signature at the bottom, no return address on the envelope.

She took a step away from him and lowered her head to read.

When she finished, she didn't look up. Eddie said, "What is it?" Hating what he was thinking. Remembering what she'd said on the threshold of Raymer's room. "I had a man."

He reached for the note, but she wadded it tight in her right fist.

"Please," she said, looking at the wall above his head. "I want you to leave."

Eddie stood there with her all over him, in him, her smell, the mystery they'd made in Raymer's pure little room, the invasion of his heart and mind by Sawnie Darrow, thinking, What's going on here?

He said, "You gonna tell me what this is? Who sent it?"

She didn't look at him. Eddie standing so close, closer to her now than he would have dared three hours ago. Her face dead gray. "Please," she said, her voice low, cold. She walked to the bedroom door, leaned against the sill, her back to him.

Eddie stared at her, angry, full of his question. He told himself not to ask it. Not so soon after his life had changed. "It's from the guy, right? You said you had a man."

She turned. And Eddie's surprise was that the question surprised her. "I'll tell you later," she said. "It's just something I have to think about. A decision I've got to make."

"Look," he said, "we have to talk."

"Not now." When she reached for the doorknob, he took her arm, stopped her.

Men, Sawnie thought. This one had refused to take Corey Darrow seriously when she'd said she was risking her life. Now he wanted to take Sawnie Darrow's life in his hands and the Governor's too.

It was funny, his guess about a man. His thinking this was a love letter. And maybe the guess was more right than wrong. It was about love. She felt the hot, hard ball of paper in her whitened fist. The note was short but not sweet:

Sawnie Darrow,

Go home *now* or face the truth about Rural Route 10, Box 7.

It was the address of her little cabin in the woods. The place where she met the man who hung his comical rubber face on the hat rack by the door.

She closed her eyes and tried to think. Maybe she could face it out, whatever this anonymous writer knew or thought he knew about a shack in the woods and two people who went there. The writer was almost certainly Coltis, a man with hundreds of connections around this state. Any one of them could have revealed to Coltis something he had seen or something he thought he'd seen or something he had merely surmised. When you were in the public eye anything—truth, rumor, or surmise—could be turned against you. And here she was in a little town in the cane country trying to find her sister's killer. Oh, how the headline writers would love it! Governor's Mistress Turns Self-Styled Sleuth!

Eddie reached out and took her hand now, squeezing it. She didn't know what she was seeing in his eyes: the excitement of the chase? More of what she'd seen back there in Raymer's room when his face had moved above her? His goodness, decency? She let him pull her down onto the love seat.

She remembered him in the bar that night, how he'd jumped over her like some combination of Baryshnikov and King Kong, grabbing Feather with strength she didn't know he had and with less concern for his own safety than was good for him. And Sawnie watching Feather's feet rise off the ground for a moment. The moment before the knife. And realizing that Feather had quit struggling, ceded the advantage temporarily, to work the knife out of his pocket. And then her own voice failing her even as she tried to reach down for the words. And hearing Raymer get there first, "Look out!"

She'd thought about that night ever since. It proved he was a man to whom things mattered. That he had too much strength and not enough caution. That he was as dangerous to himself as to anyone else. And he had already risked more for someone calling her a dirty name than he was asking her to risk right now. She could lose a lot, could lose everything, in fact, but wouldn't be risking her life as Eddie Priest had done. As Corey had done.

Oh, Corey, Corey, Corey, she thought as she lifted her hand to touch Eddie's cheek. Corey, I have to do this, don't I? Even if it destroys my future and paints the Governor black.

And in her mind's eye, she saw Corey answer yes.

Sawnie looked at Eddie for a long time.

Finally, she said, "It's blackmail. And it *is* about a man. That's all you need to know." She made her eyes fierce now, resisting his jealous curiosity.

"Somebody's *blackmailing* you?" The surprise in his face, the thing blossoming in his head. She remembered him asking, "It's from the guy, right? You said you had a man." His jealousy was a sweet thing beside the reality of Coltis's letter.

"It's from Coltis," he whispered.

Eddie moved closer to her on the love seat. "Of course it's from Coltis," she said. He could see the challenge in her eyes. The lie that kept him out and yet wanted something? Wanted it badly.

Their bodies were touching now. Quiet after a crash. She shifted away from him a little. "You're excited," she said. "You want to know. I can understand that. But this is my life."

She tried to rise again, go to the bedroom, but Eddie held her. When she stopped trying, he put his hand over her mouth. Enough. Over her eyes. Enough. He whispered, "People make mistakes."

"That's easy for you to say."

"I say we don't cut and run. Whatever this is, it doesn't have to hurt you."

"*We,*" she said, laying on the bitter grind of her sarcasm. "*We* don't cut and run?"

"That's what I said, 'we.' " Eddie played his trump card. He kissed her.

She wavered, then pulled out of the kiss, leaving him in the warm mist of her breath. She looked at him like he'd just offered her some shares in an old bridge. A beautiful old bridge in Manhattan. Like he'd said, "Trust me."

Sawnie didn't like this. It was revealing too much too soon. But she had to go on now, if not all the way, then most of it.

"There's going to be a new seat in Congress," she told him, "a new district. The Governor wants me to run. He'll back me. And his backing is almost a guarantee. All I have to do is file for it."

She leaned, kissed him hard, deep. Then she drew back her fist and hammered him hard in the middle of his chest. Right over his heart. Maybe her fist was a little harder with the ball of paper in it. She hoped so. "You'd make a good politician," she whispered.

He rubbed the spot where she'd hit him. She thought maybe she could see tears in his eyes. She was glad her punch had hurt.

"I was a good lawyer. Same thing."

Sawnie said, "The last thing the Governor said to me before I left Tallahassee was 'no mud on your skirts.' Even a hint of scandal—me throwing my weight around down here, stirring up trouble—and I'm dead. Coltis sends me this . . ." She raised the fist with the note in it. "Then he finds out from his buddies in Tallahassee I'm running for Congress . . ." She shrugged. "All it takes is a phone call to the *Miami Herald.*"

She watched Eddie. Was that disappointment in his face? Disappointment because she hadn't let him read the note. Hadn't named the man. She couldn't read his eyes.

He smiled. Rubbed his chest where she had ripped him.

"If Coltis talks to the papers, you do too. Turnabout's fair play. You talk about the big grower who had something to gain from your sister's death. I say it's a standoff."

She shook her head, looked at him like he was crazy. "Wrong," she said. "I get into a pissing contest with Coltis before an election, I'm dead. Coltis knows that."

Eddie closed his eyes now. She watched him spin the possibilities. He said, "Coltis did it. Had Corey killed. We just don't know why. We haven't got anything until we know that."

He reached over and took her hand, the one that held the wadded note. He tried gently to pry it open. "How long did he give you?" he asked. "They usually give you some time to think about it."

"What it says"—Sawnie looked at him, cold—"is *leave now*. I'd say that's pretty unequivocal."

But he only stared back at her with that stubborn hope in his eyes. And that thing that had made him grab Harry Feather by the front of his silk suit. She said, "The deadline for filing—if you plan to stand for office, you have to file a letter of intent—is next week."

"Then we've got a week," he said, grinning. "Give me a week. Promise me?"

Sawnie looked at this man carefully. She saw something new, something mean in that grin. A thing that was good and mean and all for Coltis and Feather. She liked it. She didn't know what to say. She had to decide what to do. Maybe she'd just whisper a promise to him and let him go. Send him back to Raymer's with the promise he wanted and then pack her bags. Get in that car out there and make good time back to Tallahassee like the note in her hand said to do.

There were promises in life and promises in politics. Maybe this was just politics.

But there was another promise. The one she'd made to Corey.

33

▲▲▲▲▲▲▲▲▲▲▲▲▲▲▲▲▲▲

Harry W. Feather cleared the drainboard in his little kitchen. He propped two books open on the windowsill above the sink. The first was a text entitled *Techniques of Taxidermy for Larger Mammals.* The second was *Indians of the Southeastern U.S.: Religion, Lore and Legend.* He heaved the panther up onto the counter in Moira's Barnard College raincoat, head down in the sink. He opened the coat and slit the garbage bags with his Buck knife.

The coat's label said Aquascutum. Harry had no idea what an Aquascutum was. Maybe it was a fish. Moira's name and New York address were hand-lettered in India ink on the back of the tag. Thrifty Moira, stylish Moira, the scholarship Indian girl.

Well, Harry W. Feather had never won a scholarship, but he knew how to do things. Witness this panther here. And what he didn't know how to do, he could find in books. Harry W. Feather, autodidact and proud of it.

234

He opened the taxidermy text to the chapter "Flaying the Larger Mammal" and started to work. He read both books as he went, alternating chapters. Harry didn't know which book fascinated him most. But he knew that everything he needed was here: two books and the body of the beast. The books were his Indian past and the scientific present. The panther was experience. Harry W. Feather, elbow deep in the blood of a fresh kill.

Harry slit the panther from anus to chin, spilling what was left of its entrails into the sink. Following the diagram on the page in the window, Harry worked the knife under the skin at the top of the panther's right foreleg. He cut a straight line down to the dark, heart-shaped pad of its foot. Experience, he believed, was the best teacher. And death was a big part of experience. Harry's method of death? Go with what they give you. Always do that.

With the Cowgirl, Corey Darrow, they'd given him the night, the highway, the canal. He'd used them. Nothing interventionist. Nothing from left field. He'd wanted the Cowgirl to take the Ford Explorer in without his having to touch her, but it hadn't worked out that way. Nothing was perfect.

They gave you Boner's infection, you follow nature's direction. You add a little biodiversity. Give the man a whopping hybrid infection, he sets a national indoor record for death by toxic shock.

Harry had his theories. But he'd violated them with the panther. He slit the skin inside the other foreleg and worked the knife down, exposing the bone. And there it was, the healed fracture Moira had told him about. She had, or somebody had, brought this big cat back from a broken limb. Yes, he'd violated his theory, but then, what had nature given him with the panther? Moira had taken the panther out of the woods, out of nature. Turned it into a pussy-whipped trailer kitty. Harry had done a little checking up on panthers. He knew that, even though he'd killed the panther in a very interventionist way, a crude and unsubtle way, there was very little Moira could do about it. The law was clear on that point. Nobody, not even a Native Ameri-

can activist with a Barnard College degree in social action
and shaking the power tree until the moneyfruit fell out,
not even a girl with those credentials could capture a Florida
panther and keep it as a pet. It was just flat against the law.
No, Moira wasn't going to say anything. She was going to
scrub the big cat's liver and lights off the walls of her trailer,
save what papers and books she could, and get on with her
life. That's what old Moira would do. Moira Big Breath.

Harry severed the panther's neck and tail, cut all four feet
behind the pads and lifted the carcass out of its skin. It
wasn't all that difficult, really, flaying the larger mammal.
You had the right book, the right tools. You had the will,
there was always a way.

He lifted the carcass, still holding some of its warmth an
hour after death, and carried it out to the deck overlooking
the canal. He laid the panther down and hit the light switch.
The gator's eyes immediately returned their red beams to
him. The gator started to move, only its eyes, snout, and
the tip of its tail breaking the surface. The powerful wash
of its tail telling you just how much gator there was under
that glassy, black surface.

Harry decided not to toss the panther in whole. He'd
make the gator work a little. Toss in bite-sized chunks and
watch the action. Stir up the water. Let that big gator's lousy
table manners scare the little creatures in the canal. Bump
them a couple notches back down the evolutionary scale.

Harry W. Feather walked over to the little pile of firewood
by the kitchen door. Picked up the ax. You didn't want to
treat a gator too good. Keep the gator guessing, that was
his theory. Keep him coming back. He chopped the panther
up into six chunks, threw them in one at a time. Watching
the gator thrash and fight to swallow each piece. He had
read that gators sometimes dragged their kill back to under-
water stashes and kept it there for days, letting it ripen,
sweeten. Not this gator.

It ate the whole panther. That meant the gator wouldn't
eat again for some time. After the gator finished, the red
eyes moved off down the canal, the powerful tail spreading

its serpentine wake to both banks. Harry hosed down the deck, turned off the lights, and went back inside to confront the problem of the panther's head. How to get those brains out of there without destroying that scary light in the big cat's eyes.

Raymer said, "She got that letter and she didn't run? That's pretty amazing, my friend. That's contrary to self-interest as most folks would see it. How'd you stop her?"

Eddie had spent an anxious hour waiting for Raymer to get home. Marking off Raymer's apartment with his feet, his head full of plans that disintegrated under the hot light of logic. His heart fighting its own worst impulses. He knew he'd said some of the right things to Sawnie, but he hadn't said half of what he was thinking.

She'd said, "I had a man." The verb tense was past, but the tone was elegaic. Like she'd only just gone from *have* to *had*. Like it was very recent and it still hurt. And so Eddie's heart had told him to say, "Not anymore. He isn't in your heart." So much for what hearts said.

Eddie had left her at Corey's, hadn't asked to stay the night. Had asked and received only her promise that he'd find her there in the morning still hard in her resolve to see this thing through. And he hadn't called her. Every time he crossed Raymer's floor, he stopped short of the phone.

When Raymer came in at midnight, Eddie was sick of the apartment, sick of running in place. Raymer was back from a meeting with the insurance company's lawyers in Stuart. Something about the legal grounds for withholding payments on the dead Key Men.

And Raymer had asked him how he'd stopped Sawnie from running.

Eddie said, "I asked her to trust me. I told her it didn't have to hurt her career."

"She believe you?"

"She's still here. At least I think she is."

"She's not as smart as I thought she was."

"That's a little harsh, Raymer. We're talking about doing

the right thing here." After he said it, Eddie knew he meant it.

"Staying alive is always the right thing," Raymer said. "It keeps you equipped for doing all the other things you have to do." Raymer let that one sink in.

Eddie and Sawnie had talked about her career, her reputation. The Governor. They hadn't talked about lives. About what Feather was capable of doing.

Raymer went to the window and stuck his sad, hounddog face out into the muggy night. He came back, stood over Eddie. "Let's say she doesn't go milky and run. Let's say she stays, which is entirely contrary to good sense. What do you do now?"

"I don't know, Raymer. That's why I'm putting up with you. I thought you might have an idea?"

"You want an idea? There's a good highway out there. It goes back to where things get a lot saner. Get on it."

"Come on, Raymer. You got me into this."

Raymer didn't like that. It was only partly true.

"Let's back up here," Raymer said. "What were you two doing? I mean before that letter came."

"I told you we went out to talk to Coltis."

"A mistake, in my opinion." Raymer tightened his fleshy lips, his eyes full of reproof. "After that? After you talked to Coltis?"

Eddie feeling his face go red. "We came here." Unable to keep his voice from squeaking a little with the memory of Sawnie in Raymer's bedroom.

"So," Raymer said, "I'm talking to a guy whose judgment's a little clouded."

"What are you talking about?"

"I got eyes. I got a nose too. I can tell when someone wears perfume in my bed. Unless we've had a home invasion or you got tendencies I don't know about, Sawnie was in there. And I don't think she was alone."

"It's not your business, Raymer."

"Then don't ask me what to do next. You got your foot

on your dick and no idea how to get it off and say it's not my business. I can't be in halfway, Eddie."

"All right. I'm in love with the woman, Raymer. It happens. Now you're in."

"Is that why you think she can get out of this without getting dirty? Love does that to a man's brains?"

Eddie pushed up. "I got to get out of here."

Raymer stood. "I'm going with you."

"You're in, Raymer. We're old buddies. You used to knock people down so I could catch footballs, but you're not going with me."

"Funny," Raymer said. "Funny man." Raymer looked hurt. "Tell me where you're going."

"I'm not going anywhere, Raymer. I'm just gonna drive. It's what I do when I'm not going anywhere."

"Don't do anything stupid. I mean anything *else* stupid."

"Of course not."

34

▲▲▲▲▲▲▲▲▲▲▲▲▲▲▲▲▲▲▲

It was three in the morning when Eddie found the little house. He'd spent two hours searching, driving out to Indian land, stopping at a couple of all-night convenience stores, asking directions from sleepy men who woke up fast at the mention of Harry Feather's name. Following their directions as the night got longer and the lights winked out along the lonely mud roads. Finally, in the dead dark, with no one left to ask, he turned down a narrow cutoff into solid scrub, pushed into a clearing, his headlights washing a little frame house. The sudden smell of moving water at his windows.

The old Caddy stood in the dooryard, its new paint gleaming. The porch light was burning, the center of a constellation of moths. The house was dark.

Eddie turned off the engine and sat in the quiet of the car with the night rushing in. The spicy smell of insects and the muddy odor of the canal moving there beyond the little levee where Feather's house perched.

Eddie planned to look around if Feather was out night-crawling somewhere. Maybe he'd find something interesting, something that connected Feather and Corey. It was worth a try. And if Feather was home? Eddie planned to confront the Indian, ask him some straight questions. Maybe finish what they'd started in the Cane Cutter. Get it out of him, whatever it was that linked him to Coltis. Do it down and dirty. Best man wins. And do it without Sawnie here, like she'd been when they'd talked to Coltis. Standing there writing a review in her head. Reading it to Eddie later in the car. "He ate our lunch."

Fuck it, Eddie thought. He got out of the car and walked toward the door. Imagining Feather inside the house, rising at the sound of Eddie's car door. Feather disoriented for an instant, then clearing, reaching for the pistol under the pillow. Feather moving to the window, looking out at Eddie walking toward the porch light. Feather thinking how easy Eddie had made it. Feather raising the pistol, sighting.

On the porch, still, Eddie could hear no movement. He shaded his eyes and looked into the front window. A little moonlight sifted through at the back of the house, probably a kitchen window. Otherwise, darkness. There was no bell. He stepped back, thinking Feather wouldn't shoot him in the yard; too hard to prove trespass.

He called, "Feather! Harry Feather! It's Eddie Priest. We need to talk."

Thinking Feather wouldn't shoot at all. That he liked to work in close with the knife. That he would talk first. He'd do a lot more than talk, a lot worse, but he'd talk first. The kind of guy who liked to hear the sound of his own voice.

No answer, no movement. Eddie rapped on the door. Rapped again, the sound of his fist on the doorframe rattling off into the scrub. A heron out on the canal waking up— "scrawwwwk!"—at the noise. Eddie tried the door and it opened. He stood with his hand on the loose latch, his heart beating too fast, too fast. Thinking, Slow down, Eddie. Think about this. Talking's one thing. B and E is another. People get shot out here doing this. Eddie stepped into Feather's house.

The panther was a pelt with four feet and a head. Harry W. Feather had rubbed salt brine inside the panther's skin and it was slimy. Harry threw it down on the canal bank and put down the lantern, bucket, and cast net beside it. He'd sewn up the gaping exit wound with fine monofilament line. Now in the light of the hissing Coleman lantern, the panther's back looked almost right, the ridge of dark fur down the center only a little roughened and puckered at the seam. The head, the freight of brains that would begin to rot soon, were Harry's problem.

He had done the crude work. Broken through the base of the skull with a hammer and chisel and scooped what he could. But how to remove the balance of gray matter without destroying the panther's essential self. Its personality. Harry had parted company with the taxidermy text. The text advised flaying the head, stuffing it, reconstructing the soft tissues—eyes, nose, tongue—with precast polymer pieces. But Harry needed it real, authentic for what he planned to do. Like it would have been for the Indians of the southeastern United States. In 1850, you didn't send away for mail-order plastic eyeballs.

Harry cut a stalk from the stand of bamboo that shaded the bank. He hooked the lantern on the end of the pole and swung it out over the water, bedding its thick end in the muddy bank. He sat down with the cast net in his lap to wait for the bait fish to rise to the light.

The panther lay on its splayed, empty belly, facing the water, its eyes gone dark and milky inside the plastic bag Harry had carefully taped behind its ears. When the surface of the canal under the hot hissing lantern began to roil with minnows, Harry reached into his pocket for some cornmeal. He threw a handful at the lit circle, watching the surface stir.

From Feather's kitchen window, Eddie thought he could see a light, maybe two hundred yards north, up the canal.

But maybe not. Maybe it was a trick of moonlight. He stood in the kitchen in the powerful odor of something he'd never met before, something animal, gamy. Something you didn't want to smell up close in the dark. He took his Bic from his pocket and lit it. Blood and organs, slick and oozing in the sink, glittered in the small circle of flame.

Eddie's heart and lungs had almost found the calm rhythm of this search of Feather's house. Now this gore. His pulse jumped. He'd checked the living room, the single bedroom, for Feather. He knew Feather wasn't here. Was out somewhere, but where without the car? And now, Christ, Feather had killed someone! Murdered someone and was cutting up the corpse, disposing of the pieces. Every sense told Eddie to get out.

The lighter burnt Eddie's hand and he cursed, dropped it, knelt, picked it up, tossed it from hand to hand to cool it. Was rising to light it again, to look again at this slaughterhouse sink, when he heard the sound of a weapon cocking behind him. "I'm going to blow your fucking head off."

Eddie dropped to the floor, scuttling away from the sound, the lighter still hot in his palm. He pushed his back to some cabinets, his brain trying to tell him something, trying to stop his panicked search for a hard thing to put between himself and the muzzle flash, the concussion, the drilling bullet. He could hear her moving now, her feet scraping on the floor.

The message clearer: *her?* God, yes, it had been a woman's voice. Not Feather's, a woman's voice.

"I'm going to kill you, Harry Feather." Whispering. "You're going to die right here."

Eddie breathed deep, the blessed breath of belief in his living. "I'm not Feather," he said. "Feather's not here."

The woman said nothing. Eddie tried to make out her shape against the weak light from the front windows. Maybe he saw her move, crouch. He could smell her, maybe a sweet odor on the sharp reek from the sink. Maybe some of her fear. He said, "I swear I'm not Feather." Trying to control

243

his voice, keep it from shaking. "If you know the man well enough to shoot him, you know his voice. I'm not Feather."

Every breath tasted better than the last. The woman said, "No. You aren't." Big disappointment in a small voice. Eddie had never been so glad in his life to disappoint a woman. He pulled his legs up under him, his back to the cabinets. "Can we have some light here, do you think?"

"No," she said. "He'll see it. He's around somewhere."

Eddie lit the lighter anyway, the blood-spattered kitchen materializing, his own feet, outstretched hand, and a woman's dark, pretty face, crouching body, extended arms. And a shotgun, there in the space between the refrigerator and the kitchen counter.

"Off!" she hissed. "Now!"

Eddie did it, seeing her afterimage fade to orange, black, a woman in a traditional Indian blouse and skirt, buckskin boots. The shotgun an old single-shot with a sawed-off stock, makeshift pistol grip. A gas station stickup gun, certainly not a woman's weapon. She'd pull that trigger and the recoil would break her wrist. This woman was serious about killing Harry Feather. Eddie said, "Why don't you point the shotgun away? I can see it's cocked."

"You damn right it's cocked," she said, "and I know how to use it."

He could hear her shift a little in the dark. He said, "You don't have to know much to kill a man with the pattern that thing throws."

Harry W. Feather threw the cast net at the circle of lantern light and drew the line that pursed the net. He pulled the net to the bank and emptied its struggling silver contents into the bucket filled with water. He'd caught more minnows than he needed, but what the hell. Take care of nature and she takes care of you. He pulled the panther over to the bucket and immersed the animal's head, its eyes and ears and mouth wrapped in water-tight plastic. Its cranial cavity gaping. Harry W. Feather leaned over the bucket watching the minnows roil in panic, then settle, then begin to eat the panther's brains. Harry wasn't sure why he looked up.

The big gator was there at the edge of the lantern circle, its red eyes large, glittering, prismatic in the light. Two small puffs of steam rising from its nostrils. Harry thought about the steam. Gators were cold-blooded, but a small difference between internal and ambient temperature would account for the steam. Harry knew the gator could be on him in a whiptail and three lighting strides, on him in a shower of water and a blur of webbed feet and yawing jaws. And he knew the gator would only watch. The gator had eaten too recently to want an Indian. Harry and the gator were in symbiosis.

She'd told him her name was Moira, she was a Native American, she'd been hiding in the little utility room off the kitchen, waiting for Harry Feather. She was going to kill Feather for some very good reasons. Reasons she didn't care to share with a white man. She wasn't sure yet whether she wanted to kill Eddie. She might do it on the general principle that he belonged to the same gender as Feather. Now what was Eddie doing here?

They were sitting across from each other on the kitchen floor, the Bic in Eddie's hand, the shotgun in the woman's lap. Every time he lit the Bic, she raised the weapon, cocked it. He turned off the light, she eased the hammer down. He'd lit the lighter twice to see her face. To try to read this thing he'd stumbled into. This vendetta between Feather and a beautiful Miccosuki woman.

"I came out here to see him," Eddie said. "I guess you could say I have a bone to pick with him, too." It was a bad choice of phrasing, considering what was in the sink. "Would you really kill him?" Eddie asked.

"I think so," she said. Her musing tone was from some argument she had with herself. As though she had this, among other things, to prove to herself.

"Well," Eddie said, "if you don't know, I wouldn't recom-

mend you try. Not unless you two got some kind of thing
going that ...."

"We don't have anything going. He killed a friend of
mine. You saw it."

"You mean ... in the sink? That was a friend of yours?"

"It was," she said. Her voice tight, mean. Eddie thinking,
Thank God for balance. Feather's got an enemy.

Eddie wasn't sure why he looked up, saw the light, barely
a wisp, playing on the kitchen ceiling. He jumped up, heard
the shotgun cock again behind him, looked out the window.
It was coming, a lantern or a big flashlight. A hundred yards
up the canal and making steady progress. Eddie turned from
the window and knelt. "Ease that hammer down. He's coming. Somebody is. We don't want to be caught here."

"I do," she said. "It's his ass gets caught, just one time."

But she uncocked the shotgun. When Eddie heard the hammer rest, he lunged, jerked the shotgun from her hands.
"Hey!" she said. "Goddamn, what you doing?"

He pulled her up straight in the dark, her face close, their
breath mixing. Eddie's anger was for Feather. He didn't
want this woman hurt because of him.

He said, "We're getting out of here. You can kill him
some other time. He catches us here he's got some legal
rights we don't want him to have." Eddie started for the
door, pulling the woman with one hand, the shotgun in the
other. She fought him, but not hard. The light was getting
closer. Maybe she realized her life wasn't worth what was
left in that sink.

When Eddie had her in his car, the shotgun between them,
the engine fired, he could see her face better. Could see she
was a lot to lose. When he'd driven across the clearing and
made the entrance to the narrow cutoff, the lantern was in
his rearview mirror, coming up the canal bank, entering the
clearing. The man in the light stopped, extended the lantern
toward the house, its circle of light swinging. Then the man
turned, shoved the light toward Eddie's car. Lifted his
other hand.

Oh, shit! Eddie pushed the Celica, its wheels slewing in

slick mud. Eddie thinking, A gun, he's got a gun in that other hand. Waiting for the flash and glass breaking, the rear window imploding into the back seat.

The Celica's wheels caught and Eddie powered out of the clearing. In his last glimpse, the man with the light was running toward them. Full tilt, coming, trying to catch the car. And it was Feather. He was sure of it, though not sure why. Maybe because the guy would chase a car on foot at night. Didn't care who was in it, what they might have for him when he caught them. By the way the guy just didn't seem to care.

35

▲▲▲▲▲▲▲▲▲▲▲▲▲▲▲▲▲

Ten minutes down the road, Eddie pulled over. He didn't think Feather was following him. He was certain he was hopelessly lost. He told himself, You're never lost with an Indian. He sat listening to the engine tick as it cooled, looking at the woman. Still as pissed off as when she'd cocked the piece on him. Still eying the Savage twenty-gauge on the seat like she wanted to blow his head off, take his keys. Go back and deal with Feather.

"Who was that?" Eddie asked. "In the sink back there. I need to know."

"I told you, a friend of mine." She spoke low and even, staring straight ahead. Eddie's headlights shooting down the canyon of sugar cane. He turned them off.

"Does this person have a name?"

"Who are you anyway? A cop? Bureau of Indian Affairs? You look like a Bureau guy. All buttoned up. Got your head poised to enter your asshole. I guess right?"

Still not looking at him. In profile, Eddie decided, she looked a lot like Rita Moreno, younger of course. She had that same in-your-face feistiness.

"I'm not a cop. I'm just a guy with a bone to pick with Feather. I told you the truth back there. It's a habit I picked up somewhere. Gets me in all kinds of trouble."

She looked over at him. He couldn't see her eyes, but he guessed they were saying she wished she'd capped him with a load of double-ought buck. Put him in the sink with the rest of the guts. "It wasn't a person. Not in the usual sense. It was a panther."

"Holy shit! You're telling me Feather was cutting up a Florida panther?"

"I'm telling you he killed one. I can't prove it, but I know he did."

Eddie said, "There can't be more than a hundred left, and this guy kills one. Why?"

"There aren't fifty left and I couldn't tell you why." The voice different. The Indian woman not looking at him now. Eddie knew she could tell him why. It had to do with her and Feather. They sat quiet for a space.

She broke it. "You gonna tell me why you were there, sneaking into Harry's house in the middle of the night?"

"I don't think so. I don't think it's in your best interest to know."

"White man!" she snorted. "Got my best interest at heart. Look out, Moira!"

"Where can I drop you, Moira?" Eddie fired the Celica. Brought the cane canyon back into his lights.

"I can walk." She opened the door. Letting in the curious, moldy smell of the cane.

Eddie reached over, took her arm. "Let me drop you," he said. "Truth is, I'm lost. Maybe you live near some landmark I can recognize."

"All right." She closed the door. "Take the next right at the big cypress tree."

Driving, Eddie decided to push her a little, see what he

could get. And he knew he'd have to give to get. "You read the newspaper?" he asked.

"I read it."

"You see the thing that was in a while back about the guy who disappeared?"

"I didn't just see it, I saw *him*." Eddie's heart jumped into his armpit, pumping the mean blood of the search. Pushing the adrenaline to his brain so that his foot nudged the gas pedal and the Celica lurched.

"He was poking around out where I live. I stopped him one day, asked him what the hell he thought he was doing on my land."

"What did he think he was doing? Did he tell you?" Eddie trying to keep the taste of that blood out of his mouth, keep his tongue calm.

"He told me. What's it to a Bureau man what he told me? You think the Indian people had something to do with this guy disappearing? You gonna try to stick that one up our butt too?"

It was time to give, and Eddie knew it. But the giving came hard because he wasn't sure of this woman. Who she was. What she would do with what he told her.

"Look, I'm investigating the death of a woman named Corey Darrow. I think her death and the disappearance of this bicycle man are related in some way."

"What way?"

"He came to her office at Water Management. He asked for some information about local soil chemistry. Corey Darrow gave him the information he wanted, but we don't know what she told him because a computer file she wrote about him has disappeared."

"Hoboy," Moira said, a cold glee in her voice. "White people got some real messed-up affairs. It's a wonder you don't ask the Indian people to come in and straighten things out for you. Why don't you hire me as your group dynamicist? Hell, I studied that stuff in school."

Eddie took a deep breath. He pulled his foot off of the

accelerator. "Can you tell me about the conversation you had with this man? Tell me everything he said."

"Sure I can tell you *everything* we said"—Moira was annoyed now, her voice sharp, a little pissy—"because we didn't say all that much. He was looking for a plant. It's a little vine grows around here. The Indian people call it *tokeepah*. It means 'burns the tongue.' A long time ago, we used it for medicine, but I don't know what for. Nobody around here knows that anymore. That's lost like so many of our good things. Anyway, this funny white man, he had a name of his own for that plant. Some Latin name you choke on. I can't remember the word. He showed me some drawings he'd made of the vine.

" 'Sure,' I say, 'that's *tokeepah*.'

" 'You know where I can find it?' he asks me. He's getting all excited, his face getting all hypertension red.

" 'Sure,' I tell him. 'I know where you can find it.' "

She stopped, looking at Eddie in the dark front seat. The cane whispering past their windows, the insects darting into their lights like tracer bullets. She was going to make him ask. Hell, he'd ask. He'd beg if he had to. Stop the car and kiss her buckskin boots, anything.

"What did you tell him?"

"It's on Coltis land. That's what I told him."

"Coltis land, you sure?"

"Of course I'm sure. I told him exactly where to find it. I knew where it was because I been out there on that land Mr. Coltis Almighty thinks he owns. I been out there and I've seen it."

"Where exactly? Where did you see it?"

She went coy, cold. Her eyes narrowing to a calculating squint. Eddie slowed down, looking at her.

She turned and looked out at the dark wall of cane. "Why do you want to know where it is? What does that plant have to do with this guy disappearing and this Corey Darrow?"

Eddie told her he didn't know. He'd have to think about that. Could she tell him exactly where the plant, *tokeepah*, was found on Coltis land?

But she was closed up now. Her suspicion of his white face had fallen like a curtain between them.

"No," she said, "no, I don't think I can do that. Not till I'm sure who you are, what your agenda is here. Maybe you're a Bureau guy. Maybe I already told you too much."

"Did he tell you *why* he was looking for this plant?" Eddie asked.

"No," Moira said. "Maybe he wanted to burn his tongue." She laughed quietly at her own joke, looking out at the cane.

Eddie dropped her at an intersection of 41 and some secondary road. She wouldn't let him take her any farther. When she'd walked a few strides up the road, no good-bye, the shotgun in her hand, Eddie called out to her. "You bent on this thing? Killing Feather?"

There was a certain mean pleasure in thinking she might be. No pleasure in knowing she'd bungle it.

She stopped, looked back. The colors of her folk art skirt and blouse brilliant in his headlights. "I might be. I probably am. You sure you're not a Bureau guy? I know who to call. I know how to find out if you are. If you are, you got to report that panther." She touched herself between the breasts. "This is the new Miccosuki, here. The one that knows how." She turned, walked off.

Eddie called after her. "I was you, I'd stay away from Feather." It was the same advice Sheriff Nailor had given Eddie.

Sawnie surfaced from restless sleep at five o'clock and dialed the Governor's private number. It was dark outside. Not yet a hint of light in the east. She could see the Governor sleeping as clearly as if she were there beside him. Could see it because she had lain beside him so many times, although not often in the mansion.

She knew he'd be lying on his side: that he started the night flat on his back with his right wrist flung over his eyes and midway, maybe three A.M., rolled onto his belly. That he finished on his left side, facing the edge of the bed, as though impatient for the floor, the beginning of a new day.

Hearing the phone ring for the second time, she could see him reach for it, pull it to his ear, clear his throat. And the words came to her again: "I've got to warn him." The words had made her lie unrested all this night. She couldn't go further with this thing, the thing for Corey, without warning the Governor.

"This better be important," the Governor said, his voice steady, not fogged by sleep. "You better be somebody I want to talk to at five in the morning."

"You're awake," she said. "You wouldn't know what time it was if you weren't. The clock's behind you and you don't wear a watch to bed."

His laugh was a low, affectionate rumble. She waited while he yawned, stretched, cleared his head a little more. "So," he said, "how are you?" He sighed. "I miss you, Spin-babe." His tone urgent. "What's taking so long?"

"Oh, just some details," she said, trying to stay in the range of drowsy affection, delaying the thing she had wrestled with in her fitful sleep. "Things to settle. For Corey."

"I see," he said. She imagined his face there beyond the staticky rasp of the wires. He was thinking. Finally, he said, "You know I'll help you any way I can." His business voice. The Governor very much awake. "All you have to do is ask."

And she almost did it. Pour it out to him, to his warm voice, to the picture firm in her head of him in the big bed by the window with the light cracking just now over the hills east of town. Pour it out and wait for her punishment, her banishment, her help. Whatever came. But how to start? What was the first word?

She didn't start because she couldn't bear to kill the hope he had for her. His projection of himself through her into the future. Congresswoman Sawnie Darrow, descendant of Governor Billy Miles. A mercy to let it live another day.

He said, "I guess it's rough down there?"

A second time the words were on her lips: *Governor, I am*

having second thoughts about running for Congress. Why not?
A woman could have her second thoughts. He could say,
Well, come home and we'll talk about it. And she could
come home, stand firm in her self-doubt, and finally, he'd
back off.

She was about to say, Yes, there is trouble, but no more
than I can handle. That's what you pay me for, isn't it?
Handling trouble. Was about to when she heard, "Who is
it?" A voice in the bed, a woman's voice. Sawnie flashing
anger. Old goat! Dirty old . . . Then thinking, No, hold. Hearing the Governor's hand cover the phone imperfectly, his
hoarse whisper. "Hush, Martha. This is an important call."

The woman's wounded voice. "You want me to leave,
Bill? I can get dressed and go downstairs if you want me
to." Some woman named Martha.

No one called the Governor Bill. Well, no one but . . .
Martha.

Governor Billy Miles uncovered the phone. Before he
could mint some lame excuse, Sawnie said, "Taking some
comfort in my absence, are you?"

He paused, laughed.

"You randy old dog."

"Not a pretty picture, but . . . I am what nature made me.
I lie here discovered in the light of your wrath. I wish it
was you here."

"Don't tell Martha that."

"She's in the bathroom. She'll be back. Shall I put her on?"

Martha, off: "Oh, Bill, stop it. Don't you have any . . . ?"

Sawnie didn't hear what it was he didn't have any of. He
certainly lacked many of the essential assets of God's Good
Man. She said, "Well, how is she? Is Martha, I mean?"

His voice low, a raspy whisper. "Gallantry forbids me
telling you that she is no S.D."

Sawnie's initials. "I guess I'll thank you for that."

"Come on home, woman. I can't run this state worth a
damn without you."

"It's just other things that go on pretty much
uninterrupted."

"Nature's way."

"Well," she said to the man who still lived in her heart, "get some rest. Tell Martha I said not to wear you out."

"I'll tell her."

"You do that." It was getting full light outside. Somewhere in the scrub east of Corey's bedroom window, Sawnie heard a heron's rusty cry, then its big wings crashing up through the palmetto fronds. She said, "I'll be back when I can."

The Governor cleared his throat. "There's something you're not telling me," he said. "Isn't there?"

"When I can," she repeated.

It was almost light when Harry W. Feather parked in front of Moira's trailer.

He didn't much like it that they'd been in his house. He'd seen two people in the car. He was sure one was Priest. The other probably his buddy, Raymer. Harry coming up from the canal with the bucket and lantern, the Celica hauling ass off his property.

He'd long ago learned to keep nothing that could connect him to the necessary things he did. No cop, searching for something specified in a warrant, was going to find anything else that would make Harry a ward of the state. No illegal firearms, no drugs, no contraband of any kind, no souvenirs from the things Harry had to do. No probable cause. All those things were long gone. Compost.

And the panther? What the hell, the panther was Moira's problem. Harry had tossed the last bits and pieces in the canal. The skin, with the head dried now, its cranial cavity marvelously scoured by those little minnow mouths, was on the car seat beside him.

Harry got out of the Caddy and stripped. He'd fashioned a lanyard for the Llama nine-millimeter. It hung by its trigger guard down his back. He stood naked except for the handgun and a pair of Nikes, shivering, watching the trailer for lights.

Another twenty minutes or so, the sun would break over

the roof of the trailer, hit the tall treetops on the western side of the clearing. Harry reached into the car and pulled out the panther. He slung it over his back, cold-slick and raspy with rock salt, sticking to his skin. He shrugged, adjusting it. He pulled the left foreleg into his left hand, extending the strip of fur along his arm, did the same with the right foreleg. Then he bent at the waist until the panther's heavy head fell forward across his own crown. He snugged his forehead into the cavity of the panther's evacuated cranium.

Harry W. Feather stepped into the swept, pine-needled circle in front of the trailer's door and started to do, as best he could remember it from the Indian book, the circle dance. The great universal dance of despair and hope. The dance of courtship. Holding his arms out like the wings of a bird in flight, bending his knees, clumsily at first, but with increasing skill, he did the deft little jig-step, and made the sounds. Under the wet, gluey skin, he felt himself becoming the panther. His spirit brother.

"Ai-yai-yai-yai," he chanted, a little embarrassed at first, but getting into it. Feeling himself get the rhythm, matching the sounds to the movements of his feet. Starting to move the panther's head in slow circles that meant it was reading the wind, searching for a mate. The panther's necessity was to mate and die. The panther risked death, fought its brother panther, to mate. Harry had taken the life of the panther, and now, according to the book, he owed a debt to its spirit.

When the light was lit inside, Harry was far away from the swept clearing in front of the trailer. He was out in the deepest woods, under a triple canopy of dripping green, roaming with a pride of panthers, bristling at the insults of the alpha male, preparing to unseat this King Cat.

Moira's first shot ripped the loam at Harry's feet. Needles and earth and smoke in a hot spray. He felt the sting of a pellet in his right ankle. It brought him back, back from his spirit journey on the far savanna. He stopped the jig-stepping, the chanting, stood facing Moira, looking up at her from under the panther's chin

"You dirty, filthy fake," she hissed. "You shit-brained, drugstore Hollywood Indian."

Moira struggling with shaking hands to get another shell into the smoking breach of a sawed-off twenty-gauge. From what had hit him, Harry knew she was using bird shot. The twenty was a dirty little weapon, very interventionist. The best intentions in the world sometimes couldn't overcome inferior equipment. On the other hand, Moira's trembling hands had finally fitted the shell. She snapped the breach, cocked the piece. "You killed him. He was worth a hundred of you. He carried genes that went back to unconscious time and you killed him. I'm going to . . ."

Harry raised his arms, moved them like wings in flight, took a firm wide stance in front of Moira, giving her his chest, expanded, the biggest target she could ask for. "I did it for you, Moira," he said. "I killed my spirit brother for you. It is the way of our tribe."

She extended the gun toward him, both her small hands on the pistol grip. All of her, woman and weapon, trembling. "You disgusting piece of mongrel filth," she hissed.

"Go ahead, Moira, take my spirit. I am the panther. I offer it to you." Harry knowing she couldn't do it. Believing the first shot had been a warning, an intentional miss. Maybe so close because Moira didn't know about the shot patterns of short-barreled fowling pieces. But only her ignorance was dangerous. Fear, anger, and the wrong equipment should always be respected, but Harry W. Feather was willing to bet his life, bet this new-born Alpha Panther Man, that Moira Big Breath couldn't shoot him in cold blood.

She aimed at him, hands shaking, pulled the trigger. In the flash and roar and shock, Harry knew it was all right. At the last instant, she'd pulled to the right. He could hear the pellets rattling off the tin roof of the potting shed, twenty yards behind him. He could see it in her eyes.

He remembered the Cowgirl out there on 41, the road Moira wanted to take back for the tribe. He remembered when he knew he had the Cowgirl. It was when she swerved, almost did herself in to keep from hitting a rabbit. A goddamn scrub bunny. Now he saw the same thing in Moira's eyes. He saw mercy.

And Moira's eyes were crying. She lowered the shotgun, trying to get another red shell out of her skirt pocket, trying to fit it into the breach. And crying. She moaned and Harry noticed the white lump rising on her wrist. The gun's recoil had bruised her good, maybe broken one of those delicate wrist bones. Harry had read about them: radius, ulna? One of those, maybe? Moira couldn't hold the gun up anymore. It hung at her side, smoking, the red shell rattling at her feet, rolling down the trailer's stoop to rest at Harry's feet.

Harry did the dance for Moira. "Ai-yai-yai-yai," but she didn't look at him. At Harry wearing the panther skin, doing the circle dance. She looked off at the tree line like she expected something, someone. He took a step forward, held out his hand to her. "Come on, Moira." Looking up at her from under the panther's face. Those milky eyes, that tongue hanging down Harry's forehead. "I'm offering you my panther spirit." He took the shotgun from her hand, dropped it by the stoop.

She backed away, holding her hurt wrist, moaning. She lacked the heart to make it any harder. That was good.

Harry drew her down the steps into his arms, sheltering her under the panther's skin.

"Where ... Where ... Where are you taking me?" she whispered. Not so hard anymore, Moira. Not so Barnard College tough, Moira. Reduced to the essence of her own worst fears, Moira. Going with Harry now.

He led her around the trailer to the path, led her to the clearing in the woods behind the trailer. In the clearing, she seemed to know. Seemed to guess what would happen.

She said, "Please, Harry, don't. In the name of Jesus, Harry."

Harry held her by her shoulders, lifted her chin with his hand, careful not to shake her, hurt the broken wrist. "Jesus?" he asked, his voice firm. "Jesus, Moira? Jesus is an idea you gave up a long time ago. You went to New York and learned that Jesus was a mechanism of white oppression. Didn't you?"

She nodded. She was gone now, was Moira. Far away. Maybe she'd gone out to the savanna, out there under the canopy of green where the panther pride was lazing in sunlight that filtered through the pine boughs. Maybe she was sleek from a supper of white-tailed deer and ready to entice the alpha male. Back up to him, taunting, biting his flanks a little to excite him. Swipe at him with her claws half sheathed. Ready to present. Harry hoped so.

"What about it?" he asked. "Moira?"

"Whatever," she said. Barely audible. Gone. Far away.

Harry helped her get her clothes off, helped her kneel, let her put her right elbow down, even though it skewed her a bit, so that she wouldn't suffer from the broken wrist.

It was sunrise, a golden light brushing the waving tops of the Australian pines, a morning breeze making the needles hiss and rush, when Harry entered Moira. Working, lifting his head to the warming heavens, concentrating until he was out on the savanna again, the Alpha Man, surrounded by lesser males who carried the long scars of their submission to him. With the females of his choosing, he was lying in sunlight, the intoxicating perfume of his favorite female coming to him on the breeze. He was rising, rising to meet her, to mount her. To make her his, to make her bear, to pass the spirit to her. The spirit he had taken. Rising to pay that debt to a spirit brother.

Moira fell under him, under the weight of his frenzy, his clarifying vision. She fell just as Harry came. And came out, projecting his seed in diminishing arcs at her buttocks, then at the dark loam plowed by his urging knees. Moira lay there trembling, cradling the broken wrist under her. She'd ruined it. Humiliated him again. Just when he'd married the world and myth, was rising heroic to become the Panther God, she had let him down.

Harry threw off the panther skin, shrugged the Llama around to his chest, and felt it cold and exact in his hand.

He worked the slide. Saw the glint of brass jacket between bolt and barrel.

Moira heard. Moira said, "No, Harry. Please." She sounded tired. Worn out. And then she seemed to realize something.

"My God, Harry, you're doing this for him. Aren't you? You're working for Coltis. Don't do it for him, Harry."

Harry was past talking, almost. She had his curiosity up now, did Moira. "I ain't ... I'm not saying you're right, Moira, but for the sake of discussion, why not? You tell me why not, Moira?"

Was that a smile that wrinkled Moira's mouth? Even now, a smile? Harry didn't think so. He didn't see how it could be. She said, "Because, Harry, he'll do the same thing to you. Isn't that obvious?"

Harry didn't think so and told her so.

She said, "Harry, listen," her voice all weak and pleading. "I can give you something on Coltis. I swear I can. You just give me some time, some time to think about it. I can put you up on him. I swear it, Harry."

But Harry was tired of this, of Moira. Old Going-to-Parties Moira.

The pistol shot was dampered, contained in the clearing. Like a shot fired down a well, like the sound of a pile driver thumping a pile into wet earth. Moira lay in a spreading pool of blood. Cordite smoke rose to Harry's nostrils, pleasant and thrilling, drifting past his eyes, thinning into the lower branches. Harry W. Feather covered Moira carefully with the panther skin, placing the animal's head over the wound at her temple. Taking the spent brass casing and Moira's clothes, he walked naked down the path.

It was clean inside Moira's trailer. She'd scrubbed everything. Harry hoped she'd done her work well enough to eliminate his own fingerprints. But what the hell, everybody knew that he and Moira were friends. No reason he should worry about being here.

He took the sawed-off twenty-gauge and the shells Moira had dropped and put them in the Caddy. Then he went back into the trailer and did a very careful search of the documents Moira had neatly stacked back on the table. She'd told him she was writing a book, all about that common language she had with the panther. Who knew what was in Moira's book? Hell, maybe she'd written about Harry W. Feather. If she had, there might be some, well, embarrassing things in it. Harry couldn't take that chance. And maybe he'd find something interesting to show to Mr. Coltis: Look here what the woman was doing to you. This is your land she's writing about here. Look what I did for you, Mr. Coltis.

Harry put the documents and all of Moira's computer diskettes in the Caddy. The shotgun would go into a canal along with the Llama and Moira's clothes.

Harry took the plastic Baggie from his glove box and walked back to the trailer. Using the tip of his Buck knife, he reached into the Baggie and lifted out the Bic disposable lighter he'd found on his kitchen floor. Left there by his visitors. He dropped it just inside Moira's door.

Harry thought it was a very good bet that even Bryce Nailor would notice it. Even Bryce would have the brains to send it to the police forensic lab, see if it had Raymer Harney's prints on it. Or, better yet, much better, the prints of the Former Great. Prints from the hand that had snagged the One-Second Pass.

36

▲▲▲▲▲▲▲▲▲▲▲▲▲▲▲▲▲▲▲

A ground fog had come in fast, as it sometimes did in these lowlands. When Lofton Coltis heard the rumble of Harry Feather's preposterous old Cadillac, he walked out into the gray mist to meet his man. His man who had called and asked to speak to him this morning. Passing Feather's car, he kept on, fast, toward the old shed where the ancient sprayer lay on its punctured tires. Feather got out and hurried to fall into step. Coltis liked it that the smaller man had to skip every third or fourth stride to stay with him.

Coltis had been reading Machiavelli, a favorite of his, who said that a prince should be loved and feared. And if not loved, certainly feared. Coltis's long strides wouldn't make Harry Feather fear him, but they'd take him faster to the place where fear waited.

Coltis expected Feather to start jabbering, but Feather was silent. Maybe the boy was learning something, getting somewhere after all. Stranger things had happened. Coltis had to decide if Feather was to be kept or discarded. If kept, in what capacity; if lost, cleanly and quickly.

Inside the close, hot shed, Coltis turned and looked down at Feather. "What do you want?" he said. "Tell me now. I have to know and it's in your best interest to be honest with me." The fog was already solid outside.

Coltis looked across Feather's shoulder at the bench where the big rubber glove lay, thick and stiff, a fresh black gouge of parathion lying in its palm.

Harry W. Feather tried to keep his breathing level, his eyes straight on Coltis's own flat gray disks. But it was hot in the shed and his silk suit was sticking to him all over and he could feel the beads forming with an oily heaviness on his forehead. He wanted to take out his long silk hanky and blot them, but now, in Coltis's presence, the hanky and the suit he wore seemed strange, silly. Coltis wore his usual simple white shirt, khaki pants, scuffed work boots. Coltis walking him out here through the fog like he was a little dog that needed to shit but not too close to the house. Bringing him into this shed with its smell of something very unpleasant. Something Harry didn't like at all.

When Harry had finally called, suggested they meet to talk about his future, it felt very strange. But then, Harry was tired. He'd had a busy night. And first, he'd called Amelia W. Feather.

"Tell me, Momma. What's he gonna say to me? What should I say to him?"

Harry with that empty feeling in his belly, hearing his old mother breathe on the other end, the television muttering in her shitty little room in Coltis's house. Some cop show she liked to watch. His mother, old Amelia, Lofton Coltis's devoted housekeeper, had said a strange thing. "You watch out, Harry. You talk to Mr. Coltis? You ask him for something? You watch out."

"Why, Ma?" Harry trying to keep the excitement out of his voice. The strange thing he felt. "Why should I watch out? What's old Bull Sugar got up his sleeve?"

His momma wouldn't say more. Harry trying everything to get her to tell him what she's thinking. This watch-out thing. Finally Harry realizing his mom's got a conflict of interest. She's talking to her offbeam boy, Harry, and she's feeling maybe some little tickle of mother love down there in her withered old belly. But she's got her own interests to look out for. Her bottle of Lemon Pledge and that ham gravy she's gonna microwave all over Mr. Bull Sugar's eggs in the morning. A conflict of interest.

Finally, Harry had to get that thing in his voice. The thing that always worked. He hated to use it with his mother, but business was business. He said, "Ma, you don't tell me what you mean here, I'm gonna have to fire up the Caddy. Come over there."

Not the words, but the thing that did it. The thing in the voice.

Finally, his mother said, "Clinton. He didn't watch out. He took his stupid redneck self into that shed. That shed where Mr. Coltis keeps that old tractor. They went in there together. You be careful, Harry."

All he could get out of her. The hackles rising on the back of his neck. Harry remembering how Coltis had asked him, all nice and solicitous, about Clinton's health. That whopping case of brain dysfunction. Old Clinton finally dying in convulsions that lasted ten hours. The doctors watching him buck like a slaughterhouse pig and saying they wished his damn heart wasn't so strong. Wished the electricity that kept lashing his limbs would just blow out his damn heart and let him die.

And finally old Clinton bucked himself to death. Old Clinton who had gone into a shed with Mr. Coltis. Mr. Coltis and an old tractor. Clinton saying those strange things at the end, things about Mr. Coltis. It was a mystery. Or maybe old Amelia had gone around the bend. Sniffed one too many dust rags soaked with Lemon Pledge.

Now Harry considered Lofton Coltis's question, thought about it, shifting his eyes from Coltis's flat, gray disks to

the old rusted tractor that rested nearby in the puddles of
its blown-out tires.

"Like we said, Mr. Coltis. I want to move up. It's the
American dream. Be upwardly mobile. Get a promotion.
You decide what it is. I'm reasonable. But, hey, you got to
know my worth. You got to know my capabilities. What I
can do. What I've done already. We got to talk about that
too. We get all that out, about, you know, how I'm valuable
and all, then we decide what's next for me. Is that fair?"

Jesus, Harry, shut the fuck up! What is this, verbal prema-
ture ejaculation? Don't overwhelm the man. Less is more,
Harry. Jesus! Harry trying to stay calm. Not let his hand
reach for the hanky. Feeling the sweat run from his temples
down into his collar. Wondering why Coltis didn't sweat.
Why he didn't say anything. Why he was smiling.

Lofton Coltis took a step back, leaned against the bench,
the black glove lying palm up an easy distance from his
right hand. He rested his arms across his chest, took a deep
breath, composed his face in patience. He said, "Tell me,
Harry. Tell me about what you are worth to me. Tell me
everything you've done." Feather relaxed a little and that
was good. Feather started to talk.

Harry W. Feather told Lofton Coltis about how he'd gone
to Corey Darrow's house the night he'd killed her. Going
in the back window, leaving no signs of entry. Very careful,
Harry, looking for that computer file. Knowing that Coltis
would like it if he found it. Got it the hell out of there in
case there was an investigation and the cops came looking
for it. Harry watching Coltis's face all the time. Liking the
way the man was calm, ready to listen. The way he leaned
back against the old bench, relaxed, his eyes on Harry's face.
Taking it all in. Weighing it.

"I was gonna tell you about that, Mr. Coltis. The day I
came out here and you was, I mean you were, in the cane
field and those busses arrived. You didn't treat me too good
that day. You were real short with me that day. So I just

didn't say anything about going the extra mile for you. Looking for that document."

Coltis nodded, smiled. The smile like something that crawled out of his mouth to rest on his lips for a second or two, then went back inside. Harry couldn't tell what Coltis thought of his saying that, about the way he was treated. Another guy, most guys, they'd say: Sorry, Harry. I was having a bad day. Didn't mean anything by it. Not Coltis. Coltis just listening.

"There's this other thing," Harry said. Time to let Coltis know what kind of a guy he was, how he was always thinking. Doing the benefits, the costs. Like they taught in that Harvard MBA.

"There's this Indian girl, this woman I know. Moira Breath is her name." Harry suddenly ashamed to say it, Moira's whole name. To say it out loud, Moira Big Breath. Ashamed because it was just another stupid-ass Indian name. Just like his own name, Harry White Feather. Harry closing his eyes and seeing Moira now, lying out there where he'd left her. Dead how long now? He couldn't calculate it exactly.

"Anyway," he said, "this Indian girl, Moira, she's got all these plans. Says she's gonna take your land away. Take the road, you know, 41, and all the land on either side of it, miles in both directions. Says she's gonna deal with you like a sovereign nation. I tell you, Mr. Coltis, I think this woman plans to give you a very good fucking. And she's educated, Barnard College. She's nobody's fool, old Moira."

Harry saw it then in Coltis's eyes. That thing you got from living on the same land for generations and watching generations of people like Harry come and stand in front of you and shift their weight from one muddy boot to the other and ask you for things, little things. Or tell you exactly what you wanted to hear. This wasn't what Coltis had wanted to hear. Harry lost the heat when he saw the thing in Coltis's eyes. Coltis didn't let it show long. Coltis beat the thing back into its cave after only a second or two, but Harry had seen it.

Harry went ahead and told Coltis all about Moira's plans. And he made his offer. "I can take care of the woman for you, Mr. Coltis. Just say the word. I can take care of her and you won't have any more problems from Indians around here. Not after this Moira is gone."

Coltis was shaking his head now. Shaking it slow, his eyes closed. Harry didn't like it. He'd fucked up some way he didn't understand. Jesus, he wished he knew what Moira and Coltis had talked about that night at the party. He was soaking now in the shed, and the smell, that chemical smell was making his head light already. He wanted to get some air, and he wanted to wipe the sweat off his face, and he wanted Coltis to open his eyes and say something.

He said, "Mr. Coltis, what you say we finish talking about this outside. It's hot in here."

There was a big black rubber glove on the bench next to Coltis and it held something. Something that looked like axle grease. That glove lying there palm up like somebody had cut off the hand of a large rubber man. The Michelin man. Harry remembered Clinton, what Amelia W. Feather had said about Clinton and the tractor.

Lofton Coltis liked the fumes, that heady, stringent smell, the concentrated power in that gluey substance blooming into the room. He said, "Harry, I told you we can't afford to be seen together."

Feather smiled or tried to and said, "Mr. Coltis, my car is right out there in the yard. Anybody comes by here, they gotta know I'm here. If we're taking, what you call it, precautions, we need a better plan."

Feather had seen it now, seen the glove. Feather took a step back, glanced at the glove again, rubbed one finger under his nose as though trying to stop the fumes from entering his body. And what Feather had said about the car out in the yard was not lost on Lofton Coltis. But the car was lost in the fog.

Coltis hadn't told Harry Feather about the computer file. Certainly hadn't suggested that Feather search for the file.

The possibility of the girl's holding some hard copy had been a risk Coltis was willing to take. Coltis had accessed the Water Management database himself, used his own utility software to remove Clinton's user code and deep-six the file Corey Darrow had input. He'd done it even before Feather had killed the girl. Feather must have picked it up around town, the idea about the file. Coltis didn't like it. Feather deciding on his own to go see what Corey Darrow had left lying around her house.

And now, this thing with the Indian woman. Coltis remembered her at the party. Her pretty face and legs and that glowing ocher skin. Skin like the leather covers of some of his books, books that told the stories of what men like him and women like her had always done together. They had always agreed, eventually. Moira Breath, the Barnard beauty. Coltis had endowed her scholarship to Barnard, it and many others for members of the local tribes. He had considered telling her so that night in his study. He took a deep breath of the sweet, powerful effluvium from the glove behind and said, "Leave the woman alone, Harry. You don't need to do anything about an Indian with a crack-brained plan to take away my land. Things have gotten very strange in this state in the last ten years, but they aren't that strange yet. You just sit tight where the woman is concerned, you understand me? Feather?"

Feather took another step back. Coltis could see in his eyes the natural hatred his kind held for a Coltis. And something else. The gathering recognition of what was here in the shed, what had waited here for him. Maybe how close he had come to that thing.

Feather's eyes sly now. Feather said, "Mr. Coltis, did you hear about Clinton Reynolds? He died, old Clinton. He died in convulsions and, what I heard, it wasn't pretty. They think it was some, what you call it, real *old* kind of poison he got into. A kind that nobody's used around here in a long time. That's what I heard anyway."

Feather glancing at the glove again, holding a finger under his nose like a man trying not to sneeze. Coltis considered it again. The lunge for the glove, the leap at Feather. The gloved hand tight over Feather's mouth while he struggled. Then letting go, stepping back. Letting Feather run if he liked running.

But it wasn't going to work, not now, not this way. Coltis knew it. Feather's hand was in his pocket now, where, most likely, a knife rested. Best now to make a graceful exit.

Coltis shifted his weight away from the glove. "I want to thank you, Harry, for telling me about the Indian woman. I'll look into it. What you suggested is just not necessary."

Another step backward and Feather would be out of the shed. Coltis couldn't let the man walk out on him. He shoved off from the bench and walked fast past Feather into the heavy fog. Heading for the house. Feather following, catching up.

Coltis said, "I'm going to take care of you, Harry. You think about what you want. Submit a specific request, we'll see where we can fit you in. We'll talk again when your position solidifies. For now, I just want you to know I'm going to take care of you. All right, Harry?"

Coltis stopped beside the preposterous peacock Cadillac. He bent and opened the door for Feather. Feather standing there trying to get as much fresh air into his lungs as he could. The gaudy silk suit dripping off him like so much purple gruel. Feather got into the car.

"All right, Mr. Coltis. Maybe it wasn't such a good idea about Moira. I just wanted you to know I was thinking. Had our best interest at heart. Like that."

"Thank you again, Harry." Lofton Coltis closed the car door.

When Harry W. Feather started the Caddy, Coltis was already halfway to the house. Doing that straight-ahead military walk of his. Harry leaned back, rested his dizzy head, and sucked a lungful of the foggy morning air.

Jesus, so that was how Coltis had done Clinton. Why hadn't Harry gotten it when his mom had talked about the shed, about Clinton going in there? Harry thinking, what the hoo-hah, this guy's got a thing for old tractors.

Harry closed his eyes and saw that glove Clinton had worn, a white cotton gardening glove. Clinton looking like some cartoon character, wearing a white glove two or three days before falling on his ass, raving in his office at Water Management.

Jesus, Harry, the guy was gonna do you right there in the shed the same way. Changed his mind, that's all. For some reason, decided not to. And now he's gonna take care of you. You just consolidate your position a little and he's gonna take care of you. Right.

Harry started the engine, his head clearing, the sweat drying on him. He saw Moira again, out there where he'd left her. Her pretty head in a pool of black blood. He'd figured it wrong with Moira, thinking Coltis would like his idea. Well, to Harry's way of thinking, Coltis just didn't know what was good for him. Guy hadn't done costs and benefits the right way. Old Moira, she would have made it hot for Mr. Coltis. Very hot.

In this state, Mr. Coltis, things are stranger than you think.

Harry pushed the Caddy out to the hard road, getting some rubber, punching her through a big bank of ground fog. And getting stranger. Oh, yes.

37

▲▲▲▲▲▲▲▲▲▲▲▲▲▲▲▲▲

Eddie took a quick shower at Raymer's apartment and read the note Raymer had left him. "Where are you, buddy? Keeping out of trouble? Call me at the office."

He drove to Corey's house, half expecting to find it empty. But Sawnie's car was there in the yard, soaked with dew. The house was quiet, sleeping. Eddie raised his hand to knock. The door opened.

"Jesus, what are you doing here? You scared me."

"Sorry. You don't need to be scared." She looked like hell, but she was smiling.

"You look tired," she said. "No, I take that back. You look like hell."

Eddie laughed. "I came to take you to breakfast."

"Twenty minutes to get ready," she said. "I'll meet you at the hotel."

It was a ground-foggy morning, the streets of Okee City shrouded, the trees dripping. The lighted restaurant of the

De Soto Hotel a beacon in the gray mist. Eddie parked beside Bryce Nailor's cruiser.

Inside, it was warm and full of the good smell of coffee and frying bacon. Eddie took a table by the window, watching cars and people swim past in the fog. Nailor sat in the back, same booth, hunched over pancakes and the *Miami Herald*. He looked up, double-took Eddie, then nodded.

Sawnie drove up in the rented Chevy. She got out, looked around her at the gray cloak of fog, and then sighted Eddie through the glowing window. As she walked toward the door, Eddie let himself think about a future. Years of the two of them meeting like this, her coming to him tired but smiling. Eddie rising to pull out a chair. She sat down across from him.

"So," she said, "you still want to go see Feather?"

Things to do before they could have that future. Eddie said, "Maybe he'll tell us something. Something he thinks makes him look good."

"The guy's crazy," Sawnie said, "and we don't know where he lives." She gestured toward the phone on the wall. "I doubt he's in the phone book."

"I know where he lives," Eddie said. He told her about his night's odyssey. How he'd started out driving just to drive, letting her guess his reason for that. How he'd decided somewhere in the middle of the night to find Feather. The directions from scared guys in convenience stores, guys who'd sold cigarettes and dirty magazines to Feather. Guys who had looked into Feather's eyes.

He told her about Feather's strange dark house, the rows of books, everything in its place, the compulsive neatness, and then the kitchen sink. As though the heart of order were violent death. The reeking blue and red entrails Eddie had thought were human. About the Indian woman, Moira, mistaking him for Feather in the dark. Putting the chopped shotgun in his face. About her promise to kill Feather.

He told her about the strange little red-faced man Moira had met who had told her he was looking for a plant the

Indians called *tokeepah*. Burns Your Tongue. A folk medicine
of some kind. About Moira's telling this guy where to find it.

"Where?" Sawnie asked.

"She told him he could find it on Coltis land."

"She say where? Where *exactly* on Coltis land?"

"She wouldn't tell me that."

"Coy little tart."

"Something like that. We've got to talk to her. She's the
only person around here except Corey who ever talked to
this mystery guy about what he was doing in the county.
Maybe this Moira will get a little more communicative when
she meets you. You tell her about Corey, what you think
Coltis has to do with all this."

"A girl-to-girl type of thing, right?"

"It might work."

"Jesus." She whistled. "And I thought I had a night."

Eddie said, "I had your night *and* mine, Sawnie." His
head singing with lack of sleep and coffee and thinking
about verb tenses.

She looked at him for a long time. "I hope that's your
way of expressing empathy."

Eddie nodded, sipped the good black bean. "It is."

"Look," she said, "you didn't think I was a virgin, did
you?"

Eddie shook his head. What could he say? Feelings were
irrational. He was worried about the man in her heart and
couldn't say so. Later maybe, but not this morning. This
whole thing was about as irrational as it got. Maybe that
was what made it so powerful.

Eddie tried to smile right. He said, "I didn't think you
were a virgin. And you sure didn't think I was either." He
picked up a napkin, took out a pen, and scribbled "Sorry"
on it. "Look," he said, "I'm issuing this blanket apology."
He handed it to her.

"Covers everything past, present, and future. Doesn't ab-
solve me of any on-the-spot de facto necessity to apologize.
It's really just a gesture of ongoing goodwill. It's good any
place I have good intentions on deposit. It's like a letter of

credit. You carry it with you wherever we go. I'm an ass-hole, you take it out and show it to me and I make good on it." He was rambling, it was crazy, but he was smiling right. He could feel it.

She laughed, folded it. Put it in her purse with a ceremonial flourish. "Okay," she said, "for now. But this thing runs out, I'm gonna make you write me a new one." She put her hand over his on the table. "Now what do we do? We go see this Moira?"

"Not yet. I say we stick with the original plan. We go see Feather."

"Let's call him," Swanie said. "Wake his ass up and get this show on the road."

"Sure," Eddie said. "I call him, or you want to?"

"You call him. You were his guest last night. He's used to having you around."

Eddie went to the phone. Feather's number was not in the white pages under Feather, Harry White.

Eddie decided on directory assistance. His quarter was in the slot when the big Caddy stopped outside. Feather looking out his window at the rear end of Eddie's Celica. Reading the tag number, looking at a piece of paper in his hand, back at the tag, then up at the restaurant window. At Eddie. Feather smiling through the fog.

Eddie went back to the table. "No need to call Feather," he said.

Harry W. Feather saw Bryce Nailor sit up straight back there in what the town called his home away from home. His throne room, old Bryce. Bryce gave Harry the usual hard look. Tough, that look, steel Rebar in there, under the concrete. Look that said: *Fuck with me and you go to slamtown.* All cops had it. Harry wondered if they practiced in the mirror. Took a course in cop school: Hard Look 101. Advanced Hard Look.

He winked at Bryce, walked to the counter, and ordered coffee. Checked himself in the mirror behind the counter. He'd changed out of his sweaty clothes after talking to Coltis. He was wearing his best suit, a lavender silk number he'd picked up on Calle Ocho in Miami. Set him back a bundle, that suit. But damn, he looked good in it. Sure as hell lit up this shitty place.

He was wearing it special for the Former Great and his girlfriend. Returning the visit actually. Guy comes sneaking into Harry's house at night, dressed to creep, lighting his Bic to look around. Harry W. Feather returns the favor, only he doesn't creep. No sneaking for Harry. Harry comes to the front door, knocks, dressed in his best like a gent. Only there's nobody home. Not at Raymer Harney's rat-hole apartment, not at the Cowgirl's house.

A little drive through town had done it. Small towns had their advantages. Everybody knew everybody. Here they were, Bryce Nailor, only law west of Stuart, and Harry's two new friends, Priest and the Cowgirl's sister. Harry picked up his cup, nodded again to Bryce, and walked over to sit with the cute couple. Halfway there and you could hear pins dropping all over the De Soto Hotel.

Sawnie watched Eddie stand as Feather approached. She didn't like this, even if the fat sheriff was there. Even if Feather wouldn't do anything stupid in a public place. Eddie's standing was what men did when a woman approached a table, at least some of them still did. And come to think of it, there was something feminine about Feather. Maybe something only a woman would notice. In the way he mixed colors, in the smooth young skin of his face, the fine long eyelashes, the scooped hollows under the cheekbones, the way he seemed to flow across the floor, his knees barely rising.

Sawnie had to keep herself from edging a few inches away from the table when Feather sat down. She could see Eddie looking him over, his eyes searching for something. She remembered the knife coming out of Feather's pocket in the bar. Just suddenly there. Feather risking his neck literally, so that he could slip the blade out of his silk pants. And he was wearing silk again.

* * *

275

"Sit down, man," Feather said, "you making me nervous standing there like that."

Eddie sat down, pushing his chair back, giving himself room to rise. He looked at the table in front of him—a plate of congealed scrambled eggs, coffee, half a glass of juice. Near his right hand, a kitchen knife. He said, "So, what can we do for you, Harry?"

Feather looked at Eddie for a beat, then at Sawnie. Eddie remembered him apologizing before leaving the Cane Cutter. Telling her that living with trashy people made you forget how to act when you met somebody decent. Now, Feather's eyes treated Sawnie like a centerfold, ate her like a dirty movie. Going over her inch by inch, a sneaky little smile growing on his face. Sawnie taking it as long as she could, then looking away at the fat sheriff, who was frankly watching them now. Feather finished the inspection and moved his eyes to Eddie.

"I had a visitor last night, two actually." Feather put a slip of paper on the table, put his hand over it like it was a playing card he wouldn't show yet. "Somebody driving some Japanese hunk of grunt. Some kind of Nagasaki Nutbucket. Tag number"—Feather took his hand off the piece of paper, turned it over, pretended to read it—"tag number FG 260 Q." He put the slip in the breast pocket of his pimp suit. Both hands under the table. "You recognize the number?"

"No," Eddie said. "I'm one of those guys who doesn't go around with a lot of useless information in his head." Eddie touched his temple. "I need to know my tag number, I go out and look."

"You got a head full of important stuff, right? Educated stuff? Legal stuff?"

"That's right."

Feather lifted his hands slowly above the table, showing them to Eddie, then picked up his coffee cup. He sipped, looked at Sawnie. "How 'bout you, Ms. Darrow? You recognize that tag number?"

"I'm like Mr. Priest here," she said, her voice low and steady. "I try to keep it swept out up there."

Feather shook his head, gave a sad smile. "Facts, important figures, state matters, am I right?"

"That's right." Sawnie's smile was sad too.

Feather shook his head. He was the poor, sad slob. Completely outclassed by two city folks who didn't remember a tag number.

"Well," he said, "these visitors I had, two of them actually. They went in my house without being invited. I guess they had a look around, I don't know. I don't know what they thought they were gonna find. Wasn't anything *to* find, but anyway ... So, naturally, I'm a little disturbed about this. It's rude. People going in a man's house when he's not there. Looking around. It's rude and people ought to know better. People driving shitty Japanese cars."

Feather looked at both of them, his eyes as methodical as if he were aiming, pulling a trigger, hearing some silent explosion that obliterated both of them. He blinked and said, "And leaving things lying around. People stupid and discourteous enough to leave things lying around."

"What kind of things?" Eddie asked. He knew it now. Feather had more in mind than simple harassment. More method than the snake that stares at the nest for a while, making the little birds get very still. Then crawls away.

Harry W. Feather shook his finger slowly at the Former Great and said, "Things, man. Things lying around in my house, man. It's disgusting. It's rude and it's not ... clean. You know what I mean?"

Harry could see that the Former Great was in a new place now. Harry wasn't sure where. It wasn't the land of very scared, but it was way beyond worried. It left worried way back there in another time zone. And the Cowgirl's gorgeous sister, she was turning Harry on big time. Frightened women just had that effect on him. Harry remembered that night on the highway. Flying along in the dark, window to window with the Cowgirl and suddenly getting that old familiar feeling. That wouldn't-it-be-nice feeling. That soft and sweet idea about pulling her over and suggesting that the two of them do the Big Horizontal. Harry had missed his opportunity with the Cowgirl, but here she was, replicated like in some sci-fi flicker, right here in front of him. Right here in the De Soto Hotel.

Harry decided to ignore the Former Great for a while. Harry could do that as well as he could do anything, ignore. It could be a damned useful skill. Ignore pain, distraction, annoying people. It was all part of the Indian thing, the warrior thing.

He said, "So, Ms. Darrow. Did you come out last night in a 1990 Toyota Celica, tag number FG 260 Q, and invade my home? Because if it was you, it's all right. I don't mind that. I'm still feeling a little bad about what I said in the bar the other night, so I figure I owe you one. I don't even mind you leaving things lying around my place. I don't like you bringing any football pussies with you and like that, but, hey, what the hoo-hah, right?"

Harry smiled, big and bright, not looking at the Former Great. Ignoring. Watching the woman carefully.

And very, very surprised at what she did.

Sawnie picked up her coffee cup, stuck her middle finger in it to test it for heat. She flicked the finger in Feather's face and when he closed his eyes, poured the rest of the coffee into the cut between his pectorals. Right where the pink silk shirt with the palm trees on it was open to the second button.

Feather went to his toes and grabbed his shirt with both hands trying to keep the hot brown coffee from getting to his trousers. Too late for that. And Eddie rising too, Sawnie catching the glint of a knife in Eddie's hand. And then the fat sheriff, moving faster than she'd ever seen a fat man go, with his two hammy hands on Feather's upper arms, holding him, whispering in his ear. "Easy now, Harry. Just take it easy. It's just a little coffee. Nothing to get excited about."

When Sawnie looked at Eddie again, the knife was back

on the tabletop. She looked back at Harry Feather and watched a hurricane of emotion fly through his eyes. From shock to fury to resistance of Nailor's hands to something sly and even a little excited. The kind of thing you saw in the eyes of the person who had recognized an escalation and admired it. A person who liked a good scrap.

Sawnie hadn't risen, hadn't moved. She lifted the finger that had flicked the coffee into Feather's eyes and sucked it. She smiled and said, "Mr. Feather, you promised the other night you wouldn't talk that trash in front of me. I took you at your word. I even forgave the insult. I don't understand your behavior at all. Do you want to sit down and explain it to me?"

She looked at Eddie, who shook his head and sat down again.

She looked at Sheriff Nailor, who let go of Feather's arms, brushed the sleeves of Feather's jacket, plucked at the wrinkles his big hands had made.

She looked at Feather, who was smiling now and picking at his floppy silk trousers, lank with the long, steaming stains down the legs.

A waitress appeared at Feather's side with a wet cloth.

Feather said, "Yeah, let's all sit down here. Let's finish talking. That's what we need to do."

He looked over his shoulder at Bryce Nailor. "It's all right, Bryce. You can go on back to your office." He looked at the waitress with the cloth. "'No, Celia. I'm wet enough already."

"You sure?" the waitress asked.

Feather smiled at Sawnie. "Celia here doesn't recognize dry clean only. Do you, Celia?"

Celia rolled her eyes, departed.

Eddie looked at the knife on the table. Lifted his right hand and looked at it, thanking the good reflex that hadn't even asked him if he wanted to pick up the instrument. He'd jumped when Feather did, better prepared than he'd been the last time. He looked at Sawnie, trying not to send

her a message he'd regret. That she was matching Eddie
mistake for mistake. He'd gone out to Feather's house on a
whim. He'd left something there apparently. Or somebody
had. Maybe the Indian girl. And now Sawnie had assaulted
Feather in front of the county sheriff.

The three of them sat in the quiet. Then Sawnie said, "No,
Mr. Feather. I didn't go to your house last night. And I
don't know anything about anybody going there. Anybody
leaving anything there."

Feather nodded, looked down, plucked at the crotch of
his wet trousers. His wet shirt. He shook his head. Gave
Sawnie the you're-quite-a-gal grin that country boys know
from very early. Before Feather could open his mouth, get
the madness rolling again, she said, "But Eddie and I had
planned to see you today. We'd like to ask you some
questions."

Harry Feather pushed himself back in his chair, plucked
at his wet shirt again. "Ask me. Harry W. Feather at your
service."

Sawnie looked at Eddie, giving him a chance to go ahead.

Eddie said, "'We'd like to talk to you about your arrange-
ment with Lofton Coltis."

There it was. Eddie's breathing quickened, his stomach
contracting unpleasantly, meaningfully. He liked the surprise in Feather's face. Feather wondering what they knew.
How they'd gotten from a dead girl in a canal to Lofton
Coltis to Harry Feather. What had Eddie picked up from
his midnight visit to Feather's house?

Feather stopped it, the thing in his eyes. Steadied his
smile. "Listen," he said, "I got to get out of these wet
clothes. Why don't you come on out to my place. This time,
I'm inviting you. Tell you what. I'll show you what my
visitors left last night."

38

▲▲▲▲▲▲▲▲▲▲▲▲▲▲▲▲▲▲

I've got to warn him," Sawnie said.

Standing with Sawnie at the pay phone, Eddie watched Feather through the glass doors of the De Soto Hotel. Out in the fog, Feather smiled, waved as he walked to the big white Caddy. Before getting in, Feather plucked at the crotch of his coffee-soaked silk suit. He shook his finger at Sawnie. Naughty girl.

"Why now?" Eddie said. "Why not wait a day?"

Sawnie had told him she had to warn the Governor before they went to Feather's house. Before they went any further with this thing. If she did, Eddie thought, the Governor would find some way to stop them. The Governor would start damage control, compromise, politics, and they'd end up with nothing.

"Look," he said, "I understand your . . . loyalty. But can't you wait? See what Feather has to say. Maybe he's worried under that silk suit. Maybe he'd like to deal. Give us Coltis. You never know what he might do."

"Yeah," she said, standing at the phone in the hotel lobby. "I get that impression real strong. That's why I'm gonna warn the Governor."

"Okay," Eddie said. He left her, stepped out on the street. A block down, Feather's Caddy rocked to a stop at the town's one traffic light. The light changed, and the fog closed around Feather's red taillights as he headed out into all that cane. Feather going to get out of those wet clothes.

Eddie turned back to the hotel, watched Sawnie through the glass door. Her lips moving, head nodding yes, then shaking no. The stricken look coming to her face. She hung up, pushed through the door into the fog.

"He didn't come in this morning. Missed a breakfast with the Speaker of the House. They don't know where he is. They're all scrambling like crazy to rearrange his schedule. Keep the media out of it. Hell, they thought I knew where he was. When I said I didn't, you could hear hearts stopping all over the office."

"What does it mean?" Eddie watching her, seeing what was in her eyes. The same look she'd had when she'd said, "I had a man." Something there bigger than loyalty, a lot bigger.

She said, "I don't know. But I'll tell you one thing. The Governor doesn't do anything, not even disappear, without a damned good reason."

Inside the hotel, Sheriff Nailor pushed up from his breakfast, adjusted his pistol belt, and walked to the cash register. Eddie waited to catch his eye. He wanted to nod his thanks to Nailor for checking Feather. For those two or three seconds it took Feather to calm down. But Nailor didn't look at him. Just stood in front of the cashier, fascinated by the contents of his own wallet.

Harry W. Feather had tidied up a bit, arranged some of the better reading matter on the coffee table in the living room. Out on the deck, the fog was so thick, you had to lean over the railing to see if the black water was moving. Harry liked the fog, the way it parted and closed in behind you, hiding you, turning the world ahead of you into undiscovered country. The world you had seen a thousand times could surprise you in the fog.

When the Cowgirl's sister and the Former Great drove up, Harry put the kettle on. He'd picked up some special Cuban coffee on his last trip to Miami. A little shop called Calle Ocho not far from the house where he visited his pay-as-you-go lady. He was going to serve *café con leche*. He was going to laugh, shake his finger real slow, and tell Sawnie Darrow not to throw any more coffee on him. Not *this* coffee because of what his dry cleaner had told him. It was the milk that made it stain, the scalded milk. You'd never get that stuff out.

When they drove up in the shitty rental, Harry was ready for them. Ready to be Harry W. Feather, autodidact and proud of it, with all the good manners and brains a man needed in an uncertain world.

Eddie braced himself as Sawnie braked the Chevy in Feather's yard, the tires slipping on the fog-wet grass. Eddie shifted on the seat to look straight at her. "Don't lose your temper," he said.

"Look who's talking." She stared at Feather's house like a kid looking at a circus tent. "Did I grab the guy by his shirt and try to stick his head through the roof of the Cane Cutter?" She turned off the engine, started to get out of the car.

"That was before we knew what he was like." Eddie reached over, took her arm.

She looked at the place where he held her sleeve until he let go.

"Look," he said. "Try to let me . . ." He was about to say "handle this." Something like that. But John Wayne and Jane Russell stepped into his vision. Jane Russell melting in the heat of Wayne's power and authority even though she was six feet tall, wearing body armor lingerie designed by Howard Hughes and three times as smart as the Duke.

Eddie said, "You know what I mean. I've had . . . experience with people like this."

"Listen, Perry Mason," she said, "we got assholes up in the capitol that make this guy look like he memorizes Bible verses for pennies."

Eddie said, "Jesus wept."

"Right," Sawnie said. She looked at him. "Hey, what can happen? The sheriff knows we're here."

"Maybe so," Eddie said. Then, "You didn't see what Feather had in that sink."

"No," Sawnie said, "I didn't. And you don't have a sister in a hole in the ground two miles from here." She was out of the car and walking toward Feather's door. Eddie caught up, saw that the door was ajar. Something weird about that. Always. Always the weird, the strange from this guy. Never let you get your balance.

Feather stepped out on the porch, the fog cloaking him. He smiled. "That car you're driving has weak headlights for fog like this, but I saw you coming. Welcome to Harry's house."

Feather did a little bow, stepped aside to let them in, Sawnie first. As she passed through the door, Eddie saw Feather lean forward and smell her hair. Close his eyes and breathe her in. It wasn't much, wasn't obvious, but it made Eddie's heart race, his fingers flex. It lit the source of that ugly heat in his chest. Made him want to stick his fingers in Feather's nostrils and jerk them up to the top of his head. Damn it, he thought. The guy just has to be in somebody's face.

Inside, Feather went to the kitchen, came back with a tray. A bunch of mismatched mugs and saucers, a plastic sugar bowl and milk still in the carton. Even the plastic spoons were white, yellow, and blue. Feather walked past them smiling, put the tray on the coffee table next to a copy of the *New England Journal of Medicine*. Feather sat down, proud as hell of himself. He patted the greasy sofa. "Sit with me," he said to Sawnie. "Have some coffee. Made it special for you."

284

Eddie took the place next to Feather. Sawnie took an over-stuffed chair. Eddie said, "You want to tell us about Mr. Coltis? What you do for him?"

Feather looked at him, shaking his head as though Eddie had violated a protocol known only to sociopaths. Feather lifted his finger, wagged it slowly. "Hey," he said, "let's drink the coffee here. Let's savor the bean, the roast, the grind. Do this thing right. What you say, football man?"

"Sure," Eddie said, "whatever's right." He lifted his cup, sipped. He didn't think Feather would poison them. On the other hand, the idea didn't pass that easily. The coffee was good. Eddie nodded, smiled. "Good coffee," he said.

Watching them, Sawnie shook her head. Eddie knew what she was thinking: about the male ritual, the display, the dance of puffery before the lunge. Something like that. Thinking they ought to just get on with it.

"Harry," Eddie said, "look, man. We know you had something to do with Corey's death. We know it's you and Coltis. We were thinking you might want to deal. You give us the upscale asshole and we work something out. You know how it goes. You know the process. A guy like you knows things, right?" Eddie sipped, watched Feather's smile.

Feather shook his head, put his cup down, and waved his finger again. "You don't want Harry's hospitality? You don't want to do this right? I ask you out here nice. Even after you break in, violate my privacy, I ask you out here nice. See if we can't make up, be friends, get this idea out of your head I had something to do with this lady's sister going into a canal. All you talk about is what you know. You don't *know* anything."

Eddie was going to say that maybe they didn't have proof, but they knew. And what they knew they would eventually prove. That was how it worked and Harry knew it. But he didn't say it, because Feather started leafing through the medical magazine like a kid about to do show-and-tell. His tongue stuck in the corner of his mouth, stiff with concentration. Feather saying, "Aha! There it is. Hey, man, what you think of that?"

Feather shoving the magazine under Eddie's nose. A glossy, greasy mass of something that looked like pasta, tomato sauce, and some cheese maybe, maybe some meatballs in there. But wait a minute: The thing had eyes. Blue. The thing coming into focus and Eddie recoiling from a hideously burned human face. The face of a child, before and after reconstructive surgery.

Eddie's eyes still stuck in the picture as Feather kept ratcheting that voice. ". . . what you think of that, man? Because I always been interested in medicine, and hey, I read, you know. I been a reader, you know, voracious, since I was a little kid." Feather sweeping his hand at the bookshelves, the weird collection of medical and legal periodicals, wrestling and skin magazines.

Feather putting the magazine on the table, open, shoving it across to Sawnie. "What you think, Ms. Darrow. Ain't it something what these doctors can do nowadays?"

"Jesus," Sawnie whispered, her hand going to her mouth. "Jesus Christ."

It was quiet. Eddie looking at Feather, wondering if the guy was always this way. Or if today was some kind of one-way trip. Going way out there today, farther than he'd ever been. Maybe not finding the way back.

Feather closed the magazine and said, "You don't know shit, excuse me, ma'am. You got some idea I work for Mr. Coltis, you go look at the man's taxes. Tell me if you see me listed as an employee. Find some paper that says I'm on the man's payroll. Come on, man, you ain't got anything."

Eddie was about to say it again. About the deal, about an early solution to this problem, about giving up the big wealthy grower so that the little guy, Harry, didn't have to sit on a steel crapper all those cold mornings up at Raiford. Didn't have to worry about that famous oak chair and that funny Flash Gordon hat they put on your head with those crazy corkscrew wires attached to it. But he didn't because a car pulled up outside.

Harry Feather looked at the door, at the sound, and smiled. When the knock came, he called, "Come in. We got Cuban coffee and good conversation in here. More the merrier."

Bryce Nailor walked in carrying a manila folder. His deputy, the tall, rat-faced man who had shown them Corey's Ford Explorer, stood blocking the door with his thumbs hooked in his belt.

Bryce Nailor said, "Counselor, I need to talk to you."

Eddie stood, looked at the back door. The crazy impulse to run came and went when he saw the deputy's eyes measure the distance too.

Eddie said, "What about, Sheriff Nailor?"

"You know a woman named Moira Breath? Indian woman? About twenty-seven years old? Lives near here?"

Eddie thought about it. He'd seen the woman once, here in this house. He'd given her a ride, saved her neck, he figured. Stopped her half-assed attempt on Feather's life. He'd dropped her off in the middle of nowhere. The middle of the night. Reasonably sure no one had seen them together. Had she accused him of something?

Nailor waited, something certain growing in his eyes as Eddie's silence elongated.

The first rule was keep to the truth, or as close to it as you could and still save your ass. Eddie said, "I met her once. I gave her a ride. That's about it. What's the problem?"

The sheriff took a photo from the folder, handed it to Eddie.

She was lying on her stomach, her eyes blackened by lividity, the look of surprise fading from her milky eyes. The pool of dried blood was three feet wide around her head. A dozen fat brown palmetto bugs were feeding at the edges of the blood. Some kind of animal skin lay across the margin of the picture. The glossy boot and pantleg of a deputy was visible in an upper corner. Moira Breath seemed to be lying in a clearing in the woods. Eddie couldn't tell for sure. His stomach swelled and contracted. When he closed his eyes, he saw the greasy red and brown of the burned boy in the medical journal. He opened his eyes to Nailor and that certainty. It scared him now more than the two pictures.

"Like I said, I met the woman once, gave her a ride. That's all there is to it."

"I'd like you to come with me, Mr. Priest. I want to ask you some questions."

"Look, sheriff," Eddie said, getting back some of his balance, thinking, This is ridiculous, some kind of cheap harassment thing. Coltis is behind this. But Nailor's hand went into the folder again.

"No," Nailor said, "*you* look." He was holding out a plastic Baggie. The red Bic lighter in it was smeared with the black dust they used for latent prints. And there they were, obvious even at this distance, a couple of nice clear prints.

"We found this in the woman's trailer, Eddie. Just inside the door. We figure somebody dropped it. The lab boys in Crescent City did me a special favor dusting it, running a computer check. You lawyers all get fingerprinted, don't you, Eddie?"

"Yeah," Eddie said. Remembering how hard it had been to wash the ink from his fingers. And thinking then, if they found his mutilated body somewhere someday, they'd be able to identify him. If he still had his fingers. "I was printed," he said. "You practice in Florida, they require it."

The certainty was in Nailor's eyes like the powder and shot in a gun barrel. "We figure you dropped this on your way out. What do you say about that?"

Eddie looked at Sawnie. Maybe they had some assholes up in the capitol, but her face told him she'd never seen anything like this before. She looked at the Baggie dangling from Nailor's fat hand, the red disposable lighter in it, then at Eddie, the question growing in her eyes: What the fuck is going on here? Then she seemed to understand something. She looked at Feather. Eddie hadn't thought Feather's smile could get any bigger.

"How'd you know we were out here, Sheriff Nailor?" Eddie asked. "How'd you know where to find us?"

288

Feather's lips closed over the smile, his tongue licking his teeth. Feather suddenly absorbed in the photo of the burned boy on the table. Nailor's eyes clicking to Feather for an instant before he said, "Back in the restaurant, you said you were coming out here."

Nailor turned and walked through the door. The deputy stepped aside for him, then looked at Eddie. The man's face said Eddie could go easy or hard. In hand or not. Eddie nodded, walked outside, hearing Sawnie rise and follow.

The fog was clearing. Standing by Nailor's cruiser, Eddie said, "When did the woman die?" He didn't like it, calling Moira Breath "the woman." Didn't like the picture in his head of that black face glued to a disk of congealed blood. Those greedy palmetto bugs. Not liking any of this. But his mind working now, starting to think lawyer thoughts.

He'd dropped Moira off at three A.M. or thereabouts. He'd been back at Raymer's by three-thirty. A few hours of fitful sleep and he'd been at Sawnie's by seven o'clock. "When, sheriff?"

"We'll talk down at my office."

Nailor opened the back door of the cruiser. The deputy stepped up behind Eddie and lifted his hand to cup Eddie's head. Sawnie walked to the opposite door. Eddie got in, looked across at a door with no handles, no locks, no window crank. Sawnie stood outside, her hand on the door. Eddie heard Nailor say, "No, ma'am. We won't be needing to talk to you." The deputy got in beside Eddie, shoving him over.

Eddie lurched forward, grabbed Nailor's suety shoulder. "Don't leave her out here."

Bryce Nailor turned, squinted at him. "What's wrong with you, counselor? She's got a car. She knows how to drive, don't she?"

Nailor started the cruiser and backed up in a wide arc. Eddie shifted to look out the back window.

Sawnie standing about twenty years from the house. And Feather coming outside now. Feather walking slowly toward her. Sawnie lifted her hand to wave. Eddie waved. She smiled.

39

▲▲▲▲▲▲▲▲▲▲▲▲▲▲▲▲▲▲

When the sheriff's green and white cruiser disappeared in the cane, Sawnie walked to her Chevy. She'd be right behind them, talk to the sheriff, use her influence. Whatever this thing was Eddie had gotten himself into, she'd see to it there was no home cooking. No Okee City legal voodoo. She didn't think it was anything more than a second attempt to put the fear of God into them. The fear of God Coltis, God Sugar. Get them to leave town. But she'd be ready to call down a hard rain from the state capitol if she had to. She could still make rain, even with the Governor missing. Maybe not for much longer, but for the time being, she could do it.

She had the car door open, when Feather said, "Hey, wait a minute, you didn't finish your coffee." Feather closer than she'd thought. "I made that coffee special for you. I went all the way to Little Havana for that coffee."

She felt him behind her, like a puff of warm air from a

sewer grate. She didn't look at him. When he pushed the car door shut, touched her arm, she wrenched away from him and ran.

Harry W. Feather wasn't going to chase the woman. Oh, he had chased pussy in his time, chased plenty of it, in a manner of speaking, but he had never actually run after it. Never had to. It was a point of pride with him. He watched her sprint straight to the house, running well, lifting those pretty knees and digging in with those expensive black pumps, curly hair and black skirt flying behind her.

She ran through the front door and he heard her inside, rattling things around. Maybe she was looking for a weapon, for the keys to the Caddy. What the hoo-hah. Harry didn't know what she was looking for. People did strange things when they panicked. And when they panicked, they were dangerous.

He remembered Moira's trembling hands on the shotgun. Knowing she wouldn't shoot him intentionally. And knowing that didn't mean she wouldn't shoot him at all.

Ms. Sawnie Darrow wouldn't find a gun in Harry's house. The guns were well hidden. And if she found a knife, Harry wasn't worried about that. He knew knives, knew how to work in close, knew he could take a knife away from a woman quicker than a goose could do the two-step.

Eddie said, "You got my prints on a lighter she could have picked up anywhere."

He was trying to keep his mind straight for Nailor's questions, but he kept seeing Sawnie. Or kept trying to see her in his mind's eye driving the Chevy fast out of Feather's way. On her way here now.

He was alone with Nailor. On the other side of the door, the rat-faced deputy was leaning back in a chair. When the deputy moved, the ladderback chair tapped the door. Like someone knocking. A crowd of uniforms out there, including two state troopers, smoking and talking in low tones. Maybe they thought Nailor was inside with the kidnapper of the Lindbergh baby. The Crime of the Century right here in Okee City. All of them out there cutting the tension with cop talk.

Nailor hadn't read him his rights. There was no tape recorder, no stenographer, no warrant. He hadn't been charged.

Nailor said, "There's only one set of prints on the lighter, Eddie. They ain't Moira's and they don't belong to some third party. They belong to you. You want to tell me how they got there?"

"I told you I gave her a ride. She could have picked it up then. Isn't it *obvious*, Sheriff Nailor?"

A mistake. Eddie feeling it even before his mouth shut on the last word. Never mention stupidity. A mistake because he couldn't concentrate. Kept trying to see Sawnie turning off the mud secondary road onto the asphalt leading to town. Wondering what Feather had said as she was leaving. Wondering if he had ever stopped smiling.

Nailor leaned forward, his face swelling red. "She picks it up so careful she don't leave any prints. What she do, use tweezers?"

"Somebody else put it in her trailer."

"Who, counselor? You want to tell me that?"

"I don't know," Eddie said. "The guy who killed her."

Nailor looked at him hard, leaned back in his chair. "Well, at least we agree on that."

"Who found her?" Eddie asked. "When? How long was she dead?"

"You know I can't tell you any of that."

Eddie said, "You don't even have a time of death and you're questioning me. I can prove my whereabouts from seven o'clock on."

"We'll know when she died soon enough, counselor, and this old boy is betting it was before seven in the morning."

Nailor took out a pocketknife and probed under his left thumbnail. Eddie hoped for good science here in Okee County. An M.E. who could accurately place the time of death.

Feather had killed Moira Breath. Killed her because he'd recognized her there in Eddie's car or for reasons of his own having nothing to do with Eddie's midnight visit. He had killed her and left the lighter as a calling card, the lighter Eddie had apparently dropped in his haste to exit Feather's bloody kitchen. If he told Nailor he'd last seen the lighter in Feather's kitchen, he'd be admitting to trespass, harassment, and worse: to being there with a woman who intended to kill Feather. A woman who had turned up dead.

Nailor dropped the pocketknife on his green blotter, bit his thumbnail, then sucked it. Eddie flexed his fists, shook his head, sighed, and told himself, Think straight. Don't think about Sawnie, think straight.

Eddie said, "All you've got for sure is that I touched that lighter. Somewhere, some time. I'm no criminal lawyer, but I know that's not much." Eddie softened his voice for the hint that he was on Nailor's side. "Did you find anybody else's prints in that trailer?" A citizen doing his civic duty. Two heads always better than one.

Nailor gave him a cagey look. In his eyes, concealment fought with a small-town cop's willingness to bargain.

Eddie thinking, Talk to me, sheriff. You've made mistakes already. I'll grant you the presumption that a lawyer knows his rights, but there may be a taint on the lighter. You picking it up out there, sending it to the lab. I wonder if you took the time for the photos, had somebody with you to establish its presence in the trailer. I wonder if the chain of custody is as tight as a good prosecutor will want it to be. And I wonder how many other visitors Moira Breath had. People who left their prints.

Eddie said, "If I didn't drop it, how'd it get there with my prints on it. Maybe somebody *did* use tweezers."

"All right, counselor. I told you we're just having a talk here. We wouldn't be talking if you'd left when I told you to. After that business with Feather at the Cane Cutter. What am I supposed to think when I find you out at Feather's house? You and him ain't exactly buddies. Maybe you got a thing against Indians."

Eddie thinking, You're supposed to see that Feather had me right where he wanted me. Where you'd find me after the lab results came in. Where I'd look bad and he'd look good.

Eddie said, "So, we've had a talk." Not seeing Sawnie anymore. His mind's eye failing him. Going blank.

Sawnie ran down the little levee and made a choice. She turned right, up the canal bank, slipping in the mud, knowing that her heels left her sign behind her, unable to control her speed or her rolling thoughts. She'd spent seconds that seemed like hours in the house looking for a phone. Thinking, Who will I call in this one-stoplight town? This town I thought I'd left behind me. The sheriff's office?

But there was no phone. All the phone jacks, three of them she could see, bare. A man living all the way out here without a phone? She felt her knees loosen, turn to water. It frightened her more than the cold she'd felt at Feather's approach, the bad-earth smell of him, like the smell she imagined would come from Corey's grave. And then the feel of his hand closing on her upper arm. Warm, gentle, like the hand of a boy helping his girl out of a taxi. That was why she had run, why she had been unable to control herself. Because the touch was gentle. God, a loving touch!

A hundred yards up the canal, her shoes already soaked, loosening on her feet, her stockings wet almost to her knees, her breath coming like scalding water in her chest, she stopped and looked back. Feather breasted the rise, not hurrying, walking slowly. He stopped, saw her looking back. He waved. Goddamn him! And she saw that he was carrying something. What was it? A bundle of something? But what? She turned and ran on.

Eddie was driving fast, hoping he would meet Sawnie on the way. But she'd had plenty of time to drive to town. The fact that she hadn't could mean anything. He hoped she hadn't stayed to question Feather. He stared down the narrow road that wound through the gray cane. Soon their two cars would pass. They'd stop, pull off for a reunion.

Nailor had given Eddie the ritual warning: how he couldn't leave town now. Nailor would want to know his whereabouts at all times. Eddie had pushed out of his chair and said, "Sheriff, if I'm a suspect in a homicide, I want you to tell me that right now."

When Nailor had only smiled into the teeth of his question, Eddie had pulled open the door fast. The rat-faced deputy had fallen assbackward into Nailor's office. Eddie walked through the crowd of uniforms, cutting the smoke and the conversation, out the front door and across the street to the De Soto Hotel where he'd left his Celica.

He pushed the four-cylinder engine up to a rattling eighty and watched for signs of Sawnie.

Harry W. Feather knew the woman would go until she ran out of fuel or courage. Then she'd hide. She had only two other choices: up the levee and into the cane or swim the canal. He didn't figure a city bureaucrat for braving the snakes and rats in the cane or the canal with its host of wet troubles. He took his time, carrying the army blanket under his arm. After a hundred yards or so, looking at the wet ground, he could see the woman's strides get shorter. To his left, in the canal, a serpentine wake moved along. Two periscope eyes. A slotted, steaming snout. Old Gator Ray out there expressing his curiosity.

It was why they put up those signs: Please Don't Feed the Bears. You chum a wild animal and he'll develop a dependency. He'll expect you to come back with the head of a sheep or a dead possum you found on the road. You don't come back, he goes looking.

Harry had read in a psychology book about something called intermittent reinforcement. The idea was that you fed an animal on a random schedule. It didn't have to be food. It could be anything the animal wanted—sex, rest, your positive regard. You gave it things any hour of the day or night. You didn't let the giving fall into a pattern. You could drive the fucker crazy. Make it yours for life.

And hell, it didn't have to be an animal. It worked with

people too. Old Coltis, he understood the principle. Probably just understood it naturally. He liked to give Harry things with one hand, take them away with the other. Call him all hours of the night. Treat him like a son and like a bastard too. Old Coltis was nobody's fool. Up ahead, the woman's strides shortened, her tracks stopped, sinking deep, then starting again. Terminating in a stand of bamboo. She hadn't chosen the canal or the cane. She'd done exactly what Harry had thought she'd do.

Crouching in the bamboo, Sawnie pressed both fists to her swollen eyes, unable to tell sweat from tears. She had tried to quiet her heaving chest, to think. She had searched the mulchy floor of the bamboo brake for a weapon: something to use to stab or slash.

She remembered now, as though it were a long time ago, standing on the bank below the cane brake trying to make herself jump and swim. And after she could not, telling herself it was no matter. Feather would only jump and swim too and then she'd be on the other side with him. Even farther from ... from what? What was there now? She thought of Eddie. Saw him far away, his hands gripping the bars of a country jail cell. The look in his eyes that said she had abandoned him.

She pressed her fists harder into her eyes and tried to think. Where were her resources? She, who had held the reins of power, had whipped the horses into a hard run, a hard driver she had been. Now she crouched, trembling in the hot bamboo, unable to think, unable to pray, simply ... unable. After those bare phone jacks in Feather's house, there was no power. Power was a phone in your hand. It was government, the law, the favors and customs of the capitol. Those wires were the reins and they had been cut.

Harry W. Feather stopped ten feet from where the woman's tracks went into the bamboo. He spread the army blanket at his feet, regretting that the ground was wet, that the water would soak through the coarse green wool as soon as his body touched it. "Hey," he called into the brake. "You didn't drink your coffee."

The woman didn't answer. Harry stilled his own breathing, listening for her in there. It was the Indian thing to do. Stand here still as a heron perched on one thin leg and cock an ear to the bamboo. Tune that ear to the woman's rhythm, listen with the ear of the mind. Pretty soon, he could hear it, the murmur of her terror. The music.

Keeping his voice low, sweet, soothing, he said, "I know where you are. Hell, in this country—one of the beautiful things about this country—you always know where your friends are. In this country, you can shoot the fucking president if you want to. We know that, right? It's all set up so people can't hide from people. Vulnerable is what I call it. What do you think about that?"

She didn't answer. The ear in Harry's mind hearing her in there, her terror rising to a fine soprano. Harry unbuttoned his shirt and dropped it on the blanket. Took off his pants, socks, shoes, put them all neatly around the edges of the blanket, leaving that nice wide space in the middle.

"Ma'am?" he called.

Using her name. "Sawnie?"

Off in the distance, Harry W. Feather heard an airplane, a crop duster probably, nearing. The engine pop-popping the way some of them, the older ones, did. He looked up into the gray sky, saw nothing. Looked back at the bamboo. He was naked now, the song of the woman's terror soothing him, making him erect.

Sawnie heard it, far away, an airplane. It sounded like the one she'd heard the day she and Eddie had talked to Coltis, the red crop duster. Off there on the edge of her consciousness, beyond the shallow stabbing of her breath, it popped and droned, getting closer. She thought of Eddie again. Wished him close, knew it was not possible. Wished she'd lived a less complicated life so that her time with him could have been better. Felt herself calming now, no reason for it but that she did not want to die with a scream in her throat.

Then she saw her courage coming to her, a visible thing, tall and lean and as beautiful as it was useless now, striding toward her on the plain of her steadying mind.

She wasn't going to stay in here and be rooted out like something with fur or feathers, something from a trap, something caught and cowering. Through the green stalks, she could see Feather, naked in the bath of sunlight that fell through the broken clouds. The sun starting to clear away the fog. He stood with his arms spread wide in cruciform, his pretty, terrible, bronzed face raised to the sky, his white teeth shining, his right ear cocked toward her. She parted the bamboo a little and watched him slowly kneel.

He lay down facing her on the blanket, his penis long and hard. Without thinking, she stepped out of the bamboo. She stood in front of him, ready now for whatever he would do. Glad she was not hiding, glad she was facing him with what she had, nothing but wits and will. She saw him as two people now and this as two times. He was an insane Indian named Harry W. Feather and he was Coltis. This was a godforsaken canal bank in the middle of a sugar nowhere. And it was that night on a lonely road when Corey's life had ended.

It surprised Harry when the woman came out, standing there looking down at him. That look on her face. It made the blood stop pumping to his hard one. She looked up the bank toward Harry's house and across the canal. Harry saw the shock in her eyes when she saw the big gator there waiting, only feet from the bank. Only a few quick gator strides from Harry's own bare back. Above, the airplane was louder, closer.

Harry touched himself. It felt good to be bare in the sun. Adam and Eve good. His touching brought the hard thing back. Harry looked down at himself, at the angry red streak across his lower stomach and onto his genitals where the woman had thrown the hot coffee. "Look what you did to me this morning," he said. "You burnt me good with that coffee." He held his penis out to her, to let her see the red hurt.

The woman's chin quivered a little when she spoke. "Good," she said, "you piece of shit."

"Hey now," Harry said, touching himself. Watching her. Wanting to know if she was impressed by what he was showing her. Seeing her eyes lift to the gator, jump with dizziness, then settle on him again.

"Hey now," he said again, "you got all over me for talking like that to you. Using those nasty words."

What was he waiting for? she wondered. Did he know about the alligator, the biggest one she had ever seen? She'd had no idea they even got that big. Had the animal seen them? It was obvious what Feather wanted, what the blanket and his nakedness meant, no mistaking that, but what was he waiting for? To tease her, make her beg, see her kneel and pray to his nakedness? Well, he'd have to wait a long time for that. He'd see her die before he'd see that.

If she ran, he would catch her. She had no weapon but her own hands. She could try to talk him out of it, but that was what he wanted. Part of it anyway, the long sickening conversation that ended in tearful begging. Then it came to her. The airplane motor loud now in her ears. Harry Feather looking up, confused, searching the sky. It came to her what she would do. A small chance, but a chance. At least he might die with her. She could take some pleasure in that. She closed her eyes and thought of Corey. Maybe Corey would know, be pleased too. She looked at Harry Feather, at the alligator, back at Harry. It was time.

Eddie skied down the canal bank on muddy soles and looked both ways. He could see them, he thought so at least, about three hundred yards down. Where the canal began to bend. The sound was loud, coming, an airplane. He turned and ran toward them, looking up at the heavens. Seeing nothing there.

*　　*　　*

299

Harry W. Feather realized what it was, knew his position was bad. Very bad. Why hadn't he thought of it? A mistake. A bad one. The airboat rounded the bend of the canal, roaring like the end of the world. Two men in camouflage suits and caps, both holding shotguns between their knees. The big radial aircraft engine spinning a steel propeller in a blur behind them. Their white bow wave spreading. Harry glanced back toward the house, saw Eddie Priest, the Former Great, running hard. He started to rise.

Sawnie leapt for him. To grab his ankles. Two, three strides and all the pull she could summon would take him, and probably her too, into the canal. Into the gator's reach. After that, she didn't know. She was already moving when the engine sound burst over them. Why was there no shadow in the sky? No matter. No matter. She had work to do.

Eddie ran with his hope out in front of him, pulling him forward against the pain in his chest and his bad knee's threat to buckle. He saw Sawnie go for Feather, the beauty and stupidity of it, tried to scream, "No!" saw her dragging him toward the water.

Didn't understand it—then, fifty yards beyond them, saw the man in the airboat point at the roiling water. Saw the water heave up like somebody was driving a pickup truck under the surface. And knew it. Sawnie was trying to kill Feather. Gator-kill him.

Damn, but this one was full of surprises. The woman had him by the ankles. Harry smiled, admiring her guts, her intentions. She was trying to feed him naked to his own gator. Didn't seem to care whether she went in with him or not. The airboat, full of what the law liked to call witnesses, was fifty yards away and coming. Harry kicked himself loose from the woman, rose, and sprinted past her, stiff-arming her down. He dug his feet hard into the soft loam of the levee, heading for the cane.

Naked as the truth, old Harry, stopping to look as the two men slowed the boat, their mealy faces opening black holes of surprise, one of them pointing at the naked man, the woman, and, holy shit, Delvin, look at the size of that gator. A geyser of water where Gator Ray had done a surface dive. The man, Eddie Priest, running like hell for Harry. And Harry, slick as you will, fast as a fox, into the cane.

Eddie dug up the bank and dove for Feather's running legs, felt the ankles, hard, slippery with sweat, in his hands. The shock of them crashing into the cane. He wanted to crawl up Feather's back, flatten Feather's head with his fists. But the ankles kicked, slipped away, and Feather was up, running like the lean, young animal he was, sleek and ocher in his nakedness, dodging the green rows.

Eddie got up, ran a few strides after Feather, then heard Sawnie call him. He ran back, lifted her, took her in his arms. The men in the boat, circling now. Even at idle, their propwash strong enough to blow Sawnie's hair straight back from her head. One of the men called out, "You all right?"

Eddie waved, looked over her shoulder at the man's surprise, his gathering interest. Eddie waved them away this time. Turned Sawnie, started to walk her back toward Feather's house. Hearing one of the men in the boat say, "I bleeve she was going to feed that naked feller to a gator. I bleeve that's what she had in mind."

Eddie stopped, left Sawnie hugging herself, looking at nothing or maybe inside, into the place where she had found the courage to drag a man into a canal. Eddie went back and kicked Feather's clothes and the blanket into the water and returned to her. He put his arm around her, walked her. She said, "He chased me. He was going to ... I don't know what he was going to do."

Eddie said, "Never mind. You can tell me later. Let's get out of here."

40

▲▲▲▲▲▲▲▲▲▲▲▲▲▲▲▲▲▲▲

Harry W. Feather limped down the road. His progress was slow, but he would make it. He had given the pain to his spirit brother. The panther loped along ahead of him, occasionally looking back with that question in its milky eyes. The panther carrying Harry's pain, taking him home.

Harry had made it all right into the cane, running down the rows, slipping sideways through the razor-edged leaves. Maybe a little cut here and there, nothing big. Feeling good as he ran, making his plan. Maybe it was a little humiliating to retreat, but sometimes it was necessary. Harry had let himself be caught buck naked on a blanket by the Former Great and two bubbas in an airboat. A woman trying to drag him into a canal. Harry had thought maybe the Former Great was carrying a piece. He couldn't take a chance on that, getting shot as a rapist with two witnesses looking on. So it was up the bank, into the cane.

And running well for a while, making that big circle

around to the spot where Harry planned to peer out through the green leaves as the football star and the bureaucrat drove off together. Harry was slowing down, down to a good strong lope, sucking in the hot, spicy air down here in the cane. Moving along at a steady clip when he'd plunged into the hornet's nest. A big one, an entire underground complex, and Harry down almost to the waist. Only a moment of ignorance, then a moment of panic, then ploughing his way out with those boiling, buzzing bullet-tailed birds all around him. He'd got the right leg out first, up on solid ground, used it to propel himself up, but the left had stayed down a second too long. Taking the hits. Twenty mean, sizzling stings.

Harry's panic run had lasted another hundred yards, until the last of the hornets had disappeared behind his flailing hands and arms. Then he'd stopped to look at the damage, the rising red welts, each crowned by a bleeding white blister. Harry feeling his body swelling, the roaring in his ears, the dry mouth, and the constriction at his throat. And Harry thinking a lesser man, a man with no mission, no desire to rise in the world, would have dropped right there.

Harry kept walking. His throat closing, breathing through a thimble-thin aperture, dragging air into his lungs with long convulsive wheezes.

Harry W. Feather was lost for a while, wandering in the cane, making circles for all he knew, fighting the panic. Then the panther had come. His spirit brother. Those milky eyes searching his, the ragged repair Harry had made to the exit wound in its back. The panther had taken Harry's pain and turned and walked on. Harry following, his throat easing a little. It wasn't long before they came to the road.

Inside his house, Harry emptied a box of baking soda into a hot bath. The panther sat silent and staring, one forepaw raised in supplication beside the old claw-footed tub. Harry didn't like the way it looked at him now. Goddamn reproach. He lowered all but his nostrils into the scalding water. He held his penis, feeling the big sting just behind the glans. God but it hurt. And how long before the poison lost its power?

Harry W. Feather had things to do. There was Mr. Coltis to see. Mr. Coltis who had planned to do Harry in that shed. Something about a rubber glove and a handful of poison. Something that would look like an accident. Harry ending up flopping like a fish on a gurney in the county clinic while a bunch of medical chickens clucked about crop dusters missing the fields.

Harry W. Feather had always known Coltis was dangerous. Hell, that was where they had started. Two dangerous men in symbiosis. What burned him was that Coltis hadn't recognized his worth. The genius of his natural, noninterventionist methods.

Thinking about it, his eyes shut tight in the cloudy heat of the bath, holding his wounded penis, Harry found himself getting hard. It hurt to be hard, but it was happening anyway. Harry W. Feather was hard for Mr. Lofton Coltis. And Mr. Coltis thought he had seen strange things.

Harry had read the documents he'd brought home from Moira's trailer. He'd looked at the maps, seen the sites she'd marked on them. He knew some of the places himself, the old mounds where the Indians whose history nobody knew had left their clay pots and sometimes their dead. A lot of what Moira had written was just political doodah. The kind of shit Harry supposed they taught an Indian girl up there at Barnard. Lot of stuff about oppressed peoples and revolutionary theory. It bored Harry to the soles of his feet. But Moira had written one thing that interested him.

Moira was on to something. She was on a scent, het up like a quail dog with its nose to the ground. One passage in particular interested Harry. Something about Coltis's eyes, what she'd seen in them when they'd talked at that party. How she was sure he was hiding something from her. Something about one of those mounds. It hadn't been all that hard for Harry to figure out what she was talking about. On her map, Moira had marked one of the mounds with a big red star. And she'd printed under it in red block letters: "Swap this for a boat landing?"

Harry happened to know this particular mound. It was

on Coltis land. He knew it because he had snuck out there
and looked at the gravestones, reading the names, wondering about the Coltis family, wondering if they were his family too. Hell, Harry had even thought about being buried
there himself someday. Why not? Stranger things had
happened.

Harry hadn't read any of Moira's computer diskettes. He
wasn't what you called computer literate. He planned to go
down to Miami, get himself a computer. Learn how to run
it. Get into those files, see what else Moira had written about
him and Coltis and whatever it was she was on about. And
Harry had another plan. He was going to take a closer look
at that graveyard mound. See what he might have missed
the first time he'd been there, reading the names. Imagining
himself a Coltis.

Harry heard a car door slam out in the yard. Someone on
the porch, a knock. Coltis, he thought. Mr. Coltis here to
see me. To make it right between us again. The thought that
it might be Coltis, that hope, made Harry lift his burning
body into the air. He stood up, steaming. "Come in," he
called.

There was a shape at the bathroom door, the light behind
it confusing Harry's swollen eyes. "Hello," Harry said, trying to make his voice right, pulling the words through the
little hole in his throat.

"What *happened* to you, Feather?"

Raymer Harney, the fat fuck, stepped past the squatting
panther and stood looking at Harry. He said, "*Jesus*, look
at you."

Harry was embarrassed, tried to cover himself, then remembered his dignity and sat down in the hot bath. Looking
up at Raymer Harney. Up at that half-smiling fat face, old
Raymer taking advantage.

"What do you want here, Raymer? Can't you see I'm
busy here?"

Raymer turned his back, letting Harry have his privacy.
He walked to the sink and picked up Harry's tortoise shell
shaving brush, an antique Harry had bought in Miami. Ex-

amining Harry's things, taking advantage of a man in a bathtub with hornet stings all over him.

Raymer turned around, looking at him with those investigator eyes. "I don't know, Harry. I thought you might have company."

Harry could see that Raymer didn't want to ask the next question but thought he had to. Necessity, it could be a man's downfall. Raymer said, "You ain't seen Eddie Priest, have you, Harry? I thought maybe he might be out here talking to you."

Harry smiled, stretching the stung skin of his cheeks. The idea, a beauty, had just come to him. "No, Raymer. I haven't seen the better half of your old football career, but I got something I want to tell you."

"Tell me then." Raymer smiled. "I'm all ears." Raymer pushed his big butt off Harry's sink and stood looking down into the steam that held Harry W. Feather. And, oh, how Raymer's little pig eyes lit up! Harry said, "Go find your sidekick, Priest, and we'll have a talk."

Raymer's eyes clouded. Raymer didn't know where his boyfriend was.

Harry decided to use a little of what he'd learned from Mr. Coltis. That can't-be-seen-together thing. "Raymer, you go get Mr. Gridiron Glory and you meet me at the old Warner house. Noon. You do that, I'll give you something interesting."

And Raymer: "Why can't we do it right here, Harry? Why drive all the way to Everglades City?"

Harry just shaking his head down there in the steam. "I got my reasons, Raymer. There's something in that house I want you to see. You want to talk, that's where we do it. It's a nonnegotiable item."

Oh yes, Harry had an idea. A good one.

Eddie wanted Sawnie with him and didn't. Never wanted her out of his sight again and knew she'd be in danger with him.

He'd decided to ask her to come back to Raymer's when

Sawnie said, "I have to rest. Will you follow me to Corey's house?"

Eddie didn't want to go to Corey's and sit with her. His superheated brain was jumping with ideas. Feather was running, vulnerable. Sawnie could charge him with stalking, indecent exposure. Hell, she had witnesses. Two grits in an airboat had seen Feather streak, buck naked, into the cane. Eddie wanted to press the advantage.

But he looked into her eyes, saw what was there, and followed her back to Corey's. She had to collect herself. Maybe later, he could talk her into a visit to Bryce Nailor, a little talk about a naked Indian. An Indian who might make a deal if Sawnie agreed not to press charges.

In Corey's living room, Eddie told her what he'd been thinking. She shook her head. Said, no. She just needed to rest. Think. Consider what to do. Things had gotten a little crazy. She had to call the capitol again, see if they'd located the Governor.

Eddie checked all the locks, took the shotgun from the cabinet, checked its load, reminded Sawnie of the safety. He showed her how to firm the butt between her right elbow and side, put her left hand on top of the receiver to suppress the recoil.

"Just aim at the thickest part. Nothing fancy. Anybody comes, don't talk, shoot. I'm gonna go find Raymer. I'll be back in a little while."

She leaned the shotgun against the wall and went to the bedroom. Eddie picked it up, followed her in, and lay the gun down beside her on the bed.

"Feather's not coming here," she said, her eyes already closing. "He's had enough of me for one day. Me and that big gator."

Eddie smiled, nodded. "Feather's probably still bare-assed somewhere out there in the cane." He hoped so.

A note, written in Raymer's big, scrawly hand, lay on the kitchen counter beside a pot of cold coffee.

Eddie buddy:

I ain't seen you since you left in the middle of the night
promising to stay out of trouble. (Your promises being
what they are, I'm a little worried.) Anyway, I'm thinking you might be out messing with Harry Feather. I
don't advise it. If you get back here, stay put. Let's do
this thing together, buddy.

Raymer

There were two messages on Raymer's answering
machine.

"Eddie buddy, Feather wants us to meet him. A place
called the old Warner house. Noon. Says he wants to talk.
I don't know what this asshole's up to, but I figure I got to
meet him. You get this in time, be there. It's an old cracker
house off 41. Turn right on a secondary road about a mile
before the cutoff to Everglades City . . ."

The excitement of the chase in Raymer's tone. Alone in
some phone booth, traffic noise outside. And the tape ran
out.

Eddie waited. The second message was brief. "Eddie. Got
to go now." The tone hotter, more urgent. "If you don't get
this in time for the meet, let's get together, say, noon-thirty.
Place called Daddy's Bait and Tackle. Everglades City, not
far from the Warner house. They got a little snack bar. You
get lost, ask. Everybody knows where it is. Try to make it."
Raymer's voice going quiet with excitement. "Maybe
Feather will give me something interesting . . . BEEEEP."

Eddie looked at his watch: 11:30. Time enough if he could
find the place. If he didn't get lost.

At 11:30, Raymer Harney parked in front of the little
cracker house where a pioneer family named Warner had
lived, propagated, grown old, and died. He didn't see Feather's car, and that was good. It meant he had beaten Feather
here. It meant he could have a look around before Feather

arrived, maybe find out what was worth seeing in the old Warner house. Raymer's hound-dog nose was twitching. Raymer would swear it was a real odor, a little like fresh tarragon and sweet basil when you lifted the crushed leaves to your nose. When Raymer got close to an answer, found something big in one of his insurance investigations, his nose did this thing. He'd started getting the odor when he'd seen Feather in that tub full of hot water and hornet stings. Feather acting different somehow. Not just distracted, in pain. Raymer didn't know. There was just something new in those cocksure, buzzed-up eyes. Something promising.

Raymer got out of the car and looked at the house. He unbuttoned his coat and hiked his trousers up. He touched the small of his back, the butt of the old thirty-eight Chief's Special. He hadn't fired it in years, hadn't cleaned it, hated carrying it. The house looked empty, but Raymer's nose was going crazy with basil and tarragon. He slipped around the side of the car and walked cat-quick to the front porch. He could hear music now, coming from inside. Some heavy metal shit. Some guy screaming about Satan so loud his nuts were about to explode. It made Raymer step back and look up and down the black dirt road. The long hollow of steaming scrub oak and palmetto. Nobody, nothing.

Raymer was amazed at how fast the story had gotten around town.

Two men in an airboat stop at the boat landing west of town jacking their jaws about a huge gator, a beautiful woman, and a naked Indian. A white guy chasing the Indian into the cane. Raymer had heard it from Bobby Deal, the kid who pumped gas at the Mobil station in Okee City. The kid laughing, telling it like he would any curious story, but Raymer realizing what he had. What he had made him go to Corey's empty house, then drive out to Feather's, looking for Eddie. What he had was Feather's reason for wanting this meeting. Feather's ass was in a tight sling and he wanted to talk.

The porch floor was soft and punky. Raymer's two hundred fifty pounds brought last night's rain up out of the spongy pine boards. Raymer knocked, waited. Tried the door. It wasn't locked.

Raymer looked over his shoulder again at the mud road, the way back to Okee City. Eddie wasn't going to make it in time. Probably off with the woman somewhere. Consoling her. That consoling could get a man in all kinds of trouble. Raymer rubbed his nose, put his hand back on the doorknob, and reviewed his thinking on this thing. Feather wanted to talk, had to be interested in some kind of deal, ready to give something up. Feather was mean and crazy, but today he was dealing. Raymer and Eddie were the deal makers. Raymer opened the door.

Inside, the music was loud. Raymer saw the boom box playing on a littered kitchen counter. Castrated voices screaming about the devil. The spice smell stronger, mixed with the odors of garbage and mildew. Raymer reached into the small of his back, squeezed the hard rubber grip of the Smith Chief's Special.

Holding the pistol at arm's length in front of him, he walked through the rubbled living room—empty bottles, packs of cigarettes, reeking beer cans stuffed with butts, syringes, and crack vials snapping under his heels. Peeling drywall, a mattress disgorging its yellowed padding, a standing lamp with no shade. He tried the light switch at the entrance to a narrow hallway. Nothing. Ahead of him, two rooms on either side. Raymer moved down the hall in the dark, coming to his choice.

The odor was strongest to his right, a bedroom.

"Hello, Raymer."

Raymer whirled, raising the gun. Saw Harry Feather's mean, smiling face. A face covered with red swellings. And saw the big stainless-steel Colt Python in the Indian's hand. Feather holding the pistol down at his thigh. Raymer smiled back and lowered his own gun.

"Hello, Harry."

Raymer was reaching back to settle the Chief's Special in his trouser waist when he saw the quick whip of Feather's arm, the bright metal pointed at him.

Light and smoke erupted, but Raymer didn't hear the sound.

Harry Feather walked over to Raymer Harney and pointed the Colt Python at his face, aimed it at Raymer's big mouth, and closed his eyes. Then he thought, No, hold it, Harry. You going to get it all over your suit, your shoes. Splatter it everywhere. Restrain yourself, Harry. The man is obviously dead.

Raymer's eyelids fluttered, his limbs twitched with that last serious electricity, but his chest wasn't moving. No breathing down there. Oh, the politics of up and down! This is what I owe you, Raymer, Harry thought. This is for coming into my bathroom and looking down at me sitting in the hot water with a hornet sting on my dick. This is for being your fat self all your useless life. This is for being half of the local football team.

Harry reached down and touched Raymer's cheek with the pistol barrel. It was the thing he had wanted Raymer to see in the old Warner house. He pushed Raymer's head to one side, then the other. It rolled like an empty bucket.

Harry would have to take the long walk now to the place where he'd hidden the Caddy. Get rid of the Python. Filling the local swamps with hardware, was old Harry. Expensive weapons used once and then tossed. It was all part of being professional, doing things the right way. Harry was sorry the Priest guy hadn't come along, but there was plenty of time for Harry and Mr. Gridiron. And this thing with Raymer would dead-sure piss the guy off. Make him unstable, cloud his thinking, make his pass-catching hands shake. Harry wanted him cloudy, shaky, the next time they met.

41

▲▲▲▲▲▲▲▲▲▲▲▲▲▲▲▲▲▲▲▲

On the outskirts of Everglades City, Eddie started asking people. Where was Daddy's Bait and Tackle? Twice he stopped to talk to cane-pole anglers, a Latino family all the way up from Miami, a couple of buck grits named Cobie and Pritchard. They wouldn't say where they were from. They were pot-shooting cooters with a .44 Magnum handgun, one of those big telescopic sights fixed to it. Cobie said he could hit the cooter but couldn't figure how to get it afterward.

"Yeah," Pritchard said, "what's left of it after you hit it."

They both laughed. Neither of them was going to wade into any canal after a dead cooter. Eddie could see some of the damage they'd done. Two busted, red-oozing black turtle shells on the opposite bank. Cobie offered him a drink from a paper bag and said he thought you'd find Daddy's Bait and Tackle another two miles on down, then left, then left again at the sluice gate. He thought it was gate number 27, but he wasn't all that sure.

Eddie thanked them, got back in the car. He shivered a little when he turned his back on that Dirty Harry handgun. Lacking any option, he followed their directions, five minutes on a stretch of two-lane blacktop that hugged another canal. And then, Raymer's car coming at him.

Raymer's big old Buick resolving itself out of the shimmering heat straight at him. A roadside shack—had to be Daddy's—about halfway between them. Their two cars converging. Eddie happy to be making the meeting on time. And Raymer not coming straight anymore.

Raymer's black Buick swerving into Eddie's lane and then back again, catching some of the shoulder and throwing it back in a spray of muddy water and scrub grass. Raymer taking the whole road now with his big serpentine rolls. Roostering up foot-long gobs of shoulder from both sides of the road. Eddie imagined Raymer's face. Some happiness, excitement, making him drive like that. This was Raymer's form of celebration, of greeting Eddie out here in the middle of nowhere. Raymer came on, closing the gap. Eddie could see, by the way the Buick's front end bobbed, that Raymer was tap-dancing on the accelerator too. Shooting up the speed and letting off. Two hundred yards between them now and the shack splitting the difference. Its sign visible—Daddy's—big bleeding red scrawl on plywood. Eddie pulled over and stopped.

Raymer was still eating up both lanes with those scary swerves, the Buick rocking on shocks Eddie could hear groaning above the squealing tires. Old Raymer, he thought. Crazy Raymer. It looked like Raymer might not make the turn to Daddy's. Looked like he might pull up beside Eddie and stop. But God, Raymer, you better slow her down now, boy. This is getting . . .

Raymer cut hard to the left, rocketing the Buick across the ditch, only his right wheels catching the culvert. He chewed gravel across Daddy's parking lot and Eddie saw his wheels, all four, stop turning. And the momentum, two thousand pounds of Detroit hog sledding on molten mud and rubber, vaulting the two white-painted logs that marked the parking lot and ... up. Airborne into the glass and plywood of Daddy's Bait and Tackle.

What Eddie remembered later were telephone wires and power lines. Attached to Daddy's, they whipped great crackling, sparking waves up and down the road. Eddie hearing them sizzle as the shock wave rushed past him. He pulled out again, stood on the gas, saw the bleeding red Daddy's sign whip, then topple forward. Saw the roof lift, blow dust, then collapse. The Buick's brake lights burning red, disappearing into a mass of four-by-eight plywood sheets popping from their studs and joists. A fuzz of insulation, dust, and fishing tackle rising, spreading, falling, and finally, the front end of Raymer's Buick punching through Daddy's back door.

It hung, front wheels spinning, over the black canal. Its frame rested on a cypress deck between two tables wearing frond-thatched umbrellas. One of the umbrellas, a big thatched dunce cap, settled on Raymer's roof.

Eddie left the Celica rocking against the restraint of its hand brake. He sprinted around the collapsed building, shielding his head with his arms. Falling fragments pocked the surface of the canal for fifty yards in both directions. Broken fishing rods, bright lures, and plastic worms raining. He stopped ten yards from Raymer, fear unstringing his knees, drugging him. The deck groaned under him. Settled. The Buick wanted to take it and Eddie into the water. Raymer not moving inside, head back on the rest. His face white from fear or worse. Eddie thinking: Just stunned, just resting, just amazed. Just wondering how it happened.

But there was something wrong, very wrong with Raymer.

When Eddie opened the door, a sheet of fresh, frothy blood splashed his thighs. He leaned in to Raymer, whose upper chest still pumped blood, but faintly. Eddie saw how it had been. Raymer's right hand still on the wheel, frozen there; his left, holding a blood-glutted handkerchief, fell away from the lung wound. His fist spasming so that the handkerchief oozed blood into his lap. Eddie said, "Raymer, hold on. Hold on, buddy. There's a phone in this mess somewhere. I got to get to a phone."

But Eddie couldn't leave. He tore off his shirt and wadded it, pressed it to the wound Raymer couldn't tend anymore. The wound had stopped pumping now. It drained. The blood not so frothy now. Raymer's head rolled forward onto his chest. His eyes tried to open.

"Easy, Raymer, buddy. Just take it easy. We'll get you . . ."

Eddie's eyes shuttered: the canal, cane fields, empty road, and blue-white sky. He didn't know what to say. What could he get for Raymer now? All the way out here? The phone was buried, the nearest rescue unit twenty miles away, and Eddie had never seen so much blood.

Pressing his shirt to Raymer's chest, Eddie wondered what Raymer believed. What peace Raymer might want to make. Thought about saying, Pray with me now, Raymer, like he knew his father would have done.

Then he saw Raymer in the huddle, three yards from the LSU goal line. Raymer muddied and bloodied, saying, "I don't know about the rest of you girls, but I'm gone grab a handful of grass and pucker up my ass." Then Raymer dropping into a three-point stance. And the running back, Tully Beauchene, going over Raymer's ass for the winning touchdown.

Raymer said something. A gout of blood erupted from his mouth with the muffled word. A bubble formed, enlarged, broke, spattering Eddie's face. Raymer gagged.

Raymer let go his wheel hand and clawed at his coat pocket. He pulled out the pad and pencil he used in his work. He said the word again, "Better."

"Don't, Raymer. For God's sake just take it easy."

"Is he hurt?"

Eddie spun. The old man tugged at Eddie's elbow, watching Raymer with a vulture's interest. Bald as an egg, sunburnt to the color of fresh engine oil, and wearing cutoff khaki shorts and a filthy T-shirt, the old man tugged at Eddie's elbow. Eddie grimaced at nature's random stupidity, looked behind him at the tunnel the old man had made, crawling out of the wreckage. A ten-penny nail dangled from the old man's scalp, oozing blood. The old man reached up and pulled it out. "Shit!"

Eddie said, "You got to get to a phone. Is there a phone in there?"

The old man smiled, shook his head, looked at the nail, a single drop of blood hanging from its dull point. "And *you* got to be kidding. It *was* a phone in there. A minute ago, I had a phone in there. Hell, I had me a bait shop a minute ago." With a quiet fury, the old man threw the nail into the canal.

Eddie held the wadded, engorging shirt to Raymer's chest. There was nothing. He understood that now. A curious quiet covered his senses.

The bullet had gone in an inch below the left collarbone. Another two inches higher and it would have missed the upper lobe of the lung. Quietly, Eddie said, "Take my car, the key's in it. Go. Go for an ambulance." The old man took a step back, more from the quiet in Eddie's voice than toward any rescue.

Eddie reached out and helped Raymer's right hand hold the pencil, positioned it above the page.

"Raymer, who did this? Who?"

Raymer said the word *better* again. Raymer tried to write on the pad. The first large, childish letter, an *F*, confirmed what Eddie already knew.

Raymer had taken a large-caliber hit and somehow still had the mind and heart to write an *F*. The word wasn't *better*, it was *Feather*. Raymer had brought it to him, had driven here, doing the last two hundred yards in those big swerves, to give him Feather's name.

Raymer said it again.

"I hear you," Eddie said. "Keep writing, Raymer buddy. You can do it." Eddie was no criminal lawyer, but he knew that the name of a murderer, written in the bloody hand of his victim, was evidence. "Come on, Raymer," he urged, watching Raymer's hand release the pencil.

When it was clearly no use, Eddie took the pad from Raymer's bloody fingers and held it up in front of Raymer's eyes. "Feather?" he whispered, but Raymer's eyes were closed. Raymer muttered the word twice more before his voice stopped. Eddie repeating it with him. "Feather. Feather."

Eddie removed the wadded shirt from the wound and saw that no more blood came. He lifted Raymer's white face and looked at it. Saw that it was empty. Its last gift, a name.

42

▲▲▲▲▲▲▲▲▲▲▲▲▲▲▲▲▲▲

Eddie's headlights washed the front of Moira's trailer. The small, neatly swept yard was enclosed by yellow plastic ribbon stapled to surveyor's stakes driven into the ground. Eddie got out and looked at the tape. Every few feet, the words Crime Scene, Keep Out were printed in the fluttering yellow plastic. He looked down at himself. The thighs of his trousers were covered with Raymer's blood. He plucked the sticky fabric away from his legs and shivered.

After the rescue truck had taken Raymer's body, Eddie had told the story to a tall, bow-legged sheriff's deputy. How he'd planned to meet Raymer for lunch, didn't know where Raymer had come from. Had no idea who'd shot Raymer or why.

Writing it down, the deputy had said there'd be a murder investigation. Eddie would be called by the county detectives. The uniform walking off to his cruiser, muttering about damn city people.

Eddie had found himself standing on the sagging deck above the black canal with the old man. Daddy. Eddie's blood-soaked shirt, the shirt he'd used as a compression bandage, still in his hand. He tossed the shirt into the canal and watched the bait fish rise to a shimmer of blood.

On the way to Moira's trailer, Eddie had bought the only T-shirt he could find in a convenience store. It said, Key West, the Last Resort.

Eddie took a screwdriver and flashlight from the Celica's trunk. He turned on the light, playing its beam across the chalky white aluminum walls of the trailer. In the gray brushstrokes of fingerprint dust left behind by the crime techies, he could see ten or so palms and fingers and thumbs. The hieroglyphic mystery of Moira's death.

Eddie wrapped his left hand in a handkerchief and held the doorknob while he jimmied the latch with a screw driver.

Everything was neat and clean inside, except for the greasy fingerprint dust, those fingers and thumbs, making their strange signals. Eddie found a dish towel in the little kitchen and wrapped his right hand in it. He began shuffling through the papers and books.

Moira had told him the plant *tokeepah* was on Mr. Coltis Almighty's land. She'd said she'd seen it there. Maybe she'd written something about that plant, kept a map with a mark on it. Maybe there was a picture of the plant, something to show what the plant had meant to a little man with a red face. A little man riding a bicycle around this hot, wet county asking about soil pH levels and showing people his own drawings of a medicinal vine.

Eddie started with the books, leafing through them by flashlight, looking for book markers or turned down pages, maps, anything. Mostly, they were government reports from the Bureau of Indian Affairs. They didn't yield anything. Eddie went through Moira's loose papers, examined some

U.S. Geological Survey maps on the walls, and searched the drawers and cabinets for anything that might be hidden in them. Then he saw the computer.

It was a laptop, sitting on the little dinette table. His eyes were passing over it, nothing strange there, when he realized that he hadn't seen any diskettes. He'd looked everywhere they might be kept but hadn't seen any. And that was strange.

Harry W. Feather started at the top of the mound, in the tall grass that grew up around the Coltis family gravestones, searching with his flashlight for ...? Harry wasn't sure. Uncertainty, in moderation, excited him.

The oldest graves were on the highest ground. Harry's flashlight showed him the old, quaintly carved stones, but most of the words had been rubbed off by the grass that grew here. It was a strange thing to think about. A thing as soft and temporary as a blade of grass sweeping away what the Coltises had carved in stone.

Harry worked in circles, each circle wider, farther down the grade, taking his time, staring at the ground with his light, looking for anything unusual. Concentrating on details was good; it kept him from thinking about the pain that sang in his ears from the hornet stings.

He had brought with him a steel rod sharpened at one end. It was the six-foot-long walking cane he sometimes carried when he walked the canal banks near his house. It was good for snakes. A whack and a skewer and he'd have a moccasin writhing in the air in front of him. He didn't think he'd encounter any snakes tonight, but it paid to be prepared. You didn't have to have a cigar box full of merit badges to know that.

Harry W. Feather was going to do this as thoroughly as it needed to be done. There was something to find here and he was going to find it, no matter how long it took. He was halfway down the grade now, almost to the edge of the Coltis burial circle, when he tripped and fell, the steel rod clattering in the quiet night. Harry got up and brushed himself off. The ground here was clotted with some kind of vine. It grew so thick that you had to lift your feet high to walk in it. High like you were wading in knee-deep water.

Eddie had tried to plug the computer in, but there was no electricity in Moira's trailer. The persistent smell of kerosene from her hurricane lanterns should have told him that immediately. He was no computer whiz, and it took him a moment to notice the computer's battery pack.

Now he opened the computer and turned it on, careful still to keep his fingers wrapped in the handkerchief and dish towel. The computer had a 3½-inch floppy drive, but he'd found no diskettes. That could mean only one thing. Moira had done her writing on the hard drive. Eddie sat in the blue glow of the little screen, his flashlight turned off, his fingers playing the keys. Maybe he could blunder into Moira's files, maybe she'd written something about the disappeared man. The place she'd told him to visit on Coltis land. The place where he'd find the plant *tokeepah*.

Harry had found it finally as much by luck as by method. It was artfully concealed too. He was all the way to the bottom of the mound, on the far side, away from the road that ran through the cane field and well outside the boundaries of the little graveyard. What he'd noticed first was that the cane was dead. Two rows of stalks ran through the place where he stood now, but they were dry and rustling in the night wind. All the cane around was green and growing. It wasn't particularly impressive in height or health, but at least it wasn't dead. When Harry stopped to consider this, he noticed that he was sinking. Not the kind of sinking you always did in this wet, spongy soil, but a faster, deeper thing. The earth where he was standing hadn't just been ploughed and planted, it had been dug deep. So Harry took the long steel rod and speared the ground. If his theory was right, if someone had dug here, the rod would go down easy. Down through the layer of black topsoil, down through the layer of sand below that. Down as far as the digger had gone. Harry began to probe.

He worked for ten minutes or so, getting into the rhythm of it, enjoying his own sweat in the cool night air, when he realized that he had outlined the edges of an excavation. It was, by Harry's estimate, three feet across and maybe six feet long.

When Eddie found it, he remembered the day they had talked to Coltis in the cane field. The way Coltis had stared off into the cane as though he'd gone catatonic. And then the tall, good-looking grower had given that strange salute to the marching rows of sweet plants that made him King Coltis. Eddie and Sawnie standing there baffled. In the passage Eddie had just read, Moira had written about Coltis's eyes, how they'd changed, how she'd seen fear in them when she'd mentioned the mound on his property. How the fear had seized her too and made her shiver. Eddie didn't know if she was writing about the mound he'd seen that day, standing there with Coltis and Sawnie. Hell, there might be a hundred mounds on Coltis land, but Eddie was going to have a look at the one he'd seen himself. The one with the little graveyard on its crest. Maybe he'd find that plant, *tokeepah*. Maybe he'd find something there that had gotten at least four people killed.

He turned off Moira's computer and wiped the keyboard clean. Taking the flashlight and the screwdriver, he walked out to his car.

Harry probed the center of the rectangle he'd outlined, realizing that at a depth of about five feet, he occasionally struck something hard. He stuck the probe into the center of the rectangle, drove it deep, and rocked it back and forth as vigorously as he could, then drew it slowly out, and . . . Hoboy, Harry's Luck! The thing that greeted Harry's nose made Boner Harkness's leg seem like a bottle of Eau de Midnight in My Boudoir. Christ and Oh My Jesus, what a stench!

It knocked Harry back on his haunches, made him scuttle away into the cane. When his senses quieted a little, he realized that he could actually hear the hissing gases escaping through the half-inch vent his rod had made.

In his first confused reckonings, Harry thought maybe the disputed thing, the thing that Moira had found on Coltis land, was a well of natural gas. Some kind of gorgeously foul methane that was worth money, and lots of it. But then, crouching on his dew-wet haunches, his eyes watering with the stench, Harry realized that he'd discovered something entirely other. Oh, it was natural gas all right. Natural in the way that Harry loved best. But it wasn't dinosaur carcasses down there making that scary little hiss. It was death, the Big Morbus, El Snuffo Grande, Mr. Corpseus Erectus. This was the Coltis family plot. But that was no Coltis down there.

Harry cleaned up the place a little, concealing as well as he could the probing holes he'd made, then he walked fast out to the Caddy. He had to go home and get cleaned up. He had to look nice for the talk he was going to have with Mr. Coltis tonight.

Eddie's flashlight tracked the man's footsteps as they went straight into the cane, heading toward the high ground. He followed them, pushing through the rows of cane. At the top of the mound, the man had stopped and then begun a slow circling decent. The signs were clear. The man had stopped every ten yards or so, turning, kneeling, poking with some sharp instrument, then going on. At the bottom of the grade, on the far side of the mound, Eddie found the place where the man had stopped circling. The ground had been trampled and rooted up here and then an attempt had been made to erase these signs. A few feet away in the cane, Eddie found a large clump of weed that had been torn up and used as a broom to sweep away footprints. Clearly, the man had spent some time here investigating a piece of ground about three feet across and six feet long. Then he had tried, crudely, to conceal his efforts. But why? Looking for what?

Eddie picked up the broom of weeds the man had used and examined it. Some kind of vine. Maybe it was *tokeepah*. But the vine grew everywhere on this mound and this was the spot where the man had chosen to spend his time. Eddie put the improvised broom back where he had found it. He aimed his flashlight beam at the trail the man had made straight off through the cane. After stopping here, rooting and brushing, the man had gone straight away. Eddie followed the tracks back down to the road. The man had walked to a set of fresh tire tracks. And, good-bye.

Eddie walked the man's original pathway back up to the top of the mound and tore up a handful of the vine. He'd take it back to Sawnie now. She'd been alone long enough. In the morning, they'd try to find out what it was. If it was *tokeepah*, the Indian medicine, maybe it would take them to some healing for Corey and for the little man who had searched this county for "Burns Your Tongue."

43

▲▲▲▲▲▲▲▲▲▲▲▲▲▲▲▲▲▲

There was a car ahead of Eddie's on the road to Corey's house. Eddie had gotten close enough to see that it was a Plymouth with rental plates. Some out-of-towner was lost. Or Sawnie was about to have a visitor.

Eddie held the Celica back two hundred yards. When the Plymouth pulled into Corey's dooryard and stopped beside Sawnie's Chevy, brake lights blinking red, Eddie pulled over and turned off the ignition.

A tall man got out of the Plymouth. In the glow of the lighted windows, the man stood watching the house for a long moment. It wasn't Feather. It might be Coltis. Eddie got out and jogged toward the man, moving from clump to clump in the palmetto scrub. The man turned and looked west, then east at the dark walls of pines and cypresses that circled the farm. He was tall, like Coltis, Eddie guessed one hundred seventy. But there was a stoop to his shoulders. Maybe Coltis had hired someone for this job.

The distance was fifty yards now. Eddie could see nothing in the man's hands. But he had to assume the man was armed. Easy, Eddie told himself, his thighs burning now from the running crouch. He wanted to take the man by surprise, take him before he got to the door. Before Sawnie knew she had a visitor.

It was too dark inside the house. Carrying the shotgun, Sawnie went from room to room, turning on lights.

After Eddie had left to see Raymer, she had tried the Governor again. Panicky, Lucy Watkins had answered. Told Sawnie they'd put out the story that the Governor was suffering from gastroenteritis. He'd be back on his feet soon. The press didn't like it. They could smell a dead grouper.

"Gastro what, Lucy?"

"Enteritis. We looked it up in a medical book somebody found over at the FSU library. It's vague enough, we figured we could get away with it. Basically, it means he's got a case of the trots."

"Jesus," Sawnie whispered.

"Right," Lucy said. "Listen, I'm trying to convince Dr. Bream to support the story. Can you help?"

Lucy saying she had invoked every quail the doctor and the Governor had shot together, every pot-bellied bass they'd caught, all the fundraisers their wives had attended together.

And the good doctor, the Governor's personal physician, had told her he didn't need to be reminded of his friendship with the Governor. He wasn't planning to sink a better than average medical career in a swamp of scandal.

Sawnie said, "Put him on."

Bream's voice was deathbed quiet and doctor's orders stern. "Sawnie, where are you?"

Sawnie made her own tone match it.

"I can't tell you that, Doc. The Governor and I are doing some extremely sensitive state business."

She told the good doctor that the Governor would swear he had been in the mansion, sick as a dog, when the doctor arrived. All the doctor had to do was corroborate. Go out and tell the press that the Governor was sick to his stomach.

Using the voice she saved, honey in a steel container, for times when nothing else would work, Sawnie asked Bream to do it as a personal favor to her.

"Put the Governor on, Sawnie. Let me talk to him."

"I can't do that, Dr. Bream. He's not available right now."

"I don't know what you're up to."

She heard the doctor sigh.

"I guess I don't want to know."

Silence on the line.

"Do I have your personal assurance that the Governor is all right? And he'll swear he was here when I came?"

"You have it."

Another sigh. "All right then. I'm an old man. I won't have to live *that* long as a disgraced pauper."

Sawnie heard the doctor's dry chuckle. She thanked him, thanked Lucy.

By the sound of her voice, Lucy's panic had eased. "Hell, Sawnie, thank *you*. Nobody up here could get him to do it."

Sawnie knew it was true. "I gave him my word, Lucy. You've got to make sure nobody up there leaks this." Before hanging up, she asked for the tenth time. "Where *is* he, Lucy? Hasn't anybody got an idea?"

Lucy said, "I wish I knew. We all do."

Sawnie said, "Hold the fort," and cradled the phone.

She closed her eyes and in her mind's eye, she saw Coltis talking to the news stations. But he wouldn't do that, would he? He'd stay out of it. He'd send his sneak letter to Bob Dollar, capitol news hawk. The anonymous note would read: "I thought it was in the best interest of the state to call your attention to something that's happening in Okee County right now. Signed: Ever Vigilant." Something like that. Something with Coltis's own mean twist.

She imagined the Governor's face when he heard. Sawnie Darrow, his chief aide and political heir, was tearing up Okee County with an amateur murder investigation. She *had* to warn him. She owed him that much. She owed him everything.

From twenty yards, as close as he could get, crouching behind the last palmetto clump at the rim of Corey's yard, Eddie watched the tall man circle the house. He walked slowly, careful but not stealthy, stopping at each of the lighted windows and trying to see in. His movements were a little stiff. It was definitely not Coltis. Had to be a guy Coltis had hired. *Tell the woman to disappear. Give her one last chance before we go to the press.*

The man had a high, bald forehead, ringed by a monk's tonsure of rough-looking brown hair. In the glow from the window, his face had that weird sheen Eddie had seen in the photo Harry Feather had shown them. The picture of the burned boy in the medical magazine.

Eddie took a deep breath and let it rise, and with it his rage at Raymer's death, at Sawnie's near-rape, for Moira. It was a rage that burnt all the way back to Ernesto and Martha Weinstein. He blew the breath slowly, shuddering with it. He had to think straight, get close. The gun would be in the man's waistband—the man's coat was buttoned. Or in a shoulder harness.

Eddie dug his feet into the soft sand beside the palmetto clump. The man was completing his circle of the house, approaching the front door now. Eddie would do the twenty-yard sprint in three seconds and stun the man with a forearm shiver to the back of the head. He'd ride the man's back, work his coattails up over his head, frisk him.

Then it was whatever the guy wanted to do. They'd talk, get to the bottom of this, be reasonable. Or Eddie'd give the guy his measure of Raymer and Sawnie and a bit of Ernesto too. Do it like a chain letter. Paybacks.

Eddie went down into a three-point stance. He grabbed a handful of grass.

When the shadow crossed the front window, Sawnie parted the blinds and looked out. She hoped it was Eddie.

She was over the shock of confronting Feather there by the canal. She had her courage with her now. She wanted to get this thing finished. However it came out. Whatever it did to her. Eddie had said maybe they could cut their losses, keep the Governor out of it. It was time to get serious about that. Find the Governor, give him his chance to publicly repudiate Sawnie, fire her, consign her to memory before Coltis did it for him.

Sawnie's eyes caught the shine of a face, turning away from the house, a man turning to look behind him. Not Eddie, but something familiar about him? She grabbed the shotgun and switched on the outside lights. Flung open the door.

Eddie's knee had tricked him. Halfway there, it fired a searing bolt of pain, slowing him, making him grunt involuntarily. And the tall man heard him. And turned so that Eddie had to take him face on, a flying tackle. Eddie's head butting under the tall man's chin and the two of them down, kicking, gouging, grunting in the explosion of light from the house.

Sawnie stood over them, Corey's shotgun cold and lethal in her hands, trying to make out who. Two men, one of them covered with blood and wearing suit pants and a white T-shirt. The other grunting, rolling, gasping, calling out, "Hold! Hold! I demand . . ." Then a hand over his mouth, closing it. And . . . the tall man's face. My God, his face coming off in the other's hand.

Eddie grasped the thing for a moment, cold and greasy, then jumped up, shuddering in disbelief. A face hung from his hand. An oily-looking mess of skin and hair in the flood light. Eddie's stomach rolled, settled. Not a face! A mask. Exactly that and not a very good one. And the man on the ground, turning over now, looking at him in outrage and shock and exhaustion. Eddie knew the man. Sawnie stepped forward, lowering the shotgun. The look on her face as strange as the face Eddie held in his hand.

He remembered her in Raymer's neat, bare room that afternoon not long ago. That long, slow, sweet afternoon. All the planes of her body married to all of his. He remembered her saying, "I had a man." The past tense. All the problems that came with it. The possibilities too. Now she took another step toward the tall man on the ground. She said, "Eddie, I want you to meet Mr. Wright. Mr. Effingdam Wright."

And then she laughed.

Like a fool, Eddie held out his hand. The man took it and Eddie pulled him up into the light. And it wasn't any Mr. Wright. The man who held Eddie's hand, shook it once firmly, and then let it go. The man who turned to Sawnie and embraced her now was Governor Billy Miles.

44

You should have told me," the Governor said.

"I didn't want to get you involved. Deniability. Remember it?" Sawnie's head was bowed. Her words came from behind a curtain of brown, curly hair. Her hands were under there too, rubbing her eyes.

"You should have told me," the Governor said.

The Governor had asked to talk to Sawnie alone. Sawnie had said, "Eddie stays."

Eddie spun his glass of Early Times in its wet circle on Corey's dining room table. The whiskey was burning off his embarrassment at mugging the Governor—a man he respected as much as he could respect any politician. But whiskey could do nothing to the rage he felt when he closed his eyes and saw Raymer's drained, white face.

Sawnie and the Governor had been over it and over it. The Governor saying he didn't care what she'd done, planned to do, what rights she had. She should have told him. It was the first rule of political life. You don't go into a secret circle without bringing your skeletons.

"Everybody brings their bones. We all rattle the bones together," the Governor had said, his voice, that famous musical voice, rising to the rhetoric. "We have our bone show and we decide which ones we can bury, which ones we show the public, and which ones'll be sticking their icy fingers in our backs every time we put our asses on the line. If you got too many you can't bury, you get out. Damn it, woman, you should have told me what you were doing down here."

Sawnie bowing her head and the tears coming. The first time Eddie had seen her cry, this tough pol. The Governor's right-hand woman. Crying because he was right. Because she'd wanted something so bad. Because she'd believed she could have the congressional seat and her revenge, too. Eddie still thought she could.

The Governor said, "I'll tell you what I can't forgive, woman. You didn't trust me to help you. If you'd talked to me, we could have worked something out with this Coltis."

Sawnie said it again, looking into the Governor's cold eyes. "I don't want to work something out with Coltis. I want his balls in my fist. I want to shove them up his ass. No politics. No compromises."

The Governor winced and Eddie looked deep into his drink. The Governor muttered, "There's got to be a way." Eddie bolted his bourbon and poured himself another one.

"Look," he said, "I'm just a guy who reads about this kind of thing in the paper, but I think we can cut our losses here."

"Like hell you do," the Governor said. "I've heard about you, Eddie. You weren't exactly shy about that construction scam up in Calabria County. You got some ink for that one. 'Environmental Crusader,' I believe they called you."

The Governor shoved that famous grown-up boy face at Eddie, those bulgy eyes saying, Don't jump in this water, son, unless you can backstroke with the big fish. Sawnie watching him too, her green eyes swollen, lips trembling, raising a hand to wipe her wet cheeks.

Eddie stood up, showing his blood-drenched pants. The Governor and Sawnie stared at the life that had pumped out of Raymer while he drove fast to meet Eddie. Eddie said, "Wait a minute. I have to go get something."

He walked out to his car and removed the sheaf of green vine from the trunk. Back inside, he dropped it on the table.

The Governor reached out and pulled the sheaf to him, looked at it, at Sawnie, his eyes asking for the tenth time if he should trust this boat salesman from St. Petersburg. Sawnie nodded, clear at least about one thing. The Governor said, "So what?"

Eddie took Raymer's notebook page from his pocket and held it up for them to see. One of Raymer's fingers was printed in blood above the single letter F.

"See it?"

Sawnie gasped, sagging. "God," she whispered. "That poor man."

The Governor leaned back, looked at Eddie like this was poker or some back room political standoff. "I see it. Now what?"

Eddie told the Governor the whole story. What he and Sawnie had discovered about Coltis. That they believed Feather worked for Coltis. About Moira's death and Eddie's short, violent meeting with Raymer.

"Raymer tried to write the name of the man who shot him. Feather's name. He died before he could finish it. There's a message on Raymer's answering machine that says he was meeting Feather today."

The Governor squinted at him. A country lawyer rising to cross-examination.

"All right," he said. "You're a lawyer, Eddie. There's a piece of paper with the letter F on it. Some blood, possibly a legible fingerprint. Your friend's, I take it. A phone message and you say you heard him say the name Feather. Explain to me, counselor, the evidentiary value of what you've got? Is there a murder weapon? Did anybody *see* the two men together?"

The Governor was looking at the leaf from Raymer's notebook with a high, haughty contempt in his eyes. Eddie folded it, put it back into his pocket.

Raymer had given his last breath to say Feather's name, but the law needed a long, logical tale full of explicit connections and corroborating witnesses. It was damnable, but the Governor was right.

Eddie had an idea.

"Look," he said. "You're the Governor. Even if you are window-peeping in a Halloween mask. Even if the TV says you're still in the capitol shitting water. You got ways to find things out, don't you?"

The Governor rubbed the jaw Eddie had butted, looked at him for a long time. The Governor's eyes lit up hot, then the anger subsided. He nodded, twice, sharply. "I got ways. What do you want to know?"

"Anything we can find out about *this?*"

Eddie shoved it across the table, the handful of weed he had taken from the mound on Coltis land. He explained what he'd read in Moira's files about *tokeepah.* About the disappeared man she'd sent to Coltis land looking for it. About going there and discovering that someone had been there ahead of him.

The Governor said, "Where's the phone?"

"There's one in the bedroom," Sawnie said.

When the Governor was gone, Eddie reached out and took her chin. Lifted it. "He was the one, right? The man in your heart?"

He said it gently, neutrally. But, by God, past tense. They could talk about it later if she wanted to. For now, he just wanted the fact. Wanted it on the table.

She nodded.

"Good," Eddie said.

Sawnie stood at the window, staring into the darkness. Eddie stood behind her listening to the Governor muttering low on the phone in the bedroom, making the music of urgent secrecy. Then silence. Then the phone ringing, someone calling back.

And Eddie thought, She's been through a lot. Maybe too much. Corey dead, Feather's shadow in her life, and tonight, facing the Governor's drumhead inquiry. No wonder she's numb.

The Governor came back to the table and Eddie poured him another bourbon.

"I called a friend of mine," the Governor said, "Mr. Arthur Deems. He's the curator of the State Museum of Natural History in the capitol. I asked him about this *tokeepah*. He knew some interesting things. Like you said, Eddie, the Indians called it 'Burns Your Tongue.' Apparently, they used it for a variety of ailments. They made tea out of it and drank it for the bellyache and chewed it for toothache and sores in the mouth. They mixed it with black bear fat to make a poultice for battle wounds. Arthur says they got results too. Or at least some of the accounts, William Bartram's among them, tend to indicate they did.

"But here's the interesting thing. This plant grows down in South America, mostly in the Amazon basin. The scientists call it . . ." The Governor stopped to consult some handscrawled notes. ". . . pittisspasium, something like that. Latin. Anyway, my friend Arthur knows all this because he's received requests for interlibrary loan materials from his folklore collection."

"Requests from who?" Eddie asked.

"From the drug companies. Apparently, they're on to the plant. They don't know, according to Arthur, whether it still grows in the southeastern U.S. or not. Apparently, they don't think so. And here's the kicker."

The Governor smiled that political smile, the one he used when he was about to bestow something on the undeserving but very lucky. Eddie had seen the smile on TV.

"The Amazonian version of this plant has been tested by the drug companies as a cancer cure. Specifically, according to Arthur, ovarian cancer. They think it's a wonder drug."

Eddie looked at the mat of green vine on the table. "And worth a lot of money to the man who finds it?" He looked down at Raymer's blood on his pants and back at the Governor.

"Arthur didn't say so. He's a scholar and they don't quiver at the thought of treasure. But one might safely assume that a wonder cure for cancer is worth money."

Eddie looked at Sawnie. She was still at the window, looking out. Her back to them like she didn't care anymore. Like she was worn out with them and just didn't care. The Governor followed Eddie's eyes to Sawnie. He reached out his hand to her back, held it there outstretched.

As Eddie watched, burning inside, Sawnie's back softened. Somehow, somehow, she knew the Governor's hand was there. She turned, laced her fingers with his, and let him pull her to his chair. She stood beside him for a moment, resting a hand on his shoulder, watching Eddie. Then she drifted out into the kitchen.

In the kitchen, Sawnie looked at her sister's coffeepot, thought about brewing some for Eddie and the Governor. Do *something* useful. Some woman thing. No, forget the coffee. They were drinking whiskey, going down, they wouldn't want to go back the other way, not just yet. Let them talk, make plans, with the whiskey light in their eyes.

Sawnie's eyes fell on the cabinet by the door. She saw herself in a bamboo brake by a canal. Nearby, a naked man lay on a blanket calling out to her, "You didn't drink your coffee." Showing her the burn she'd put on his dick, holding it out to her.

"Goddamn it!" she whispered. No more. No more of this. No more bad men winning. Men who killed for a plant that women needed. Men who killed women for that plant. God, what nonsense. What vile, filthy nonsense it all was. Then she knew that more was exactly what she needed. To replay some scenes. Do them differently this time. Change her own part.

She opened the cabinet by the door, slipped on Corey's

quilted hunting jacket, and lifted the Remington pumper
gently out of the corner. She liked its cold, serious weight.
She took the box of federal number 6 shells from the shelf.
Six was duck shot. She remembered that much. More punch,
a tighter pattern than the more common number 8 used for
quail. Sawnie would have preferred double-ought buck. But,
hell, you get close enough to them and anything will do.

She looked down at her feet, her Ann Taylor pumps. She
couldn't risk the trip into the other room for Corey's shit-
kickers. You go in your own shoes tonight, Sawnie Darrow.

She listened to the low music of the men talking in the
living room. Her heart failed for a moment within her, and
then she saw it again, saw her courage coming toward her,
tall, long-legged, and walking fast across the windy fields.
She eased open the back door and slipped out into the night.

Eddie said quietly, "What about her?" Nodding toward
the kitchen.

"What *about* her?" The Governor's eyebrows rose.

Eddie looked at him. "You and her. You know what I
mean."

"Oh, I see." The Governor's eyes registered damage. "She
told you?"

"She didn't tell me. I guessed. It wasn't hard."

The Governor thought about this for a moment. Clearly
didn't like it.

The Governor seemed to realize something. "*You* and
her?"

Eddie nodded. The two men looked at each other. Finally
the Governor smiled. "I set her free. She'll tell you that if
you ask her. She doesn't need an old man like me."

Eddie still didn't like it. Knew it was a small way to feel,
but couldn't help it.

"I *will* ask her," he said. He spoke from the burn. The
place that hurt from watching the Governor and Sawnie
together. This old man who lived in her heart.

Eddie wanted to get out of this house. Out into the windy
night where actions happened without thought.

The Governor said, "What are we going to do about all this?" He leaned forward, giving Eddie the full benefit of that famous appeal. Those eyes that said: Come let us reason together.

The Governor said, "Eddie, I don't want you to do anything until Arthur Deems gets here. He'll know what the plant looks like. He'll find it for us if it's around here. And he's going to call the drug companies, find out who asked for the materials, make some discreet inquiries as to who might have disappeared. We'll go on from there."

The Governor watched while Eddie took this in. The Governor's power could summon a museum curator in the middle of the night. The Governor said, "And I still think we can reason with this Coltis."

Eddie looked at the Governor, then at the kitchen where Sawnie waited. He knew now what had been written in the letter Coltis had sent to Sawnie. The one she'd wadded in her fist. Somehow, Coltis had found out about Sawnie and Governor. The Governor had a lot to lose.

Eddie said, "You can tell me what you think I ought to do, but unless you plan to leave here with that rubber face on, that's *all* you can do. Anybody sees you here and you're finished. Now I'm listening."

"Oh, yes," the Governor said. "You're right about that, Mr. Priest. I'm either flat on my back in the Governor's mansion with a bellyache or I'm here asking you to do what's right. It's a hell of a position for an old man to find himself in."

Eddie wanted to know what Sawnie thought. They'd done this thing together so far. He wasn't sure if she'd say anything now, but he knew there'd be something in her eyes. Something he could trust. He wanted to see that thing. He didn't think she'd go for compromise. Talking to Coltis about a murder he'd committed? She'd go for the throat or the groin but not for politics as usual. Not this time.

He looked at the kitchen door. "Sawnie," he called.

Sawnie didn't answer.

45

▲▲▲▲▲▲▲▲▲▲▲▲▲▲▲▲▲▲

Harry W. Feather slowed the Caddy, centered her on the muddy road and pulled the rearview down, looked at himself. Maybe he wasn't going to be Handsome Harry anymore. No more passing for a tanned Anglo. No more heads turning on Calle Ocho, people nudging each other, whispering, "Hey, isn't that *him? Don Johnson?*"

The hornet stings were about the circumference of a quarter. They rose three-eighths of an inch from the plane of his skin. Each one had a clear blister at its center. The blister full of lymph. With time, the lymph turned cloudy. Became pus. Harry wished he had time to take pictures, send them in to *The Lancet.* Good shots of multiple hornet stings. Hell, they'd publish in a minute, those guys. Harry W. Feather, a self-portrait.

Harry was thinking that the theory of death by nonintervention was big enough to include the possibility of his own monstrous face. They give you hornet stings, you use them.

339

Use them to scare the living shit out of your adversary. Thinking about some of nature's uglier surprises. The hagfish, for example, a creature that oozed slime when attacked, that had a system of grinders and suckers for a mouth, that fixed itself to the anus of its prey, ate its way in, and killed from the inside out. The efficiency of ugliness. They give it to you, you use it.

Harry had first heard about the hagfish from a fisherman. A guy who did some longline work out in the Gulf Stream. Guy told how he'd hooked some very nice tuna one day, big ones. Pulled them in and there it was, sticking out of a big bluefin's anus, the *tail* of this thing. The guy telling Harry how he'd gutted the tuna. What came out. This thing from hell with a big chunk of intestine sticking out of its mouth. Only it wasn't really a mouth.

The guy going green at the gill slits telling about it, knocking back his Cuervo and lime in a hurry. Harry asking, "You didn't have a camera out there, did you, man? You didn't, like, get any pictures?"

Fingering the white pustules on his face, Harry closed his eyes and counted the bones. The bones he had to pick. There was the Priest guy, Former Great. Hagfish Harry wanted him for meddling and simply because he was there. Like that mountain in Tibet.

The Former Great deserved the hagfish the same way the tuna did. For being stupid enough to get caught up in all of this. Stupid enough to get hooked on the Cowgirl's line. Hooked again on her sister. For embarrassing Harry in the Cane Cutter, grabbing his shirt like that. Lifting him off his feet in front of all those people. Bone number one, the Former Great.

Sawnie Darrow was another sweet little bone. That high chin, hard voice, cold pussy from the capitol. It had done Harry the Hagfish no end of good to see her running scared down that canal bank, slipping, flopping in the mud. Hiding in the bamboo, waiting for old Harry. Old Harry still pretty then, taking his time, then doing his striptease to give her what she'd wanted all along. Since they'd met in the bar and he talked dirty to her and she loved it so much.

Sure, she'd tried to drag him in with the gator. That wasn't so bad; he admired it. It showed imagination. It was pathetic in just about every other way, and Harry had to admit it embarrassed him to run bareassed up the bank in front of two rednecks in an airboat with the Former Great after him like there were still touchdowns to be scored and Harry had the ball. But it showed imagination. Harry didn't like stupid women.

Maybe he'd make Sawnie part of his price with Coltis. Tell Coltis he wanted her. Let Mr. Bull Sugar figure out how to arrange it. Hell, she'd learn to like it, living with old Harry out here in the cane. Living that lonely, monastic life with the books and photographs and the gator in the canal. It would be pure. It would be primal, and if she didn't adapt or if Harry just got tired of her, there was always the hagfish. Resourceful, efficient. Nature's way.

Coltis was a bone, a big one. Harry hadn't decided yet what he'd do about Coltis. After the meeting in the shed, Harry was pissed. Coltis trying to do him with the big rubber hand, looked like it came off some giant Michelin man.

When Harry had tapped into that natural gas in Coltis's family plot, he'd put it all together, the who, the what, and the where. Maybe he was a little weak on the why, but that would come tonight, along with a few other details he hadn't placed yet. Like exactly what the Cowgirl had done that had put her between Coltis and that secret out there in the mound. And what had made Coltis put the secret there in the first place. Harry's anger had cooled now. Now he figured it could go two ways with Coltis. Either the guy stayed in his face, Mr. Obdurate, Mr. Stuck-Up, Mr. In-the-County-Since-They-Invented-Gator-Shit, in which case there would be consequences. Or the guy came down to Harry's level a little. Just a little. Gave Harry his due, acknowledged him as an intellectual equal, put him in the organization on an equal footing. Harry figured he had Coltis by the sweetmeats. Hagfish Harry.

Harry W. Feather rocked the Caddy to a standstill under the Australian pines on Coltis's dark home acre. He was parked a good distance from the house, behind a shed where the Caddy wouldn't be seen from the road.

He looked around, saw the light on in the kitchen. Amelia W. Feather would be in there humping the ham gravy. Maybe she'd let him hunker down and stick his eye to the pass-through again. Get himself another big pain in the neck. Or maybe Harry wouldn't do that this time.

He reached under the seat, getting a good hot jolt from his hornet-stung leg. He found the Steyr Parabellum. He checked the clip, chambered a round, set the safety, and snugged the cold black bitch at the small of his back. He got out of the car.

Harry had to steady himself for a second against the roof of the Caddy. He stood letting the night wind dry the sweat that had come instantly to his face when his swollen foot hit the ground. It made him think of Boner Harkness. People said what goes around comes around. Or was it the other way around? Harry couldn't remember now. He figured the first guy to say it had been some dick-brained loser in a correctional facility. Who else would have the time to sit around and think up pseudophilosophical shit like that. Harry flexed his toes or thought he did. He couldn't really feel them. Leaning on the Caddy, Harry took a deep breath. The wind was blowing harder, cooler, a storm coming from the south. A squall. He reached back and rested his hand on the cold butt of the Steyr and hauled another deep breath. This was it, his moment.

He was going in the front door. This time, the front door.

Lofton Coltis said, "Get to the point, Bryce. I'm busy tonight. I've got work to do."

Bryce Nailor began a lengthy apology for taking up so much of Mr. Coltis's time. Lofton Coltis put the phone on the desk and went back to the column of figures in front of him. When Nailor's whining stopped, he picked up the phone again.

"... the point is, Mr. Coltis, *somebody* killed the woman. It wasn't that Priest. Hell, I never thought he done it. We don't have any evidence on him that'll stand up. He was with her, that's all we know."

Christ, what was Nailor saying? What woman was dead? Coltis wished now that he'd listened.

"Wait a minute, Bryce. Slow down here. Who *do* you think killed the woman?"

Silence on the line. Coltis couldn't help smiling. He'd had these weekly talks with Bryce Nailor for years, from the beginning of Nailor's tenure as sheriff. A tenure Coltis himself had financed. He'd always told Nailor that if anything important happened, he wanted to hear about it first. For years, Nailor had been making these dutiful reports, telling Coltis the rumors and the gossip, about the gator and cabbage palm poaching and the marijuana growing and about anything the migrants did or said, especially anything political. Now it seemed that Nailor's voice had dried up. And *what* woman was dead?

"Well ..." Nailor's reluctance was gargantuan.

"Well what, Bryce? For God's sake, stop wasting my time."

"Well, it's what people are saying, I guess, Mr. Coltis. It's just rumors, that's all. I wouldn't ..."

"Goddamn it, Bryce, what rumors?"

"Well, they say she was at a party at your house. I don't know, Mr. Coltis. I find that hard to believe, personally, but ..."

Coltis's heart stumbled, a stream of adrenaline burnt the column of figures from his mind. What party, who was ...?

"Hell, Mr. Coltis, *I* wasn't invited to that party. I told the missus, I told her you sure wouldn't invite no Indian woman if you didn't invite her and me. But, anyway, that's what folks are saying."

Coltis was starting to get it. His heart speeding now, pulling his thoughts along. Bryce Nailor was saying that Moira Breath was dead. He was saying people were talking about Moira and the party Coltis had given.

"Bryce, are you telling me that people are saying *I* had something to do with . . . ?"

"Not *saying* it, Mr. Coltis. No, sir, it's just something . . . a rumor. She was talking about taking land back from you, or that's what folks are saying. Then she goes to a party at your house and next day . . ."

Oh, Jesus, Coltis thought, Oh, Harry Feather. Feather coming to him and offering to kill the woman. Offering to do something he'd already done.

46

▲▲▲▲▲▲▲▲▲▲▲▲▲▲▲▲▲▲

Sawnie stood at Lofton Coltis's front door, the shotgun
butt snugged under her arm, the cold barrel riding her thigh.
Her courage had brought her here, striding ahead of her,
just beyond the Corsica's headlights. She'd thought about
going to Feather's house. Knocking on his door, asking him
if he'd like to brew some coffee now. If he'd like to show
her his dick now. Invite him to stick it in the barrel of Mr.
Remington's finest. But she'd tossed that idea.

The heart of it all was here, was Coltis, and she knew it.
Coltis owned Feather, controlled him, as much as anyone
could control a sickness. She had come here because the
question had been asked here. The question: What do you
do about a young woman named Corey? A young woman
who knows too much. Maybe she'd need the shotgun tonight, and maybe she wouldn't. She planned to talk to Mr.
Coltis woman to man. The kind of conversation he'd never
had before in his life. Ask him her own question.

Sawnie opened the Remington's breech. She looked at the bright brass band at the top of the chambered red shell and gently closed the bolt. She shrugged Corey's jacket off her shoulders and tossed it into the darkness. Shivering in the rising wind, she stepped into the light above Mr. Coltis's front door.

Harry W. Feather touched the Steyr to the back of Sawnie Darrow's head and said, "Hey, what is this: ladies' night?" Thinking, Indians go first now. We go in the door first.

When she tried to turn the shotgun in the tight space by the door, Harry dug the Steyr hard into her nape, reached around, and grabbed the shotgun. "Look," he said, "this is fun, but it's the wrong time, wrong place."

Harry thinking hard now, his leg hurting. A lucky thing he'd parked where he did. Seen the woman drive up in the shitty Corsica.

And what was this cheeky bureaucrat doing here carrying a twelve-bore Remington pump. Jesus, Harry thinking of Moira: all kinds of women after him with shotguns. Whatever happened to those pearl-handled European .25 autos the bitches used to carry in their pearl-studded clutches. Like in the movies. Well, Harry, you get a low class of woman out here in the cane. Woman who doesn't appreciate the aesthetics of confrontation.

Harry twisted his fingers into the hair at the back of the cold pussy's neck, rubbed her temple hard with the barrel of the Steyr, and said, "We're going together and we're going quiet. Nothing's gonna happen if we go quiet. You understand me?"

She didn't answer. Harry didn't like that. He remembered her eyes when she'd stepped out of that bamboo brake, that strange look. Looking at his dick like it was a piece of lint in his hand. Then jumping at him, grabbing his ankles like some kind of midwife trying to get him born again in a gator's mouth.

Eddie pushed the Celica hard. He knew where she'd gone—for the straight answer to the heart of the matter. The

woman of politics finally getting tired of subtlety. Damn
her! He knew she'd gone to Feather's house.

Eddie didn't want to think of what Feather might do; the
possibilities were too many, they required imagination.
Eddie tried to shut down his mind's eye, let the good lizard
rise to the bath of hormones in his scared brain. Let the
creature perch there and flick its tail. Let it grow.

Sitting in the living room, Eddie and the Governor had
called out to Sawnie, asked her to come back, join them.
Then they'd looked at each other, both of them thinking,
Let her alone. Let her stay in the kitchen, out there in her
own thoughts. She's been through a lot.

They kept talking for a while. Until Eddie knew it was
just too quiet.

At first, thinking she'd gone for a walk, leaving the back
door ajar, the rising wind whistling across the jamb. Then
he'd seen the open cabinet door.

It was dark in the shed and there was a smell, some chemical that kept getting stronger. It made Sawnie's face numb,
almost as numb as the hands tied behind her back with
baling wire. From where she lay on the floor, she could see
Feather making his way back across the yard. He carried
the pistol he'd held to her head low at his thigh. And carried
something else under his arm. Feather out there walking
like an Indian, toe to heel in that weird parrot-green silk
suit. And with a new face. A face like the pictures he
showed people in medical magazines. Like mustard and
hamburger.

Sawnie was surprised to be alive. She'd expected to die
quickly and loudly and have an ugly corpse. She had welcomed it. A way out of all this, better than waiting for her
own long dissection in the press, the Governor's political
death.

When Feather had thrown her down in an oil stain on
this dirt and straw floor, had knelt by her, turned her over,
rested the pistol in the small of her back, whispering, "You
feel it?" When he'd wrapped the strangling wire around her

wrists behind her back, she had thought, Now he'll put the gun to my head. The wind is blowing hard. No one will hear. A single shot, muffled. She saw herself rising in a starburst of light and sound, rising to meet . . . Corey?

But Harry Feather had said, "You just wait here. I'll be back for you. We got things to talk about tonight."

Sticking that horror-show face of his close to hers, using his cigarette lighter to let her see the thing he had become. What had happened to him? Had the festering inside simply erupted to the surface?

Now she wiggled, jackknifed her body in the oily dirt. Hating the embalming smell that seemed to come from the bench above her. She remembered two things about coming here. Feather had thrown her shotgun to his left as he'd dragged her inside. She'd heard it clatter against the corrugated tin wall. And he'd done something behind her. Something after tying her hands.

She tried to wallow toward the place where the gun would be lying. She made some distance and then came up short. Feather had tethered her. She struggled back and felt it, the yard-long double strand of wire that tied her to a . . . what was it? She touched it, her numbing hands only able to move a few inches to either side, losing their sense of shape. A tire? Yes, a tire. An old car? A tractor?

What was it she had seen her father do with wire? If you bent it back and forth at the same spot, it got hot. After a while, it broke. Sawnie grabbed the tether and squeezed the double strand into an L. Straight again. Bent again. Her hands aching, begging her to stop, to lie still. Her face numb, her lungs cold from that strange, evil odor.

Harry W. Feather opened Coltis's front door. He'd been in this living room maybe twice before watching his mother push her dust rag. To Harry, it was like a place from a movie. The lights were low. The leather and mahogany furniture, the Persian rugs, were all clean and, Harry supposed, tasteful in some way he didn't understand. Not yet anyway. He had pictured Coltis sitting in the big chair over by the fireplace, looking up from the *Wall Street Journal* with that pissy, impatient expression on his face. Saying something like, "Feather, what in God's name are you doing here? Haven't I told you not to come here unless I invite you?" Well, Harry had sent himself an invitation. He shifted the big can of poison to his left arm, with his right hand touched the pistol snugged to his back. The element of surprise was all-important tonight.

He found Coltis in the study. The man was standing when Harry opened the door, looking at the dark windows. Exactly where Moira had stood that night. Harry outside cooling his heels, wondering what the big deal was. Well, Moira and Mr. Coltis wouldn't be making any more deals. "Lofton," he said, "you got a visitor."

Coltis spun, surprised in a way that Harry liked. Coltis's eyes swept across Harry's hornet-fucked face and double-took the big can of parathion under his arm.

Harry closed the study door behind him. He walked over and dropped the can of poison on Coltis's desk. Put it—thud—right on the green paper blotter with the fancy leather borders.

"There's my ante," Harry said. "I'm in the game. What's yours, Lofton?" How he loved that word. *Lofton*. How it rolled off his tongue. And he loved the overload in Coltis's eyes: just too much data for Mr. Corporate Genius to process. Coltis shook his head like he was trying to get water out of his ears.

Harry W. Feather sat down in the big leather wing chair opposite the desk. He'd thought about taking the desk from Coltis, but what the hell. He didn't want to overdo it. Surprise, confusion, all in moderation. And all for the other guy.

"Sit down, Lofton," he said. "We got to talk."

Coltis recovered himself a bit, narrowing his eyes and putting some stiff into his back. As he stepped to the desk, sat down, he looked across Harry's shoulder at the door and then at the phone. Old Lofton surveying the highways of hope. Who did he think he was going to call? Did he think Amelia W. Feather would walk in and scold her bad boy? Tell him to get out of Mr. Coltis's life? Coltis looked at the big can of gluey poison, then his eyes settled on Harry.

"My Lord, Feather, what happened to your face?"

Harry got up, pulled the Buck knife, and pried the lid off the can. Careful to lift the lid with the knife blade, to lay it neatly on the green blotter, dirty side up. That dangerous, mind-altering odor bloomed into the room. Harry took a sniff, then a deep breath, another. Maybe he could enjoy that smell. Just like he could learn why those rugs and lamps and that furniture were pretty. He said, "Lofton, you were gonna do me in that shed the last time I was here. You were gonna hand me a glove of this evil shit just like you did Clinton. Old Clinton too scared to talk about what you did to him. Old Clinton betting he had a better chance of getting well than he did if he talked."

Harry watched Coltis's eyes. Eyes that told him he had it exactly right. Maybe not the particulars, but the essentials.

"All right, Feather." Coltis pushed back in his chair, away from the open can. "What now? Where do we go from here?"

"I don't know," Harry said. "We could go lots of places." Harry pressed some fingers to his temple, acting it up, doing the young-man-reviews-his-options. "How 'bout we go out to that cane field of yours? About a half mile up the road there on the right. The one with the high ground. Grows lousy cane, that field. The one where you got all your family buried. We go out there tonight, you and me? We take a shovel with us?"

And, oh how Harry loved it! Mr. Unshakeable. Mr. Rugged Indivisible under God. Mr. King Cane breaking out in a sweat. Reaching up to wipe his forehead with the sleeve of his shirt. Hell, even Harry knew that wasn't tasteful.

Coltis said, "It won't be necessary to go out there. Just tell me what you want. If you'll think about it, you'll recall that I've asked you that question before. I've promised to take care of you."

Lofton Coltis wiped his forehead again, hating the way this felt. Everything he'd stood upon was soft and sinking.

The things he'd done, the people he'd had to do them with. All of it leading to this. His sitting here doing business with a homicidal maniac, a deranged Indian in a Harlequin suit. Doing business that would save him, save everything, and condemn him to a thousand conversations like this. A lifetime of looking straight at Harry Feather.

No, it wouldn't be straight. Coltis would be looking *up* at Feather from now on. The very floor under him seemed to slant now, and Feather seemed to rise. Coltis fought for time, for the world as it had been, for vision.

"Tell me, Feather. How did you figure it? What took you out to that field?" Let the Indian gloat a little while Coltis thought about this. While his mind cleared if it would.

The Indian looked annoyed, then his eyes, those terrible blank eyes, burned bright. He said, "Let's just say Moira told me. She had you figured out, Lofton. You should of let me take care of her. I'd have done it sooner, we wouldn't be sitting here like this. Think about it." Feather smiled, played with the open Buck knife. A little of the black parathion smearing the blade.

Coltis thought about it. How had it come to this?

He'd wanted to shut Clinton up, scare him into the kind of obedience that would last. The poison had done more than Coltis had wanted, but so be it. Clinton was no loss.

And then there was the woman, Corey Darrow.

Coltis remembered the night she had died. How he had been awakened by a wailing siren out west of town. How he had dismissed the siren as the probable fate of a drunken cane cutter. A man lying in the back of an ambulance with his bowels spilled by the knife of another one of his kind. A human cipher that Coltis would write off his ledger, a Juan or José or an Etienne. Blood as replaceable as the oil in a tractor engine. And learning the next day from Feather that the siren had been for the Darrow girl.

After Feather had stood in front of him in the cane field in those dancing shoes and told him the story, Coltis has gazed to the west, the highway. He'd imagined the girl, Corey Darrow, lying in a hot and steaming trap of steel and rubber. A pretty girl. Beautiful and doomed by her own curiosity. And by the inexcusable stupidity of her employer, Clinton Reynolds. Coltis thinking, There is not enough beauty. This loss is too bad. I will suffer for this loss. Suffer in my soul.

Finally he had told himself it was a justifiable thing when seen, as he had always tried to see things, from the high ground, that terrain from which men of vision looked down upon the common run of humankind.

And now, tonight, he had learned that Moira Breath was dead. It was all too much.

Coltis looked up, yes up, at Harry Feather and thought, One more decision can end this. One making up of the mind. One more grave in the cane can cover this trouble. All it takes is that resolve you learned the day the Gypsy Botanist looked with government eyes at your land.

It's the land, Coltis thought, that must be protected. The land that grows the cane and sleeps the dead and makes me what I am. A Coltis. Without the land, I am vapor. Coltis looked down at his own hands. They had done only what they'd had to do. He looked at Harry Feather's throat, at the knife that Feather held. At the can of poison in front of him on the desk.

It wanted will, that was all. Where there was will, anything was possible.

Harry W. Feather reached down and wiped the knife blade on the carpet, closed the Buck, and put it back into his pocket. Coltis smiled when he put the knife away.

"So," he said, "Lofton, I'm going to take you up on your offer. You're gonna take care of me. Maybe not the way *you* planned."

He got up and stood in front of the desk. He stuck out his hand, a big, oozing hornet sting on the back of it. He said, "Let's shake on it. I'm gonna work for you, white collar now. Do a little of this, little of that, whatever you need. You understand what I mean? I'm gonna be your facilitator. Experience enhancement. Like that."

Coltis just stared at his hand, didn't shake it. And that did it. Harry reached back, pulled the Steyr Parabellum out of his waistband. He leaned across, grabbed Coltis's right hand, and stuck the pistol barrel into it. "How come," he said, "I offer to shake hands and you don't give me nothing ... anything back? What the hell's going on here, Lofton?"

Harry W. Feather liked it, the old farmer with the hot, sharp hawk's eyes, the sneering lips, patches of skin cancer on his nose, the old guy looking down at that cold, blue barrel Harry'd stuck in his hand.

"Shake it," Harry said.

Coltis shook it.

Harry said, "Okay, now we got the amenities out of the way."

Way back in there, in those cold, pale blue eyes, Harry could see the change. Coltis finally revising his vision of Harry W. Feather, Expediter. Harry thought it was the beginning of respect. He liked it.

"All right, Mr. Feather," Coltis said, "you'll work for me."

Oh, how Harry liked the sound of it. *Mr. Feather.*

Outside, it had started to rain. Big drops plopping on the roof now, pelting the windows. Wind lashing the Australian pines. Old Nature out there getting excited, congratulating Harry W. Feather.

47

▲▲▲▲▲▲▲▲▲▲▲▲▲▲▲▲▲

Kneeling in the rain at Coltis's front door, Eddie picked
up the wet hunting jacket. It put Sawnie here somewhere. He
remembered her wearing it the morning she'd held him at
shotgun point in Corey's yard. He'd lost valuable time going
to Feather's house, finding the place empty, running the canal
bank a hundred yards in both directions before driving
demon-crazy to the only other place Sawnie could be. Eddie
hid the jacket and made his way to the back of the house.

Through the window, Eddie could see them, Coltis watching as Feather waved the pistol, conducting some silent
music. They were in a library or study, a small room lined
with bookshelves, leather chairs, a sofa. In the corner, a
standing cabinet full of shotguns. Two reading lamps on.
Harry Feather waving the pistol as he talked. Coltis with
that sneer of command on his face. A big, rusted tin can in
front of Coltis on the desk. And no Sawnie.

* * *

She worked the wire, worked it through the pain, the exhaustion, the swelling of her wrists, the hot spurt of blood that had come after only a few seconds. She worked it through the heat of the L where it bent, the heat that burned her fingers until she smelled cooking flesh. The heat was her hope. She worked it hard, her whole body flexing and releasing with each bending and straightening of the wire. She was bathed in sweat, breathing like a sprinter, her body making greasy mud on the shed floor. If she did not work the wire fast, the heat at the L decreased. Whole mind on the heat, she worked the wire.

The Indian woman, Feather's mother, was in the kitchen. Eddie stood in the hammering rain, watching her clean the counters. Did she know her beamish boy was in the library holding the boss at gunpoint? Maybe she knew and just didn't care. That would be one way to live with Harry Feather. Carefully, Eddie tried the kitchen door. It wasn't locked. If he could get in quickly, maybe he could silence the woman. But she might scream for her boy, Harry.

When he saw the woman wipe her hands on a towel and leave the kitchen, he counted to twenty. The wind rose, moaning loud behind him. He opened the door.

In the kitchen, he found the big Henckel carving knife, hefted it, weighed the possibilities.

He didn't know where Sawnie was. That coat lying out there in the rain? Maybe Feather had killed her already. And what was happening in the library? Two men, the crazy one with a gun. Feather's back was to the door. Eddie could walk in, demand Sawnie, and be shot down like a pig. He could try to take Feather without hurting him. He could rush Feather, bury the knife in his neck. And what would Coltis do? Fight with Eddie or with Feather? The pictures sickened him. Too much mind's eye.

Eddie stood shivering in the kitchen remembering those midnight phone calls. Ernesto's lovingly detailed pictures of mutilation. Unless. Unless Eddie did what was required. Eddie had done what was required, but only after it was too late for Martha Weinstein. And Sawnie? Maybe she was alive in the kind of trouble that didn't tolerate scruples.

With the knife for Feather's throat, Eddie started toward the sound of Feather's voice. To hold the knife there tight and ask once for Sawnie. His voice calm: Where is she? Ask just once. After that, he didn't know. He didn't want to think too much.

Coltis said, "Look, Feather, be reasonable. I've said I have important plans for you. Isn't that enough? We'll get the specifics down later."

That was when Harry reached out and screwed the barrel of the Steyr nine-millimeter autothumper into Coltis's forehead. He was tired of this. What would he have when he left here tonight? A bunch of promises? Oh, he had Coltis by the short and curlies as long as that body was out there in the cane. As long as Coltis didn't move it. The night Coltis moved the body would be the same night Coltis sent a man to Harry's house. The man would tell Harry that Mr. Coltis's plans had changed.

There was only one thing for it: Harry W. Feather had to move that body. Tonight.

But first, there was the thing Harry had promised himself. The Big Thing. The thing that would make them close.

"There's something I want to know, Lofton. Something I always wanted to know about you and me."

Harry cocked the sweet German piece. The pistol barrel drawing its zero in the center of Coltis's forehead. Let Coltis feel the vibrations of the mechanism against his brainpan, that melodious clickety-click. Harry touched the safety off, another pretty little note. Coltis getting sick in the face, breaking out in that greasy fear sweat.

"How come I look so Anglo? Where'd I get this straight nose? You know who I think I look like?"

Coltis looking at him now like he was crazy, the thing Harry hated most in the world. A person thinking he was crazy.

Coltis swallowed, or tried to. A dry sound coming from

his throat. Coltis lifted both hands like he wanted to touch the pistol. Harry tapped the trigger with his finger and watched the hands fall back into Coltis's lap.

"Tell me," he whispered into Coltis's face. "Tell me I'm your son."

And before Coltis laughed, he said something. Harry thought the word was *pathetic*. Wasn't sure, but thought that was it. Then Coltis laughed.

Harry felt the guttural vibration of the scream before he heard it. Felt it in his chest like some deep-burrowing parasite taking its first bite of his heart muscle. Amelia W. Feather hit him hard from behind, shoving him into Coltis.

Half of his mind could hear his mother screaming, "Get out, get out! You not mine! I don't know what you are! You something that crawled out of me and died! You been dead since the day you was born! Get out!"

That low, growling lament and all the time pounding him with her ham-smelling old fists. The rest of Harry's mind telling him that Coltis had grabbed the Steyr. Coltis was trying to wedge his finger into the trigger guard. Turn the pistol toward Harry's face.

And Harry feeling sad, getting disowned from both sides.

Harry jacked his left elbow backward into his mother's soft middle, shocking the voice out of her. He heard her hit the wall and slide down it. But the time it took to get her off his back gave Coltis what he needed.

In this strange dance with Feather, Lofton Coltis's right hand was locked in Feather's left. His left hand owned half the gun with Feather's right hand. Coltis tried not to think about the strength of a young man's right hand. Summoning his guts ball, he forced the gun downward. And—oh, sweetness!—his finger penetrated the trigger guard.

The gun went off loud, concussing his ears. He looked down at the torn fabric and black powder burn at Feather's thigh, then farther down at the spray of blood and meat on the oak floor with a bullet hole in the middle of it. As he felt Feather's spasm of pain and outrage, all four of their hands on the gun now, Coltis was sorry that the shot had not hit something vital. Sorry that he was giving up twenty years to Feather. In his own youth, this would have been no fight at all. Now it was every fight he'd ever fought, everything that mattered, and Feather, with that maniac grin, those bottomless eyes, was slowly bringing the gun up between them. For the land, Coltis thought. This is for the land.

Harry shot Coltis once, neat, and shoved him back into the desk chair. Coltis's chest pumped a dark red jet six feet across the desk, steaming onto the Persian rug. Squeezing his wounded thigh, Harry jumped away from the stream of hot blood. Coltis's eyes all astonishment, his hands clawing at that big hole, trying to stop that red cataract in his chest.

All of Harry's behind-you bells ringing now.

Harry turns and Priest is prone in midair with a butcher knife in his hand. Aimed at Harry's eyes.

Harry spins and the knife misses. Priest doing his best as he passes, a big grunting swipe at Harry's windpipe. Harry pumps a round at Priest, the guy scuttling behind the sofa. Harry puts two more, tight pattern, into the sofa, turns. And Mother is coming at him with that big bucket of parathion. She's got it up over her head like a bundle of wash and she's going to brain him with it. Harry covers his head but the big bucket stuns him, knocks the gun out of his hand. And Priest, Mr. Touchdown, has him by the ankles, twisting him. Crawling for the Steyr. Harry knows it's time to punt.

Eddie grappled for the pistol, but Feather got it. Eddie rolled to his left, behind the sofa. He heard Coltis sigh. The sound of the infinitely tired. The infinitely confused. Eddie slipped trying to get his feet under him, slipped in hot, pooling blood. He heard glass and metal crash. And then the rain.

Feather had thrown a chair through the window and followed it. The curtain blowing out, the rain slanting gray

outside. Eddie got up, checked Coltis. Nobody home. Ozy-
mandias, King of Kings.

Eddie jumped through the window. In the slashing rain,
a muzzle flash from Feather, running for the Cadillac. A
bullet thumping into the wet sod at Eddie's feet. The Caddy's engine coughed, backfired. Feather, fifty yards away
and firing from the car window, the shots singing off into
the night. Then Feather drove, not toward the highway, but,
slewing mud, rooster-tailing gouts of grass, toward a row
of outbuildings. Eddie sprinted toward his own car, stopped
when Feather circled back, aimed the big smiling Detroit
grille at him. Feather standing on the accelerator, trying to
run him down. At the last chance, Eddie leapt from the
chewing tires.

The heat was hope. The heat was hope. The heat was
hope. There! The wire broke, and Sawnie, a bloody, muddy
thing, jackknifing like some larvae sprayed with poison,
crawled toward the dark place where she thought the shotgun lay.

Eddie watched Feather rock the Caddy to a stop at the
shed. Feather got out and ran in. Why? It made no sense
unless ... It had to be Sawnie in there. Feather going in
there for her. Wanting her more than his own escape. The
Caddy stood idling in the rain, its lights burning. Eddie
expected Feather any second. But Feather didn't come out.
Eddie turned and ran toward the house.

The bitch had broken her tether. When Harry got to her,
she was lying with her back to the shotgun, covered with
sweat, stinking of that bug spray Coltis, Mr. Massive Heart
Attack, had loved so much. The woman trying to do something pathetic with a firearm. Harry jerked it away from her.
Harry thinking about Mr. Bull Sugar's last word. Pathetic.

48

▲▲▲▲▲▲▲▲▲▲▲▲▲▲▲▲▲▲

Eddie vaulted through the window of Coltis's study. The Indian woman knelt at Coltis's head in a pool of blood. The blood leeched up her skirt, darkening the hem. She was rocking and keening, a low, cold, wretched noise that Eddie hated as much as the whine of the wind and the drive of his own blood in his ears. The gun cabinet was locked. Eddie ripped a book from a shelf and punched it through the glass.

Behind him, the woman screamed at the noise, then went back to her sorry rocking song. Eddie pulled drawers in the cabinet, knowing it would be quicker to match the shells he could find to the bore of a gun. He found a scattering of shells, mostly sixteen-gauge number 6. Duck shot. A couple of useless number 8's and one rifled slug. He chose a Browning Sweet Sixteen semiautomatic. He loaded the shotgun and stuffed his pockets with shells.

He vaulted the window again, running hard. As he ran, he muttered his list of saints: Corey, Martha, and Raymer. But not Sawnie. Not yet.

*　　*　　*

In the shed, with Feather kneeling over her, she said, "Loosen the goddamn wire!" Her bloated hands were ice cold.

He said, "I do, you be nice? Promise?"

"All right. Promise." Her hands were already crossed.

She rolled, offered him her back. She heard him search his pockets. Then the scratch of a lighter and the weak flame.

"Jesus," he said. "Look at that. Baby's hands are all blue."

She heard him take out the big knife, open it. It went through the wire like it was nothing, like it was thread. Her hands were free but she couldn't feel them. She sat up and crossed them in her lap, waiting for the rush of warming blood.

Eddie started the Celica, turned on the lights, and then turned them off again. Feather would want him to come straight in. Would wait for him that way. Feather had Sawnie in that shed, and he'd be coming out with her, using her as a shield to get to the Caddy. For some reason, Feather was taking his time.

The lizard, in its bath of adrenaline at the base of Eddie's hypothalamus, flicked the tip of its tail into a pool of pure aggression and licked a sweet drop from it. The thing to do, the lizard said, is surprise the surprise.

Sawnie said, "Let me look at it."

Feather lit the lighter again and lifted his hand from his thigh. Dark blood oozed from the wound. Blood covered the dirt floor. Some of it had run back under Sawnie's own buttocks. Feather said, "It's nothing. What we call a through and through in the business. You like it?"

In the flickering light, Sawnie examined the wound, a rough gouge of blue and red meat with a cauterizing furrow through it. A bullet wound. She wondered who had shot him. Anyone would do. Lying in this shed with the wind ripping outside and her own every fiber concentrated on breaking the wire, she'd heard no shooting. She wondered who was out there. Who might be coming. Or who was dead now and wouldn't come.

Feather watched her look at his leg like she was looking at one of his magazines. Wanting to know if she liked it.

"Yes," she said, "I like it," wondering if he knew what she meant. "What are you going to do?" She rubbed her hands in her lap. Bringing back the warm.

"I don't know," Feather said. "Take you to my house. I got to do something about this leg. Things get infected quick in this climate." He smiled, let the light go out. But she remembered his face. It looked fire-scarred. Or like somebody had thrown acid. He said, "Maybe we get to my house you can do something for me. You know anything about first aid? CPR, that shit? You wanta tear your slip, make some bandages like in the movies? Do that for old Harry?"

Sawnie didn't say anything. Rubbed her hands. When they got warm, she was going to do something.

Let him keep talking, playing with her. Trying to do things to her head. It didn't bother her. She'd turned the head corner long ago. Emptied it all out while she tried to break that wire tether. She had no head now, only hands, here in her lap. She touched the wire cuts, too deep to think about. The warm was coming back and with it the pain.

Feather lit the lighter again and pulled a pint bottle of rum from his back pocket. He set the bottle in front of her and smiled. He set the flickering lighter beside the bottle and opened the knife again. She watched him start sawing the parrot-green silk of his trousers away from the thigh wound. Stripping it back, exposing the oozing, seared furrow. He looked up at her, framed the wound for her with his fingers. "Lucky it missed the femoral."

Sawnie rubbed her hands together. They were almost ready.

Feather said, "Pour," nodding at the bottle of Mount Gay, then at the wound. She picked up the bottle, thinking maybe she could break it, shove a glass shard into one of his eyes. Something. But she cried out at her hands. The bottle fell. Feather caught it.

"Shit," he said. "Your hands, huh? I can understand that."
He tilted his head back and swallowed rum until the ar-
teries bloomed in his neck. His neck was about the only
place that wasn't covered with the poxy-looking risings. He
wiped his mouth on his bare forearm.

When he poured the rum into the wound, he lifted his
face and screamed like some animal from the sewers of hell.

Eddie stopped the Celica thirty yards from Feather's
Cadillac; the Caddy was parked parallel to the shed, its engine grumbling, lights blanching the old tin walls of the
outbuilding. Eddie got out and stood behind the open car
door, the Browning in one hand, the other hand on the
Celica's headlight switch.

The scream was long and full-throated and like something
from a terrified dream. And it wasn't Sawnie. At least he
didn't think so.

The lighter would run out of fuel soon. Harry W. Feather
examined the woman in the little flame. It was time to get
up and drag her to the Caddy, get out of here, but Harry
was tired. The thigh wound sucked at his strength. It made
the dark of the shed a better thing than the wild night outside with the big jock in it somewhere. Watching the
woman, he began to think about Moira. He reached out and
put his hand over Sawnie's eyes.

He remembered Moira's eyes at the moment when she'd
understood what would happen. How they had clouded. All
the fire of her expensive education and her Native American
agenda dying out of them. And then the gunshot, muffled
under the trees.

Harry lifted his hands from the woman's eyes. She looked
tired and stunned and hated his touch. She'd gone down
dull and hard and simple. Down to what Nature had given
her. Nature had given her that thing he'd seen when she'd
come out of the bamboo. That dangerous thing he admired.

Harry bit hard on the scream that wanted to rise again
from his throat. He took the woman by the arm, careful of

her wrists. "Come on," he said. "We don't want to be caught sitting in here." He wanted her with him. Wanted her to watch Harry's movie: The Former Great Meets Harry W. Feather, Experience Enhancement Facilitator.

He liked the woman better all the time. She was scary with that midwife look in her eye, that look that wanted to get old Harry born again into some hell she was making in her head. She was the perfect woman for a panther god. She'd give him half-man, half-beast children.

Harry snuffed the lighter and drank the last of the Mount Gay. He told the woman what he was thinking. "Your former friend, he's out there in the rain. He's gonna come straight in. Call me out like we're a couple cowboys in the streets of Laredo. He's got a knife, knows I got one. He's gonna want to fight me fair and square by the rules. Some guy in a striped shirt with a whistle standing over us. Throw a flag if anybody grabs balls in a pileup."

Harry felt the woman move. He couldn't see it, but knew she was rubbing her wrists, shaking her head at him. "Oh," he said, "I forgot. You don't like that kinda talk."

He reached out and found her cheek, caressed it. She shrank from his hand like a wild animal. He said, "Old habits die hard. I got a habit of not going with the rule book. Got a theory about taking what Nature gives me. Using it to my advantage. When Mr. Touchdown comes, I'll show you how it works."

Harry was tired. He had no idea what he would do when Eddie came. Nature would give Harry his surprise and he'd use it.

Eddie had watched the flame go off. Come on again. Go off. The little flame weird in the darkness and the rain. What was Feather doing in there? Eddie shouldered the Browning and fired the first shot at the Cadillac. The right headlight exploded in a shower of glass and sparks. The Browning's muzzle flash blinded him for a second. He blinked, sighted, and took out the Caddy's left headlight. Next, the right front tire. His fourth shot flattened the right rear. He jacked four more shells into the Browning and wiped rainwater from his face, listening as the last of the air hissed from Feather's radials. Michelins, Eddie thought. That new set of tires for Corey, for those trips down to see her.

Sawnie stood behind Feather, her hands limp at her sides. The warm wouldn't come back. When she tried to flex the fingers, nothing happened. Corey's Remington was somewhere here in the dark. Wherever Feather had tossed it. Maybe she could find it. She didn't know now if her hands could hold it. She knew her head could, and easily.

Feather touched her cheek again, stroked her. When the shots sounded outside, four of them, spaced, loud, flashes of light from the gun punching through the open door, Feather jerked away from her. He pushed her back into the dark behind him, moved toward the door.

"Where's Eddie?" he whispered. "Where's our hero?"

Crouching behind the car door, Eddie leveled the Browning at the open door of the shed. In a flash of lightning, he saw Feather standing there, the automatic pistol in his hand. Feather was watching the Cadillac. The car's radiator jetted steam through a half-dozen pellet holes. When the coolant was gone, the engine would overheat and seize. Good.

Eddie had seen Feather for an instant, standing there. And no Sawnie. Eddie tried not to hear it again, the scream that had threaded its way through the rain a moment ago.

He aimed the Browning at Feather's vague half silhouette, closed one eye, stopped his outgoing breath. Duck shot wouldn't kill Feather at this distance, but it would cut him awful. With luck, blind him. Damn it! He lowered the gun. She might be there behind him.

He'd hoped Feather would take the bait. The car was his vanity and his ticket out of here. Come out and fight for the car, Feather, or come and take mine. We'll do it right here, gun to gun. But Feather was holding his advantages, the shed and Sawnie.

Eddie counted the shells in his pockets and tried to remember Feather's shots. He'd seen Feather's pistol in Coltis's study, knew it was some kind of European nine-millimeter. One shot for Coltis, then three flashes outside in the rain. Feather burning at him in the Cadillac, trying to run him down. Or was it four?

Over the rain and the shotgun shock in his ears, Eddie heard Feather call, "Come on, Mr. Touchdown. Harry's waiting for you. *Mano a mano* if you got the stroke. You got the stroke, Mr. Three Yards in a Cloud of Dust?"

Light and thunder erupted from the doorway of the shed. Feather firing the nine-millimeter, bullets splintering the Celica's windshield, thumping the mud at Eddie's feet. Three, four, five, six shots.

Eddie waited, crouched behind the door, considering what was between his belly and Feather's bullets. A thickness of window glass and some Japanese sheet metal. Feather was pacing back and forth in the doorway now, exposing himself, daring Eddie to shoot. Feather pumped another round at him, still yelling about dueling it out, *mano a mano*. Was that eleven from a fourteen-round clip?

Eddie wanted Feather out of that doorway. Wanted Feather looking for him, thinking maybe he'd hit something out here with one of his wild shots. Let Feather imagine Eddie's punctured corpse bleeding in the mud beside the Celica. Eddie wanted a clean sightline.

He touched the rifled slug in his shirt pocket. A solid lead pellet the size of his thumb, it was rifled to spin down the smooth bore of a shotgun barrel. It would take off an arm, explode a skull like a ripe melon. A center shot was certain death. Eddie knew he had to save it.

Harry W. Feather had been surprised at first, the guy not coming in the front way. The guy hiding out there, shooting his car. Must of picked up one of Coltis's shotguns. And Harry could see from the holes in his sad old Caddy all the guy had was bird shot. All it could do at this distance was sting a little. Hell, Harry's face was fucked already, he was willing to risk it.

Harry knew the guy wanted him out in the open. He checked the clip in the Steyr Parabellum. Five rounds left. He raised his finger to his lips and turned to the woman standing behind him in the dark. "You be quiet now," he said to her. "You stay where you are and I'll be right back."

Harry remembered those useless hands hanging at her sides. He hadn't planned to hurt her hands like that. A woman with no hands wouldn't make it out here in the cane. When this was over, Harry would have to reconsider the whole thing. Her being the wife of the alpha panther, giving him the feral children. For now, he didn't want her hurt anymore. Didn't want her shotgun ugly if he could help it.

Harry edged into the doorway. He knew where the guy Priest was. He was tired of this. They could be here all night. And time was not on Harry's side. His thigh was hurting. His head ached where Mother had whacked him with that big can of poison. The rum had taken the edge from the pain for a while, but now he could feel it coming back big and grim. Harry had a plan. He would draw fire, then shoot the muzzle flash. It would be a difficult shot at night in the rain, but Harry had done better.

When Eddie saw Feather leave the doorway, he turned on the Celica's headlights, freezing those eyes in the beam, red eyes like a gator's. Eddie tightened his finger on the trigger. And there was Sawnie. Feather lurched backward and pulled her out, holding her in front of him, one hand over her mouth. Feather leveled the pistol across her shoulder at Eddie. Started walking toward him.

Eddie turned off the lights, saw the flash, felt the cut and burn at his side. He spun and fell.

Sawnie saw Eddie fall. She lifted her hands when Feather loosened his grip on her face. He moved around her to peer at Eddie's car, crouching, aiming the pistol. She held her hands straight out in front of her. They were numb, dead as two sash weights. Lightning flashed, and she saw Eddie lying still.

Eddie rolled and felt the splintered rib and ripped meat where the bullet had crossed his side. It burnt, but he knew it wasn't a killing hit. And knew that Feather would shoot again. He scuttled back toward the car, the headlight switch. He tore the rifled slug from his pocket, chambered it, and turned on the lights again.

Feather stood frozen in the light, Sawnie beside him. "Sawnie, get down," Eddie screamed. Feather raising the pistol. Sawnie still there, still standing, Feather's left hand holding her up. Feather thinking Eddie wouldn't shoot: The spread of shot would take Sawnie too.

"Get down," Eddie screamed again as Feather's face opened, smiled in the bright beam. Feather walked slowly toward him, pulling Sawnie alongside. When he'd closed half the distance, he let go of her, steadied the pistol with both hands, taking careful aim.

She hit Feather with everything she had. Watched him ski on the rain-slick grass, the pistol up, flaming. She lost her own footing, fell, crawled madly. Then she heard Eddie shoot, once, deliberate. She covered her head, waited for more. Seconds. She lifted her head. Feather lay face down in the mud, the gun still in his hand, his body twitching. She saw Eddie off in the rain. Watched him reload the shotgun and walk forward, his eyes never leaving Feather's face.

She looked back at Feather and saw that she'd been mistaken. Feather had no face.

49

▲▲▲▲▲▲▲▲▲▲▲▲▲▲▲▲▲

The sailboat rocked gently at anchor. Eddie sat in the cockpit watching a blood sun set over Shell Key. In the weeks since Okee City, he'd hurried up the work on the *Sight Unseen*. She was a proud thing to see now. Everything topside, from stays and shrouds to cleats and winches, new or restored. Aloft the new brass telltale pointed dutifully west, and the new spreaders were painted a gleaming white. Over the side, reflected in the moving blue, the boat's bright colors shimmered. Down below, she was as new as an old boat could be. All teak-paneled and carpeted and fitted out with a tiny kitchen and a sea-going water closet. And her mysterious name painted on the transom.

Eddie set aside the law book he was reading and opened the cooler at his feet. He popped a Beck's and swallowed half of it, loving the way it cut the heat and salt from his throat. He stood and stretched in the falling light. It was mid-September and cooling a little. Over the mainland to

369

the east the rising thermals were starting to pull in the cool sea air.

Eddie took a second beer from the cooler and slipped forward along the rail. Up on the bow, in a nest of cushions and a crumpled genoa, a beautiful woman was sleeping. Eddie knelt and touched her cheek with the cold beer bottle.

Sawnie didn't open her eyes. "I felt you coming," she said.

She opened her hand and Eddie put the bottle in it. She sat up, shaded those explosive green eyes, and sipped the beer. He moved between her and the slanting sunlight.

She reached out with the Beck's and touched the cold green glass to the ragged red and blue rip where Harry Feather's bullet had scored Eddie's floating rib. That was Eddie's luck, the bullet smacking that rib and not digging in, not taking half of his liver with it.

The cold bottle should have felt good, but it didn't. Eddie couldn't feel anything there now and never would again.

He reached out and took Sawnie's hand and lifted it, took the bottle from her, and set it on the deck. He closed his eyes and kissed the scars on her wrists. The sad thing was that they looked like a serious attempt at self-extinction. She'd have to keep them hidden, or she'd have to explain them. Either way it wasn't good.

Kissing those ridges of scar tissue, Eddie thought about the irony. This woman had fought harder to live than most people would ever have to, and the fight had made her look like she'd tried to die. He knew there were things inside, invisible things that had become stronger after the fight. Sometimes, he thought, too strong for him. For them.

"I had a dream," she said to Eddie's closed eyes. To his kisses. "It's a dream I've had before. I'm making a speech. You know, politics. In the dream I'm on a platform somewhere. It's outside, a sunny day. There's a good-sized crowd and it's about their faces. Not what I'm saying. That never makes any sense."

Eddie couldn't stop the laugh that came. "Politics," he said, "you know."

She took her right wrist away and gave him her left. With his eyes closed, he kissed it.

"Anyway," she said, "it's about the people, the way they look up at me. What they want from me. The hope they have, the faith they're ready to give me. It's a scary thing. But good scary."

Eddie opened his eyes. "Is there room for one more there among the cushions and the sails?"

He looked around. It would be dark soon. There was no boat traffic nearby and Shell Key behind him was empty. Sawnie undid the front of her bikini top and let the two sides slip from her fingers. Elastic did what it was supposed to do, and the fabric slid away from her breasts. She hooked her fingers into the waistband of Eddie's swimsuit and he stood up slowly, letting her strip it down across his thighs, his shins. He stepped out of it and knelt over her.

He made his right hand into a bowl and covered her breast. They were still new to each other. The first touch sent a thrilling sting to his loins. He kissed her, drinking the air from her lungs, that deep identifying thing.

She pushed him gently away. "First," she said, her breathing ragged with the wanting. "First tell me why the law book. Does it mean what I think it means?"

"Never mind the book."

"No, tell me." Mock-stern with him as though she might really withhold herself.

"All right, congresswoman, it means that my law practice, which was permanently temporarily closed, is now temporarily permanently open."

Eddie pressed his lips to hers. She held him that way, then opened, opened everything.

It was dark when they finished making love. They lay for a while letting the strong land breeze dry them. When Sawnie shivered in his arms, Eddie rose, took her hand, and led her back to the cockpit. He wrapped her in a jacket and took two more Beck's from the cooler. He opened the beers,

371

gave her one, and they touched their bottles together. "Time to do it?" he asked her.

She hugged the jacket around her, took a long pull of the beer, and nodded. He couldn't see her mouth but knew she was smiling. Couldn't see her green eyes but knew they were a fighter's eyes.

"Just a minute," he said.

He went down below and came back with the package. He bowed to Sawnie in the gently rolling boat. "Do the honors now, congresswoman." He handed it to her.

Sawnie opened it, a box about two feet square, and took out the wreath of pittisspasium. She held it up to show him.

Driving out of Okee City, leaving town, she'd made him take her to the field. The middle of the night, Eddie bandaged and hurting. Sawnie sitting beside him with her dead hands in her lap, staying in the car while he climbed up to the little mound and identified himself to Sheriff Nailor's forensics team. Eddie had looked at Sawnie from up there, a woman staring straight ahead, her eyes boring into the future. Then he'd looked down the other side of the mound at the diggers in their pool of lantern light.

There were two corpses, not one.

The strange little man who had started all this, who had come to Corey and asked about soil and sealed her fate with his question, was already zippered into a black plastic bag. And beside him, in pieces roughly reassembled, was the small, blackened skeleton of a prehistoric nomad. An Indian man or woman who had lain here for a thousand years at least among the rubble of shells and pots. Waiting, Eddie fancied, to see the light that revealed the folly of ownership.

Eddie had knelt and gathered a good armful of the green vine Sawnie had asked for and had walked quickly back down to the car.

Now he looked at the wreath Sawnie had woven and placed in a box. It reminded him of a flower box full of dead mangrove shoots, of a man named Ernesto. Maybe this wreath would heal that memory a little. Sawnie had said it would.

Holding the wreath, she leaned out over the railing in the strong breeze, her foot slipping a little on the wet gel coat.

"Careful," Eddie said.

"Oh, I'll be careful." Her voice was full of experience now, of reverence. "I know what that means now."

"What does it mean?"

She had tied a simple black ribbon around the wreath. She let the wreath go over the side.

"It means sometimes you risk everything. It means you owe your friends the right thing, even if it hurts you."

Silently in the dark, Eddie told the names of his saints. Martha. Corey. Raymer. He couldn't see Sawnie's tough, soft smile but knew her well enough. They touched their bottles together again and drank to the future.

Eddie didn't start the engine until the wreath was gone on the falling tide, until he'd asked Sawnie if there was anything she wanted to say. She'd stood staring off at the last deep red of a fading horizon and whispered, "Goodbye, my dear sister."

Eddie held her.

She was getting her staff together, raising funds, laying the groundwork for a campaign. She'd even asked him to come on board as advisor, speech writer, position paper man for ecological issues. She'd said Eddie could name the job and his price. Of course, he'd declined.

She'd go a long way and there'd be more trouble. Maybe there'd be more ceremonies of grief and shriving.

Yes, she'd go far, but tonight she was going home with him.